D ... me

DEADLY THYME.

Published by SkipJack Publishing.

First edition: January 15, 2014
Second edition: April 11, 2014
Published in the United States of America.

Deadly Thyme/by R.L. Nolen
ISBN-13: 978-1-939889-14-0 (SkipJack Publishing)

Book design by www.merakiediting.com

For my mother

she liked this one

CONTENTS

WEEK ONE

Time Is

Oh more than moon,
Draw not up seas to drown me in thy sphere,
Weep me not dead, in thine arms, but forbear
To teach the sea what it may do too soon.
– John Donne 1572–1631 –

When Annie Butler opened her eyes, she could see nothing but the dark. Nothing. Her face warmed up to a sob, but she squeezed her eyes shut against the tears. It was no good being a baby. She had to think about how to get out of this mess.

A deep breath turned into a gag because something smelled gross. Where was she? It was freezing. And why couldn't she move?

In an effort to shift away from the cold, and the smell, and the heavy something holding her down, she only managed to turn her head to the side. When she did, pain shot through her skull and a deeper darkness came and took her so she didn't know anything more.

I

CORNWALL, ENGLAND
Ten hours earlier

Annie Butler loved to stand on this rock promontory, arms outstretched to grab the wind. The sky lightened with the promise of a new day. She and her friend cut across the brilliant green field, a stage set high above the sea where heaven touched earth.

There had been a storm the night before, the kind that brings shells to the shore. They were on a mission to collect them.

Annie caught up to her friend. "Dot, you didn't say a thing about my new shoes. Look!"

"Yeah. So?"

"My mother didn't want me wearing them till tomorrow's school."

Dot laughed. "Why are you wearing 'em, then?"

"Couldn't wait, could I?" Annie paused to swipe at a wet leaf stuck to the toe of one of them. "Come on. Don't be such a slow coach." She ignored her friend's disbelieving face and navigated the overgrown path where it dropped through the bracken to the first tier of the village roads. Her mother would worry, as she always did. She pulled out her mobile to text: **W Dot @ beach.** She sent it to her mum. Tromping down a side street, she cast a glance toward her home where her mother would keep breakfast warm until she returned. A tinny note sounded, and she glanced at her mobile. The new text read: **Thx. C u.** As she climbed down to the path that led to the beach, she caught her shin on a jagged rock. She rubbed at the sudden burning pain, but a little blood didn't dampen her resolve. She slid the rest of the way and then jumped to the pavement. Her shoes clattered across the stones.

Dot kept up, but just barely, finally saying in an overloud voice, "You'll wake the village, yeah. See what your mum says then, naffo."

"Ha." Annie squeezed around an old black car taking up much of the alleyway. A thought passed briefly that she had seen that car before. Did it belong to that odd man who kept hanging about? He reminded her of a crab the way he sidestepped away when she stared at him. She tugged open the gate above the beach, glanced back at Dot, and then hopped down two steps. "We're going to find bags of decent shells, you know. I feel lucky today."

On the beach, hidden in blue shadows cast from the abrupt wall of rock, Charles sat on an old crab sack in the middle of a circle he'd drawn in the sand.

His hands clenched and unclenched. He looked at them and imagined them on Cecil's smooth neck, saw in his mind the look in her eyes, and he wanted the past back so badly it hurt.

Above the seawall, cottages stuck like limpets against the rock. They belonged to people who hated him and he them. Among them was the American woman at this very moment in her pert little cottage. Why had she come here? She had brought back the old trouble, ruin his life. He had to do something, but what?

Rocking, rocking, he closed his eyes, and fought the pain in his gut while bile scorched the back of his throat. The hiss of waves formed words.

"Don't. Do. Something. Stupid."

He dug his fingers into the sand, took a handful, and threw it at the seawall where the soft pellets stuck. He hated his mother's voice.

A commotion above him … Someone was coming. Footsteps pattered lightly down the stairs, and just in time he stood and pressed his body into the recesses of uneven rock. To be caught here would be disastrous.

The footsteps slowed to a stop. He did not want them to stop. *Walk on. Walk on!* He peeked over the edge of a step at the two girls with backs to him.

One girl pointed at something in the distance. They took some time to gather shells. The girl with the sack said something he couldn't make out. Then the other girl took off across the sand, and disappeared around a jutting shelf of granite.

The girl with the sack half-turned and Charles choked back a gasp. The American woman's daughter! He pushed back into shadow. That woman brought the voice back. Now he couldn't remember things, couldn't think, *couldn't* be blamed. And her daughter was here, a few feet away, and they were alone. It must *mean* something.

Then it came to him. He could use her.

The girl moved into his line of vision and he could not help but watch her. Her dance fascinated him. A flash of sunlight transformed her hair to spun gold. He edged back, but if she turned, all the shadow in the world would not hide him. Hide him.

"Don't. Do. Something. Stupid."

The gurgle of waves—it would not stop. The breeze lifted his hat brim. He jerked it lower. A flutter of black and white, and a magpie swooped down at the girl while she sent up a shrill noise and dropped her sack. The bird pecked at the sand and took flight again.

With bag in hand, the girl smiled and stepped into a waltz timed with the surf. He despised her pleasure. She sang the magpie song. "One for sorrow, two for joy, three for a girl, and four for a boy, five for silver, six for gold, and seven …"

"… for a secret never to be told," Charles said aloud, because he had a plan.

With a gasp, the girl pivoted to face him.

He stepped forward. "Up and out a bit early?"

"Who are you?"

Charles said nothing. *She knows. I can see it in her eyes.*

Slowly she backed away from him. "You've been following my mum, haven't you?"

"Don't be ridiculous."

"You were at the market yesterday, staring at her. And the day before I saw you outside our house, on the street."

He stepped closer. The surf hissed.

The girl turned away. "I'm going home."

"Your mum shouldn't have come here. Don't you understand?" *Brat.* He grabbed her arm. It was thin, as fragile as a bird's leg. He could snap it.

"Let go!" She broke his grasp.

He stood between her and the stairs and held out his empty hands. "I only want to talk."

She stood her ground. "I'll scream."

"No, no, you mustn't. I want to explain. Wait!"

She zipped around him and up the steps.

She might have tripped.

Or had his hand squeezed onto her ankle?

He didn't know. He couldn't recall. But she now lay very still at the base of the steps. This wasn't the plan. He hadn't meant to kill her so soon.

Everything disgusted him—the way the wind blew, the way the waves sounded, the smell in the air.

The other one might be back at any moment. The girl's hair lay in waves. Hair and sand, sand and hair—it was the color, the same color. What was this? He could see a vein pulse on her thin neck.

The voice in his head snapped, *"Don't stand staring, idiot!"*

He didn't have to listen. He had to think. He couldn't leave the girl to wake up and tell. She would tell. He snatched up his large crab sack, and fit it over her head. He worked to stuff the rest of her in. The smell from the damp burlap—wet hemp and shellfish—clung to the back of his throat.

With a glance up at the closely shuttered cottages, he lifted the lumpy sack. She was not heavy. He lurched up the steps and through the gate to his car, and as he dumped her in the boot, her body noodled limply out of the bag. Her sweat and female scent were loathsome. He slammed the boot closed with a thud that matched his heartbeat. He climbed into the driver's seat, and took a breath before releasing the brake. He was free. Then a wheeze in his ear made him cringe.

"Something stupid!"

He closed his eyes for a second. He snorted back a retort and slammed the car into gear.

Ruth Butler couldn't shake a sudden uneasiness. She plunged the shovel into the stone-hard earth with a clang that set her teeth on edge. She studied the ground. Her efforts had made not even a dent. She lifted her shovel and then, as if her arms hadn't the strength to hold it, she let it drop. Cold penetrated her jacket and made her shiver. The last week of March had brought a week's reprieve in weather, but now, in this first week of April, it seemed winter would give them another gut punch to remember it by.

Where was Annie? She stared down at the bare-rooted fern. Something was wrong. She glanced at pots and creeping ivy and the way the light from her kitchen window tinged her drive yellow. Everything looked in order. So why this sudden worry?

She dropped her gloves at the back door, switched on the electric kettle, and stared out the kitchen window to wait for hot water. She picked up her cell phone and reread the text from Annie. She was fine. So what was wrong? She grabbed the duck mug, one of the items she had managed to save from her grandmother's belongings and just about the only thing to survive in one piece from Texas to Cornwall. She set it on the counter and rubbed her hands to work the cold away.

The kettle whistled. This worry was silly. Everything was fine.

She plopped a tea bag in the hot water and wrapped her fingers around the mug. She backed up and almost tripped on Annie's tennis shoes. If she wasn't wearing the these, then it stood to reason she'd gone out this morning with her new shoes, the very shoes she'd told her not to wear until tomorrow. She huffed. What was she to do with a ten-year-old who wouldn't listen?

Ruth took her tea to the window that overlooked the road to watch for her.

The doorbell rang and she jumped. She hadn't seen anyone come up the walk. She set the untouched tea on a side table.

On the porch, out of breath, her daughter's friend Dot huffed, "Where's Annie?"

"Wasn't she with you?"

"I lost her! I thought she came back here."

"Weren't you at the beach?"

"For about five minutes."

"She must have come another way."

Dot's expression made that seem like a ridiculous response.

Ruth's thoughts raced. There were so many places on the beach to get hurt, like the caves that were only empty of water at low tide and the unstable coastal rock that was scarred with deep clefts. "Let me grab my jacket." She texted Annie: **Where r u?** and took off with Dot toward the beach.

The village was Sunday-morning silent. People would be at home with the paper, or asleep, or bustling kids into well-dressed bundles for early services.

Ruth and Dot searched up and down the streets. They looked around corners, and peered down alleys. Ruth's skin crawled with fear. All she could think about was that this couldn't be happening. They were safe here.

A walker with a dog came up the street and Ruth stopped him. "Do you know Annie Butler?"

"No."

"A girl, have you seen a girl with a pink jacket?"

"No, no sign of anyone. Sorry."

Ruth nodded, numb with anxiety. In the ten years they had lived here, hadn't they always been safe? She caught up to Dot. Couldn't Annie have stopped by another friend's house? No, Dot explained, all of their other friends lived too far away to walk.

Ruth didn't scream bloody murder. She didn't beat doors down. She didn't stomp her feet and throw things because the world hadn't produced her daughter immediately. But all the worst questions came full circle in her mind: What if? What if? Could it be happening again? She couldn't stop checking her phone. Why didn't Annie answer?

At the beach, sheer rock rose from the sand in a jagged edge of land as if the Almighty had used a saw to sever the coastline from the sea.

"Annie!" she called.

The cliffs cast her cries back at her. Gulls screamed, and flapped up from their perches.

Dot returned from the other end of the beach. The thought crossed Ruth's mind that she would hear bad news. But the child said, "No one's seen her, Mrs. Butler."

"Why, Dot? Why did you leave her?"

"I just ran round the other side of the rock there for a second. I thought there might be prettier shells closer in."

Ruth took a deep breath and stared at the jutting, sheer wall of rock. On the other side were the stairs. *Be patient with Dot, she's just a child, too.* "Where was Annie?"

"I thought she was behind me, but then she wasn't there. But she had said she would get more shells farther down, while the tide was out. Then I couldn't find her. She didn't go to the water."

"How do you know?"

"She wouldn't have wanted her shoes wet. Her footprints stopped at the bottom of the steps. That's why I thought she went home." Dot's china-doll face glistened with tears. "I don't know why she left me."

"Go tell your mum. Run!" Ruth heard the panic in her own voice and wondered, *When should the official time for panic begin?* Her life wasn't what it appeared to be, and she could never talk about it.

Annie was old enough to walk with a friend without a mother that hovered like a crazy. She didn't want Annie to grow up afraid of her own shadow. She trusted Annie to know what to do in a bad situation. Hadn't she taught her?

The morning sun had hardly moved. How could that be? She stood on the beach and stared back up at the village sprawled up ruffled hills away from the sea. The River Perrin cut down between the cottages with their higgledy-piggledy roofs and tumbled into the surf.

She and Dot must have caused a stir as they ran around and yelled because two couples and several teens came scrambling over the rocks from different directions.

Many voices blended into the beat of surf. Ruth heard, "… looking for your daughter … called police …" Her legs went wobbly. She sank down on the cold sand. *Oh Lord! Don't let me fall apart. I'm overreacting. Surely, I'm overreacting. There is no way he could have found us.*

2

The Mini Cooper zipped along the road between brown hedgerows, popped into view occasionally like a white rabbit with a propensity for tardiness. The car trailed a hint of music in its wake. Inside the car, Detective Inspector Jon Graham gripped the wheel. One finger tapped out the rhythm coming from the radio.

He braked as something tiny started across the road ahead. The little creature stopped midway across the road. Jon slowed to a stop. The young fox stood upright like a rabbit, stared at his car, then turned and bounded back up the steep incline to the hedge. Jon pressed on, thankful there was one less dead fox in the world.

The opportunity to travel south had come as a relief. His job in the fraud division of Complaints usually involved sifting paperwork and unbearable bureaucracy, so he'd grabbed the chance at this assignment. He shifted his legs in a cramped stretch. The investigation of a corrupt police officer shouldn't take long. He figured to have the fellow in custody within a week—two, at the outside.

The West Country coast curved along dramatic cliffs that were wrapped in white streamers of surf. The sun grew bright with the promise that today might develop into a lovely day which meant that, if the stars were aligned correctly, it might not rain much.

Perrin's Point boasted a legend that had proven lucrative to the spotty village. Four centuries before, Douglas Perrin, a bloodthirsty blackguard, walked into his castle fortress and vanished. Jon wondered how the pirate might have felt about the tourist industry that was captivated by his disappearance.

A distant foursquare church tower showed well against the verdant green hills. There was a gap in the hedgerow, and the sea view flashed past again, closer this time. Jon observed striations of deep amethyst in the pale gray water.

His mobile sang out its own beat, and he switched his satellite music over to the phone.

Superintendent Bakewell's voice blasted, "Well, Jon, hope you're getting on with that little trip to the south. How's the weather?"

"I haven't actually arrived. The sky is only partly cloudy this morning. Maybe it'll clear before long. You're up early, sir."

"What is your scheme of action for today?"

"I'll settle in and get the lay of the land. Then tomorrow when the shops and local savings and loan are open—"

"Hold on. You don't have tomorrow, you have today."

"Are you seriously telling me I have one day in Cornwall?"

"Your man should have all the particulars in order for you. You're to be done and dusted by day's end and back in London by tomorrow. See you then."

"Super, the officer assigned to this nearly died." Nothing's as dangerous as a half-cooked micro-dish of fish.

No reply.

"Sir?"

Jon listened to phone air, so he disconnected. "One day here? He's daft as a brush."

It was a distasteful mess when one got right down to it, a DCI involved in scandal—with the officer's savings account suddenly filled with riches (and with no explanation, according to the anonymous bank official's complaint). Direct questions would create more problems, the Higher Powers decided. So for the general morale of the police force, the investigation would be kept low-key. Broadcasting such an investigation would alert the DCI, and he would likely find a way to hide the money.

Jon had one day to play catch-up and come to a conclusion. But he intended to stay until the job was complete, so Bakewell and his "one day command" could jolly-well stuff it.

He reached to switch to the radio again. Being Sunday, not many people would be out and about. His assignment demanded he act as any other tourist, and that meant get in and out with as little notice as possible.

Just as his Mini swung into a blind curve, a dark blur of a car shot out straight at him.

In the second before Jon swerved and rammed his car up against the hedgerow, he heard the horrific squeal of two vehicles make paint-scraping contact. His car sashayed as the tires slid across a muddy verge to stop short and sudden. Earth's longest minute was over. Silence. He took that first, deep breath, and another breath, and realized then that it was okay to unclench his fists from the steering wheel. He set the hand-brake and switched off the motor.

And then he thought with regret, *So much for a quiet entrance into the village.*

8:00 a.m.

Shit!

Charles rammed his car forward to get away from the car he'd just sideswiped. It would take some time for the other car to shift round and come after him. The grumming hum of his car assured him that the car could carry him away. If it would only go faster.

Some miles later, he zigged left into a narrow lane and rolled to a stop in a dip of land behind some trees to wait. The adrenaline rush subsided, but the pain in his stomach remained. What next? This girl, this bold chit of a girl, had stood up to him, challenged him, like the others. His gut burned when he thought about the others. He'd naught to do but implement damage control. Unless—unless he could talk her into cooperation.

He tugged on the rearview mirror. Blood dripped where he had bitten his lip through. What else? He imagined his wide eyes were those of a stranger caught in headlights before the car's wheels thumped over him. He must calm down.

He exited the car and opened the boot, reached in for the girl, and held his breath so he wouldn't have to smell her. Still as death, yet a pulse. Why did this have to keep happening?

"It is your eternal punishment before your eternal punishment."

No! It must be that the girl was his salvation. But could she save him—save him from … from being overwhelmed with the terrible tortures that pressed against his life at every turn, the burn in his gut that seared with every breath? Could she bring back his life with Cecil?

He didn't want to kill the girl. He wasn't like that, not really. He only wanted the peace he'd had when he was young. Before his mother ruined his life.

The girl's mother would surely come to save her. She would come and he would make her tell him what she was supposed to tell him. She would say it.

He didn't want to kill the girl. Death was messy and he hated messy. Her living blood would take the place of the blood he couldn't have any more. But the child's mother—he would have to kill the woman after she said what needed to be said.

He used an old cord to bind the girl's hands and feet so there would be no mistakes. He secured her and climbed back into the car.

"What's wrong with you, Chubby? Why didn't you do that earlier?"

Charles jerked. He muttered, "Whatever I do, it's useless!" With barely restrained anger, he answered, "I didn't carry string with me to the beach, Mummy."

He propped his head on the steering wheel and moaned, "Crying peace. When there is no peace." He lifted his eyes, saw nothing.

The girl had recognized his proclivity, fascinated as he had become with her mother. His world unraveled when he spotted the woman at the fete and knew her for what she really was. His mother had come back. This time he would be more thorough, and wring the confession from her before he killed her a second time.

He held his hands up like a shield. "Shhhh. Mother, don't say it. I know I should have gotten it right the first time. I never did anything right, is what you always say. But I *have* changed, you'll see."

The asthmatic wheeze in his head quieted. He could feel her still there, watching. *Oh God!* Perspiration soaked his shirt. He struggled out of his coat and glanced at his watch. Forty-three minutes since he'd first spotted the girl. The white motorcar hadn't come after him. It was a reprieve.

After a few moments, he reversed the old car and drove back up onto the blacktop.

The dark car gone and away, Jon Graham sat, dazed. Why hadn't the other motorist stopped? Must have been drinking and driving—on a Sunday morning and all. He pushed the car door open, swung his legs out, and set his feet squarely into a trough of liquid black mud. He leaned back and rubbed away the tiredness from five hours of driving. He could easily have gone over the side of the cliff, never to be seen again. There likely wasn't anyone about to hear the gut-wrenching scrape of his sweet little car tear through the gorse and fly into space to be squashed on the rocks below. He was thankful.

He picked his way out of the mud and shook what he could off his shoes so he wouldn't feel weighted down. He detailed what injury his car had sustained. A smear of purplish paint from the crash-derby car was etched into a dent along one fender. A razor line of silver sliced through to bare metal. It could be easily remedied. He walked around to the hedgerow side. There was a dent the size of an orange and quite a few scratches from bracken. Fortunately the impact was not great enough to cause his air bags to deploy. That would have required immediate assistance.

He'd pinched, scraped and sacrificed to purchase this, his first car, a year ago. Though not a new car, it had been so well kept as to be beautiful. Here he'd driven all this time in London, with its racecar taxi-drivers, without a scratch. And then the first day in peaceful Cornwall and BOOM!

He looked around for CCTV possibilities and saw none, so the accident wouldn't have been recorded. The sun was under a misconception of cloud but still dazzled. The breeze from the sea was brisk. He checked the condition of his books, which he had packed loosely. He started up, pulled the car to the road and once more drove toward the village.

His baby was bruised. Everything would be fine. Hindsight being what it is, Jon honked his horn before he came to the next turn in the lane.

"Mrs. Butler …"

She was still at the beach. The policeman kept talking, but Ruth tried to hold onto her daughter's words as she walked out of the house that morning. "I'm going with Dot, Mum! See you." The flute-clear remembrance called to her like a prayer. She had been in the kitchen stirring oatmeal. She hadn't even bothered to look up.

People from the village surrounded her—bundled-up people, ready-for-anything people. Come fire or flood, they were ready, these people. Faces floated in. Faces floated out. Mouths opened and closed like fish. Words came and went like waves, close, closer, then blended into sentences.

Ruth heard, "… a description of your daughter." She unclenched her jaw. Her teeth clattered as she said, "Maybe she's back by now. Let me go home."

"But just in case we need it …"

"Hair, umm, lighter than mine, blue eyes, dark lashes."

Reed-thin Constable Stark scribbled notes.

"Did I tell you she's ten?" This panic is silly, an overreaction. "I'm sure she's home. I hate being a bother."

"No bother."

Hands reached at her—pulled her up (When had she sat down?)—wiped damp hair from her face.

"But write down she's tall for her age, though slight of build." It was Sally's voice. "And quite independent. Ruth, what was she wearing?" Ruth became aware of warmth across her shoulders. Sally's blanket. Sally, her neighbor and friend, whispered in her ear, "Yer frozen, m'dear!"

Ruth crushed the prickly wool to her face. The scent of cigarette smoke was strangely comforting.

"What was Annie wearing?" Police Constable Stark asked, for what must have been the second time. He was being patient, wasn't he?

"I know the answer." She stared down at her own cold, wet feet, to think, to be certain. "Blue jeans, a yellow shirt … a pink jacket, I think you call them windcheaters … shoes."

Sally's flannel-coated arm felt warm. Ruth turned her head. She studied Sally's eyes. She could still breathe. Another question? Ruth faced the constable. He waited for her response. She couldn't remember what he'd asked. "I'm sorry?"

"You were saying—shoes." The constable turned from her then. Ruth looked back into Sally's eyes. "Black ones, Sally. Her new black shoes. I just remembered I told her not to wear them until tomorrow." Her face burned. She couldn't breathe.

Sally looked distraught. "Steady, luv."

Ruth coughed. "Sally, tell me she's home now. That's why you're here. You came to tell me she's home. I'm so silly to get all these folks worried over nothing." Ruth clung to her bundled-up friend and studied her face. Sally's sad face meant that she had not come to tell her that Annie was home.

God! This can't be happening. Don't let this happen. Make him give her back.

A seagull's *cack, cack* sounded like a baby. Ruth swung around at the cry. Constable Stark stood bent over Dot. She heard the child blurt, "No, I ran down the beach for more shells." The child's young voice broke. Ruth looked down. She's only been gone a little over half an hour, surely. How far could they have gotten in a half hour?

Stark stood up straighter. "So did you see anyone else here?"

"Yes!" Tears cleared trails through sand dust on Dot's cheeks. "A few people up at the wall and a big black dog on the beach."

Stark's voice came softer. "You're certain you were separated from your friend for only a few minutes?"

She nodded, her face screwed up tight.

"That's all right, Dot. You're good at telling. You should be proud. Now then, what happened next? You turned back to join Annie and rounded this boulder." The constable used his pen to jab the air over his shoulder. "What did you see?"

Pointing toward the base of the steps, Dot sobbed, "The sack, the shells were dumped out, the ones we found. She said she wouldn't drop them. And she's stomped on them, looks like."

Ruth followed the direction Dot had pointed. At the base of the cement steps lay a sad heap of shells—limpets, cowries, and a few scallops in crushed pieces—along with the crumpled cloth sack that Annie kept her socks in normally. Her gaze followed the steps to the top. She knew the latched wooden gate opened into a dark alley that lead directly out of the village. It had been too easy. And she could not say a thing.

3

Jon Graham rubbed his brow. He'd left London around two in the morning, fueled with plenty of coffee made strong enough to kill any notion of sleep. He didn't want anything now but a shower. He could smell his own perspiration, instantaneous and copious immediately after the accident, but now cold and sticky beneath his jacket.

At the top of a distant hill, he saw the remains of a mine engine. He'd done his research. The husk of darkened brick marked a tin mine, now a crumbly reminder of the past. The mines were closed. Economic hard times had hit the region hard, but the Cornish had pluck, and thankfully, a tourist industry. The land had taken a strange upward turn in value after the flood of '04 and people clamored for it.

At the southern tip of England, Cornwall was a rugged triangle of man-tunneled rock, like a hardened wedge of Swiss cheese. In bygone days, pirates and smugglers found myriad hiding places in coves and abandoned mines. Lawlessness permeated Cornwall's history like brandy in a Christmas pudding.

As Jon crested another ridge, he slowed the car. Perrin's Point was perched below a steep hill on three sides and had a harbor that lead to the Celtic Sea.

Perhaps it was for the best the other car had disappeared, Jon thought. His presence would remain unremarkable. He lowered his window and breathed deeply of the briny air. Lovely. He could hear a commotion down towards the beach, people yelling. Early Sunday sunrise service on the beach? There must be a celebration, or something like.

The car descended on roads that twisted into the lane's tight curves. The village lay cradled behind arms of rocky shoreline. The bay stretched with the tides into the village. The tide being out at the time, boats of all sizes and colors lay lopsided all over the sand, moored by long ropes anchored at the shoreline.

He slowed to look for High Street and then looked down at his map for the address of the local police sergeant who had agreed to house him on the q.t. Jon was supposed to be a cousin from London on surfing holiday. *I wish.* It sounded plausible, as the sergeant had indicated he owned a surfboard or two that he could lend.

He made a right turn onto a picturesque lane with quaint, painted cottages fronted by slate porches. It was unbelievable that three slabs of stone, two of which stood upright either side and a third as a "roof," could withstand time and storms without toppling. The lane narrowed even more. Now he had a view of the rear of buildings, but had to dodge dust bins. The backs of homes or shops pressed against both sides of the road.

He slowed the car to a crawl and one-handedly poured a cup of hot coffee from his thermos. Good thing his cup had been empty during his accident earlier. The road curved and dipped. A wall sprang at him. Both feet slammed on brakes. The car ground to a burring halt.

He mopped at spilled coffee before he reversed and maneuvered the car back round the way he had just come. It was then he saw the signs that warned drivers to take another route. *Ta, very much.*

He studied the map again and turned it around. Ah, here was his mistake. He was to turn *left* at the top of the hill, then drive to the cliff lane and turn right. His cheap, internet-purchased satnav had done him even worse in past escapades, so he hadn't even taken the blasted thing out of the console.

He poured a bit more coffee and took a sip. The taste reminded him of his office, which would be brimming with activity just now. He'd been in the police for ten years and worked out of the Regional Crime Squad's London base at present. A specially selected detective sergeant from the Bristol RCS completed Jon's team. Detective Sergeant Thomas Browne was a good man. It was too bad about the food poisoning—he was still in hospital.

According to the bank official, Detective Chief Inspector Peter Trewe's deposit account had jumped from £2,000 to £982,000. A special trace on the money dead-ended at a corporation with one member of record: Peter Trewe. Something didn't add up.

Their mandate was to find the source of the money and make sure nothing embarrassing oozed from the bottom of any mess to make its way into the public forum. To keep things quiet wasn't easy, with increased public scrutiny and information handed round like bowls of spaghetti.

Jon's sergeant had been careful to keep the surveillance secret. This was not an easy thing to do in a small village. Once, an old lady with a stick, chasing a cat from her rear garden, surprised DS Browne as he installed a camera. The point of the surveillance was to see if Trewe had a secret means to replenish his monies, such as with stolen or smuggled goods. DS Browne told the old lady he was bird-watching and produced a birder's manual. She took her stick to him and chased him down the street anyway.

Despite recent setbacks on the job, Jon was determined to find answers here. He had to recover his reputation, especially with fellow Detective Inspector Bennet. Their two desks shared proximity at the London office. He could picture Bennet's sneer. "Couldn't find the source of the money could you? Worthless prat. Screw around on the job. Screw around on women. You never could stick with anything. Pun intended!"

Jon had chatted up the wrong girl, as it turned out—Bennet's cousin.

Nobody's perfect.

Another gulp of coffee, and he turned at the signpost. The narrow lane turned tricky with sudden twists, and what was left of his coffee sloshed across his shirtfront. He set the coffee in a holder.

A wooden stake in front of a gray cottage read "Frog's Turn." This was it. Yellow flowers edged the front of Sergeant Perstow's home. Sergeant Perstow and Constable Stark manned the tiny Perrin's Point Police station. DS Thomas Browne made arrangements through intermediaries, drove a caravan down from Bristol and parked it in Perstow's rear garden. The tiny home on wheels contained everything required for survival plus a bank of flat-screen monitors required for the project. With his sergeant in hospital with food poisoning, Jon would stay here. He hated confined spaces, so this would be no picnic. He'd have to think positive thoughts to be able to sleep in such a stuffy, cramped, closed-up space.

Positive thoughts, Jon thought. *Boy Scouts, camping, adventure. Right!*

He swung the Mini round the house to the rear and his tires crunched on the gravel drive. At the bottom of the garden next to a dilapidated garage sat the caravan, white and dented in places like a discarded tissue box, a tiny, enclosed box of a place. So much for positive thoughts.

TREBORWICK, POLICE STATION AND CID OFFICE
Sunday, midmorning

DCI Trewe possessed the scariest eyes Ruth had ever seen. They were ice-blue and predatory, a wolf's eyes. The detective chief inspector's skin stretched thin across his prominent cheekbones and angular chin. From a distance, Ruth had imagined his face rakishly handsome, not the cadaverous aspect in front of her.

Ruth refused another offer of tea from Sergeant Perstow. She was shaky enough. She could not absorb the fact that her daughter was missing. Missing meant disappeared. Gone. Things like this didn't happen to people like her.

"This is bad." The sturdy Sergeant Perstow sat very still next to Ruth. He seemed as wary of Detective Chief Inspector Trewe as she was.

"Perstow, you're upsetting Mrs. Butler." Trewe angled his chair around to rifle some sheets of paper on a nearby file cabinet.

"Sorry, lass." A deep shade of red flushed up from Perstow's neck.

"Please." Ruth shook her head. Nothing could upset her worse than she was already.

Trewe nodded. "I'm so very sorry. Do you feel up to a few questions?"

"Of course. I want her back. Safe."

"A little girl called Dot was with your daughter this morning?"

Ruth stared at the red pen Trewe twisted between the fingers of one hand. "They often take walks."

"Does she often disappear?"

"No! This has never happened before. She wouldn't worry me like this on purpose."

"Does she carry a mobile?"

"She isn't responding. I've called dozens of times; it goes to voice mail. I've texted her. Nothing. Now I've resorted to texting her friends and their moms. They've put out a bulletin with their social media. They're out looking for her." Ruth heard her hysteria rising with each word. *I want to snap out of thinking that he found us. Dear Lord, what am I doing here? Should I tell the police? No, don't panic. Dear God, bring Annie back. Make this go away.*

"There has been an attempt to locate your daughter's mobile signal, Mrs. Butler. But they believe the mobile's been turned off. You're on the telephone at your house?"

"Yes. I have a land line."

"We'll post a constable to listen in the event she rings your house. You have your neighbor—"

"Sally. Her name is Sally. Look, I'm sorry. I don't want to sound like a panicked … a panicked … you know … I want to help. I do. I want to help. I …" Ruth suddenly realized she could not stop repeating herself.

Trewe swung around. His chair hit the wall.

Ruth jumped into the immediate present.

He asked for details of every activity Annie had been involved with in the past three weeks. He had Perstow take notes and write a more detailed description of Annie than Ruth had given Constable Stark earlier. Ruth concentrated on every detail that she could think of. He wanted a list of Annie's friends. She had brought a recent photo.

Trewe looked at the photo. "What kind of friends does she have?"

"Good friends. I like them. I like their parents. They're great."

"Does she have a boyfriend?"

"What?" Ruth tried to understand exactly what he meant. "A boyfriend? She's only ten. Yes, yes, I know she knows about things."

"Things?" Trewe's eyes betrayed nothing. They held ice.

"The facts of life, but she isn't interested in the opposite sex, from what I can tell. She wants to play soccer—I mean, football. You call it football, sorry, I should know that by now. Boys are the farthest thing from her mind, except as friends. She has a lot of friends."

"Does she have any close friends who are boys?"

Ruth shook her head. *Why does he go on like this?*

Trewe kept on. "Is there any reason to believe she may have been experimenting with anything?"

"What do you mean by anything?"

"Drugs."

"Of course not! She is ten, not seventeen!"

Trewe's expression didn't change.

Ruth took a deep breath and started over. "I know kids are at an iffy age at ten, but Annie is different. She's … How to describe it? … She's transparent. I can tell when she's lying."

"So she lies occasionally, does she?" Trewe tapped his pen on the desk.

"Don't all kids?"

"I'm sure. But you think you could *tell* if she were doing something she shouldn't?"

"That's exactly what I'm saying."

Ruth stared at Trewe's hands. What were the police saying? Do they think she ran away? That she was involved with drugs and boys? Were they crazy?

A glance passed between Perstow and Trewe. He nodded and looked at Ruth. "Mrs. Butler, we'll do everything in our power to get your daughter back to you. You must allow us to do our job."

"She did not run away, she does not do drugs, she has no boyfriend and no enemies. Does that answer all your questions?"

"Sergeant Perstow will take you home, Mrs. Butler."

"No."

"No?"

"I want to know how you plan to find my daughter." She heard the breathless panic in her own voice.

"Mrs. Butler ..." Trewe hesitated as he studied her. At last, he turned to Perstow. "The area's been secured?"

"Yes, sar."

"Scenes of Crime Office came immediately?"

"The whole area'd been trampled by the time they arrived but SOCO worked as fast as the tide would allow." Perstow bobbed his head as he spoke. His accent was thick. His "sir" sounded like "sar" and while his "s" sounded like a "z", he pronounced his "th" like a "d."

A huge weight crushed Ruth inside. Her breath came in gasps. She coughed to clear her throat. *Don't fall apart now, missy.* "You suspect foul play. You suspect someone's taken her."

"We take every precaution in situations such as this, Mrs. Butler," Trewe said. "When a young girl goes missing, it is important we do what we do, quickly. I can reassure you, usually there's a logical explanation. I don't want you to worry overmuch. We are doing everything possible."

Ruth swallowed. *Get a hold of yourself. He won't listen if you fall apart.* The two police officers stared at her. Did her presence constrain them?

As if he had read her mind, the ice-eyed man said, "It'd be best if you were home."

Ruth took a moment to stand, and even then, she was not sure her legs would support her. She wanted to sink to the floor right there, but she jerked herself upright, chin up. "Fine. I'll be at home."

Trewe looked at the clock on the wall. Several hours had passed since the child's disappearance. So many things can happen in a moment. He didn't like to think of it.

Perstow came back into the office and picked up another stack of files. "I'll have these sorted soon enough, sar."

"Perstow, what do you think happened to the girl?"

"Heaven forbid someone took her, sar."

"I'm going to tell you something that no one else is to hear for gossip's sake. But for the record, I was at that beach this morning."

Perstow's broad face registered shock. "You were there?"

"But I saw nothing, as God is my witness, of this girl, Annie. I recall thinking that it was strange that the little girl, Dot, was there alone. I often stop for a moment at the top of the wall before I come to work. Today was not much different than any other day. That is, until I received the call about the missing girl."

"I see, sar."

"If it comes up, I won't hide the fact. I simply don't see any relevance." Trewe laid a chart across the district map on his desk. He studied it for a moment, then looked up at Perstow. "It was hard getting the mother to listen, wasn't it?"

"Annie is a good girl, sar."

"You know her?"

"She would speak if we passed."

Trewe shook his head. "Tell me what you know of the mother."

"Well, she lived here for some years before anyone knew her a-tall."

"What do you mean?"

"Kept herself to herself. Save for sending the girl for school, no one ever saw Mrs. Butler until a few years ago, when she volunteered at the church."

"So you haven't spoken to her before today?"

"I wouldn't go that far, sar. She sort of came out of her shell, you might say, here about a year ago. I don't know that I'd noticed her before then. We would speak after church services. A few months ago, she helped run one of the booths at the fete. And I saw her at the hall later. She was dancing."

"Who with?"

"Well, if ye must know, me, for one. She was only being friendly, not picking anyone in particular."

"Flirting?"

"No, definitely not. I asked her to dance."

Trewe pursed his lips, thinking, then said, "She's American. There's something she's holding back, Perstow. Knowing the villagers as you do, do you have any idea what she might be hiding?"

"I have no idea, sar."

"I intend to find out. Perstow, prepare a team. Alert the coast guard. Put out an Amber Alert. Let's jack this thing up!"

4

Sunday night

Jon Graham turned away from the live feed of the beachfront. His heart heavy, he fiddled with his cup. When he followed his sergeant's written instructions as to where all the cameras were, he had seen the blue flyers. What he had heard this morning had been no celebration on the beach. They had been searching for a missing girl.

His super would have to know right away, though he wondered if perhaps he should hold off. The girl might turn up. Offering help with this missing girl situation would jeopardize his undercover work. To make matters worse, the officer in charge of finding the girl was the officer he was investigating.

He pulled his bowl of rice from the micro and cleared the table of Detective Sergeant Thomas Browne's old mags, remotes, empty cellotape dispensers, and stacks of blank notepads. The monitor hooked up to the lone DVD player was the closest to him. A lot of the newer cameras recorded directly to the computer. All the VHS tapes would have to wait until he could locate a VCR. Who uses such outdated equipment anymore?

The video would recycle itself unless he took the pertinent footage and archived it. He'd gone through and archived footage taken at the time the girl disappeared to flash drives. The only thing he could do nothing about was the VHS tapes. There were two of them. He wondered what was on them. He was that knackered. Everything blurred in his mind.

He cleared his disposable dish out of the way. The flatware he tossed in the sink amongst other unwashed dishes. His predecessor was not much in the cleaning department and he'd been here two weeks. He grabbed a bin bag and cleared away rubbish to make needed surface space.

He wanted to replay the footage he'd seen of the two girls on the beach. One of the cameras caught the girls as they rounded a rock outcropping. Both girls had been in brighter light, but when one girl disappeared back around the rock, there was too much shadow. He couldn't see.

Now more awake, he pressed "pause" and switched his attention to another computer screen. The other camera set face the steps the girls had taken may have caught something more. He set it to play back at the same time, then he clicked "back" on both of them and watched the camera's clock. He pressed "play" just as the girls stepped away from shadows into the light. The video from the other side of the beach made the girls look minuscule. The missing girl had gone back toward the steps as if she'd seen something.

The VHS tape recorders were closest to the stairs. It was dark there, but the really important things might be on them. *Blast it!* As he pounded a fist on the table, an errant paper cup tipped over. A muck of old coffee spread out and he had to grab his police notebook up. He stopped the play by play and stared at the images frozen on the monitor. He soaked up the mess and pulled out another notepad for unofficial scribbles.

Conclusions? The girl had seen someone off-camera, against the rock wall, apparently hiding in a natural crevice where he wouldn't be noticed. This means there was a possibility that the person had not planned the attack, that whoever had been there had arrived before dawn. The cliffs faced west. Before the sun was higher in the sky everything on the beach was dark. It wouldn't have been difficult to remain hidden. So why had the man spoken? Unless he wanted to get the girl's attention and so, kidnap her? An involuntary shudder took him.

Jon turned to the other monitors, which had footage from the live CCTV cameras set up on the roads to and from the farm where Detective Chief Inspector Trewe lived with his son's family. By special dispensation and in conjunction with the UK Highways Agency, Jon's sergeant had been able to set up a wireless link to the traffic observing stations. In the same vein, Jon had been able to recommend that a few fixed cameras be strategically placed in the Active Traffic Management system around Perrin's Point. Why hadn't the local police department requested more cameras before? Answer: Money—always the issue, and damn the results. Jon had used the argument that Cornwall wasn't as inundated with traffic cameras as were other areas and that traffic accidents did occur here.

He wanted to check to see if the dark car that hit him was recorded. The road footage showed a lot of nothing but dark strips of pavement augmented on one side by stacked rock walls and on the other side by hedgerows. Except for the seasonal influx of sun-and-surf revelers, what was there to see? Hedgehogs, sure. Rare wild ponies would be a definite highlight. And grab your hats and hold your seats if a walker with dog happened by.

He backtracked to the time of the girl's disappearance, then decided if the fellow who hit him had driven out of Perrin's Point, he had likely driven into Perrin's Point, so he backtracked even further until he did catch the dark car enter the road to the beach. The footage was too dark to read the registration tags. He fast-forwarded through darkness, and there it was, the car leaving. Not much to go on. The driver gripped the wheel; there were no identifying marks on his knuckles and his face was hidden beneath a hat. Then he saw the time. The exact time the girl had been reported missing. Coincidence? He thought not.

He should get the VHS tapes to the missing girl's investigation team. If he took the VHS tapes to the local police, the entire force would be at him about his role in it. He'd have to return to London a failure. On the other hand, if he didn't report the footage this moment, he would be accused of withholding evidence, surely a reason for dismissal.

His boss, Detective Superintendent Bakewell, had experts that could help out with shadows and lightening and enhancing even VHS footage. But time was of the essence with a missing girl. "A simple reporting of the facts," he murmured, as he slipped the DVD he'd just created into a sleeve and labeled it "Beach Footage."

What would Bakewell say when he heard Jon's story? He would say, "If you report the tapes, we'll have no choice but to stitch up this business with Trewe, and *that* would put him in a position to withhold information, which would then afford him opportunity to hide the money."

Jon would make the argument about the missing girl and time, etc. etc.

Bakewell would tell him to send the flash drive footage by email, copy the flash drives and keep them to hand over to DCI Trewe when the time was right, and send the VCR tapes by post first thing in the morning.

Of course. That is exactly what he would say.

He sent a preliminary email to explain the situation and hoped it sounded lucid, given his lack of sleep. He then packed the two VCR tapes in a big envelope and the flash drives in a separate, smaller envelope. Done and done.

He cracked a window and closed the door.

A full twenty-two hours had passed since he'd last slept. The best sleep-inducer would be to read the reports his ailing sergeant had left behind. He picked up the reports, lay on the sofa, and within an hour sat up again. The most remarkable thing about all the information in the reports was that there was nothing remarkable. What had the man been doing? This lack of progress meant that he would have to go to the hospital and interview his sergeant. It was past visiting hours, so he couldn't do that until the next day. His stay in Cornwall just grew one day longer. Ha!

He fell asleep with an open book of Shakespeare on his chest. *Come what come may, Time and the hour runs through the roughest day.*

❦

Ruth pressed the toothbrush harder against the tub grout. The toothbrush was a frazzled mess. She was told to stay put and wait for a call, but she couldn't just sit. So she cleaned. She stared up at the mirror above the sink.

The day before, Annie had called, "Mom! Come see!"

Ruth had gone into the bathroom. Her funny, creative daughter was sitting on the sink, her feet in the bowl, drawing faces in a smear of shave gel. "Annie! I said *clean* the mirror."

"But Mom, this is you. Look," she drew her finger through the gel, "a smile!"

"Oh? And why am I smiling?"

"Because I made two goals in the practice game today, and straight away Mr. Sawyer told me I was brilliant. Real praise—coming from him, that is."

"Great! I'm so proud of you."

"Yeah, and Caroline was furious about it, jealous prat."

"Annie!"

"She was."

Annie had tackled her school papers the night before so she wouldn't have them to do the last day of her weekend.

The mirrors were fogged now with hot water steam. She felt inclined to clean the mirrors until she noticed the tiny smears left from the gel. No. She wouldn't touch them.

Ruth got up from beside the tub and took her gloves off. She'd been at it since coming home from the police station that morning. She took up the bottle of cleaner and squirted it on the sink. The sink was already desperately clean.

"Dear Lord Jesus."

It sounded odd. She hadn't really prayed in such a long time.

She wandered out to the living room. She couldn't vacuum; the phone might ring and she wouldn't hear it. Beyond the picture window, the front yard was dark. It was night? When did that happen? The clock on the wall ticked. Was Annie hungry? Cold? What was he doing to her?

Earlier that day, Sally had held Ruth's hand, answered the phone, fixed meals Ruth couldn't eat, then left to care for her own family, promising to come back and spend the night.

Ruth lay on the couch and hugged her knees to her chest. The flowers in the vase looked orderly, but they smelled bad. They reeked. She stood and yanked the flowers from the sour water, stumbled into the kitchen, rammed them into the bin, bent over, and retched.

She made her way back to the living room. *He meant to kill us. No one would believe me.* Now she had to tell. Everyone here would find out what a liar she was. But it didn't matter. He still meant to hurt Annie.

"Please Lord, not my Annie." She looked at the mug of tea she hadn't touched since this morning. The room closed in. She couldn't breathe properly. She paced—back and forth, back and forth. She hit the wall with an open hand each time she came to it. Pace, slap. Pace, slap.

She looked at the clock again. It was eleven forty-five. Why hadn't she heard anything? With a cry she fell across the couch. *No, no, no! Annie!* She rubbed at her face until it hurt.

She needed to wait. Something would happen. She reached for the box of tissues from a side table, turned off the lamp and sat in the dark. She picked at her nails as she stared out the window.

Riverside was the name of her cottage. It lay nestled in a quiet neighborhood with the River Perrin, which was more like a stream, running along behind. She was four blocks from the sea with several rows of cottages or businesses between, but sometimes she could swear she heard the song of the waves, as she did now. She went to the window and cracked it. No. It was, of course, only the river she heard, and yet—

the rhythm, the ghostly echo of drums—and she was back on the beach surrounded by people. They were calling for Annie.

Across the village, in the harbor, searchers' lights flashed like fallen stars, pieces of hope that spread farther and farther out of her reach.

She paced some more, then crumpled to the couch again. Mandy, the cat, jumped up and settled herself on the back of the couch behind Ruth's head. Somewhere, Ruth had a picture of baby Annie sleeping on Mandy. She remembered taking it—in the picture Annie's baby drool dripped onto the ferocious-hater-of-water-turned-pillow. Despite being ten and too "cool" to be sentimental, Annie loved her Mandy-cat. Ruth leaned back against the cat and let her purr drown out the ticking of the clock.

A melodic ring woke her. She sprang from her seat and a billion pieces of shredded Kleenex scattered. The tinny notes of "Annie Get Your Gun" grew louder. Her cell phone! *They call them mobiles here, mum, remember?* She snatched up her purse and dug into it.

How hard could it be to find a phone? She flipped the purse upside down. Everything fell out. The cell phone clattered. She grabbed it up and unlocked the screen. The incoming number!

She screamed, "Annie where are you?"

"Hello, Mother." It was not her child's voice.

Her legs gave out from under her. "Where's Annie? Where's Annie?"

"Tell me you love me."

It didn't sound like the voice that she remembered, but it had been years since they'd spoken. "What are you saying?"

The connection was cut.

5

Annie Butler took a few deep breaths. Her head hurt. She tried to move. She choked back a sob. It hurt. Where was she? She couldn't think. She lay very still, scared of the pain. But the darkness frightened her worse. It was a dark that she couldn't understand. It took away her sense of sight and hearing and smell. She was cold, and yet, she was wet with sweat. She couldn't stop shaking. Her breath came in gasps because everything hurt and she hated this horrible dark.

She coughed. The noise was a foghorn to her ears. So, her ears did work. She whispered, "Hello?" Her voice trembled like the rest of her.

Nothing.

She listened. Water dripped. She lay on something soft, like a mattress. She flexed her fingers. One hand wasn't held down and she slid it to her chest. On top of her a huge, flat something pressed into her from head to toe. She took a chance of pain to strain against it to shift it away. The thing was soft but unyielding and it smelled bad. She forced her breathing to slow and for the rest of her to remain calm. *Think.*

Don't panic.

Don't cry.

It did no good, this pep talk. Heat flushed up to her face and tears burned her eyes. With her free hand, she rubbed her eyes to force the tears away. She couldn't move, she couldn't see, but she could breathe.

Her stomach cramped. How long had she been here? Mom had breakfast waiting.

Mom! A blubbering sob choked her and she coughed and coughed and couldn't breathe. Pain shot across her skull and the dark inside her head took her away again.

Monday, 3:03 a.m.

Charles didn't want to move until his eyes became used to the darkness. He stared around the murky garage to discern familiar shapes. He wiped the cold sweat from his oily face. The choppy lass had it coming to her. He made his way past the old canvasses where turpentine permeated the dust and petrol smell.

The wife had been fast asleep for a little while. He'd added that special something to her nightly glass of red wine.

To see the time, he punched a fist into the moonlight streaming through the window. He must judge the tide well. Can't keep the girl's body around here forever. The Wife might find her.

He'd had no choice but to end her pitiful life. To clean up the filthy mess was the first order of business.

Then to deal with the American woman. A travesty, to allow foreigners into this country without restitution of some kind. If he were in charge, things would certainly be different. And this mess was all her fault. If she hadn't resembled Mother so closely and flaunted about so he would notice—stupid get!

His mother's voice rasped inside his head, *"If I could have undone you from my womb, I would have."*

"Why have you always hated me? Cecil was your fault. Your fault. You. You!" Tears rolled down his face. He held his stomach and took a slow breath.

A gossamer thread caught the moonlight. He watched the spider, mesmerized, but he grew bored with the creature's exacting ministrations. So, as each strand was cast he took control, and, line by meticulous line, he disassembled the web. With one finger he smashed the helpless creature. He used the spider's remains to draw the letter *O* on the windowpane. The moonlight broke through the clouds and silvered the opaque smear.

He opened his cold storage box, took out a jar of her blood, dipped his fingers in, and smeared it across his face. He drank the remainder.

From inside, he shoved the garage doors open. He started the car and reversed. He prayed silently to the only god he believed in, *Lady Luck, you've been there for me, be with me now.* He drove along B3263 south away from the village and, finding a certain private road, drove until he could park with a view of the sea. Colored a gray sepia wash, the entire world lay open around him, barren and desolate. The moon outlined each scuttling black cloud with white. He watched and waited. There was a storm coming. One huge cloud in particular moved closer and closer to the awful lunar spotlight. As he examined the landscape and waited, he hummed.

Demon arms of black stone jutted up from the sea, gnarled hands clutched at the water's surface. As waves washed over them, he could almost imagine the desperate movement of the damned and drowning.

"Hurry!"

The voice. Always the voice. Always interrupting.

He got out of the car and went around to the boot. He leveraged the girl's body from the car, checking to make sure the cloth sack tied around her head would not slip off. He did not want to see that face again.

He pulled her to the edge of the grass verge above the beach and propped the body up beside him, like a plastic mannequin. He slid with it down the side of the steep embankment. Her leg almost tripped him up at one point, but he caught himself. He let their weight work and they reached the beach somewhat together.

Above the crash of surf he heard, *"Evil will slay the wicked; the enemies of the righteous will be condemned."*

He doubled over, curled up on the wet sand, and covered his ears with his hands.

He pushed against his ears, harder and harder, until a groan squeezed out of his throat. He whined, "I try to do good, Mummy. I try."

Nothing.

He rolled onto his back, held his breath and counted to thirty. Into the ensuing moment of silence, he gasped, "All I've ever wanted from you … Just tell me you love me."

Inside his head, the grate of labored breathing diminished. His racing heart calmed. Standing, he shoved the girl's body with his foot. "I hate you."

Lifting the stiff, angular body roughly to his shoulder, he carried it to one of the dozens of outcrops of rock. The tide would take care of everything. Chances were, only a few minutes remained in which he could do this without being seen. Damned early commuters. He wedged the body between two jagged rocks.

In a hurried frenzy, he took a leafy sprig out of his pocket and tucked it into the string around the neck. In the old days there had been meaning in things.

Charles stood as tall as he could. The wind buffeted his body. Normally wound around, plastered to his bald pate, his thin, gray hair flew in long, gray Medusa-like strands around his ears. He spoke out bitterly, fist to the sky, his words spit at the sea, "The young live forever. Do you hear? Forever."

He glanced up toward the cliff's top. His heart skipped a beat, then jolted through his body. Had something moved up there by his car? He sidled away from the body and quickly made his way crab-like across the rocks. He jumped down to the sand. The waves muffled any noise he might have made as he scrambled up the steep embankment. The grasses stretched without end like a large swath of deep-purple crushed velvet. In the distance, barely discernible, a black dog ran towards the village church whose square tower was visible above a line of rock and hedge. Charles let out a long hiss of breath, then got back in the car and drove back the way he'd come. His breath came in heavy gasps. His heart thundered in his ears, all the winding way. He secured the car in the shed. He had to keep it hidden, and surprisingly, his mum remained silent.

Once inside the house, he cleaned his face and relaxed. He tilted his watch face to the moon. It had taken him forty minutes to rid himself of the body. After a little while, the tune "As Time Goes By" played in his head and he murmured the words.

6

Monday, before daybreak

Boom! Boom! Boom! Somewhere in his dream, DI Jon Graham shot at ducks on a lake. The birds flew up, and millions of wings stirred the scorching breeze. Palm trees swayed.

A loud thud, then a metallic explosion jolted him awake. Without reason, he found himself on the frigid floor of the caravan, one leg hung up in the blanket. Light flashed—on, off, on, off—from his alarm clock next to his face. The electric mini-heater whirred a blast of heat. The heater did little good. He had left a window open. It just made sense in the tightness of the place. He wrapped covers around his body and grabbed the clock to make out the time. Did the thing actually read 4:30? Already?

Boom! Boom! Boom! The caravan's fabricated walls shook. What stonyhearted villain banged on his door at this ungodly hour?

"Coming! I'm coming!" he called out, and massaged his scalp to rub some awareness through to his brain. The cold sliced through him as he pushed the duvet aside. He stood, slipped, and jammed a toe into the wire grate of the heater. "Oww!"

He yanked away. The grate popped off, and the heater fell forward. He flipped a light switch and saw that the old appliance head melted into the flooring. He jerked the plug from the socket.

The caravan's door handle wiggled. *Bloody-minded hell!* "I said I'm coming!" he shouted, limping two hops across the narrow space to peer through the curtained window at a fellow he didn't recognize. He popped the door open. "Hello?"

The rotund chap on his doorstep smiled. He carried a lumpy dish-towel-draped tray. "Sorry, sar. Thought you said, 'come in.' Weather's turned sketchy. Does sumin to my ears."

Jon gritted his teeth to keep them from chattering. "It's half-bloody-four."

"Oh … er … Sorry. I'm oaf to work. Thought you'd wish to know what's what."

Jon was awake now and realized this must be Perstow, sergeant of the local police and owner of the house occupying the other half of the garden. "Of course. Yes, come in. Sergeant Perstow, I take it." Jon grabbed a torn shirt up and threw it on.

"Sure, sure," Perstow groaned as he climbed the step. "Ow. Her Indoors is on me 'bout me weight. I tell her it's her fine cookin' and it calms her right down. She'll fix you a meal once she settles to the new face."

Perstow was short, not much over five feet, and built like a brick. He set the tray on the table and managed to squeeze his backside into a swivel seat. He drew the towel away from his tray. "Somethin' warm fer braxis."

"Thank you very much!" Jon rubbed his hands together and sat across the narrow table from Perstow. He cleared away the notes he'd taken the night before, and pushed a stack of his books aside, effectively hiding the mail package that contained the two VHS tapes.

Perstow looked around the confined space and sniffed the air. "Somethin' afire?"

"The space heater melted into the floor a bit."

"Sorry to hear it, sar. Milk?"

Jon nodded.

Perstow poured. "In for a mort o' weather."

His accent was thick but manageable; it held the sing-song quality of the local dialect. Jon briefly wondered what he'd meant, but he nodded in agreement, which was an acceptable answer to a weather statement this early in the morning.

Jon rubbed away at his eyes and studied the sergeant. The gray-haired man had the kind of jolly face that meant unlikely advancement in the ranks. He didn't have police eyes—the shrewd, cynical look of a person accustomed to being lied to. His round cheeks had a rosy blush, and his belly jiggled at every word. The tea was passed over. Perstow took a sip of his and an expression of pleasure swept over the man's good face, smoothing the lines and taking age from his years.

Jon eyeballed his tiny caravan. Not even here a day and the place looked like a clothes bomb had gone off in it. "Excuse the mess."

Perstow glanced around and said, "Your note mentioned you hated closed spaces, but I'm afraid the missus 'ud get a bit teasy 'bout the loan of our settee."

"No worries. The window's open. My therapist friend ..." Jon looked at the open face of the other man and wondered if he had disclosed too much information about himself. Even in such cold weather, he always kept a window cracked. Perstow seemed a good listener so he'd have to watch himself. "Enclosed spaces don't sit well, is all. My friend Steve suggested I take up spelunking."

"Sounds adventuresome, sar." Perstow had a habit of tossing a crinkle-faced smile upon every other sentence.

"But I said no way in bloody hell could anyone get me in a cave."

"You'll have to watch it round here with the mines. Sometimes the rock falls through from up top, and if you happen to be on the spot, you'll find yourself in a cave, right enough." Perstow drew the corners of his mouth down. "The other thing I need to tell you—no doubt today you'll observe the posters of the missing girl."

Jon adapted his well-used reserved look, "Oh?"

"Went missing yesterday morning just before seven." He glanced around at the monitors. "Did you happen to notice anything?"

"Sorry." Jon studied the man's face, then said, "No … No, I shouldn't be so cagey, what with your taking me in, so to speak. I … I have footage of the girls on the beach. I'm sorry to say the cameras aren't state of the art, so there isn't much to see."

"You saw …" Perstow leaned back as if he'd been slapped. "I'll need to see it." He added a "sar" as an afterthought.

"Here, I've archived the footage to these drives. You can look through them. Believe me, if even the slightest hint was on them, you'd have seen them right away. There isn't a thing. My super will get the experts on them. Trust me. The footage shows nothing, past the girls arriving on the beach, no one else, a lot of shadows. If I hadn't arrived when I did, and with DS Browne's food poisoning—"

"How is he?"

"He'll be fine, with a few days' rest. But what I was going to say is I'm here to complete the assignment."

"And the missing girl will not interfere?"

"She doesn't have anything to do with my investigation. I'm only interested in Trewe. We must know the source of this money."

"Oh! Aye. The money."

"And—" A clap of thunder like a gunshot made Jon duck. He'd have to speak softly, as noises seemed to carry through the caravan's walls. "And he's never said a thing about his new-found wealth?"

"Never." The tragic look that overcame his face under other circumstances might look comical. "I'd like to know, too. Our chief inspector seems to be a chap with worries."

"Odd. Very odd."

"DCI Trewe is certainly more on edge about the missing girl than anythin', though."

"How on edge?"

"He said, and I'll quote, 'the girl's American. The implications! International scandal. The newspapers. Bad for business, worse than the foot and mouth ever was in '01.' At least, that's what I remember he said. But … it was the way he went on."

"A coldhearted beast."

Perstow shook his head, "Oh no! I wouldn't say it like that. But I've never heard him *quite* as bad, sar. He's desperate, pulled in a profiler. The profiler said that there is a forty-four percent chance the child will be dead in the first hour, and the best chance of bringing her back alive is within the first three hours. The way our Chief Inspector went on … Where's the mercy in him, I ask meself. It was as if there was something else botherin' him."

Like nine hundred thousand somethings, Jon thought. "Keep me informed, as you are able. It is imperative you let no one know about me. I'm your cousin, on holiday, remember. And your wife must play along. She will, right?"

"Don't worry."

"I must concentrate on DCI Trewe, not a missing girl investigation. Hopefully, she'll show up with a good story and nothing amiss." Jon didn't believe it for a moment. The man in the dark car would not have been barreling out of the village quite so fast if there had been nothing to hide. He set his cup down with a definitive thud. "In the event the girl's body is found, the police will saturate this place. I'll have to make my presence known. If it comes to that, it would be expeditious to drop my investigation momentarily. Meanwhile, I'll send the footage in an anonymous package to DCI Trewe. I can't help but think it is the proper thing that he get it."

"I'll follow your lead, sar." Perstow nodded, eyes averted, as if he was well aware of his standing and didn't want to step beyond his bounds by getting chatty with a DI.

Jon had taken an immediate liking to the fellow but wondered about him a little. He seemed too nice to be true. The heaviness of an impending storm added to the burden he carried inside himself. He hoped against hope the girl would be found soon.

Outside, the storm pounced, but inside the caravan, Jon and Perstow sat hunched, intent upon the archived footage from the beach. Blue-white light from the monitor flashed across their faces and danced shadows around the caravan. Outside, the wind moaned and shoved against the tiny abode.

From the upper corner of one of the live monitors—one automatically controlled by computer at the monitoring station so any motion had it zooming or panning and focusing on minute detail—a large black dog darted into view, stopped, stared toward the camera, turned and took off.

Monday, daybreak

Rain and hail bulleted across Ruth's front window and the glass was rattled by inconstant wind. In those first few seconds of awareness Ruth wondered why she wasn't in her own bed, why she had slept in her big easy chair. Then came the heart-stopping memory of Dot's voice asking, "Where's Annie?"

Movement under a blanket on her couch caused Ruth to sit straight up. "Annie!" she whispered, heart beating wildly. Sally's curly red hair spilled from under the blanket. Ruth fell back, hope dashed. *Dear Lord Jesus, bring her back and I'll be a better Christian. I promise.*

She must have drifted into sleep again, because when a knocking woke her, the window was a dull rectangle. Here it was, another day, and no Annie to get up for school. Annie wasn't a morning person and the routine for school readiness was quite a production. She liked her sleep after her night hours of reading by flashlight. As far as Ruth knew Annie was unaware that her mother knew she was staying up, and that Ruth used to do the same thing.

In the corner of the dining room, the computer's new-mail icon flashed. Ruth sat up as she smelled bacon cooking. Another knock-knock, and she was at the front door.

Even in the gray drizzle, the local magistrate stood immaculate and stiffly upright. His sloping nose hooked over smiling lips. A poised fedora held his gray hair firmly in place.

"Excuse me, Mrs. Butler. I heard at the post office your daughter has gotten herself lost. I hope I might have misunderstood. Perhaps I misunderstood." Mr. Malone's umbrella dripped water in a neat circle all around him, turning the gray slate of the porch black. He stepped forward. Bushy gray eyebrows hung over his black-rimmed glasses, eyes hidden in shadow behind thick lenses. Mr. Malone gave talks on the local history to visiting groups of tourists. He volunteered at the library. He let it be known that he knew everybody.

"Thank you for coming," Ruth murmured.

"Of course," Mr. Malone said. "I've heard that your daughter is a polite young lady. Polite."

Ruth reached out and touched his sleeve. "Come in."

"Oh!" Mr. Malone stepped away from her. "Don't mean to intrude. The wife instructed me to bring you this soup she made you. Good soup." He held out a large canning jar. "I like it, anyway. She says it's an old family recipe. Yes. Mustn't stay. Mustn't."

"Thank you."

"Your Annie will come back to you, I'm sure. Take heart." Mr. Malone paused a moment, as if he was about to say something else. Then he touched his hand to his hat in a haphazard salute. "The wife and I will be thinking of you. Our prayers 're with you. With you." He made a stiff, miniscule bow, turned, and went gingerly down the two steps to his car.

Ruth called out to him, "Tell Liz thank you."

"She'll say you're quite welcome, I'm sure." He waved and squeezed gracefully into his Bentley. The grand silver car moved smoothly down the one-way road toward High Street, which was the main road in and out of the village.

Ruth leaned against the closed door. Mr. Malone was not a comfortable man. She took the jar of soup into the kitchen, where Sally wiped at the counter. A plate of congealed fried eggs sat on the tiny table where she and Annie usually sat to eat. The eggs were from the night before when hunger drove her to stuff food into her mouth. Rubber. Salty rubber. A few bites had been enough. She must have forgotten to clean up after herself. How had that happened?

Sally put her arms around her and pulled her into a motherly hug. "Hungry?" she asked.

Ruth's stomach rebelled. "No."

Sally, an expert at argument who had a temperament to match her fiery red curls, gave Ruth a look.

"I wouldn't mind tea." The British panacea had become just as much her own. As she turned to leave the kitchen and its heavy smells of food, she heard Sally say softly, "Bless yer heart."

Ruth went to the computer. She had an email from someone named Charles. The subject line said: **Tell me you love me!**

That was what the man on Annie's phone had said. She sat heavily as her knees gave way. It was her fault, hiding as she had all these years. She missed her parents, and the thought tore into her heart. Her parents—she needed them now.

Tell me you love me. He had said it on Annie's cell phone. How had he gotten her email address so quickly?

"Sally," she called out, "could you phone the police?"

Ruth stared at the computer screen. A tap at the front door made her jump. She got up and swung the door open to find no one there. With a glance down, she found a nosegay of wildflowers on the wet doorstep. She glanced up and down the street. A few cars swished by.

A card tied around the flowers with brown string read "*Fel neidr yn y ddaear.* Sorry for your loss." Her stomach tightened. She tossed the flowers on her hall table and stared at the card.

The night before—after the call—she'd dressed warmly and headed outdoors into a moonlit night, to attempt divination of the direction Annie might have gone if she had left the beach on her own. She walked to the cliff overlooking the bay. The moonlight sparkled dimly upon the waves. Silver-lined storm clouds amassed where horizon met sea.

She had paused long enough to listen to the surf before heading home again.

"Here we are, luv." Sally brought Ruth's tea in the duck mug. "The police are on their way."

Ruth smiled her thanks. Dearest Sally. The funny mug had given Annie a laugh. Sally knew things like that. When the tea is drained, sip by sip, the duck figurine is revealed. The words on the outside of the mug read, "Who's at the bottom of the well?"

A child's mug.

The phone rang. Ruth set the mug down and jumped up to answer it.

"Hello!" She listened. Nothing. "Hello?" She heard breathing. "Hello?" No response, just the sound of someone breathing, listening to her.

"Annie?" she said, unable to stop the desperate keen of her tone.

The caller hung up.

Shaken, Ruth stared at the phone in her hand. That was the second time she had answered the phone and known someone listened to her frantic questions. The day before, she had let it pass as a mistake. It had been no mistake. She shivered. Things became more horrible by the minute.

7

Even with the rain, more visitors dropped by. Sally deflected some of them so that Ruth did not have to face them all.

The postmistress, a large-boned, rough-faced busybody with a strong West Country accent, stopped by. "Andrew tol' me the child was missin'."

She gave Ruth the creeps. Something about her wasn't right, but it occurred to Ruth that today it wouldn't be so bad if the postmistress passed the news of Annie on to everyone who dropped in to post a letter or buy stamps, as long as she didn't embellish as usual.

She told the postmistress there was no news and thanked her for dropping by.

She was back at her computer staring at the email.

"Mrs. Butler?"

She jumped to her feet and turned to see the wolf-eyed officer from yesterday enter with a woman police officer trailing behind.

Detective Chief Inspector Peter Trewe's salt and pepper hair had an untamed massiveness to it, as if it had absorbed half again its own volume with the rain. "Did you ring the station? Have you heard anything? Has she returned?"

"No." Ruth gulped back a sob. She fell to her seat.

"We didn't mean to startle you."

"Last night there was a phone call. He used Annie's mobile. He told me to tell him I loved him. Then this morning I opened my email. Look!"

DCI Trewe bent over Ruth's computer. "Is this it?"

"It's a repeat of what he said last night."

"I'll forward this to a safe computer where it can be opened and examined. We'll find out who sent it. There are ways. We can't just go marching to your ISP demanding names without justification according to the Data Protection Act. If it's important to finding your daughter, we'll do it. I'll let you know. We will triangulate the mobile call from last night."

"Another call came in on the home phone this morning. I could hear him breathing."

"How do you know it was a him?"

Ruth looked down. "An impression."

"I regret some people take advantage of this kind of situation. Do you know who would do that to you?"

"I don't."

"Will you let us know about any of these types of communications?"

"It was the second one of those."

Trewe caught her glance as he handed her another of his cards. "You've been remarkably calm through this."

"I don't know what you mean."

"I don't mean anything is wrong. Just an observation." He turned and indicated the other officer in the room. "You've met WPC Craig?"

"Yes." Ruth nodded to the woman police constable, who had her notepad at the ready.

"Mrs. Butler, we'll put a stop to this. Rest assured. Anything you consider worrisome in the way of phone messages, we'll consider harassment. Ring the number on my card the moment you receive another."

"Thank you." Her voice broke. She cleared her throat. Oh, to banish this weakling inside her. Should she tell? Yes, she must. "I've got to tell you the rest."

At that moment Sam Ketterman stepped into the room from the kitchen. Ruth sucked in what she had been about to say. It was getting to be a regular feeling, this jumpiness. Sam was not a stranger. She'd known him almost from the time they had come to Cornwall. He was a solicitor. Why had he entered through the rear door? Sally stood behind Sam, making faces at his back.

Sam glared at Trewe. "I'm sorry. Am I intruding?"

"Mrs. Butler called us, sir. And your business here?"

"Pardon me. I didn't realize … Detective Chief Inspector, I am Ruth's solicitor. Is there any progress?"

"By progress, I assume you're asking after Annie Butler?"

"Exactly so."

Trewe turned to Ruth. "Mrs. Butler?"

"Sam, I did not ask you to come."

Sally intervened. "Sam, there's tea if you'll come be my company in the kitchen."

Sam looked from Trewe to Ruth and then shrugged. "Thank you, Sall."

Ruth stared at their departing backs. Sally was being kind under the circumstances. She hated when he called her that.

Trewe sighed and stood up. "We are working, Mrs. Butler. There are forty-eight officers from the Devon-Cornwall area helping with the search. Two special officers from the Bristol Regional Crime Office are here. We've had few leads."

They hadn't produced her daughter. Ruth nodded. She couldn't ask more of them.

"Mrs. Butler, you mentioned there was something else?"

"It isn't important." She choked against the lie. She cleared her throat and picked up the flowers with the odd note. "There's this. Do you know what this says?"

Trewe looked at the note. "Welsh. My gran would have known just what it meant. If you'd like, I'll take this with me and get someone who knows the language to look at it."

"Yes, please."

"Anything else?"

She couldn't say it, but yes, there was heaps more—tons more.

"Don't give up hope, Mrs. Butler. Let us know about any problems. Will you do that?"

"Yes," she said. In that moment, she thought Trewe actually sounded kind, despite his fierce looks. She studied his face for a moment. She had to tell him the most important thing of all—the one thing that may in fact be impeding Annie's quick return. Could she trust him? "Can I say something for your ears alone?"

He nodded for Constable Craig to step across the room.

She drew the chief inspector aside and whispered, "Ruth Butler is not my name."

8

The detective chief inspector's eyes went wide. He cleared his throat. "If you are in this country using an alias, you will be asked to leave."

Though he had whispered, Ruth glanced at Constable Craig who watched them without expression. She looked back into the icy eyes. "Please wait and hear me out."

He didn't respond but he was still listening.

"Could we step into another room?"

He studied her face for a moment before nodding.

They stepped from the open living area to the hall where she could close the door. She kept her voice to a whisper. "The day after graduating high school, I married. I was pregnant with Annie and thought I was doing the right thing. And … and it wasn't horrible in the beginning. Then when Annie was seven months old I noticed the bruises and took her to the doctor. There was a criminal investigation. My husband's family had connections with the county's visiting judge and my husband was found innocent of the sexual abuse the doctor discovered." She rubbed away hot tears. "I ran away to my parents' home, but he dragged us back, locked us in, began systematically beating me."

Trewe cleared his throat, obviously uncomfortable. "Mrs. Butler—"

"Let me finish. Please. I escaped. One night … he was passed out drunk. A neighbor took us to a women's shelter. *She* believed me. From there, they hid us. By night we were shuttled between Texas towns and then sent to Houston. Months passed like this. I couldn't contact my own family in any way. He would have found us. He knows people, you see. The Women Helping Women organization helped me change my identity. He is a sexual predator of the worst kind, and he was not convicted. That made him free, and me in violation of the court order to allow him visitation."

She waited for Trewe to say something. She'd confessed, and now she was in his hands.

Trewe stood back, averting his eyes.

She pressed a hand out, touched his chest, briefly. "Please. I think my identity has the sanctity of the law, but I'm not sure. I have all the paperwork. It came at great sacrifice, you know. I haven't visited my mother in ten years."

"I assume you've told me this because …"

"He's found us."

"… you believe he's found you."

"I do."

"This is quite serious."

"I realize that."

"What do you want me to do, Mrs. Butler? You've placed me in a hard place." The cold eyes again.

"Please."

"I'll be totally honest. I don't know what I need to do first: call out all the king's men to find this monster or call on immigration to find out what my culpability will be defined as if I don't report you."

She forced her hands to unclench. Her breath caught before she found sound again—loud enough to be carried into the next room. "I don't wish to get you in trouble, sir." She slammed her hands together. "*I'm* not the important thing. Finding my daughter is."

Trewe leaned away from her. His voice still low, he said, "She is my first priority, and as such, I will put out the word while protecting you, for the moment, from exposure. I need you to help me with a full name and description, and I must bring Constable Craig in on this. We will investigate your—is it ex-husband?"

"Yes."

"So, Mrs. Butler, I will need to find out more about him to check whether he has entered the country recently. I don't know how this will affect your status. We will try to keep you out of it. But then, rocks will fall where they will, won't they?"

Her racing thoughts stumbled over the misquote. "I understand."

Trewe went back out to the constable and carried on a brief conversation in low tones. He beckoned Ruth closer. "You'll share all the information you can about … this man. I want a picture, age, last known address. Constable Craig shares your concern as deeply as anyone else in the force does. You can trust her. The information will be given out as to a possible person of interest only, not as Annie's father. But if this secret of yours comes down to me, I won't be pleased."

After relaying her new information to the WPC, Ruth stood with them at the door as they prepared to leave. Someone had pulled the plug on all her feelings. She rubbed away tears. "Take me with you. I'm useless here."

Trewe held up one hand. "We'll locate your daughter."

"Call me," Constable Craig said, handing her another card, "if there's anything you'd like to talk about. And my name's Allison, by the way."

"Thank you, Allison." Ruth clenched her arms around herself. Her teeth clattered.

"Wait for me, sir." Allison ran after Trewe as he climbed into his car.

Ruth turned as Sam bounded from the kitchen to rejoin her. He must have been sipping his tea with one ear at the door.

"Why have you come?" she demanded. She tucked both the officers' cards under her computer's keyboard.

"You may need me as a solicitor, and … You know how I feel." Wandering around the room, he fussed and straightened furniture. As he moved, he moaned. It irritated her.

No, Ruth didn't really know how he felt. Not really. He was too closed up inside. She couldn't get through all the walls he put up. Good looking? Yes, he was a blond god. Ruth had been very attracted to him, so much so, something may have come of it but for his enshrouded core. Never mind that she hid something from him, as well.

She could not live with his inability to make a firm decision. He couldn't even decide what film to watch on the television. She had ended their relationship months ago. Why wouldn't he leave her alone?

Now, watching him putter around the room being useless with her, she wondered what she could possibly have seen in him. She would have told him she didn't want him there, but he had disappeared into the kitchen. Then he was in front of her with a bowl of something that smelled suspiciously of fish.

"Look what I made just for you. You should eat."

"Don't be ridiculous!"

He set the bowl down and sank to his knees. "I'm only doing what a friend would do. You should eat. What will happen when they find Abby and you're too weak to go to her?"

"Her name is Annie! Why can't you ever get her name right?" She shook her head. What was wrong with him? "Please leave."

Sally watched their exchange. When Sam left, she mimicked him. "I'm only doing what a friend would do. For Abby!"

The rain had passed. Bright sun filtered through the rain-dabbled window. Ruth could sense the spring freshness outdoors and instantly wished to walk, but the trouble it would take to don a jacket and wellies seemed exhausting. She found herself drifting in and out of the quiet sunlit room until exhaustion finally caught up. A stray chill kissed her neck and jerked her awake. She could see by the way the sun glowed from behind a mountain range of clouds that darkened the western sky that it was late afternoon. Was he feeding Annie? What was he feeding her? Was it enough? When would he make a move to give her back? She would admit to anything—plead guilty, do whatever it took—if he would only bring her back.

She called her mother in Texas. Someone had to tell her about Annie, but her mother must have gone to bed. She left a short message, the first she'd left in years. It was all she could choke out.

More people dropped by. Good people. They gave news about what the police were doing. The full force of the law with officers from all over Cornwall and Devon—and even Wales—had been and presently were still searching.

Evening brought more visitors, flowers, and teddy bears. Her daughter's school chums came in small waves. They tittered all the way to the front stoop where they morphed into a single, silent entity. Memorials sprang up across her front garden with flowers, candles, dolls, and letters.

The Women's Auxiliary dropped off two meals to heat up when Ruth wanted, and she found that her hunger became more insistent and gnawing with each passing hour. When pressed, she did eat. It didn't feel good. It didn't appease the monster in her gut, but she ate. Sally answered her phone for her. It grew dark, and still people brought flowers. None would come past the entry. "Don't want to impose." "Just know we're thinking of you." "Had to stop and let you know we care, must run."

There were three categories of people in Cornwall: the Cornish, the incomers and the foreigners. The Cornish had lived there for generations born and bred. Anyone visiting was a foreigner—including any other English. Incomers were people who had moved here as more-or-less permanent residents—incomers were incomers for twenty years or more.

Ruth and Annie had graduated from foreigners to incomers as soon as they purchased Riverside. Most of the villagers were slow to talk at first, but when they figured out she was friendly and interested in learning about Cornwall, those same villagers could become quite talkative. On the whole, the villagers were decent, hardworking people who were proud of their heritage, as well they should be. She and her daughter had loved living here.

It had felt safe.

9

Jon cut his connection to the Internet and sat deep in thought. It was too hard to believe. But there it was. He had to think it through. Thirty years. Had this been going on all this time and no one had seen it before?

The morning's search activity in the village grew at every turn. Dogs, police, searchers on horseback, and volunteers probed the countryside with poles. Parked vehicles crowded the roads and the air throbbed with two helicopters that circled like blowflies. Like that scene from Frankenstein in Technicolor, the stick-carrying crowds were out for blood. He imagined that they would likely be wondering who would harm a child—and that they would not stop until they found him.

Jon hadn't joined in the search parties, but he hadn't been inactive. He decided to take the opportunity to blend in and explore the village, from the church tower at the top, to where the river emptied into the sea at the bottom.

He had taken the packages to the post office. The county combined courthouse also housed the post office and several administrative offices. The postmistress's eyes glittered under thick brows. Stoop-shouldered and thin-skinned, she hulked over the smaller package, taking her time, she snuck a cold look at him every few seconds. Her actions were even more exaggerated with the larger package. That was fine with Jon. He didn't like her either.

While it was true, under the circumstances, that strangers would be regarded with suspicion, something about this woman did not seem right. She had two ears, a mouth, two eyes, a nose, all placed in the correct spots. But something about her left a bitter aftertaste in his mouth.

The postmistress took his money, wrote him a receipt, and carried the packages into a back room and set them on a table in full view.

He called out a half-jolly "cheers" and left to do some more walking.

Like an exhausted angel guarding the lives clustered below it, the weathered church tower perched above the village.

Jon stood on High Street. Below, he could see a squat yellow building with the word "Pottery" splashed in purple across the slate roof. Farther along the slope and as the road turned sharply to the sea, there sat a narrow stone building. A black sign above the door proclaimed it "The Spider's Web." Up the other side of the road, various shops specialized in trinkets commemorating the legend of the disappearing pirate, or, more often than not, worked to cash-in on the King Arthur lore that bounded up and down this side of Cornwall. There was a prominent sign advertising the Museum of Witchcraft, behind which were a newsagent and a tea garden.

He walked down the steep incline to the quay and decided to trace the dark car's imagined path to see where it had come from. High Street ended in a car park. There was a narrow turn around. He climbed down to the beach. He noted how the steps the girls had taken went to the top of a short cliff. At the top was a gate. He took the steps up and went through the gate. It opened upon a narrow road, more like an alleyway. Originally designed for horses and carriages, roads around the village were unlikely to ever be widened. This road would barely contain a carriage. It led upward between buildings and then turned to skirt behind the village.

He had included in his package for Bakewell the video that showed the car's movement on the morning the girl disappeared. Jon wondered what he would make of it.

He would have to include that footage in an anonymous package to DCI Peter Trewe. *No good deed will go unpunished,* he thought. He was in for it, and quite soon, unless he could find some answers to his own investigation and leave.

For the rest of the day he wandered the village and its back streets. As the sun was setting he found a shortcut to Perstow's cottage on his maps. He took the path that led along the top of the cliffs. The sea foamed below him as he took the slippery turns. Seagulls lifted away from the cliff wall below him and hung in the air at eye level. He thought he saw malicious intent in their beady little eyes. A breeze carried the faint odor of something long dead, something the seagulls were working on, no doubt. The first of April and already greening vines twisted through a thorn hedge on the land side.

His pocket trilled. He snatched the mobile open and applied it to his ear, "Jon Graham."

"Jon." Bakewell's voice. "You are not back. I'm not surprised but a bit disappointed."

"Things have taken a turn."

"I'm following the news of the missing girl. It's all over the telly. Seems there is a suspect—an American. His picture and name are on the news. I've received the email attachment of video footage. Not much to go on. I do think these should be handed over to Trewe. Use Perstow, he can make a perfunctory visit to the CCTV monitoring station and use it as an excuse. I've sent some files on Trewe's service record to you. What's Trewe been up to that you know of besides the search for the girl?"

"To and from work is all, really boring stuff. After reading Sergeant Browne's reports I've decided I need to speak to him for more details."

"Which means another day?"

"Yes, sir. I sent you VHS tapes that I have not viewed because I have no VCR. As to the missing girl, I had a run-in on the way into Perrin's

Point with a car. In the other email I sent you footage that shows the car coming and going."

"You think it has to do with the girl's disappearance?"

"Must be a reason for not stopping after hitting my car. And," Jon hesitated. "I've been doing some internet research."

"Oh?"

"Missing young women from other regions found dead in Cornwall."

Bakewell gruffed, "Another matter. This girl didn't go missing from Wales or Devon. And hasn't been found dead."

Jon's grip tightened on the mobile. "Even so—"

"You're investigating Trewe, not the whereabouts of teenaged girls."

Jon swallowed what he wanted to say. He respected Bakewell, but he found his implication offensive.

Tuesday, 11:59 a.m.

Charles stared at his wristwatch, a gift he gave himself. The just-baked bread from the steaming dishes of food at a nearby table had his mouth watering. He had only meant to stop briefly but now considered ordering. Had he the time? Would it seem strange he was eating alone? Better food here at the pub than what he would get at home. A cheddar and prawn jacket potato would be good.

He watched the regulars and wondered if they only pretended not to notice him.

The girl behind the bar burst out laughing at something one of the men must have said to her. She waved a mug. "Chris, you would-na sed sech a thing." Her face went rosy and she giggled at his murmured reply. She deposited the mug in the dumbwaiter where it clinked against the others. She slid the tin door shut.

Charles held his head up and went to the bar. With a nod to the girl, he pointed to the mugs that hung from the ceiling.

The girl asked, “Which one is it then? Fourth one back, I remember.” She reached up to the ceiling beam, counted the handled glasses and mugs hung from hooks, and pulled down the one she wanted. “Fancy that. Has yer initials on it.” She rinsed it. “The usual?”

He nodded.

She handed him his bitter, took his money, and left to collect used glasses from empty tables.

He carried his drink back to a table. Sitting heavily, he willed himself to relax. Filthy mortar outlined the painted stones in the wall at his shoulder. Everything was stained with soot and there were spider webs between the beams on the ceiling, health inspector or no. The fug in the air was a constant.

“You look like a toadstool sitting there, Chubby.”

He almost ducked, but stopped himself just in time. She had found out the kids at school teased him because of his weight. “Chubby Charlie, puddin’ and pie. Kissed the boys and made them cry.”

He stood quickly, accidentally tipping the heavy table. He caught it before the salt and pepper and open sugar bowl could slide across and crash to the floor. All conversation stopped. People stared. Not a friendly eye among them. Just as he supposed, they suspected something.

He gulped his bitter and left. Better a dry morsel in peace than a good jacket potato with the village idiots.

Ruth could hardly breathe for despair. Annie had disappeared on Sunday; this was Tuesday. She rubbed her clenched jaw. If she unclenched it the screams would come out. She checked her email again. No ransom note. Her email confidant and relative, Aunt Maybe in Galveston, Texas, emailed her not to give up hope. Ruth had called her, and, just as with her mother, she had had to leave a message.

Finally, it looked as if her aunt wanted to respond to her Skype message to get on the computer with her *now*.

Aunt Maybe, nicknamed after her reply to her future first husband's proposal, always looked the same: disheveled white hair, glasses perched at the tip of her nose, sparkling blue eyes.

"Aunt Maybe, Bubba has her."

"No, that isn't possible, Ruth."

The screen's picture pixilated beyond recognition. "Email!" Aunt Maybe yelled. Their connection froze mid-sentence.

Ruth rubbed the back of her neck. She was useless when it came to putting her feelings to paper. Sure, she could write technical stuff, but she was using words from manuals. She was an artist, not a writer. How could she write in an email that she had no hope when it came to Bubba Roy Brock? Despite his ridiculous name, he was no fool. He appeared normal. He used a charming personality to win people over and get them to trust him. At home he was a horrific beast.

Sally told her, "Why don't you go out for a walk? I'm here. I'll not let a thing get by you'll want to know about."

"Thanks." On her way out, Ruth stepped on another nosegay of flowers that had been left on the doorstep with an odd, handwritten note. She didn't understand what they meant. She left them on the stoop for the police and took off, ready to run or walk off the unrest threatening to bust out from inside. She wished there was some way to unlock the building where she'd taught kickboxing cardio classes in the village. She hadn't begun a new class since her last class ended two months ago. She could give her boxing bag a dent or two.

A cold wind funneled down the narrow streets from the north and pushed her along. She found herself in St. Nicholas's churchyard. The bells gonged the hour.

This was Thomas Hardy country. Had he helped with the design on this square tower during his architectural apprenticeship? Salt-shorn and wind-bent, trees leaned inland along the seaward side of the churchyard. She'd been brought up "chapel," not "church," but the very age of this place shouted to her soul, "Come and worship." All these years and she'd been inside two or three times for funerals and weddings and had even come to the last fete held on the bare mound of green next to the church walls, but she'd never before heard the church call to her like this.

Spring-green turf belied Ruth's dark thoughts and muted her footfall as she made her way toward the stone building. The heavy door opened on well-oiled hinges. Her steps whispered across the cavernous room, which smelled of must, dust, and dry stone. A dim, gray light fell into the chancel through a small, high-set window.

Silence invited listening.

Some small sound caught at her ear like a hook. She swung around, but saw no one. She continued down the aisle, turning once again to make sure she was alone. She left wet footprints tracked across the slate-flagged entry.

She imagined the building alive and breathing, glad to have her heart beating life into the dear room. The stained glass beyond the pulpit was a testimony to the incredible artistry of men made in the image of God.

There was a soft noise behind her, she glanced back. There was nothing there. *Not to worry,* she thought, *old buildings have mice.*

She slipped into a pew. The seats were joined to the floors and everything creaked as she pressed against the wood. She pulled out a dusty needlepoint prayer cushion and knelt. She laid her head on her hands. *Lord, why did you bring me to Cornwall just to endure my daughter being snatched away?* A chill brushed the back of her neck.

Was that a step that she heard? She looked up.

A sudden appearance of the sun sent a stab of light in through the window. It highlighted the golden cross at the altar. Her breath caught in her throat.

A scratching sound interrupted her. She turned. The church was empty. *Must be the mice,* she thought. *They should put out traps.* She would mention it to Sally who was on the board.

She turned back to attempt to reclaim the sense of repose that at last she found. A familiar sense of unease tingled against her arms until the hair rose. Had God taken Annie from her because she hadn't given Him much thought? In how long? Since her life turned sour with bad decisions? But she had never consciously blamed God. And now, to question Him was so trivial—her own fault or the natural course of events—what did it matter? She wanted her daughter back, and only a miracle would make that possible.

Leaning forward, she gazed at the cross. Her heart ached. Her parents, her God, and her church were all tied together with an unbreakable cord woven into her life. Why couldn't she have been satisfied with the safety she knew as a child? Why couldn't she have just learned contentment? Why had she not trusted her parents' assessment of the man she'd set her dreams on?

Through the memory of years, a refrain came to mind, "Up from the grave He arose …" A strong song. A victorious song. It was the only thing she missed about attending church. The music moved her, lifted her, it transcended the mundane into the spectacular.

She gripped the hard, wooden back of the pew in front of her.

Outside, the wind gusted. A low whistle echoed from the eaves. Tree branch shadows moved across the stained glass panels. The Bible characters appeared to move. The noise came again, like a shoe scuffling. A crystal clear thought burst into her head. *Get out!*

She stood quickly and turned back down the aisle. Before her, on top of her footprints, were larger ones. At the back of the room, a black velvet curtain swayed slightly. A cane with a silver handle was hooked to the pew directly behind where she had been kneeling, as if someone had stood behind her as silent as death.

With a sharp intake of breath, she burst into the cold sunshine outside.

10

Once outside, Ruth swung around in an attempt to look in as many directions at once as she could. Distant fields of new corn were visible through the beeches. Where was he? She could fight him now. She knew ways to hurt a man that she wished she'd known ten years ago.

Except for the rooks that scattered up at her sudden appearance, the churchyard was empty and quiet. She was alone. So alone. She crouched ready to meet danger.

Slow the breathing. Slow the movements. Be ready.

Sam had a cane. It was one of his affectations of gentrification that griped her. If it had been him in there, why hadn't he answered her? Would he do that to her?

When she broke it off with him, she had watched him grow more desperate to win her back, as if he couldn't stand to lose what he thought was so easily his.

What if it had been her ex-husband in the church? What if he had Annie holed up somewhere as he devised ways to make Ruth pay for the perceived wrongs she had committed against him? The divorce was final; no judge could argue her that. Annie's custody had been the issue. In any other court she would have won the right to keep Annie as far away from him as possible. But not in the family court of the small town where he and his family had arranged the hearing.

For eleven years the noise behind every closed door and the horrible things that crept into her dreams were her ex-husband. He had taken Annie to take revenge. It was working. Without her daughter she would die. Now she wished he would show his ugly face so she could get it over with, because now she knew she could kill him.

Backing away from the church door, she turned and crossed the graveyard. Dry bark and leaves crackled under her feet. A few weeks ago, rooks had fought over the best nesting spots in the beech trees, tossing pieces of nesting material at each other. Sticks rained from the trees.

Annie had called it the "Twig Wars."

In the vale below the church, where the thin line of the River Perrin flowed to the sea, sinewy beech limbs reached and twisted together like clasped, skeletal hands. Wind whistled through their fingers.

It was spring. Daffodils bloomed wild. Dark gravestones peppered the yard like misplaced game pieces on green felt. The oldest ones, green with moss, tilted into the ground. Low shrubs cast shadows that danced across the old graves. Flowers marked a new grave. She studied them, and breathed in their potpourri.

Her eyes settled upon a single piece of paper. The familiar handwriting sent a shiver down her back. Brown twine bound the note to a stone vase of fresh-cut daffodils. She stared at the words. They looked the same as she had seen on her doorstep.

A large shadow fell across the paper. She spun around.

"It is you!" Her heart beat double-time. She angled away from him.

"Sam I am." Sam hooked each thumb in a trouser pocket.

"Were you inside the church just now? Did you leave a cane?" She was shaking, fists clenched. She wanted to take him down.

"I don't own a cane."

Why did he lie? She'd seen the cane at his home. "Someone followed me into the church."

"It was not me."

Ruth crossed her arms. She felt sure he was lying. She looked away. She had to be careful.

"Would you feel better if I went in there and looked?" he asked.

"Sure."

Sam disappeared and returned a few minutes later. "No one there. Everything present and accounted for."

"Didn't you see the cane? It was black with a metal handle."

"Nothing."

Challenging him wouldn't do any good. A shudder passed through her. A knot formed in her stomach.

Sam's eyes carried a strange wariness. He put his arms around her. "I don't want you to be scared."

She shrank from his touch. "Sam."

"Ruth."

"Don't." She attempted to push away from him, but he held her tighter.

"You know I love you." He sounded desperate. "You've been putting me off."

She slammed a foot down on his instep.

"Oww!" His grip loosened.

She wrenched away. "We are not a couple. It's over."

Sam glared at her. "I'm sorry you find me so distasteful." His voice was cold.

She kept her gaze steady as she rubbed the sore out of her arms; the muscles quivered. Her heart raced. He'd never been harsh or touched her so cruelly. She hoped for something that would distract his intense gaze. He looked dangerous.

A dark car pulled along the church lane. She almost fell over with relief when she spotted DCI Trewe climbing toward them.

"Just like him to show up now." Sam's lips curled and his face flushed red.

"Fine weather for a walk in the churchyard," Trewe said between catching his breath. His teeth were not quite straight and not quite white, but nonetheless his smile was a nice addition to the otherwise ruthless face. Trewe held out his hand.

Ruth shook it, her hand enveloped in the rough, dry warmth of his comforting grip. She asked, "What made you look here for me?"

"I happened by," Trewe told her.

"So you thought you'd intrude," Sam huffed.

"I certainly hope not," Trewe said.

"Well, you hope in vain."

Ruth stared at Sam. "The police are looking for my daughter."

The afternoon was getting on and thunder rumbled toward them from far across the sea. The timbre of the wind changed and shifted direction, and brought with it the scent of more rain. The sun disappeared and the atmosphere grew heavy as dark clouds surged across the sky.

"Mrs. Butler," Trewe said, staring up at the darkening sky, "I am thankful to have run into you like this. I would like a word."

"Of course."

"Do you need a ride? Looks like rain."

Sam glared.

Ruth nodded, reassured by Trewe's help to get away from Sam. "I'd appreciate it."

"Mr. Ketterman," Trewe said, "would you please drop by my office when you get a chance?"

"When I get a chance." Sam turned and tramped down the slope toward the car park.

Ruth walked with Trewe to his old black car, the hood dented and not quite the same color as the rest of the car's body.

"What've you got there?" Trewe asked.

Ruth had forgotten the piece of paper in her hand. She handed it to him.

"Time heals," he read aloud.

"I recognized it's the same writing as the note left with my flowers. Take me home. There's been another. I left it on the stoop."

After they reached her home, she showed Trewe the vase of flowers with the odd note.

Trewe studied the writing. "*'Gofalwch Gofala!'* Strange none of the notes are signed."

"I can't even read it." She went to a cabinet and rummaged through the stack of cards she'd received so far. "I've gotten hand-written notes and lots of flower arrangements, as you can see." She made a sweeping gesture. There were fresh flowers in the room, most with stuffed bears or heart-shaped well-wishes. "But then these notes on my doorstep—I can't understand them."

"Have you received any other emails?"

"Not from anyone I don't know."

"Have you received any other communications or things which felt out of place?"

"Everything feels out of place." Ruth went to her computer. Rain gently tapped against the big window, as if asking politely to be let in. "Something happened at the church earlier."

She briefly explained the episode at the church—the strange noises, footprints, and the silver cane. She did not offer her opinion that she thought Sam had showed up a little too conveniently.

"We'll see what we can do." Trewe turned to her. "We've traced the email. The server is a free one available for anonymous users, but we have applied for a court order to examine their records."

Earlier, when Ruth arrived home and before Sally came to spend the night on her couch, she had found an envelope taped to her door. The initial shock of what was inside sent shivers over her. She had carefully taken it from the door and into the house where she burst into tears. She collapsed to the floor and held the thin slip of paper to her heart.

Annie Butler came to and felt dizzy as she tried to imagine where she was and what had happened. So, she started with simple things. First, it was still dark, but not so dark this time that she couldn't see a few inches around her face if she lifted the rag away. Second, she was on her back, face-up, more or less, and something was holding her down. What was it? Whatever it was it was soft but resisted any attempt to be pushed away. She needed more air; the stuffiness of breathing her own, old breath pressed in on her. Fighting against the thing made a larger pocket of space for her face. Near her left eye a cloth-bound button dangled from a thread. It wasn't a suit button or a button for a shirt. Some memory buzzed around her head. What was it? Why did this button look familiar? If she could figure out the answer to that, she would know why there was a button hanging by a thread so near her face. It remained a puzzle that kept her mind spinning. She slid her free hand up and batted at the button.

Was the button real? Yes, it was real. And the other real thing was that her head still hurt very much, especially above the brow of her right eye. And there was a pain in her arm, the arm that she couldn't move.

Beyond her cocoon, because that is how she would describe where she was, she heard a soft slithering. A second or two passed when it dawned on her that there could be a monstrous snake nearby. "Let me out!" she screamed, but her voice was muffled in the enclosed space like she was in a deep well. Grunting, pushing, thrashing—the effort sent her skull reeling into pain. Familiar darkness enveloped her, so she went away again.

II

Wednesday, 10:03 a.m.

Both the library computers were in use.

Charles grabbed the particular book he had stashed out of sequence off the shelf and clumped to a corner where no one would be in his way. He needed to think without any interruption.

He pulled at his collar. The heating needed to be turned off or some windows opened. The room smelt of musty books and old people. They were all for destroying the creaking place and building a new facility. He'd fought it at the last couple of council meetings. He made sure they had his opinion. The facility had served well enough the last three hundred and fifty years. Why go for change for change's sake?

He sat alone at a table, his head in the history book he had used before. It included some mention of herbs in history. Not that he needed to go over that. He had it memorized. He was good at memorization. He had been an excellent student.

Ah, school memories.

His friend Morley had once sent him a magazine at boarding school, one that his mother wouldn't have allowed if she had known. He was enjoying it immensely in the privacy of his room when Headmaster discovered him and grabbed the mag away. Charles had kicked him.

"Your mother will be displeased, Charlie," the headmaster yelled. "I shall telephone immediately."

Charles's mother hated him enough; she didn't need more reason. He spat on the headmaster's back. The headmaster turned, his ugly features stretched so he looked like a gargoyle. Charles ran. The headmaster chased him—up the stairs, all the way to the roof of the old building and across a short flat area to the parapet where the headmaster caught him by the arm and tried to drag him back. But he turned and maneuvered into position behind the old man—one shove. He then "discovered" the body. They ruled the death suicide.

The smallness of the library corner where Charles had stationed himself closed in on him. The buzz of conversation grated across his thoughts.

An older gentleman spoke to an equally older woman, "You've read them all, have you?"

The answer was a drawn-out, "Yes."

The old man again, "'Bout time to get some new books 'ere then."

For Charles, the problem was that old people couldn't hear. Charles almost screamed at the old buzzard, "'Bout time someone told smelly old people to keep quiet!"

The constant click click of the mouse from the computer nearest him set his teeth on edge. He wished he could fling the book across the room or perhaps down the stairs to hit someone's head.

Just for a change of pace.

He smirked. He had a plan. He took a quick glance around before he took up a looming position over the timid-looking oldster seated at the computer. He rocked back and forth, settling for a bit of a wait.

The thing was, he would need to keep his eyes open for a chance to let the American woman know he had her daughter—get her to let her guard down enough that he could grab her, too.

The timid oldster squirmed in her chair. Charles didn't move or make a noise. With a huff, she turned and glared up at him. "What?" she challenged.

"I'm waiting," he muttered.

She stood and glared eye to eye. He didn't give an inch.

With a final harrumph, she clomped away in her completely practical shoes.

Satisfied that she wasn't coming back, he grabbed the computer and logged on.

Ruth backed away from the window when she saw Trewe's old, black Renault at the curb. She didn't know how she felt about his arrival. Was he bringing news? Every part of her body felt as if she'd received a beating. It was Wednesday and nothing had been found of Annie. She couldn't live like this. She would rather die than not know what happened.

Trewe started up the walk. Another car pulled up. Woman Police Constable Allison Craig exited her car. The WPC's hair stuck out in wispy curls and there was a pencil behind her ear. Trewe had mentioned that he wouldn't allow questions without the constable present.

She sucked in a deep breath and opened the door.

"Mrs. Butler, you remember WPC Craig?" Trewe stood on Ruth's porch and kept his coat on while the constable shook out her coat and came to stand next to him.

"Yes. Hi, Allison. Come in. Can I offer you something to drink?" Ruth went to her drinks cabinet.

Allison shook her head and retrieved a notebook from a pocket of her coat.

"Nothing for me," Trewe said.

Ruth started to fix herself a drink then decided against it, opting to eat something first—and changed her mind again in quick succession. She poured herself two fingers whiskey, neat.

Trewe remained standing. "I still have a few questions about the morning Annie disappear—"

Ruth cut him short. "Maybe you would rather have tea?"

Trewe hardly paused. "Constable Craig could you make us tea?"

Ruth set her untouched drink down. "Please sit. I don't like it when people stand in my house."

Constable Craig exited into the kitchen. Trewe sat. "Of all the people you come in contact with on a daily or weekly basis, did it strike you that day or later that someone you know wasn't around on Sunday? Everyone in the village was out and about looking for Annie at some point. Does anything odd come to mind?"

Ruth picked up her drink and sat across from him. "Someone I know who wasn't around?"

"Yes. Someone you expected would have shown up to help out, or someone you wouldn't have expected in a million years that showed up and was solicitous?"

"Sergeant Perstow's wife. She was being too nice. She's never been the sort of person to go out of her way to be so nice to me. It did seem odd."

"Why is that?"

"Why these questions? It doesn't make any difference; she certainly wasn't the one calling me from Annie's mobile. That was a man."

"Is there anyone in the village you've had any disagreements with?"

Ruth pushed back into the cushions. "No one has ever been outright rude. Indifferent, stand-offish maybe, but most have made me feel welcome."

Trewe didn't say anything.

The silence prompted more words from Ruth. "If ever I need to know local news, I ask the postmistress. She makes it a point to let me know anybody else's business, so I wouldn't put it past her to know mine, too. I guess I don't like her much."

"You could form a club, from what I hear. But Sunday morning she was at the church, arranging flowers. Several people saw her. What about someone missing, someone you thought should be there and wasn't?"

"Sam Ketterman didn't come till around two on Sunday."

"How long have you been acquainted with Sam Ketterman?" Trewe asked.

Nothing like being direct, Ruth thought. She stared down at the amber liquid in her glass. It was early for a drink, wasn't it? "A while." She took too big a swallow. The whiskey burned its way down her throat. She held her breath, willing herself not to choke.

"The nature of your relationship?"

"Does that have anything to do with Annie?"

Trewe leaned forward. "I like to understand all of the people involved in an investigation, Mrs. Butler. I don't mean to offend."

"The first time I met him was when he asked me if he could get into my garden. He was after thyme. I remember thinking it was a novel pick-up line. I invited him into the garden and we talked. That was the beginning. We saw each other—for a short while. I don't know why he calls himself my solicitor." She tugged at a loose thread on her sweater. "There's nothing between us. I broke it off with him. I don't think he gets it, though. He has been almost what I would call harassing me since Sunday."

Trewe stood and stepped to the window, turning his back to her, and said, "I read from another report that you moved here from London. You stopped in London, coming from Texas? Then why here, Mrs. Butler? Doesn't seem the kind of place to attract a lone woman and her child." He turned to face her.

Ruth was uncomfortable. On an empty stomach, the alcohol hit hard. His words shot at her much too fast. Probably his intent. She wouldn't put it past him. She set her glass down too hard on the coffee table. Liquid splashed. Those frightful, white-gray eyes. She hesitated, measured her words. "I followed a friend to London. Found a good job, working for a newspaper … on its redesign. It was a small newspaper, one of the boroughs—Merton. I had a little to live on." He didn't need to know that her parents took out a personal loan so she could get away—that her father had to work an extra job to pay the loan back, because any money she sent him could be traced back to her—how her father died before she could even thank him. Her stomach roiled. "Annie and I came to Cornwall for a holiday. Annie loves the beach."

She rubbed her face. "I'd read Thomas Hardy's *A Pair of Blue Eyes* and had notions of becoming a writer living the romance. I read everything by Rosamunde Pilcher and Dauphne du Maurier and decided that the West Country was where I needed to stop. I'm a horrible writer. I do artwork for hire. I felt some sort of homing pull when I came to Cornwall, though. Sometimes, from the top of the cliff as I watch the way the sun sets beyond the sea—the cottages planted against the valley slopes, the wildness of the sea during a storm—I think it's like something made up, and ... such a contrast from the forest of buildings and the diesel fumes of London. But that isn't what you want to know is it?"

"I think you answered the question." He took a seat again. "So you do artwork for a living?"

"Technical stuff and advertising art, the occasional illustration job." She pointed at the mock-ups for the illustrated dictionary of herbs she had been working on that were pinned across one wall. "I have a crafting website that pulls in money from advertisements."

Trewe watched her for a moment before saying, "I apologize for asking, but tell me more about your ex-husband."

"I lied about his death to my daughter so she would never go looking for him. The hiding, the lies, the cross-world move—it was a justified deception. Stealing Annie was a necessary evil."

"I do understand, Mrs. Butler. I have family."

Ruth wondered if Trewe could picture her in a previous world—an existence more foreign than miles made. "Everything was so different."

Constable Craig entered with tea and biscuits on a tray. "You sounded very Texan just then, Mrs. Butler."

"Call me Ruth. That part is my real name. I've been hiding so long, it's hard to remember what normal could look like." Ruth didn't take the offered cup of tea or cookies, but took a slice of dry toast. "The police might still be looking for us. I'm sure we've been on milk cartons and the post office walls in my home state."

"You are a 'wanted' woman, but not in a serious way. I wondered if that response was how things were done in Texas. It called for more questions. That's really why we're here."

"I would describe the police in Texas as being a lot more aggressive." She remembered how they had handcuffed her arms behind her, cuffed her feet, and tossed her in the police car like a sack of rice. It happened after she had run away from Bubba. But those had been officers who were Bubba's friends. "They would still be the same cold arm of the law, unless …"

"Unless what?"

"Unless Bubba called off the search." A cold chill crept up from her feet.

WPC Allison Craig put her cup down with a clatter. "And the only reason he would do that?"

"Because he had found us and wanted to exact his own revenge."

Trewe leaned forward in the seat. "We are trying, Mrs. Butler. But you understand that even if it isn't Mr. Brock who has done this, Mr. Brock is now aware you are in England, as his picture has been put in the paper. I tried to keep it somewhat quiet, but when it concerns a child, these things take on a life of their own."

Oh, if only you knew! Perhaps it was the unexpected compassion in his tone of voice and the fact that after so many years, someone else knew. Ruth found she couldn't put a stopper in the flood of tears. "It's just … the feeling of losing … she seemed here a moment ago. I can't believe she's not … coming home. I keep thinking she's visiting a friend."

"Mrs. Butler, they say bad things come in threes. I'd say you've had all your bad things." Trewe's eyes were not so terrible after all—piercing, direct—but not terrible. She pulled an afghan from the back of the couch tight around her shoulders.

Trewe finished his tea. "You're young."

Ruth shook her head. "Please don't say that. It's not good enough."

"No, I expect not. Do you have any relatives here?"

"No."

"Without family," Trewe said quietly, "this must be especially hard."

"My mother is terrified of flying. Always has been, but not because of what happened in New York. 'There's terrorists everywhere' is what she says to me." She rubbed her wet cheeks. "This is when I think most about moving back. But I can't leave now … not without my daughter."

"And I'm sure you'd be missed here."

It touched Ruth that he would offer that thought.

"Would you like me to stay with you?" Allison Craig asked. The police woman's wild hair floated out from her face despite several clasps. "I could help out with the phone, the email."

Ruth shook her head. "Really, I'm fine alone in the daylight. It's at night I'm afraid of my own shadow, but Sally stays with me."

Rising, Trewe nodded in Allison's direction. "If there's nothing else, Mrs. Butler."

"Before you go there's something I should show you." She went to a bookshelf near the door. She pulled a book forward, flipped it open and extracted an envelope. "I found this taped to my door yesterday."

She handed it to Trewe.

Trewe's face closed up as he studied the photo. "This is your daughter."

"It was taken on Sunday morning, when she was on the beach. Those are the clothes she was wearing."

Allison crowded over Trewe's shoulder to view the picture. "Good detail. Perhaps an IP camera."

"Who was on the beach, this near the girl, except …" he didn't finish the sentence. He glanced into Ruth's eyes.

She knew he hadn't wanted to say, "except the one who took her."

"May I keep this?" he asked.

"I've already made a copy."

"Mrs. Butler, we've taken enough of your time. Thank you." He nodded and stepped aside as Allison passed him. He followed on her heels to his car as the rain began again in earnest.

Ruth pushed the door shut behind the two police officers. She was emotionally drained, but she wanted to check her email, just in case someone was trying to get in touch. She had a new email.

> RAB@Westco.uk.co
> Subject: For you
> Lazy Annie has grown so fine
> She can't get up to feed the swine,
> But lies in bed till eight or nine.
> Lazy Annie Butler.

She pivoted in the chair. It *would* be best for Constable Craig to stay; the police needed to have this email. She stood. She should, at least, call them back inside. She hesitated. Should she call Sally? Before she could decide, the doorbell rang. Detective Chief Inspector Trewe must have forgotten something. She would show him this email.

She opened the door.

It wasn't the chief inspector.

12

When the figure on the porch came forward from the gloom of the wet day, Ruth drew in a gasp. The short, square woman with a round, flushed face peered at her over her rain-speckled glasses. The woman's hair had definitely gone much grayer and thinner than the last time Ruth had seen her.

"Momma?"

"Well! I don't know what 'a penny for a pound' means in this gosh-darn, cold, wet place! And what in God's name is a 'Euro-dollar?' I can't even get what a 'pence' means." She shook a rolled-up newspaper in Ruth's face. "This is a great picture of Bubba—a detestable ugly mug if ever I saw one."

The harsh, bravado voice resounded against the porch's slate walls. Ruth certainly never imagined her mother would brave the seas and air to come to England, but she had never been so relieved. "Is it really you?"

Mrs. Thompson stood on the step in her red coat, the same coat she had worn when Ruth was a girl. It stretched threadbare thin in places. One of the buttons dangled loose.

Ruth pulled her mother into the house, and wrapped her arms around her. "Momma? I—how did you get here?"

Her mom returned the hug, squeezing tight. “Amazing what a little Valium can do. They should pass them out with the peanuts on planes. Thankfully, they were generous with the wine, too.”

“What?”

“Had to have something. Supposed to be eleven hours!” Her voice was overloud.

Ruth smiled to hear her mother, see her mother, for the first time in so many years and especially now. “Wasn’t it?”

“I don’t remember. Good medicine. Your Aunt Maybe’s suggestion. Blame her! Can a body get something decent to drink around here besides tea, Ruth-Ann?” Her voice rose to loud, as if she were talking through a wall. “I’ve got enough caffeine in this body, I could have carried that taxi. And there aren’t enough bathrooms to accommodate, I can tell you right now!” Her voice was gravelly. She must have been yelling a lot.

Mrs. Thompson glanced around. “My land and stars! That taxi driver is still sitting there! He doesn’t want my credit card and I don’t have the right kind of money. If that don’t beat all, I don’t know what does.”

Ruth glanced out. A rumbling taxi exhausted black fumes into the tiny street. And worse, it was a black taxi. No telling how much this was going to be because he would have kept his meter running all this time. “I’ll take care of it,” she said, and prepared herself to haggle.

“Dang! I’ve got to find a bathroom.”

“Through there, Momma.” Ruth pointed. She grabbed some money out of her purse and ran out in the rain to the taxi.

Her mother came back into the sitting room at the same moment Ruth finished instructing the taxi driver where to deposit the rest of the luggage. She shook off most of the rain inside the door. An exhilarating wave of emotion swept over her—her teeth chattered, her knees jellied—but all she could do was stand mute and stare at this pleasant-faced, frumpy woman in her late fifties. Ann Thompson wore her mousy, blond hair curly on top to hide the thin, gray roots. Her mother was here.

"All the way from London in a taxi? It must have taken forever."

Her mother laughed, "Forever. But daughter, I am glad to see you. I'm so sorry about Annie."

Ruth's voice choked with emotion. "You're here. Oh Momma, you came! Are you sure no one would trace you? Though it doesn't matter much now, with his face all over the place, he'll soon follow unless he's been here all along."

"No, he couldn't be."

"How can you be so sure?"

"I can't believe you didn't get that email."

"What are you talking about?"

"We only found out about this a week or so ago. We sent you an email immediately. Now we realize you never got it."

"Got it?"

"You're just not going to believe it!" The plump woman hugged Ruth, speaking into her hair. She choked back a loud sob. "I couldn't stay home, my sweet girl. The minute I heard, I started my plan—plane or no plane, ocean or no ocean—and despite Bubba's awful family, and the extra cost of baggage, and full-body scans, blast it, I'd get to you."

Growing up, Ruth had always been a little afraid of her mother—her strength, her commanding voice, her constant movement—the unflappable, Blitzkrieg of mothers. That remembered image could not describe this lady. Standing before her now was a short, untidy woman with tears streaming down her care-worn face.

Shaken, Ruth said, "Momma, tell me what's going on. Tell me."

They clung to each other. Her mom cried out. "Oh, how I've missed you and baby Annie!" After a few minutes, her mom kissed Ruth lightly, let her go and headed for the brandy decanter. "I was plannin' to come see you before this happened, I have to tell you. The shock of this ... Have they any idea where she is, honey?"

Ruth collapsed on the couch. "He's gone and done it. He's taken her."

"Maybe emailed you, didn't she?"

"What do you mean? You've been speaking in code or something. I'm not getting it."

"Your ex is dead, honey. Has been. For two weeks."

Climbing the windswept hills, Ruth watched white foam slash against the rocks in the surf below. She'd just come from a visit with DCI Trewe for the third time that day. She had to tell him that her ex-husband was dead, so it couldn't be him that took Annie. It couldn't be him, so it had to be someone else. Her heart shuddered deep inside. What kind of life had she brought her daughter to? Who had her? What was going on?

While walking the night before, she had thought someone was following her. It was an odd sensation. But it would explain the emails, the phone calls, and the shadowy figure that watched her house from across the street. She had heard the footfall barely in step with her own. She'd called out and no one had responded. It wasn't right. Why were they after her? Why would anyone wish her harm here? Who had a vendetta against her? Who had picked up the slack from her dead ex-husband?

She went home. Her mother was in the kitchen, scraping the stone floor with a knife on her hands and knees.

"Mom, you don't have to do that."

"It's dingy."

"You're disturbing hundreds of years of dirt."

"I couldn't sit."

"I get it, but cleaning the floor doesn't change anything."

"Daughter of mine, don't reckon you can act as if you know everything. I know a few things, too."

"I made the decision to live here. It was better than staying near Wallis. We were safe from him here."

"You were safe from him after he got sick. I told you that."

"You never could accept that he would find a way to hurt me no matter how sick he was. He's got family that's as bad as he was. He'd use them from beyond the grave if he could. That's how determined he was to hurt me and, more importantly, to hurt Annie."

Her mother pointed to one of Ruth's paintings of Annie. "She took after you in looks."

How dare her mother use the past tense. Ruth wanted to yell, but she whispered, "Takes, not took!"

"I'm not here to fight." Her mother kept scrubbing. She used a dish rag to wipe her face. Her shoulders were jerking.

"I know." Ruth took a deep breath. She realized her mother was crying. "It feels like it's all part of the same discussion. We used the same language ten years ago."

Her mother shook her rag at Ruth. "Everything I said made it worse. You told me to mind my own business. Then you went and married the bastard." She sobbed without sound as she scrubbed.

Light filtered hazily into the kitchen. Strong gusts of wind pushed against the window. All at once, Ruth sensed what her mother must have felt when her daughter left. "I was an idiot."

"Ruth-Ann," her mother rubbed her face dry, "I need to speak mother to mother. I realize that you needed to move here then. But now … with this? And Bubba dead? His folks don't care about you; they've got enough worries on their plate with Bubba's youngest sister." Her mother's red-rimmed eyes glittered with unshed tears. "Ruth-Ann, why don't you just pack up and come home? You can do it now. There is no court case against you. There will be no problems. I can arrange everything. We can leave—as soon as all this is settled."

"It sounds as if everything's settled already." Ruth stood. Nothing changes does it? Another world existed parallel to hers—the hot, muggy world of a childhood that circled her like a merry-go-round, constantly casting her back into the guilt from leaving.

Here in Cornwall, she had found a life that meshed differences into familiarities. She had never been brave enough to admit that she had left the flat landscape of the Gulf coast not only to escape an abusive husband, but to escape her mother—her take-no-prisoners, controlling mother. It had been her attempt to make familiarities from differences.

"I'm not ever going back," Ruth said.

"What do you mean? I don't understand."

"This is my home. Annie and I were—*are*—happy here." She paused to think about it. There are places in the heart, geographic places the heart knows nothing about—like rare art hidden in an attic—until one fine day, a day of exploration, those places are discovered in the real world and recognized, as if the heart had found its true home.

Her mother gripped her arm. "But you can't stay here, Ruth-Ann. There'll always be bad memories."

"There'll always be the best memories, too. I can't leave that."

"But dear, your family is in Texas."

"My friends are here. My family can visit." And until the words left her mouth Ruth had never been so certain she wanted to remain in Cornwall.

Annie Butler lay on her side. The mattress beneath her smelled like the time she forgot to tell her mother she had spilled the milk in the pantry. She remembered what the button was that dangled by her face. It was an old mattress button. She had taken it and kept it tightly clutched in her free hand. Something about it gave her comfort. She didn't know anything about where she was or what was happening to her, except that now she smelled bad all over. How long had she been here and why was it so cold? How long was she supposed to be here, and why wasn't she allowed to move? Her brain couldn't think. That was it. It was as if she couldn't wake up.

The rag on her eyes wasn't tied tight, so she could slip it to the side enough to see. There was the pale blue ticking of the mattress above her and the spotted mattress below her. It was hard to make out. A pale light came in through the cracks around her cocoon. She could bring one hand to her face and see her fingers, like she was under covers and the sun hadn't come up yet.

But no, she wasn't home. This was no place she knew. She remembered that she had been on the beach with Dot but nothing after that. She knew how to get away from a stranger and how to defend herself, so how did she end up here?

13

Thursday, 6:17 a.m.

The bedsprings squeaked and groaned as Charles shifted his weight, setting off a cacophony of gaseous outlays. He couldn't sleep. An active brain didn't help matters. Next to him, The Wife lay on her stomach pretending to be asleep. He lay as still as he could, and listened. She was awake, breathing through her pillow in order not to smell him. He smiled to himself. Damn her efforts.

He'd best rise up and get out of here before she started her insistent demands for sex. She'd been like that since their wedding day ten years before. He no longer touched her. How dare she think he desired a thirty-one-year-old bag o' bones like her? After all, with each new batch of blood, he grew younger.

He rolled onto his side and sat up. With a deep sigh, he swung his legs over the edge of the bed. He rubbed his face.

She must think he didn't know about her dalliance—the two-faced, self-righteous whore. She told him she had gone to Penzance for the day with her pals. She called it her "little fling with the girls." But he wasn't stupid. Penzance and the next farm over were entirely different locales, weren't they? She went to cavort with the gypsy who ran the stables. Did she know he knew? Did it matter? As for the dark-haired heathen, the fool never realized his prized horse didn't die of colic. The perfect result had been achieved. The heartbroken young fellow hadn't had anything to do with The Wife since, had he?

Charles shrugged. She had driven him to it.

He wondered if The Wife had been her usual blabbing self, because something wasn't right. There was a change in the atmosphere around the village. He felt the unease at The Spider's Web on Tuesday. The censorious looks, the sudden quiet conversations, and the subdued laughter didn't fool him. In the Seaside Restaurant where he ate alone yesterday, the sideways glances and smirks of the other patrons didn't escape his notice. They whispered behind his back, didn't they?

He tied his velvet dressing gown tightly around his ample middle. His soft, tattered slippers were a comfort. He slipped into the bathroom as quietly and quickly as he could.

"Not happy in your little village, Chubby?"

His toothbrush slipped out of his fingers, bounced across the sink and into the toilet. He had not expected Mother to give her opinion. His breath caught as he fished the toothbrush out of the toilet and threw it into the bin.

He shuffled into the kitchen to boil water for some decent tea, not like the usually watered-down stuff his German wife considered tea. He set the kettle on the porcelain hob to boil, then took down the tin of loose tea from the cupboard. Teabags were for infants and foreigners.

Water sputtered with a hiss into the fire. He poured a tad into the Royal Albert teapot, swished it about, then dumped the steaming liquid down the drain. He pried the lid off the tea, put three heaping spoons of it into the pot, and tipped in more hot water. He set it aside to steep. Steam rose from the teapot's spout like prayers to a god. He stared at it a moment, satisfied, then set the timer for four minutes.

He hummed to himself. He thought of words to his tune: *Some like it strong. Some like it weak. Some like it in the neck. Tweak! Tweak! Tweak!* That was good.

Timing meant everything.

Now the American woman had brought everyone down to this stinking village. Police of every kind and description. He wished he could snap his fingers and take care of the bitch—bend her to his will. In the old days women followed orders. There were real knights, cut-throat pirates, and honest-to-God kings. Men needed to be men. That's the problem with women.

That American woman looked exactly like his mother had looked in the good times. Exactly like his mother. Snapshots flashed across his memory of his mum after his father left—pictures in his mind, his mother with all of her men *friends* she called them—but he knew the truth. A familiar pain stabbed at his abdomen. His mother told all of them that she loved them, everyone who came and everyone who went—everyone but the one who stayed by her and did everything she asked him. She never told *him* that she loved him. And now the American woman had brought her back to him, so he would make her say it, if he had to chase her into eternity to do it.

Charles shuffled back into the bathroom. All he wanted was peace. He had to continue his experiments in peace. He would be successful in his quest for youth. And he would win Cecil back.

The white stomach tablets were in the medicine cabinet. He caught his countenance in the mirror, and straightened and flattened his silver hair. *It's good hair,* he thought to himself, *glorious hair.* He should be a king with hair like his.

"Chubby!"

He jerked, and bumped his elbow against the cabinet mirror. The stainless edging peeled back a flap of skin and his elbow started to bleed, the blood dripped into the sink. He mopped the bright redness away and added a plaster to the wound. He wiped the mirror of condensation and his face of perspiration.

Her dead voice made ice run in his veins. He hated when mum interrupted his thoughts.

He shuffled back to the kitchen to drink his tea.

Jon watched the flat-screen monitors like a fiend. He had set the video analysis software from America to search automatically for specific types of objects: the black car, the girl, DCI Trewe. The software could spot patterns that he might not notice. Fantastic stuff, this software. But again, he had come up with nothing.

This was one boring little village. He'd already been to the hospital where his sergeant, though still a bit green, was able to answer his questions. He had learned exactly nothing further. His mobile buzzed. He flipped it open. "Jon Graham."

"Jon?" Bakewell's voice. "I've not received the video that you wanted analyzed."

"It was sent Monday morning by overnight delivery. This is Thursday. You should have gotten it by now."

"You sent it by post?"

"The postmistress assured me on the delivery."

"And I thought you'd be back by now. Didn't we agree?"

"I've learned nothing new about Trewe, sir."

"One more day. We need you back here. There have been more developments with the officer in Lancaster."

"I realize the Lancaster case is more prominent …" Jon's ear rang with the click of a closed connection before he could finish.

Why hadn't Bakewell received the package? He walked through the village. The post office was one of the oldest buildings in the village, over four hundred years old, with only the slate roof replaced within the last two hundred years. A fine example of well-built simplicity, strategically positioned above the bay overlooking the rest of the village, it had originally been a local official's house. The woman behind the counter had a white eye-patch across an eye.

"You're the postmistress I spoke with on Monday, last?" Jon asked.

"I'm not the greengrocer. Wot-cher want?"

"Look, I'm on holiday but I'm police—"

"Natur'ly. You're standin' in the way of a payin' customer."

"The package I asked you to mail—"

The postmistress poked a finger at him. "Go-on then. Wot-cher sayin'?"

"It hasn't arrived. Was there a problem?"

"Problem is police bullyin' the innocent and don't know what they're doin'. E'en when a chile goes missin' from under their own noses. An' 'ave yer looked into them other murders?"

"Other murders?"

"Yer can't see yer own face despite yer nose." She laughed at her own joke.

"What do you mean?" Everyone else in the post office, which meant about three others, avoided his eye as he glanced around. He wondered if he should read the woman the riot act. He wondered what she knew of the other murders. Did anyone else know of the other murders, and was there a general feeling that there was a serial murderer on the loose? "And where's my package?"

"I sent it an' thet's all thet matters to you now. End o' discussion."

"But it hasn't arrived."

"It'll get there now, ne'er you mind. Get a-bootcher business and leave us decent tax-payin' volk in peace."

14

Friday morning
Day six

Jon watched the pale light of dawn filter through the trees and twist into wisps of fog that floated along a stream of water, then poured like lava over the cliff.

The stream's babbling rush was lost to the thunderous waves below. Far out at sea, a boat bobbed like a black cork on the pewter sea. Jon wondered if past wreckers had stood where he stood with their ill-guiding lanterns, to wait for ships to crumble on the straggles below.

Scruffy bushes lined the edge of the ravine. He knew his plants, having accidentally fallen in love (Can one accidentally fall in love?) with gardening after his mother begged him to plant vegetables for her. He never did things halfway, so he'd delved into all the garden manuals and books he could get his hands on and created a whopping good plot for her at the bottom of her garden. She was quite proud of the flower and vegetable beds and even the plum he kept espaliered across one wall. His knowledge came in handy sometimes. Just now he had identified the scruffy plants amongst the gorse along the cliffs as wild thyme.

The ever present wind coated his tongue with salt. The vast area of openness around him left him feeling as if he stood at the edge of the world. Below, pockmarked walls of rock lined the cliffs as far as he could see. The earth beneath his feet was rough and hummocky. The sea stretched before him, unbroken to the horizon. Behind him, the land dropped upon a meadow, beyond which hills rolled along forever. Trees grew tall only in the dips between hills; such was the wind all year long that it scraped the rounded humps bare of anything taller than a sheep.

From this vantage point, he could see Detective Chief Inspector Trewe's family dairy sewn into the windswept, patchwork quilt of other farms and estates. He'd viewed all the footage from cameras near Trewe's farm and his office at the police station in Treborwick. It had been like watching grass grow. He'd gone over records and interviewed his own sergeant, and could draw no conclusions. Why did the man continue as if he had no more than his regular salary in his deposit account?

How safe would it be, he wondered, to climb down to the beach from here? He knew he probably shouldn't get too close to the edge. Signs everywhere warned that it was unstable.

He had risen at five that morning. He'd used the time to look up details of missing persons in Cornwall. Despite what Bakewell said, he couldn't stop being curious. Obviously, if the postmistress was connecting the missing girl to the other missing girls, word was out.

Two females had gone missing in recent years between Devon and Cornwall, with the fifteen-year-old girl's body having been discovered recently. The other had been missing for six months. She was twelve and about the same size as Annie Butler.

He turned at a snuffling sound. What appeared to be the same dog he'd caught on tape at the beach Sunday morning and Sunday evening now romped toward him. His heart flipped over and beat double-time at the sheer size of the thing. He didn't have any time to run before the dog was next to him. He flinched. All the dog did was sniff his hand. The plumed tail sailed back and forth. "You seem to get around. Did you see what happened that day, dog?" He rubbed its warm head.

"Chelsea!" The stern voice, seemingly next to his ear, startled Jon and he jumped to his feet. An old man wielded a walking stick and stood not four feet from him. He spoke again, "Errr … A bit o'er friendly is Chelsea."

"A fine dog," Jon managed to sputter.

Wisps of beard framed the man's wide, square jaw like an early morning frost. His chin sprouted a smooth length of snow-white beard that was tucked into his shirtfront. He said something that sounded like "Newfoundland." Then he cleared his throat with a loud *"Aurrrrugh!"* and spit.

The dog, whose mouth spread into what looked like a wide grin, sat at the old man's feet, but occasionally glanced around at Jon. The gaze was nothing short of intelligent, and Jon wouldn't have been surprised if the creature had communicated exactly what it meant to the man. The way she glanced up at the man, it was as if she was saying, "Why don't you move?"

Jon wondered aloud, "I suppose you don't observe too many people out here this time of year."

Ramrod straight from the waist to a slight stoop at the shoulders, the man bent toward the sea, leaning against his staff. His prominent nose and red cheeks jutted from under a floppy felt hat that had seen better days. "Seen enough fer a lifetime. Just walkin's one thing. Falling off the side's another."

"Falling off the side?"

"Tourists don't read the signs, do they?"

The old man must think Jon a tourist. And that was what he was supposed to be. He wondered how many tourists had fallen off the side lately. "Walk out here often, then?"

"Often enough. Gettin' too crowded," the old man muttered.

"I'm curious," Jon said. "You're aware, no doubt, a child has disappeared. I was just wondering where she might be. Have you seen anything?"

The man stirred, mumbled some response, and then, as if he realized another human stood next to him, said, "Seen the mum walkin' 'ere." He tapped the ground with his stick.

"Here?"

"Here." He tapped his stick again. "Sure as sure." Then silence.

Jon turned. "There's a pub not far, open for lunch. If you like, I'll buy you a drink."

The man nodded assent and shoved off with his walking stick, as if the land were a great sea and he the ship pulling away from the dock.

The dog followed them, darting back and forth, nose to the ground, then ran ahead.

Jon tried to keep up with his silent human companion. He kept himself in the best possible physical condition, but the old gent battled forward at a pace that left Jon puffing.

The dog kept leaping down to the water's edge when the land dipped and would scramble back up to them as they passed. The way seemed impossibly steep in Jon's eyes, but then, he wasn't a dog. They had gone another five hundred yards when, with a low growl, the dog slid over the cliff's edge to a tiny beach below and barked twice. Jon's new companion stopped abruptly. The dog climbed to a rock shelf that jutted into the surf. Waves crashed over and sank, only to roll up and splash down again. The dog zigzagged its way toward the waves.

Jon glanced at his companion, still and quiet beside him. He had heard Newfoundland dogs were good swimmers, but the violence of the waves upon the granite shelf looked too dangerous for man or beast.

The dog stopped and scraped at something with one paw. Jon smiled. She was obviously after a poor fish trapped in a rock pool with the tide out. Something white flashed as the dog pawed.

"Tide 'll come in," muttered the old man.

A huge wave washed up and over the rock, and drenched the dog, but the animal would not give up its mission. Jon glanced at the man leaning on his stick, waiting. Surely he would not let his dog be washed out to sea, but he budged not an inch.

Time passed. Jon glanced again at the old man. His gaze returned to the black dog and then again to the man's grim face. Something told him to be patient; the man was waiting for his dog. What did the dog want so badly? Jon sighed. Nothing to do but to wait with him.

Down went the dog's nose into the shadows and out of sight. After a tug that almost landed the dog on its haunches, the black, fuzzy creature headed back. The dog pranced across the rock, head and tail up. With some effort, she crawled and clawed her way up the steep embankment, over to the two men, and dropped her prize at their feet.

It was a girl's black shoe.

15

Jon pulled his mobile from his jacket pocket and dialed. Whilst it rang, he turned to the old man, "Your name?"

"Gareth Wren Tavish," came the gruff reply. He gave the dog a rough pat on the head. He didn't touch the shoe, merely looked once again out to sea.

His name surprised Jon. First impressions were funny things. His connection went through.

"Tom Bakewell."

"Sir. Jon Graham."

He glanced up and down the coastline. "I'm less than a mile from Perrin's Point."

"In which direction?"

"Sorry, south." He watched as Mr. Tavish drew pictures in the dirt with his staff. "On the cliff top and I've run into a gentleman and his dog."

"With your car?"

"I'm on foot." He glanced at the dog. "The dog's pulled a girl's shoe from the surf."

"Floating?"

"It was attached to something."

"Have you looked?"

Jon's eyes went to the spot on the rock ledge where the dog had been. "No," Jon pushed the soft, springy sod with the toe of his shoe, "I don't think it will wait; the tide will put it underwater again."

"Discover what you can and ring me back no matter."

"Yes, sir." Jon closed the connection and turned. "Mr. Tavish, do you know what's down there?"

"Tavy."

"Excuse me?"

"People call me Tavy."

"Tavy, do you know what's down there?"

"Why?"

Jon pulled out his official identification, but Tavy motioned him to stop.

"Know yer police." He grinned. The old man sported a toothless upper palate.

Jon glanced again at the spot where the dog had been. "I ask because you looked as if you knew what the dog was up to."

Tavy studied the ground. He leaned against his staff. His hat hid his face. The white wisps of his beard shimmered in the early daylight as he gestured toward the dog sitting at his feet. "Wouldn't a-bothered about a fish."

He prodded up the soft earth with the end of his staff as if there were more answers to be found in it. From behind them, the sunlight burst through the clouds and sparkled like diamonds across the sea. The beach below was darkly shadowed.

Jon shaded his eyes with his hands to try and pick out anything he could. "So you don't know if the missing girl is down there?"

The old man's eyes were dark tunnels of unfathomable depths—unsettling.

Jon started down over the side. He didn't mind the dirt and rocks. He wasn't inexperienced with climbing—and with that thought, his foot slipped. His descent was more rapid than he had intended. About midway down, in the soil and turf avalanche, his foot caught on a rock and twisted him sideways so he hit the soft sand at the bottom of the steep incline, on his face.

Spitting sand from his mouth, Jon sputtered, "I'm fine. I'm fine." No response from above. "Hello?"

Tavy's face appeared over the edge, looking down on Jon with a bemused twinkle. "Fallen over the side, 'ave ye?"

Dignity lost in one fell swoop, Jon brushed the dry sand from his face. "If you wouldn't mind sticking around a bit ..."

Tavy made no indication to Jon that he would or would not stay.

The waves soldiered in as the wind picked up. The sun disappeared behind a cloud and shadows disappeared. It was much easier to observe everything in this light.

Jon climbed onto the rock. He didn't really want to see what he knew was there. A short phrase from Macbeth came to mind: *Present fears are less than horrible imaginings.* Only, he believed that his fears would prove true and be worse than what he imagined. From here, the incoming swell of water towered skyward, sank down, and then splashed up around him. What awaited in a crevice closer to the end of the rock shelf was far worse than crashing waves.

The slender, petite body was crammed into a wide crack in the rock so that it was almost entirely submerged beneath the clear-as-glass saltwater.

It might have been the child had fallen over the cliff and into the surf, which then mashed her body into this crack, but for the fact that the head was covered with a cloth sack. One end of the string binding the sack floated free and wiggled like a white sea-worm each time a new wave deposited more sea spray into the cauldron.

A hole in the sack over her head pulsated, and for one sick moment Jon imagined she was attempting to speak to him from inside her covering. But as he bent closer, tiny crabs crept from the hole and scattered over the rock, and dropped one by one into the foamy surf. Some creature had devoured the flesh of the part of her arm that was visible above water, exposing the delicate bones of her forearm. Underwater, whatever skin he could see was washed of any color.

Shockingly, the fully clothed body lay as if resting in the bath. One shoeless foot still had a white sock on it.

The other foot did not have a shoe or sock because it was stripped of flesh.

A gull dropped from the sky onto the rock. It waddled toward the body, sharp beak pointed skyward, wings flared out. The sight of that small skeletal foot filled Jon with rage. Waving an arm, he shouted, “Scat!”

The bird screeched and launched itself into the breeze.

Jon turned back to where the body lay. He had seen death touch human beings in many ways, but this—this horrible imagining proved fearfully real—was no good. This was no good at all. The fact that this white, torn piece of flesh had, only six days before, been a lively young girl turned his stomach. He dialed his mobile. After one ring the phone connected.

“Yes, Jon.”

“It’s a girl’s body,” Jon said.

“You’ll have to ring up the police. Tell them who you are. Stay with the story, though. You’re on holiday.”

“Right.” Jon closed the connection. He stared out to sea. “Such a holiday.”

The doorbell rang. Sally answered. Ruth stopped brushing her teeth to listen from the next room. She could still hear her mother snoring; the noise was irksome because she couldn’t hear who was at the door. She wiped her face. The toothpaste tasted salty and artificially sweet.

She tightened her robe and slipped into the kitchen to sit at the table with her tea. A shiver passed through her. She wrapped her freezing fingers around the warmth. Her legs had cramped last night and had kept her awake.

Sally entered the room followed by the same police officer who had questioned Ruth on the beach that dread morning. Constable Stark was followed by Constable Allison Craig. Each face revealed that what they needed to say would not be good news. Ruth gave a moan and fell sideways. The tea mug landed on her braided rag rug. The handle cracked and the tiny ceramic duck on the inside broke free and rolled out. The milky liquid soaked the rug.

Sally knelt next to Ruth's chair, without heed to the sticky mess. "They've found a girl's body."

Ruth sat bolt upright in the chair. "No! I don't want to hear this!" She searched Sally's face. "Don't look at me!" Ruth pushed her away and struggled to rise.

Constable Stark had paled to a dead white with twin red blazes of color from cheek to ear. "I'm sorry, Mrs. Butler."

"What do you mean? Why did you come here? It isn't Annie. Don't be silly."

He looked at the floor. "I don't quite know how to … The body … due to nature's ways … They've moved 'er because of the tide comin' in and all. We're not asking you to identify the body—just to look at some of the items recovered."

"What do you mean?" Her breath came in gasps. "What about the tide?" Her voice strained into a higher pitch and louder volume, "Why did you say tide?"

"Mrs. Butler—"

"Ruth … Ruth …" Sally shook Ruth's arm gently.

"Are you saying she drowned?" Her voice didn't sound like her voice. The truth of their words bore through Ruth's heart and left untellable pain in its wake. Her daughter had been in the water all this time? How could she not feel that? How could she not have detected through the deep blankness of space that her daughter had died? She could not believe it.

Ruth's eyes met Sally's.

"I'm sorry." Sally hugged Ruth to her robust bosom, rocked her back and forth and sobbed, "I'm so sorry."

Ruth felt sick to her stomach. She pushed away from Sally. "You're wrong! You're wrong! Annie is not dead!"

She heard her mother say, "Annie is dead?"

Ruth couldn't stop shaking. Her teeth clattered. Her throat was on fire. "No, Momma. She's coming home. She's lost. She'll come home because she always does. She always comes home."

Allison Craig reached for Ruth's mother as the stout woman slid to the floor.

"She's coming home!" Ruth yelled.

The tall constable shifted from foot to foot, clawing at the brim of his hat. Constable Craig, her hair coming undone from its clasp, face puffy as if she wanted to cry, helped Sally get Ruth's mother into a chair. The police woman spoke quietly, "Mrs. Butler, please."

Ruth took a breath. "What did you ask me?"

Allison Craig said, "We need someone to look at some clothing, and well, we do need you to allow us to take a sample of your DNA." Her voice cracked. She pushed her hair away from her eyes. "You don't have to view anything else."

"But I want to see." Her baby, her daughter … a *body* lay on some cold metal surface somewhere? Impossible. In a firm voice, she said, "I need to see."

"Me, too," her mother sobbed.

"No, Momma. No. I'm going. Alone."

Constable Stark swallowed. "There isn't enough of the face to identify."

Sally took Ruth's hands in hers. "Think what you're sayin' Ruth! Let me go … or Sam!"

"I'm going to see the body. If it's Annie—and I know it isn't—but if it is, I … This is my fault. I brought her here. I took away all her chances. It's God's punishment, isn't it? I should have done something more or different. But …" Her face set, she said in a cold voice, "I need to see."

Sally shook her head. "No. Have you—"

"Thought about this? I've spent all these nights and days thinking about it. There shouldn't be any more thinking." *A body.* She heard a voice that sounded like someone else's voice speaking. "I will go." *A body without feeling.*

Sally took her hand. "Let me go with you."

Ruth nodded.

Her mother pushed back from the table. She looked empty, deflated—not like her mother at all. Ruth put out her hand. "Momma, you stay here. There may be a phone call." She stood. Sally stood. One supported the other as they followed the constables to the waiting police car.

16

Friday, early afternoon

Jon Graham drove. The road into Treborwick was narrow, the way, short. From the direction of Perrin's Point, one had to travel east and uphill to reach the larger town thirty minutes away. An old bridge, three men wide, crossed the river alongside the newer, navigable bridge leading into town. Treborwick police station was a larger, more modern facility than the Perrin's Point police house that dated from former times when the police station and the policeman's home were one and the same.

He had reported the body. The SOCO team came while he was still there. Tavy had been allowed to leave. The body had been transferred. Now he had been invited to speak to Trewe at his office. *Great!* He'd be face to face with the one he'd come to investigate. His hands were sweaty, his stomach full of flutter—as if he had come for a job interview. He was that nervous. The door to the police station swung open. The boxy, sterile front room appeared deserted, and a glass-enclosed space encapsulated the front desk personnel.

Subdued activity could be heard from the rooms in back. Nearer at hand the buzz of conversation drew him to peek around a partition. He could see no one. He dare not walk back to the adjoining room and interrupt as if he were part of the team. Jon thumped his knuckles against the scarred counter with the immediate reaction of silence.

A uniformed constable poked his head around a corner. "May I help you, sir?"

"Jon Graham. Here to meet with Detective Chief Inspector Trewe."

"Thank you for coming." The constable conferred with someone behind him, then looked past Jon at the hard plastic chairs. "Someone will be right out."

"Thank you." Before Jon could sit, a woman police constable emerged from the inner recesses and announced that Detective Chief Inspector Trewe would see him now. Should he follow her? She gave him an odd look. Then she smiled—good smile, solid woman, messy hair at odds with her perfectly creased attire.

The large, sunless room held a gloom that had nothing to do with the weather. No one met his eyes. Uniformed police officers slumped back and forth, intent on their work. Suited detectives bent over one computer, taking notes from what was on the screen. A table stacked with papers took up the center of the room. Ringing phones, conversation, and the tap-tapping of fingers at keyboards rolled in waves of intensity—louder, then softer.

Push bicycles lined the inside wall near a back door.

The WPC leaned toward Jon and whispered, "Allison Craig." She shook his hand. "Don't misunderstand, things aren't normally this—"

An office door opened. Ear splitting shouts burst from within. "Take that bloody rubbish out of here!"

Everyone froze.

The recipient of those words backed out, and closed the door. Apparently not realizing anyone stood behind him, he turned and smashed into Jon's chest. The papers he carried scattered across the carpeted floor.

"Sorry." Jon peeled the poor man from his shirt. "Sergeant."

A flush spread from the officer's neck to his ears. Sergeant Perstow stuttered his apologies. "Should be a-mindin' where I go." The sweating older man looked around as if not quite sure what to do with himself. He started a fresh apology. "Sorry—"

Jon stopped him. The man had a plaster along one wrist that disappeared beneath his cuff. “You’ve hurt your arm?”

“I’m fine, sar.” Again, Perstow’s ultra-fair skin grew red in a deep blush as he bent down to gather papers. “Sorry, sar.”

Jon glanced over at Trewe’s secretary. Her gaze was steady as she gave him a provocative half-smile and shrugged with a shake of her head. He nodded and knocked on Trewe’s door.

The door jerked open. Trewe proclaimed, “I said no interruptions!”

A second or two of silence elapsed.

Trewe huffed. “Who are you?”

“Detective Inspector Jon Graham. I was asked to come round.”

Trewe shook his hand and fumbled with the door. He marched around his desk, opened a drawer, and popped two white tablets into his water glass where they fizzed. He drank it in one go and sat down, his face a studied picture of calm. He pointed at a chair across from his desk. “Please.”

Jon quickly scanned Trewe’s face, and noted the thin, wrinkle-free skin and palest of blue eyes, the unwavering gaze—definitely the face of a determined individual. He knew it by the set of the jaw. He sat.

Perstow seemed hesitant to enter but Trewe waved him in impatiently. Perstow eased down to sit on the edge of his seat, his papers grasped tight as if he didn’t expect to stay for long.

“Why are you here, Mr. Graham?” Trewe demanded.

“I’m the one who found the body.”

Trewe’s demeanor changed. He pushed his chair back. “A policeman finding the body. That’s novel.”

“Yes, sir.”

Trewe shuffled paper. “The officers at the scene took a detailed statement. I just want to go over a few items.”

“All right.”

“Why are you in Cornwall?”

Because where there’s muck there’s brass. He kept his retort and held his gaze level, hoping his face appeared honest and sincere as he lied. “Actually, I’m on holiday. Been planning to come down this way for a bit of a seaside holiday for years. I surf. Seemed a likely spot, you see."

"A change from ..." Trewe let the question hang.

"London," Jon said, smiling. The fixed stare threatened, the pale of Trewe's eyes as disconcerting as circles of blue-white flame from hell's bottomless pit. "The weather seems pleasant enough for this time of year."

"Usually get some kind of weather." Trewe shifted his eyes to the other man. "This is Sergeant Perstow."

Jon shook Perstow's hand, as if this was a complete stranger and he couldn't be camping, at this moment, in his garden. "How do you do?"

"Very well, sar." Perstow cleared his throat.

Jon saw the round face turn pink and thought, *the blooming idiot's giving the game away.*

Trewe glared at Perstow. Perstow looked at the floor. Trewe stood. "Excuse us for one moment, Mr. Graham. I need to speak to the sergeant."

Trewe and Perstow stepped out.

Jon glanced around Trewe's office. It was definitely as uncomfortable as the man, with nothing to indicate his new wealth here. The shelves held few books, and those amounted to procedural manuals. There were no framed family photos, no awards, no medals, no indication of any hobby. An electric pencil sharpener held down a stack of papers, and there were papers and files stacked on the desk and on the floor. Cellotaped to the lampshade was a snapshot of a man standing with one hand on a cow, the other held a blue ribbon.

He considered that with all he'd heard and read about Trewe's character and drive, he should have made Superintendent by now. Something must have happened when he was with the London Met twenty years before, because it was at that time he abruptly put in for a transfer to his birthplace of Cornwall. He never pursued promotion from that point on. What had happened? The rumors of his odd behavior and possible commitment procedures circled and flew. He knew they were wrong and unfounded, put to rest years later with an inter-departmental note about gossip. Even after a review of the files he had on the man, the mystery remained. The explanation for the transfer: personal.

The two officers re-entered the room. Perstow's hands were empty of papers, and Trewe's demeanor had changed, become sharply alert. "You work for Complaints and Discipline, Mr. Graham? And you came all this way a month before the tourist season starts—to play in the sun?"

Jon glanced at the stout man plopped beside him whose gaze seemed intent on the pencil sharpener. What game was Perstow playing? He had been sworn to secrecy about why Jon Graham's holiday spot was in Perstow's back garden, so why tell Trewe that Jon worked for Complaints? Hell, why not tell him he was camping in his garden and that they poured tea together every morning? He said to Trewe, "The job and the London weather do get a bit monotonous at precisely this time of year."

Trewe's nostrils flared. "This department operates like clockwork. Is there any question o' that?"

"Why would there be?"

Trewe's square jaw worked back and forth. Under his thin skin along the sides of his face, the rippling muscles looked as though he did a lot of teeth grinding. Trewe sat behind his desk facing Jon. "We've interviewed you about finding the body. You gave your name and rank but not what department you're with. Why the bloody hell not?"

"I didn't think my department had any bearing on your case." Jon rubbed the back of his neck. "I've seen the posters of the missing girl." *That sounded natural enough.* "I knew it was not my place to interfere with your investigation or I would have volunteered to help find her." *That sounded weak.* He'd never been completely confident that he would know what to say once he met up with Trewe.

Trewe made a noise in his throat that sounded like a growl. "On holiday, my arse! I wouldn't mind a holiday about now. A few hours ago, a girl's body—an American girl's body—turns up in the surf. The media have swarmed. Just as I suspected, this is a bloody mess. I don't need more complications, Mr. Graham. We can't even get official identification without a face or teeth." Trewe kept his gaze steady. "And now it seems we've suddenly become a favorite holiday spot."

"Planned to do some sightseeing."

"Haven't you seen enough?" Trewe's voice rose. He did not wait for a response. "Let us know your whereabouts after this."

It was a dismissal, but Jon didn't want to leave just yet. "Actually, it seems a frivolous thing to be touring with a murder investigation under my nose." Jon watched for a response. Perhaps this could be a lead-in to asking quite naturally if he could lend a hand.

Trewe angled his chair. Shadows fell across his face. "A murder such as this is very rare."

Jon cleared his throat. "You've pinned it down to murder then?"

"The child didn't put the bag over her head and jam herself into the rocks. Let me be frank with you, Mr. Graham." Trewe paused, eyes narrowed. "I don't need London, nor do I need you to interfere in this investigation."

"I spoke to Trewe." Jon was frying up an egg as he juggled his mobile against his ear. The beans were hot and he was hungry. Nothing like runny egg and beans on toast.

Bakewell asked, "Wasn't keen to include you in the investigation, then?"

"No, he was not." Jon transferred his food to a plate.

"Hmm … So Trewe's only interested that you happened into Perrin's Point just as a murder occurs?"

"As if I planned it. And he knows I work in Complaints and is suspicious why I'm here."

"Keep your head down for the time being. You've got my permission to stay as long as you need to."

"What I've been thinking is," Jon said, and with a free hand cut the toast into bite-size pieces with a fork, "if, say, I was ordered onto this investigation team, I'd have a real inside chance at figuring out Trewe."

"It *would be* the natural progression of things. I'll see what I can do."

He rang off.

Jon set his plate on the small fold-out table beneath his bank of monitors. He lined up his flatware beside the plate. If it weren't that he was trying to get close to Trewe, he wouldn't *want* to get involved in this investigation. His hand tightened around his glass of water. It's a horrible murder, and of a child. He looked down at his congealed egg. He had no appetite.

17

Friday, midafternoon

Jon sat across from Perstow in his cramped caravan. "Why?"

"I tried, sar. But he can see through me every time. Tol' him I recognized you from an interdepartmental communiqué."

"Weak."

"I could not think of a thing else. Sorry, sar."

Jon rubbed his face, weary. "You've got other things to worry about. Go about your business and don't let on about anything else concerning me. Understood?"

"Understood. Sorry, sar."

After seeing the portly man out, Jon decided to treat old man Tavy to the drink he'd promised him. Even if Jon wasn't part of the investigating team, he was a policeman. Despite a lack of invitation, he would find a way in.

"Tavy's house is at the back of the village," Sergeant Perstow had told him as he handed him a hand-drawn map of the lanes to follow.

The lane he turned on had a sign that read "Unsuitable for Caravans." The deep cuts in the lane would have made navigation by such a thing impossible. Jon drove his motorcar until he came to a rough path no wider than two people could manage walking abreast, then parked and started walking.

The lane wove downward. Hedgerows on both sides leaned inward so that the lane became a tunnel. He quickened his pace. The closing in made him gasp for breath. The wind whistled through the gorse. Several species of entangled green vines had flowers. Below the hedge was a drystone wall, the flat stones laid in a distinctive herringbone pattern. No one made them like that anymore.

Down and around, he came to a gate where he picked his way across a water-filled cattle grid and pushed aside a rusted bar. The resulting ruckus was enough to wake Hades.

The thatched cottage was nestled deep in the earth. Beech trees crowded all around it like brooding giants. The starkness of the white-washed cottage and the deeply set, shuttered windows gave it the effect of a skull peering from the shadows. The thatch appeared as worn as its owner had. At Jon's approach, rooks scattered up into the sky—black, fluttery specks picked up and carried by the wind. The birds returned with a racket like duck-hunter calls gone mad.

Slightly askew over the door, a small sign read "The Combe."

Jon knocked on the door and waited. No response. He watched a bee hover up drunkenly from beneath a window. He knocked again, listening. No sound from within. He had just about given up when he heard a step. With a loud clank and clatter of chains, the door opened and the dog's wide, black nose poked out, followed by the old man's face.

"Back, Chelsea!" Tavy's voice sounded far off and a thousand years old. Without a hat, his pure white hair, long and wispy, stood out all over his head. He could be mistaken for a Merlin wizard. From his eyebrows down, his skin was weather-wrinkled red. His smooth, pale forehead seemed glued on like an afterthought. He glared at Jon. "An' ye'd be a-wantin' … what?"

"Tavy, how about that drink at the pub? I owe you."

The door swung closed. "Don't feel ye must pay up."

"Wait! So … I want information from you. I'm buying."

Tavy smiled his toothless smile. "I does *like* an honest man."

Ducking behind the door, he reappeared with his beat-up, brown felt hat crushed to his head. He crooked his walking stick under his arm and closed and locked his door. More than happy for an outing, Chelsea did a four-step waltz around them as they made their way back down the shaded lane to Jon's car.

The dog took up the rear seat. The smell was powerful in the closed up car. Jon lowered a rear window for the dog's drool to drip down the inside and the outside of the glass.

Passing fields of green-turned-platinum-in-the-sunshine corn shoots, they drove to the Napoleon Inn at the top of the village. The whitewashed, two-storied building melded into surrounding cottages. It was hard to distinguish which part was pub and which was the rest of the neighborhood, but it looked inviting with its shiny mullioned windows and squat door. With no car park, he had to search tiny side streets for a space. They parked, locked up, and set off. As they rounded a corner on foot, Tavy paused and pointed to a wooden sign set into a wall. "You know where the name came from?"

"No."

"Long ago, a man by name of William Bone was the landlord. The story goes that one day 'e went off to thet Napoleon war. When 'e came back they called 'im the Napoleon man. 'Nother story 'twas the 'riginal name was 'Boney's Bar' till the Napoleon War, and the young men was inscripted 'ere. Anyway, any'ow we just calls it 'the Nap.' " He bared his vacuous grin again.

"Quite old, then."

"Yep."

The dog beat them to the door, her tail waving and nose pointed at the door's handle. Through an outer door and past an inner courtyard, they entered the pub. The noise of the late afternoon crowd of four dulled on their entrance. Then a shout arose from a thin-faced man behind the bar, "'Allo, 'allo! 'Ere's Tavy to grace us, lads. Who've you brought with you?"

Tavy waved an arm. He led Jon to a table by a huge fireplace where a tiny flame smoldered in the grate and blew a low whistle. "Here, Chelsea."

The dog seemed to find a familiar spot, circled and settled quickly.

"What'll you have, Tavy?" Jon asked.

"Bob'll know what I want."

Jon made his way around the empty tables to the bar. He placed his order for two, apparently the house specials. The room had a wet-cave smell suffused with the odor of cigarette smoke. A rusting, Firestone/Mobil Oil sign was tacked to a wall next to some handwritten score sheets. A dartboard had three darts stuck to it. The mantel over the fireplace held empty, dust-covered brandy bottles, brass candlesticks, and black and white, unframed photos of various people casually posed. Walking sticks and canes hung from the ceiling. There was a metal one much like the one his grandfather had used before he died. A few baseball caps hung from the canes. The place was a regular home from home.

He needed to locate the gents'. He asked Tavy.

"Ooo-er! I'll have to show you the trick." Tavy arose and made his way to the wall. Jon followed. There wasn't anything but the fireplace until the old man pressed a brick on the hearth with his foot. A part of the wall, next to the hearth, opened inward.

Jon didn't know what to think. "What's this then?"

"An old building. Shouldn't be too surprisin'. Smuggler's country after all." Tavy pointed down the narrow passageway lit by dim bulbs that hung from the ceiling. "You just follow this hall down a bit and you'll find the loo on the left. Come back this-a-way, press this knob and the door'll open."

With an inward shiver, Jon followed the instructions. He hated it. "The Hidden Loo" is what the pub should be called. After coming down the low-ceilinged hall with the claustrophobic walls, he found the gents' to be brightly lit, clean, and surprisingly modern.

The invisible hand that squeezed his chest whenever he found himself in a closed-in space accompanied him to the toilet. He did not totally relax until he rejoined Tavy. Chelsea lifted her massive head and winked at him, which left him with the oddest sensation that she understood his problem. The low rumble and occasional burst of noisy emotion from the game tables in the next room drowned out the radio that crackled from behind the bar. Jon wondered whose taste ran to Peruvian goatherd yodeling, until he observed the barman adjust the knob and heard a twanging folk song belt across the room.

"Yer don't look well, son," Tavy said as Jon sat.

He knew he had sweat marks at his arm pits. "I don't care for enclosed places."

"Eh?"

"Childhood trauma. Locked in a cupboard accidently. Mum found me catatonic or some such. That passageway to the loo gave me the creeps, is all."

"Ghoulies and ghosties an' things that go bump in the night." Tavy hooted and slapped his knee. "Should 'ave asked for the direct route."

Oh yeah! Funny, Jon thought. The barman put the drinks on the bar. Jon went up and paid for them and carried the brimming glasses back to the table.

Tavy finished his off in one go. He set his empty glass down hard, wiped his mouth with his sleeve, and gaped at Jon. "Ordered the same?"

"Yes."

"A brave soul to drink the cider."

Jon considered his drink. The murky amber liquid didn't look dangerous. "You mentioned seeing the mother of the girl, walking on the cliffs?"

"Yeah, 'er."

Jon took a swallow—bitter but not bad. Here we go, he thought, I'll have to drag it out of him. "What day was it?"

"Day tha' girl disappeared."

"Have you seen the mother more than once?"

"More 'n once."

"Time?"

"Late. Early. An' all in between." Tavy stared pointedly at his empty glass.

Jon's immediate thought was that the old man spent a lot of time wandering about. He caught the pointed stare and went to the bar to order another round.

The barman winked at him. "Watch yer pocketbook. An' watch yerself, if yer not used to the cider." The barman grinned at the room in general, which precipitated a round of loud guffaws.

Jon nodded his thanks and paid for it. The stuff seemed harmless enough, going down smooth as silk after the bitter passed. He walked back to the table and set the full glasses in front of his new friend. The room tilted. He fell into his seat.

Tavy chuckled, "Gotta take it slow, son."

Chelsea heaved a sigh and stretched out making her the longest dog in the world for a moment.

Tavy drank, slower this time. He placed his drink on the table, leaned toward Jon and laid his finger against his nose. "The first time, her looked fer the world like a lost waif—a spirit—gave the heart a rare leap till I recognized 'er."

The old man stared past Jon to some distant, unreachable point. "Late at night on the cliffs … 'tis dangerous." The words creaked out of the old gent slowly.

Jon leaned forward. "She walks along the cliffs?"

"Yeah—*aurrrrugh,*" Tavy hacked out with a sputtering, gloopy clearing of his throat, as if he needed a bucket to spit in. He made do with a handkerchief. "Can't sleep. Not as fit as I used to be. Worked the mines when I was a young'un. Closed 'em down, the mines. Took the wind out o' Cornwall's sails."

"You saw Mrs. Butler …" Jon prompted.

"Yeah, 'er."

"What did she say when she saw you?"

"Didn't see us. Didn't see t' other one neither."

"What other one?" Jon noticed Tavy had finished his drink and eyed the food being consumed at a nearby table. It was nearer evening than noon. Jon intercepted his stare. "Would you like something to eat? It's late. I shouldn't have kept you."

"No, no … well, erm … if you've time to hear more … Bob'll know what I like."

Jon went to the bar, and before he opened his mouth, the barman told him the fish and chips were sizzling in the fry vat, enough for two if he wanted. Unless, of course, he wanted crab; he could always provide a crab.

A horrid picture flashed through Jon's mind of tiny crabs exiting a hole in a sack.

"Don't think I want anything with crab in it just now, thank you."

Someone next to his elbow turned to Jon and said, "That decision 'll see ye roight." There were a few muffled snickers.

Jon told the barman whatever Tavy was having would be fine. He returned to the table, feeling as if he'd landed in a foreign country. "Didn't know what to order."

Tavy moved his head to glance toward the bar then back to Jon. "Just plain good food—the best thing 'ere."

"You were saying Mrs. Butler didn't see …"

Tavy nodded. The fading afternoon light from the windows darkened the deep-as-trenches furrows on his leathery face. "I've seen 'er walkin'. At the same time, an' so 's 'e."

"He?"

"Don't know. Too many clothes about his head, the dark … Some'pin about him, though." He shook his head; his face shuttered. "Some'pin familiar."

"Could you recognize him again?"

Tavy looked up at him, and took his time to reply. "P'r'aps."

Jon tapped his foot. "Were there no distinguishing mannerisms?"

A bell rang. Jon retrieved their food. Steam rose from the plates as he set them down at their table. The door to the outside opened. A well-dressed chap and a woman entered.

"That be Mr. Malone and his wife," Tavy muttered in almost a growl. Chelsea took the growl up, a low rumble which stretched on and on until the old man made a noise with his tongue. The dog gave him a look and a nod and put her head down again.

The barman greeted the Malones with loud jocularity. Jon noticed Mrs. Malone wore slacks and a stylish jacket just below her waist—and that she had lovely hips.

Tavy stared too.

"He seems well known," Jon said.

"Fact o' bein' gentry, innit? He's the local magistrate, a volunteer position he takes serious."

Jon changed the subject back to what he was most interested in. "Too bad you couldn't tell who it was on the cliff."

The old man gave a shrug and chewed noisily, not taking his squinting eyes from the two new customers. "Too dark."

He coughed and a piece of fish spewed out of Tavy's mouth to land on the table. He picked it up and tossed it to Chelsea. With an almost human groan, she scooted closer and the piece of fish disappeared. The dog moved closer to Tavy's chair and sat upright as if to say, "Any more?"

They ate without further conversation. Jon enjoyed the fish, done to white, flaky perfection. The chips were not overly greasy. He added horseradish to the mayonnaise. The chunks of dry lettuce on the side he could have done without.

He couldn't get away from the revelation that Mrs. Butler walked late at night alone. He had no business getting so involved, but perhaps he should warn her to stop. Someone should.

18

Friday night

Jon settled into a wooded spot above Mrs. Butler's house, and wondered why the woman left her home at night. It was dangerous, whatever the reason. Surely since the child's body had been found, she wouldn't be out wandering, but just in case, he'd sit there as an unofficial guard. With Trewe as suspicious as he was, Jon couldn't be seen to be too involved.

That was a powerful drink he'd had with Tavy—a drink called scrumpy, a type of cider served straight from the barrel. After he took Tavy home, it hit him, and he didn't trust himself to be able to navigate well. So, he had parked and taken a nap in the quiet lane by Tavy's house. When he woke, he had driven to his caravan and taken a cold shower in the cramped, toilet-shower contraption before setting out again for a walk. The brisk night air would set him right.

He hadn't been able keep from thinking about the woman. She should not walk alone at night. Period. So into the little copse of wood above the slope to the road in front of Mrs. Butler's cottage he'd gone.

Despite the cold, the rustling of something in the bushes, and the wet of the undergrowth that seeped through his trousers, he fell asleep again.

Some barely-perceptible change penetrated his sleep state. There it was again, a sort of metallic jangling. He came fully awake. The sounds of the night diminished. He jumped to his feet. He heard it again, the jangling—like pocket change or a set of keys being shifted.

He peered up and down the road in front of the woman's house in time to observe a figure in white flutter—like a spirit in the mists—round the street corner and head up toward the cliffs. Cursing to himself, he followed. He turned the corner only to catch a brief glimpse of the person, just at the street entrance to the Nap. As yet he couldn't tell if it was Mrs. Butler or not. Heart thudding, he ran after her.

By the time he rounded the last corner of civilization, she had hurried into the fog. Gauzy white strips of cloth flapped behind her. He understood Tavy's description of the lost waif. This must be Mrs. Butler.

They were close enough to the sea for him to hear the surf beat against the rock in a poorly timed rumble. He could just make out her form through the fog that crept up and enveloped the cliff. He traipsed after her when, with a jolt, he saw another figure who kept up with Mrs. Butler, pace for pace. This person was not on the path but crept along above her. He heard it again—jingle keys. The figure was not as silent as Mrs. Butler. Was this the mysterious "other" Tavy mentioned? Or was it Tavy himself?

The woman had moved too close to the cliff top. The rock was unstable; she might slip and fall over. Jon closed in. The dark other slid closer to her. Jon's mouth went dry. Was the other person going to push her?

"Stop! Police!" The surf deadened Jon's voice, but the dark figure stepped into the mists with crablike movement.

The woman turned toward Jon. The darkness obscured her pale features. "Who are you?" she called out.

"I'm a police officer. Why are you here, in the dark?"

"Walking … looking for … What are you doing here?"

"You weren't alone right before I came up. Did you see the other person?"

"What? No."

"I don't think his intentions were good." Jon sensed rather than saw a massive dark object loom on his left. He turned, instinctively defensive.

"Oh!" Mrs. Butler reached a hand toward him. "Don't come closer. The edge is tricky."

The dog, Chelsea, dipped her huge head down, and snuffled at Jon's foot. She moved toward Mrs. Butler as if it were the most natural thing to meet humans at the top of the cliff in the night—and why was everyone so excited? Able to breathe again, Jon stepped aside.

Tavy appeared, wheezing asthmatically, next to Jon. "Rest easy, Mr. Graham. We'll take care of the lady."

Jon was immediately suspicious. From which direction had the old man come? "That's okay. I'll take her home."

"We're used to doing things our way 'ere."

"I'll take her home, Tavy."

"So be it." Tavy cleared his throat with a soupy *arrrgh* and then made a click with his tongue. Chelsea left Mrs. Butler's side and trotted to her master. Tavy pointed away. With her tail wagging, the dog trotted away. The old man nodded to Jon and trailed after the dog. Within a moment, they were swallowed up into the fog.

What else could he have done? He took a deep breath, and touched Mrs. Butler's thin arm. She offered no resistance. "Mrs. Butler?" Jon asked her. "I'll take you home."

"I … I was looking for my daughter." She hung her head, hair draped across her face.

"Hold on, Mrs. Butler, I'll see you safe."

"Will you get my daughter back to me?"

"I'll see what I can do." *She must be sleepwalking,* was all Jon could think this was about.

They walked. Jon held her elbow lightly, and hoped she would understand he didn't wish to push or to pull her around.

Her voice was so soft, he almost had to stoop to hear her. "They think that body was hers. It wasn't. No one will listen."

Jon didn't say anything, but he thought that maybe she wasn't sleepwalking after all. She had a purpose, even if it was misguided.

They came to the turn in the lane that led down to the village and her house again. A sparkle caught his eye, and he watched as water trickled across their path to the sea. Upon the burbling stream, columns of thick mist floated. One after another, like a ghost army, the pillars marched downstream and slipped silently off the edge of the cliff. As he witnessed this, he could understand why people took night walks—time floated, as if suspended in this corner of the world, streams danced to sea, waves rolled to shore, and clocks ticked, for time, for eternity.

The fog grew thicker. The woman's safety was a priority.

They arrived within a few yards of her cottage, which was ablaze with light. Jon glanced at the woman next to him. She stared straight ahead; her cheeks were wet. He couldn't help his intake of breath when he saw her face. *My God! What a beauty! And so young! How does she have a ten-year-old daughter?*

"Mrs. Butler?" A woman crossed the front garden and stood on the front walk, fists resting on her hips, dark hair stood out all over her head. It was the police constable, Allison Craig. She said, "At it again, Ruth?"

"I was only walking."

"She should stay in at night." Jon told the woman, cross that this had happened with a constable in the house.

"It isn't as if she announces she'll be leaving. And what are you doing here?"

He turned and left. He could hear the woman sputtering as he walked away. He silently cursed. He had hoped it was too dark for her to recognize him. Trewe would question his interference.

Not chancing a shortcut along the cliffs, Jon took the lane. A few turns and a few tiers of road later, he arrived at Frog's Turn. His feet crunched around the gravel walk to the caravan-home. Who had followed Ruth Butler so closely? Who watched her besides Tavy?

Now that Jon had seen her—astoundingly, remarkably seen her—he had to think about this. Motives might be discovered in the shadows of the past, but what had Mrs. Butler done to provoke a stalker, besides being an attractive, young, American woman with a ten-year-old daughter? Some offenders didn't need motive. A chance phrase, a small glance without any meaning attached, and the crazy could interpret an entire notebook of reasons for harassment or worse.

The crimes in a small village could be personal, close to home; one had opportunity to become personal with the villagers. But here was a gorgeous woman in terrible trouble, and his hands were tied. The situation could become precarious balancing between impartiality and personal involvement, and he had no business interfering any more. He struggled with a desire to fix things—the harder the challenge the more adamantly he wanted to make it work—but some things were impossible to fix. One must come to a conclusion about what is and what isn't doable. He could understand how being an impartial referee of the law in a small village would be a difficult assignment.

And after his encounter with Mrs. Butler? Phew! Of course, it was a dark night. And a glimpse of face isn't the person, is it? She might be loud and obnoxious. She might be a liar, a cheat. Who's to say she didn't orchestrate her daughter's death for insurance purposes? A wicked thought, but these were wicked times.

Inside his caravan again, he took out one of his favorites from his traveling stack: *Rebecca*. He plumped his pillow, wrestling it into conformity. Nothing like a good book to let the brain relax. Ah, "the blood-red rhododendrons," which was a foreshadowing thing. He arrived at the part where Mrs. Danvers welcomed the new Mrs. De Winter, the point-of-view character, "… I could see that black figure standing out alone, individual and apart, and for all her silence I knew her eye to be upon me." Creepy.

He knew the feeling. The suspicious character had turned and looked at him before disappearing, as if whoever it was wanted Jon to try and catch him.

In a fool's paradise only the fools have peace. He slapped the paperback down on the top of the stack. He really didn't feel like reading anything creepy. Best find forgetfulness in sleep.

The next time Annie came to, the stroppy pad that had been above her wasn't there, and the cold air held a thin keening of sour. She tried to see something, but the cloth over her eyes was tighter than it had been. She had on a coat and extra clothes that were not hers. She lay on something soft and she could move more freely. She reached and pulled up long strips of cloth and soft fluff, like loose cotton wool. She pulled the cloth off her eyes just as another hand grabbed hers—a freezing hand, a much larger hand. She sucked in her breath and tried to speak, but coughed instead.

"Don't try to talk," a man said.

She recalled everything in that instant of voice recognition. It was that man from the beach, the one who had been following her mother. She had to pee or scream. What came out was a low moan, and the urgency of her body's need pressed into her brain so that she could think of little else.

The man said, "You've had a concussion. You will get better, but you must keep your eyes closed."

"Where am I?" she managed to say. Her breaths came out short and her urgency made the breaths tiny. "I need to use the toilet."

"I will help you."

The tears came then. "No, please. Leave me alone."

"It's all down to trust, isn't it?" His voice was smooth. It was a soft, mundane voice with little accent. It turned her stomach.

"No, don't t-t-touch me."

"I am a doctor. Nothing about you is shocking to me. I do not like little girls. I will not touch you without reason. You need not worry on that account. We've already done this many times. Allow me to help you to the toilet. I would rather you did not soil my lovely place again."

Warm tears flowed, and her nose was stopped up so that she could only breathe through her mouth. A noise came out like little "snicks" that sounded like a baby's cry. It hurt her ears, the loudness of her breaths in contrast to the scratchy breath sounds next to her. She wondered how she could stop the hands that touched her now, but she was helpless without sight. And she hurt all over.

With a revulsion that made her want to bend double, she submitted to being helped to stand. Her legs felt like they were wet pasta. The hands let her stand until she did not sway. There was a clanking metallic noise related to the unfamiliar bracelet on one wrist. She pulled against it. With a tight gasp she caught a chain in her hand. Chained. A claw-finger of cold dug into her thudding heart. It was hard to breathe. Her stomach wanted to be sick, but she concentrated on breathing. She wore some sort of cotton stretchy material, like jogging bottoms, instead of her jeans. And where were her shoes? She cried in earnest as the big hands pushed her forward. The chain rattled.

"W-w-where?" she managed to ask between choking sobs. She meant many things at once: Where am I? Where am I supposed to be? Where are my shoes? Where are my own clothes?

"Stop sniveling. Sit here."

She could hear his wheezing dip lower. Her trousers were jerked down. Her knickers were missing. She was pushed backward, and a rough partition caught her behind the knees so that she sat with a gasp on a cold toilet seat. She couldn't stop the spasms of tears, but she held her free hand across her mouth so she wasn't loud. The terror from the man's coarse breathing above her head and the chill air coming up and touching her private parts kept her from letting go, although by now her stomach hurt from holding it in.

His voice growled, "I don't have all day."

With fear and panic and the horror of having things that she kept private become so bare to a stranger, she let a moan escape and then let loose the only warmth left in her. She heard nothing but a slight whistling sound beneath her, and somewhere far away, water poured into water. The cold air pushed up into her and turned her to ice through and through.

19

Jon's experience with the figure on the cliff kept his adrenaline pumping. He couldn't sleep. He couldn't get comfortable, unable to turn down the volume of his thoughts. His cracker box abode jerked every time he turned over.

It was three in the morning when he gave it up, only to sit drooped across a chair trying to sort a jumble of things in his mind.

Being out of doors gave him relief from his claustrophobia and would help him come to terms with his cramped quarters. He tramped out into the night air and down the lane toward the village. He brushed past the low-hanging branches of a tree. The wet air chilled his face. Life had taken a strange turn in recent months. He hated loose ends and uncertainty.

All of his thirty-two years, he took pleasure in the process it took to accomplish tasks. He valued his job and believed in what he did. He could take orders and he liked to complete a job. In everything, he did his best. He was a committed man, dedicated to becoming an excellent police officer. So far, his personal life did not reflect that same dedication and focus.

He didn't see the tree root before he tripped over it. Picking himself up, he brushed off the knees of his trousers. Just goes to show, life doesn't always work out as expected, and sometimes things take an unanticipated tumble.

Take women. He wondered if he'd ever meet one he could actually like. And love? He'd been in love many times, but had never been successful with keeping anyone in love with him. He wondered what exactly he was missing; women were attracted enough to go out with him, but as soon as his thoughts turned seriouse, they made for the exit.

He took a deep breath of good sea air and wondered if he'd ever known any girls from Cornwall. He definitely had never met anyone from America other than older couples on holiday in London. He'd never met anyone near his age or younger from America. He wondered if Mrs. Butler liked *Dallas* reruns, too. Why was she "Mrs."? What was the story?

He spent a good amount of time outdoors, so he sported a decent tan. His last girlfriend had described him as having rugged good looks. But by the time she gave him the boot, she'd said he was grungy and smelled of dead leaves.

There was a season for everything, in his reckoning. He didn't keep a neat closet—so? The choice, in his mind, came down to comfort or ironing.

Anyway, at thirty-two years of age, any thought of settling down could be construed as a momentary lapse of sanity. He could afford a daily and he took all his suits and uniforms out for cleaning.

But he definitely didn't like being alone. There was nothing worse than going to bed in a silent flat, having had yet another cold sandwich for supper, or popping into Jack's Pulpit for a pint and finding not a single familiar face because all his mates had fallen across the altar of matrimony and moved away.

Yes, it was hell being alone, although there were perks. He could date whomever. But here lately the whomevers were hardly worth the effort. Perhaps he was too critical. Was he looking for perfection? Of course, he didn't offer perfection, so how could he expect it? Was there no woman that could overlook his idiosyncrasies and love him for everything he was?

He ducked to miss a low-hanging branch. Perhaps he needed to take a real break from the dating scene.

He came up short in his walk and found himself in a copse of trees between two street levels. On a night like this the lichen made the tree branches look like hairy arms. Something wrong with the picture jolted him—stopped his mind mid-thought—something out of sync with the dark stillness.

He turned slowly to take in the scenery, and strained to hear any sound that might seem out of place. Every hint of noise reverberated. He picked out the sound of footsteps scuffling on the road below. He peered through the trees. Someone walked on the pavement heading away from him and toward the streetlight, their face in profile—the postmistress? What was she up to? Didn't she live on the other side of the village? Why was she walking at night?

From the retaining wall, he jumped down to the road. A flush of adrenaline tingled into his core. This is where he had been earlier—Riverside, Mrs. Butler's cottage. A slight movement caught his eye. He moved closer. The object was small, level with her door. Swaying in the breeze, with a white sock stuffed inside, a girl's black shoe dangled from a string.

11:47 p.m.

Each house on the American woman's street shared garden walls, which made it easier to get into the back gardens from the alley. The houses were close together in a single row.

On the opposite side of the street, a rock retaining wall kept the hill from tumbling down into the street. There were trees and plantings in which to hide and, above that, another street and more cottages with a clear view of her garden all around.

Charles lumbered slowly back and forth. He twisted his hands together until they hurt. For his trouble, he had left the American woman one more little something to remember her daughter by.

The temperature had dropped in the night and the wind had picked up. Sapling trees slapped at him with every turn. He bent one until it snapped in his hands. He cracked the pieces into parts. Having to deal with the captive was just another interruption. He broke the parts into smaller pieces and stuck the bits one by one into the earth. He stood and ground the pieces deep into the loam with his heel.

Re-entering the street above the American woman's house, he picked up the bags, chuckling at his ingenious disguise. No one would notice a binman collecting rubbish.

With a flourish, he tossed the stinking bags into Widow Purvey's rear garden.

Tired, perhaps half-asleep, Ruth showered and put on warm pajamas. She checked Annie's room where her mother snored. She went back to her room. Her dressing table mirror had pictures of Annie stuck into the sides of the frame. Ruth took the latest school picture down. She sank to the floor, and gazed at Annie's smiling face, so confident and self-assured. She held her stomach. Her heart beat heavy and sluggish as she thought about how she would miss Annie's smile the most. Memories slashed like a raptor tearing into her chest with beak and talon.

She remembered herself at that age. She felt awkward and ugly. Was it peer pressure to be perfect? Until recently, she had continued to feel that way. Maybe it was age that made it better. Small comfort that Annie had never had that struggle with self-image, at least not that Ruth knew of. She was the most confident of girls. But then again, as a mother, who could judge until Annie was grown and able to voice how much of a mess her mother had made her life? Wasn't she guilty of doing the same to her own mother? Did all daughters do that?

The school uniform that Annie had worn in the picture still hung neatly in the closet where it had awaited that fated Monday morning five days ago—the same day the new shoes were to be debuted. Now, the green jacket would never grow too threadbare or too small. The outfit would hang there for a million Monday mornings, unless she was right and Annie was alive. But how would she get her back? What if she never got her back? Someone's daughter had been found in the surf dressed in her daughter's clothes. They would never get their daughter back.

Would she give everything away? Would she keep everything and make her room a shrine? She didn't know the answer. She never imagined she would ever need those answers.

20

Saturday, midmorning
Day seven

Jon leaned over his little fold-out table and gripped his mobile to his ear. "Still holding. This is Jon Graham. Yes. Tell them I'm ringing from Cornwall." The cold air coming from outside bit into any exposed skin, but he couldn't live in this little box of a home without that window open. *A home from home for sure this is, roight!* He wondered if he should make another pot of coffee while he waited. A harried sounding woman popped onto the line.

"Records. Cynthia Reed."

"Cynthia, love, has anyone ever told you you have a lovely voice?"

"What do you want, Jon Graham?"

"Now my dearest love, we agreed—no grudges."

"You are such a cheeky bastard."

"Yes, but you can't help but love me, right? So check this for me. I need to know if there are any samples or DNA profiles from these cases." Jon read off the case numbers.

"You do realize it is Saturday morning?"

"Yes, and any help you give me will not go unrecognized. It is urgent."

"Not go unrecognized? Why, whatever could you mean?"

"Cynthia."

"I'll see what I can do."

"You've got my mobile."

"Of course."

"You are an angel."

After a little while, he couldn't sit still any longer. He took off for the village. Most of the investigation's activities took place at the larger Treborwick police station and in the incident room they'd set up in an abandoned fish cannery warehouse building above the beach. He decided first that it wouldn't hurt to check on Sergeant Perstow, so he stopped by the three-room Perrin's Point police station and entered through the back door. The tiny police station officially closed at noon during the off season, so the sergeant might be alone. Silence prevailed, as did the odor of burnt coffee and plaster dust.

Someone muttered a curse, a metal file drawer slammed, and there was a rustle of shuffled papers. Jon poked his head around the office door. Perstow bounced forward in his seat, flung an arm out, and knocked a lampshade out of kilter.

"A pleasant surprise, sar. Come in." Closing a folder, the smiling sergeant reached to straighten the shade, his face red.

"Interesting office," Jon said. "Who's your decorator?"

"First floor's being converted into more efficient office space—new wires, the filing to be kept up there." Perstow pointed to the ceiling. "I can't imagine what it will be like hauling my girth …"

"Oh now, you want to say you're overweight, but you're not what you'd call obese."

"P'r'aps. I'm fat enough, and know my limits." Perstow shook his head as if he couldn't quite believe anyone would make him climb stairs on a daily basis. "Used to be a police house, this did. And in here was the holding cell."

"Now holding you?"

"Yes, sar."

Jon shifted some papers so he could sit on the straight, wooden prisoner's bed. "Long night last night, too?"

"Cream-crackered." Perstow rubbed his face. "As can be understood, what with the discovery a certain gentleman made in the wee hours. Do you always wander so late?"

"Couldn't sleep." Jon leaned his aching head against the rear wall. "I had your official Cornish cider yesterday afternoon, so I did take a nap soon after."

Perstow threw his head back and laughed. "They used to throw a dead rat in the barrel, sar—claimed it made the cider more potent. It is still tapped from the barrel. How'd you come to drink it?"

Jon recited the details of his dining experience with Tavy. He went on to recount his later experience with Mrs. Butler on the cliffs, including the sinister person who looked as if he would push her from the edge. "So now it's your turn. Tell me about Mrs. Butler."

"Sech a tragedy to happen to a fine, quiet lass. From all accounts, never bothers a soul, bless her heart." He shook his head.

"The loss of her daughter is horrible. How did the father take it?"

"No father living. But the woman's been on her own for ten years."

This surprised Jon. "The shoe. It was only twenty minutes earlier that I was in front of her house, and no shoe hung from that branch then. I saw paper inside the shoe and didn't dare dissect it. Trewe holds me suspect enough; I don't need to touch anything. Was it a note?"

"I made a copy. See if you can make anythin' of this."

Jon took the note handed him and read, "Little Annie Blue, / Has lost her shoe. / What will poor Charles do? / Why, give her another, / To match the other, / And then she will die in two." Jon pondered aloud. "Misquoted Mother Goose, it should say—besides the obvious filling in of names—'And then she will walk in two.' This doesn't fit the context; the girl is already dead. This shoe makes a complete pair. Mrs. Butler identified them as her daughter's. But this poem, the way he's written it, indicates she isn't dead yet."

"P'r'aps she wasn't dead when he wrote it."

"Wasn't there something about the identification? Mrs. Butler insisted on viewing the body. Claimed it wasn't her daughter afterward."

"'Poor lass. The DNA will prove the truth, whatever that might be."

"Yes, you're right, of course."

Perstow held out more notes. "And these emails …"

Jon glanced over them. "Charles. The same as on the note in the shoe. He's a bold one. What's he playing at giving us his name?"

"I s'pose. But we don't have his last name, and a bit o' worse news." Perstow's face had tragedy written all over it. "There ain't a Charles or a Charlie, or a Chuck, or even a Chas, in the entire village, nor the next village over, nor in the next hamlet. If there's a Charles nearby, he goes by another name."

Lack of sleep caught up with Jon in one terrible rush. He took a turn around the cramped office, which had been a holding cell. This was just another closed-in place. Air … he needed air. How did Perstow stand it? Even with a lamp, it was dark. The walls were mustard yellow. Puke yellow. The pain in his bum from the wooden bench matched his pounding head. "I observed the postmistress walking away. Word is she's not a pleasant person, but she's no Charles. Maybe Charlene."

Jon saw a fleeting smile passed over Perstow's face, and then his open face grew stern, as if he was reluctant to say anything bad about anyone.

"Her's from Devon originally. Been here a long while, but never has been o'er friendly. Her companion, Thomas, is nice enough for two, p'r'aps. You sent the tapes to London?"

"Yes."

"The DCI will murder me for certain when he finds out about the video footage."

"Out of your control. I'll take care of it. This morning I'm talking to Trewe about being added to the team."

"I already know, sar. He received a call from a Superintendent Bakewell."

"Good. Then I'm in?"

"As I understand it, sar. You are an observer, which means you can't be officially involved in the case in your capacity as Detective Inspector."

"Better than nothing. Tell me what we have so far."

"Every grain of sand collected near the pile of shells where the girl disappeared was sieved. The top six inches were scraped up. Every shell and scrap of material was categorized and submitted to intense scrutiny. They scraped spittle and gum from the rocks. They've done everything but remove the stone steps leadin' up from the beach. All that and nary a scrap to neither find nor convict."

"This murder, it could have been a random thing."

"Random murder in a village this size?" Perstow looked surprised.

"I suppose every loony within the region has been questioned?"

"Oh dear Lord, it's not as if we've been sittin' on our arses, is it?" Perstow stood. "Coffee 'ud wake you."

Jon shook his head. "I'm so filled with coffee and tea, I slosh."

Perstow left the room and came back with a steaming mug that he placed on his desk before he sat down again.

Jon studied Perstow. The man seemed most at ease when behind his desk. "Perstow, I've parked across the street. I need a small job. I was sideswiped by a dark car at precisely the time of the kidnapping. I'd like you to authorize having the dark paint smear on my car analyzed. We might get a make and model from that. Whoever it was, when I backtracked the likely path of the car, it could just as well have come from the alley above the beach where the girl was taken. So it might tie into the investigation."

"It does sound like it, sar."

Jon reached for the cup of pens on Perstow's desk and picked up a thin, silver tube. "What's this?"

"A penlight." Perstow pushed his girth back in the chair. "Find it comes in handy at the oddest times."

Jon reached to return the torch.

"No, sar, keep it. Please. I have more than one."

"Thank you." Jon stuck it inside his jacket pocket. "Can you give me any insight into Trewe? What should I watch out for?"

"Never volunteers anythin' personal, our DCI. He is what you'd call a closed trap. And even more likely to be so with an observer, sar. That'd be you. Only watch yer p's and q's. He's one for 'by the book,' our DCI."

"The preliminary inquest into the death of Annie Butler—I'll be there, of course."

The stout, balding sergeant pushed back his chair as he stood and leaned to grab a folder which he then stuck under an arm. "I must check on Her Indoors. She's feeling a bit teasy 'bout things—scared. If you'll excuse me?"

"Of course. Cheers." Jon wondered what the folder contained as he watched Perstow leave the room and head toward the back door and his push-bike. He didn't want to say too much, but soon after his arrival, Jon had heard Perstow's stunning young wife asking her husband, "Just how long must I endure *that* as a garden?" The door had slammed shut and he hadn't caught the rest, but he'd wondered if it foretold trouble. The woman had a tongue in her head. Later she'd turned friendly enough, a little too, but then, he was used to ladies lavishing attention on him. He didn't pay too much mind, and instead went out of his way to avoid her.

He wasn't a blinking idiot.

Just as Perstow exited the back door of the station, Jon heard the front door open. He waited a moment but didn't hear anyone call out. He was supposed to be alone in the building. He called out, "Hallo?"

Footsteps approached until Trewe filled the doorway of the cell/office. "Not much to holiday sightsee in here."

"Perstow has filled me in. I understood you received a directive."

"I did, and I'll repeat what I said before: I don't need your help."

"I don't mean to take over." Jon stood at attention.

"Directive received, I will obey, naturally. You may tag along. Don't expect I'm dancing in daffodils about it. Where's Perstow?"

"Went to see about his wife."

"The fellow's never about when you need him—has a wife from hell. That's what happens when you marry a younger woman, take my word for it."

Jon liked Perstow. What was it like married to a woman with the tongue she had? The surprising thing was Trewe had revealed something of a personal nature.

Trewe's lips stretched in a thin line in what Jon supposed was a smile. "We go back, he and I."

"Perstow?"

"No, your super, Thomas 'The Big Guy' Bakewell."

Thomas? The Big Guy? He had heard only one person ever use Bakewell's given Christian name and he had gone away with a toad in his ear for it. "I'm surprised. I've never heard him mention you."

"Oh really? Well, I'm not too surprised, considering. So have you found the secret biscuit stash in here yet?" Trewe asked.

"No, sir." Jon wondered what had he meant by the word *considering*.

"In the cupboard by the coffee machine," Trewe said. "Perstow's wife keeps him on a diet, but who can change an old dog's habit? I think I spotted a package of chocolate digestives earlier. I'll make a new batch of coffee, if you like." He grabbed a mug from a cabinet in the hall. "We've the place to ourselves, at present. And you, young sir, want to get into a murder investigation, by hook or by crook."

"Sergeant Perstow has allowed me a look at the file."

"Good. His job is here, of course. It's a mess with the plaster dust and all. The major incident room was previously a warehouse being made ready to convert to flats. There's enough room for the team to set up several computers with HOLMES II at the ready. But the activity and noise is endless. Here you can get a quiet read of the files. The interview room is still in one piece, so we may utilize it, private as it is. Just a word between you and me, Perstow needs to put a lock on that pumpkin shell of his and show up for work occasionally. And where is his illustrious community support officer, PCSO Trethaway?" Trewe asked, fishing around on Perstow's desk. "Never mind, here's a note from Perstow. Hmm." He read silently. "Some sort of crisis with Mrs. Trethaway's son and his car." Jon noticed the knowing smile sneak across Trewe's face.

Just then, the back door burst open and Perstow popped in, his face red. "Oh gov," he addressed Trewe, "the calls … I came back to leave you a note."

"Calls? The pertinent number for the missing girl is to the incident room."

"Not about the girl's death. A man …" Perstow was out of breath, "… about registering his gun."

"Patrick?"

"That was his name."

"He say when?"

"No."

Trewe turned to Jon. "He's attempted to register that rabbit gun four times this year. Always when he knows something will prevent it. As if he cares about rabbits munching his sprouts or guns being registered." In the hall just outside the door, Trewe took a package of biscuits out of a cupboard and re-entered Perstow's jail-cell office. "Likely looking for someone to talk to. Have you turned out someone's file cabinet onto your desk, Mr. Perstow?"

"I wanted to apprise Mr. Graham, sar. I noticed there was a fingerprint on the shoe. P'raps …"

Trewe pursed his lips. "The police national computer should have that information by now. They'll know if there's a match in the system or not. They haven't called."

"Yes, sar."

Trewe crumbled the rest of the biscuit into his coffee. "It's all so blasted frustrating."

Jon broke in, "I saw the collections list from the beach on that morning. The thought crossed my mind, why not create a DNA profile from the spittle scraped off the seawall? Why else scrape the spittle in the first place?"

Trewe looked surprised. He took his time answering. "We collect everything. If it isn't needed for the present investigation, it is stored in case something else comes up." Trewe held up the package of biscuits for inspection. "Someone's licked the chocolate off." He gave Perstow a look and threw the package into the bin. "Unfortunately we have nothing on the girl's body to compare it to. Chance is nothing to waste time on."

"She may not be the only one he's murdered," Jon said. He held his breath to see what would happen.

"What?"

"I've been reading about the other girls found in this area. Had some files faxed—"

"Absolutely not!" Trewe was a regular volcano, Jon thought, he seethes at something new every few minutes. "Those have nothing to do with this case."

Jon sucked in patience. This volatile individual was definitely someone to handle with kid gloves.

A knock sounded at the station door. Trewe opened it. A blond man dressed as a walking advertisement for the latest trends and fashion entered the station.

Trewe nodded toward Jon. "Mr. Sam Ketterman, this is Detective Inspector Jon Graham. Apologies for my not attending the last appointment. Thank you for taking time from your busy schedule to come back."

Sam nodded. "Apologies accepted."

"Let's go into an interview room for privacy."

Mr. Ketterman backed up slightly. "You're going to interview me?"

"This is a murder investigation, after all. Aren't you here to help us?"

"Do you mean 'assist the police with their inquiries'?" Long fingers made invisible quotation marks in the air.

"Procedure," Trewe said and nodded in Jon's direction. "DI Graham will be observing. Sergeant Perstow, if you'll remain out here in case we need you?"

"Yes, sar," Perstow said.

Trewe went into the interview room which was basically another jail cell that had had the long wooden bench removed. Jon stepped aside and gestured for Mr. Ketterman to enter. Save for the lone, high-set window opposite the door, a rectangular table and four chairs had been arranged like naked women in a cubist painting. On the table, a dual cassette machine with open bays waited for new tapes to be inserted.

Jon waited for Mr. Ketterman to sit before taking his own chair. The room didn't invite one to relax. Trewe put tapes into the recorder and switched it on. "This interview is being recorded. I am Detective Chief Inspector Peter Trewe with the Devon-Cornwall CID. Also present is Detective Inspector Jon Graham. This interview is being conducted in an interview room at Perrin's Point Police Station. What is your full name?"

"Samuel Walter Ketterman."

"The date is five, May. And the time is half past four in the evening. Mr. Ketterman, at the end of this interview I will give you a notice explaining what will happen to the tapes. You do not have to say anything. But it may harm your defense if you do not mention when questioned something that you later rely on in court. Anything you do say may be given in evidence. Do you understand?"

"Why in God's name are you cautioning me?"

"Do you understand?"

"Yes."

"You are entitled to free and independent legal advice, which includes the right to speak privately to a solicitor in person or on the telephone. This interview can be delayed for you to obtain such legal advice. Do you want to have a solicitor present at this interview or speak to one on the telephone?"

"Completely asinine."

"Do you wish to contact a solicitor?"

"I *am* a solicitor."

"You have continued to waive your right to legal advice. Would you like to tell me why you don't want legal advice? You are not obliged to give any reasons."

Sam spoke through clenched teeth, "I can represent myself here."

"You are not under arrest," Trewe said, "and are free to leave at any time. Do you understand?"

"Did you need to practice your technique and found no other volunteers?" Sam folded his arms. "I've come because you asked me."

"Do you understand?"

Sam Ketterman looked down and muttered, "Someone from St. Lawrence's needs to come with white jackets."

"Do you understand?" Trewe persisted.

"Yes! Yes! Yes!"

"Have you got anything to add at this time?"

"Yes. I'll add that you've flipped off your bleedin' rocker." Sam sat back, his lips twisted into a sardonic smirk.

"Is there anything I can get you?" Jon asked. Someone needed to keep on his good side.

"A diet cola."

Jon went to the door. Perstow was still in. He said he'd get a diet cola for Mr. Ketterman.

"Mr. Ketterman," Trewe continued, "you're here voluntarily, and we're grateful you've taken time to come. Questioning you apart from Mrs. Butler frees you to express yourself in—perhaps—a less restrictive manner."

"I'm certain that's why you put the recorder on isn't it? And I don't know what you're talking about. I wouldn't hide a thing from Ruth. She can know anything she wants to know about me." Sam Ketterman uncrossed his arms and brushed his fingers casually through his thick blond hair. "I've nothing to hide from you gents."

"Of course, Mr. Ketterman, I didn't mean to imply you had." Trewe's deep voice had turned silky. He smiled.

"The idea you would consider *me* a suspect!" Ketterman folded his arms tightly across his chest, and leaned back in the chair. "Me, with a good job and a fine roof over my head."

"Who ever told you you were a suspect? You're here to help us. In retrospect, is there anything about Annie's disappearance you recall now and haven't told us?"

"No."

"Mr. Ketterman," Trewe's words came sharp as knives, "what is your relationship to Mrs. Butler?"

"As if that's any of your business!" Sam snorted. His eyes were wide, wary as they darted between Jon and Trewe.

Trewe leaned toward him, still smiling, his voice silky again. "Of course, it isn't. Would you answer the question?"

Sam's arms went limp. "I hoped to ask her to marry me."

"Why haven't you?"

"I haven't found a good opportunity." Sam grabbed the edge of the table. "But what has this to do with Annie?"

"Where were you on the morning of the twenty-eighth? It was a Sunday."

"Asleep. And unfortunately, I was alone."

"How did you feel about Annie?"

"She was a lovely child, I suppose."

"Suppose? You suppose? You don't know, Mr. Ketterman?"

The sweat stood out on Sam's brow.

"Was she sweet, Mr. Ketterman?"

"Of course. She was a good girl."

"A really good girl?" Trewe said, "Or did she just bat those pretty lashes at just about everyone?"

Sam went pale. "What are you implying?"

"Did she get on your nerves, Mr. Ketterman?"

"No more than any other kid."

"Oh!" Trewe pressed, still smiling. "Kids get on your nerves, do they?"

"Of course not! You've only got to be patient. I haven't thought about my feelings towards Annie. Not to put into words."

Trewe's face darkened. He leaned to within inches of Sam's face and lowered his voice to a growl. "You haven't thought about it? You want to ask a woman to marry you, but you haven't thought about how you feel about her child? I wonder about you, sir." He leaned back, keeping his icy gaze centered on Sam.

Sam let go of the table. He glared at a corner of the room.

"Did you think she was a problem, Mr. Ketterman? A problem that would go away if you didn't think about it?"

"You're reading more into this than there is."

"Do you wish to add anything?" Trewe asked.

Sam rose from the table shakily. "I do have a solicitor, as a matter of fact. And you'll be hearing from him. You'd better watch it. I can make something of this, you just wait and see."

"I'm sure I will, Mr. Ketterman," Trewe said. "Do you wish to clarify anything you've said?"

"No."

"This," Trewe waved a sheet of paper, "is the notice I told you about at the start of the interview."

"Yeah! Yeah! Good-bye!" Sam stalked out.

"Thank you for coming." Trewe called after him. "Interview terminated at sixteen forty-two." He switched off the recorder.

The diet cola had arrived and dripped condensation in a neat ring onto the interview table.

Jon leaned away. "I'm certainly glad I'm not a suspect."

Trewe gave a brief shake of his head. "He deserved it. I have questions about his purpose in the entire scheme of things. He's a bad penny. Let him stew. He's all talk, no action—a man of thirty-five and never married. A bloody old maid is what he is."

Jon squirmed in his seat. "Well—and I was going to ask how you *really* felt about him."

"We all have our prejudices about something." From his pocket, Trewe produced a folded piece of paper. "Don't be so quick to rule yourself off my suspect list, Mr. Graham. I think you know who gave Mrs. Butler this photo. Am I right?"

"Perhaps."

"I have questions about it, such as where and when and how?"

The phone jangled.

Trewe stood abruptly and walked toward the front. "Perstow! Answer that. I'm not here."

The slam of the front door left Jon wondering how in the world Trewe had gone on this long without splitting in two.

21

THE COUNTY COMBINED COURTHOUSE
Saturday afternoon

Jon had to report on the discovery of the body, hence his inclusion in the inquiry into the death of Annie Butler. Though this building adjoined the old post office, the post office was the newer part. This part of the edifice had originally housed a castle's garrison and had withstood several centuries to become a combined courthouse that held the magistrate's courts and the postoffice.

In the open foyer was a souvenir shop the postmistress had cleverly opened as part of the postal cubicle. Today, a "closed" sign across the darkened window reflected the general atmosphere.

The inquest would likely be well attended. He glanced around at the white walls, dark floors, and threadbare carpet strip that ran up the center aisle to the coroner's podium which stood like an exclamation point.

The coroner sat behind the podium like a sleepy bullfrog. His round, puffy eyes barely cracked open, and his broad mouth stretched across the lower half of his face in a thick-lipped frown. At the side of the room, behind a squat partition set in place to disallow a peek up skirts, the jury was seated.

Jon picked out the people he knew by name. His sergeant had left excellent notes, with photos. Mrs. McFarland, the hostess of the Hasten Inn B&B, sat next to Mr. Little, the potter. According to his notes the bright-eyed and rosy-cheeked older woman was a regular whirlwind of movement. Today, she sat very still, her pale face staring straight ahead, while the very large Mr. Little, notorious for being taciturn, appeared to be entangled in animated conversation with the barman from the Spider's Web, Harold Sonders. Harold held a hand across his mouth and his shoulders jerked in mirth at something Mr. Little said to him.

He continued his scan of faces. Tavy gave him a nod from the back of the room. He wondered if the dog lay by his feet, because he could not imagine the man without the dog. His gaze continued all the way around to the man seated next to him, a lanky, middle-aged man with white and green paint splotches on the shirtsleeve of his training suit. Jon had no idea who he was. A squat, typically thick-set Cornish man of indeterminate age sat in front of him, a tear in the shoulder of his knit cardigan and the words "Trevellen Paint Works" in faded script across the back. His dark, wavy hair stood on end at the back of his head as if he'd just removed a cap.

In contrast, he recognized county magistrate Mr. Quentin Malone, neatly trimmed in a gray, worsted suit. He sat in the front row, next to his perfectly coifed blond wife. The magistrate's head turned and Jon saw he had glasses perched low on the bridge of a distinctly sloped nose, an odd hook at the end like the beak of a gull.

Jon's attention was drawn to an acrid odor. He leaned forward to look. A girl a few seats away from him had begun to varnish her nails. Cheeky. Across the aisle all in a row were four young girls possibly Annie Butler's age, possibly school chums. Two of them cried and held hands. He wondered at parents who would allow their children to attend such a gruesome thing as an inquest. A funeral yes, but this?

The coroner opened with the warning, "This is not the investigation of a crime but of a death, in order that the manner of the death of Annie Grace Butler be decided." The coroner's wheezy, falsetto voice squeaked. He didn't pronounce his *r* so he wasn't from the West Country.

Jon shifted in his seat.

Massed at the back of the courtroom, other spectators were silent. Jon glanced around. Titillation rippled at the expected horror of the day's proceedings. The day before, he had overheard the postmistress state this was the most sensational happening since old Mr. Poindextor drove his BMW over the cliff in a botched suicide attempt in 1993. The old man had lived; the BMW had died.

Full of helpful information, the postmistress knew a lot about people in the village. It was the perfect job for a spot of blackmail on the side. Given her demeanor, he wouldn't put it past her. It was a surprise she hadn't been a victim of murder.

The inquest was in progress. Trewe was speaking. The man was an enigma. After their first encounter, Jon had decided the cold bastard could steal the crown jewels without a second thought. But since then, he'd seen flashes of humility and perhaps even humanity—quite a puzzle.

Trewe explained the police investigation, cutting to the chase, which was definitely his style. He mentioned that he himself had been at the beach briefly that morning and had seen nothing. He said it was a regular habit of his to stop before traveling on to the Treborwick station. If only to stay in the loop of information, Jon listened, all the while wondering how to get around Trewe's obtuse lack of sharing.

A commotion arose from the back of the courtroom. A troop of parents marched to the row of young ladies and motioned for them to leave. One man leaned forward and whispered loud enough to be heard down the row, "This is not the place for you." There were squeaks of protest and tears shed. But in the end the parents won out, and the girls filed out behind their red-faced parents.

It was a good thing. The soft-spoken doctor, pathologist Roger Penberthy described the condition of the body. Jon had seen the same report. He could hardly bear it.

"... crabs. There is no identifiable face. Cause of death ... is undetermined." His description was incongruous coming from a man who looked like Father Christmas, with his silver hair, rosy cheeks, and white brush of a mustache.

Jon wondered how cause of death could not be identifiable with all the forensic experts there were in the world. He glanced around hoping Mrs. Butler didn't have to listen to this.

"Cuts and small incisions covered what flesh was left. There were needle marks. Chemical analysis of the flesh showed signs of long-term narcotic use. The toes of one foot on the body were printed as there was not enough flesh left on the fingers for fingerprints. The front teeth were gone and the molars had never had any dental work; consequently, dental records are moot. The body had been drained of blood, which is a possible cause of death. A tissue sample was taken for DNA. What blood there was type-matched Mrs. Butler's. Clothing, size, and hair color matched Annie Butler's."

The part about long-term narcotic use doesn't fit, Jon thought. The torso, though intact, offered little more information except that she had never had sexual intercourse. Jon knew from discussions with officers assigned to the case they took solace in the fact that the monster who killed Annie hadn't made things worse. He knew most of the investigating officers couldn't help but think of their own loved ones. That night those in this room would go home and make a special effort to give their families extra attention.

Impotent anger had him picking his nails until they bled. He sat up straight with a quick intake of breath. His eyes burned. He thought about the comparisons he'd made between the old case files he'd requested from London and the missing persons notice he'd found on the Internet. There were discrepancies, but there were also similarities. It was truly bizarre.

The noise in the room turned predictable and the building was warm. He hadn't slept well and desperately needed rest. He fought weariness by focusing on things around the room. On the ceiling there were fourteen light bulbs in each of four chandeliers. Eight light bulbs were out and two were flickering. Woodwork around the windows and doors gave an air of elegant respectability to an otherwise unremarkable room. He concentrated on the words from the various officials at the front of the room.

"... could not yet determine exact cause of death as loss of blood ... exsanguinations such as this are rare ... Exsanguination is the process of blood loss, to a degree sufficient to cause death. One does not have to lose all of one's blood to cause death. Depending upon the age, health, and fitness level of the individual, one can die from losing half or two-thirds of their blood; a loss of roughly one-third of the blood volume is bad. The loss of quantities of blood over time can cause a degree of instability of the body's normal antibodies and cause a reaction that looks very much like starvation, which can in turn cause the loss of hair and teeth that we found present."

He told himself to listen and discover exactly what matched this girl's murder to the others. What was it? Time. That's what it was. This girl had survived over time a difficult process of having her blood drained. That's what they were saying.

The sun shone through a tiny window behind and above the coroner and shown like a spotlight upon an empty chair at the front of the room. He could dream it might be hot out. It wasn't true. There was a stiff wind. Good weather for country walks. Would the weather hold? This time of year one could never tell. The sun might shine for a few hours, and then a tremendous storm might sweep out any remembrance of warmth, like the tale of Beira, queen of winter, who always tried to stave off spring with fiercer and fiercer storms. Greater and more potent each would be until the last, greatest storm of all when all her strength would be used up. Her power spent, she would go into hiding to let spring and summer have their seasons.

The creak of wooden chairs under heavy bottoms, low mutterings, and shoes scuffing on the wooden floor ceased abruptly. The silence jolted him from his daydream state. He turned his head and watched Annie Butler's mother, accompanied by another woman, walk down the aisle to a seat near him. He leaned forward to facilitate a better view.

She brought her head up and her dark, shoulder-length hair parted. Jon's heart did a flip-flop. *God!* Though her face was colorless and puffy from crying, she was even more striking than he imagined from his first glimpse of her the night before. Framed under glamorous brows, her eyes were a splendid dark brown. Her pale lips were full and expressive above a well-defined chin.

The droop and visible shake in her shoulders spoke of sorrow. Tears ran unchecked. She covered her eyes with a hand as if shielding herself from everything.

He'd always wanted to visit the states, the land of cowboys and Indians and craggy, cactus-covered mountains. He had watched the westerns as a child, and wished he could be a cowboy. He had set up his room with his bed as a rock shelf to hide from the bad guys. They always wore black hats.

He wished it were so simple. These days it was hooded windcheaters and balaclavas.

So, after he'd heard that the victim's mother had left the States, the first thing he wondered was why such a woman had come to hide away in Cornwall. Had her past life anything to do with the murder?

Jon watched as one after another of the villagers gave testimony. Ruth Butler was not called immediately. Her friend Sally and other people who were near the scene gave details of what they may have noticed at the beach after Annie disappeared.

Sam Ketterman, a more circumspect man after Trewe's interview with him, described Annie as independent and bright, though headstrong. He was not being used as Ruth Butler's solicitor and this made Jon wonder. Usually the relative of the victim has a solicitor present, but the coroner conducted the entire proceeding.

He noted the honorable Mr. Malone, esteemed magistrate, being called. He was a dapper man, handsome at one time perhaps, but he had run to middle age, if his large midsection was any testimony. Malone claimed Annie had been in his last history lecture. After he was sworn in, the poor fellow found a sidetrack where he expounded on the evils which can befall the innocent. Soon thereafter, he was interrupted and told to step down. He literally huffed on his way to his seat.

It was Jon's turn to testify as the person who found the body. He kept to the facts, glad he wasn't asked about his presence in Cornwall. As he stepped down, duty done, he noticed Mrs. Butler's seat was empty. *She doesn't like me.* The painful thought cut to the quick. *Wait. I am being a self-centered jerk. This isn't about me.*

The sunlight streaming through the window disappeared. The room's atmosphere changed into a gray gloominess under a rumble of thunder. He wondered if winter wasn't through with them yet. *Send your worst, Beira,* Jon thought, *you can't make that woman's pain any more devastating.*

Annie learned that the slithering sound she had thought was a snake was a doorway covering. It was made of leaves. When it rustled it meant the man had come back. She couldn't count on regular times for his visits. He muttered about the heater and fire and his precious jars. She could count on food being fruit and raw vegetables, sometimes a sandwich. He brought it in plastic containers. She wouldn't eat when she knew he was nearby. But as soon as he'd leave she would devour it. She didn't want to be caught awake because he might touch her and she didn't want him to touch her. As she was usually flat on the mattress, it wasn't difficult to freeze if she suspected he was coming. When she heard the door leaves rattle, she steadied her breaths to fake sleep.

When he found her in what he thought was sleep, he would grumble incoherently, his voice whispering rasps. He would stumble around the cave rearranging. She couldn't see well because she was pretending to be asleep, but she would crack her eyes and watch through her lashes. Sometimes his weird words would turn into a conversation with different voices that really made the hair on her arms stand on end, and even after he left those voices would creep uninvited into her dreams.

She didn't know who he was or where he was from, but he was no doctor. Doctors didn't act as he did, and the knowledge that he was a regular person who had stripped her of her clothes left her shaking with fury.

22

Saturday, 4:55 p.m.

"Hallo, old friend."

"Charles."

"And see, there's the problem. We need to talk."

"I've no call to hide from truth."

"I've suspected it. You've known me the longest of anyone. You know why I couldn't let my past trip me up."

"You needed a chance to come into your own, though I've never understood how it happened that you are able to live as you do."

The dog growled deep in her throat.

"Call yer dog back. I have money that you didn't know about. I'll share if you'd like. You could use a new roof."

"I don't ask for what I can't pay back. Tell me about yer mother."

"I never laid a hand on the old woman. You knew her—why would I? I was framed for it. You of all people have understood the way things work in this country. You believed me."

"I tried to help you."

"Are you going to let me in?"

Chains clattered loosed, the heavy door creaked open.

"Ye'll be wantin' tea?" Tavy asked.

"Sure, sure." Charles made his way to the kitchen table, alert to any possibility. "I'm wondering why it is you've never said anything about my name."

"Never have gone out o' my way to stir up trouble, have I?" The older of the two men lifted the kettle off the Aga. "I saw you at the inquest. I suspect it is you on the cliffs at night. Charles, did ye murder this child?"

"Of course not."

"An' I'm to take yer word fer it?" The older gent set the kettle down and put the teapot on the table, already laid with a single table setting, the breakfast fry-up ready to eat.

"All I can give," Charles grumbled. "You've no choice."

"All of us have choices, Charles Darrin. Just as you had the choice when you moved here whether to use yer real name or not. If I hadn't known you from Carmarthenshire …"

"Only a temporary place until I moved here and decided to settle. I live free with the name I use and I intend to keep it. I've helped you out before. Do you need money now?"

"Nae, I need nothing. I understood it then, I understands it now. But because I understands, does not mean I believe it is right for you to hide behind a different identity. Do you worry about your past—is that it?"

Charles wondered what he was on about. "I hate my past."

"Revenge only delays the pain."

"Fine talk."

"I've tried to reach through to that dark soul but you seem harder than the stone this house is made of." The old man turned his back, as he reached hands for the tea mugs. "I want you to know I'm not afraid of death. There's forgiveness through prayer."

Charles lifted the heavy iron pan from the table. "Praying never helped me, old man."

Ruth knew where she was and what was happening. She was in a car—sounds of swishing tires because of the rain—on the way home from her daughter's inquest, where she had identified the black shoes she had bought for her daughter the week before. There were quiet sobs from the back seat where her mother sat. The proceedings in the coroner's inquest were suspended until after the final outcome of any criminal case was known. She'd heard the words "open verdict" and couldn't believe it. Dead is dead isn't it? They couldn't bury her daughter-who-wasn't-her-daughter because of all the legalities that she couldn't understand now. All she knew was that the body would not be released.

Swish-rack was the sound the old wipers made as they scraped against the windshield. The noise she noticed, but not much else. There were times the numbness dulled even the noise. Days passed and she hadn't noticed them as days, only the passage of light to dark to light. Emotions were scattered, but horror or numbness prevailed, and there was not much else that she could recall with clarity. She floated, alive and not wanting to be.

Waking up to that first shattering pain of awareness every day since, she choked down food that was as tasteless as cotton, washed up dishes and tried not to remember. But she couldn't do anything else but remember. She showered in the hottest water possible. It numbed her skin to match her heart.

She had no desire to be around anyone who didn't know. She didn't want to see that look on any other face again, that look of pity and sadness from hearing for the first time that the poor lady's only child was dead. They always tried to cover it up with words, with platitudes, but she knew—and she never wanted to experience that look again.

Swish-rack. Six days. Seemed forever. Seemed yesterday. Where was the order of things? For a child to die before a parent—it wasn't right.

The sky rumbled and growled—so like that Detective Chief Inspector. His bushy gray hair stuck out in a fringe above his ears. He had a way of staring. Almost clear, his piercingly unemotional eyes frightened her.

The inquest had adjourned so the police could "identify the killer and look for more evidence to secure the necessary conviction."

Swish-rack. The wipers barely cleared anything on her side. She looked through the windshield and saw only the gray and wondered how many other mothers had lost their children to blood-drained starvation. Drug dependent? It wasn't Annie. To think it was was more than ludicrous.

The rain fell with a steady roar on the car's roof. Her mother moaned, then whispered, "I'm so sorry, Annie."

Swish-rack. Rivulets of silver whipped across the windscreen. The car insulated by rain smelled of wet dog hair and muddy shoes.

Shoes.

Was it just last week? She had told Annie she could take a day off from school just that one time, as a treat. Why work so hard to exist if they couldn't take a moment to enjoy their lives? *A special day, just the two of us, Mummy?* Yes. That was Thursday and they had gone up to London by train from Exeter.

The quiet train had moved steadily with smooth stops and starts. They'd seen short scrub trees and bare, green fields dotted with sheep and crisscrossed with trimmed hedgerows. They could take the countryside all in as it flashed past in that moment, in that 'twinkling of an eye', and they did. *Look! Mum! A pheasant! There by the other track!* Indeed there had been a pheasant just then, sneaking, neck extended, back into the undergrowth. They had passed the canals, the rear side of flats and their garden allotments, with views gradually changing from field to steep sides of earth. Then the steep sides of earth turned to brick walls splashed with bright graffiti, and they'd arrived in London. London! They got off the train at Paddington Station where pigeons flew indoors, its noisy crowds and loudspeaker announcements, its smell of train diesel, coffee and frying sausages, and its odd outdoor feel with the light from the glass ceiling. Then they'd gone to busy Oxford Street and stopped at Selfridges where they bought the shoes. The next stop was Marks and Spencers to buy a treat to take back for tea, just the two of them—all the luxurious day. They went back by train to Exeter. "Out of Devon and into heaven" was how she'd first heard it upon her arrival. Then they had driven on the A30 past Henry's trees, a tall tight-knit group of them. *You know that story, Mum. He said those were his trees. He told us at school.* Next they were on the way home on the 3266 with glimpses of the sea. She had told Annie then to put away her shoes. She was not to wear them until school on Monday.

The one shoe she identified at the inquest had been scuffed and torn and damp. The other had been pristine, as if Annie had not worn but one shoe that morning. Everyone said they were Annie's; she'd even said they were Annie's. But surely not. They couldn't be. She'd seen the body. She would know if that was her child, and she knew—she knew without a doubt—the body was not Annie. It was not her daughter who had died. It was the horror of some other parent, someone she didn't know. It was their daughter on that slab at the mortuary, not hers. Swish-rack.

23

Saturday evening

The inquest over, Jon watched seagulls float between village and cloud as he stood on the beach below the village. Pastel cottages dotted the dark hills like Easter eggs hidden in folds of earth. The afternoon rain had passed on and left a sharply briny smell in its wake. The sun sank lower. The last of its rays tinted cottages and businesses orange. Windowpanes sparkled. The glint of muted gold played off wet slate roofs.

He wondered if the delay in confronting Trewe had been the best course of action. He sorted in his mind the details he'd learned about Annie's death, adding things together. The girl hadn't injected herself with drugs. She'd been injected. The killer took her blood. Why? The abuse must have lasted more than a week. There was no way a week of drug taking and bloodletting had produced the body he found in the surf. That body had been suffering for a lot longer than a week.

He hung back to take in the huge sky and the salt air before going home. The piles of paperwork in his caravan were growing. He had the files Bakewell sent him about Trewe. He hadn't learned much he didn't already know. He had the computer print-outs of missing-persons reports—useless information if Trewe wouldn't consider them.

He took the road from the beach, past the Spider's Web. He would stop in for a pint, then head for home.

He hadn't meant for the mother to be distraught because of the photo of her daughter that he'd left at her house, but what had he expected? It had been a stupid, impulsive thing to do. He wasn't normally given over to stupid, impulsive things. So why had he done it?

As astute as Trewe seemed to be about those around him, why would he not be forthcoming about his sudden wealth? With so much money in the bank, why did he work so hard? He worked as if his life depended upon it. Perstow let slip that Trewe had been on the beach that morning but had not seen the girls. How had he missed them? What was the real reason Trewe had been on the beach that morning? He said it was habit to stop briefly above the beach before work. Was it really? Or had he only told Perstow about this to cover himself in case someone else saw him?

Ruth brushed her teeth. She would sleep on her couch, the farthest thing from Annie's room. She didn't feel like changing so she lay down fully clothed. Her mother was asleep in Ruth's room, unwilling to spend this particular night in Annie's room. She had hit the brandy before the inquest and hadn't stopped. Her drink habits were worrisome, but she was a grown woman. She didn't need her daughter to say anything.

Detective Chief Inspector Scary Eyes had tried to assure her they were doing everything possible. But the problem was this: the body was not Annie's. They thought she was in denial. Was she? No, she would never forget the foot. It was horrible. A foot—the only thing left whole and untouched. But she knew when she saw it. It wasn't her child. A mother knows her own child. She'd seen her daughter's feet for ten years, and that wasn't Annie's foot. For one thing, it was flat, and the toes long and narrow. Annie had perfectly shaped feet with short, fat toes. Annie had a high instep, not flat feet. She tried to tell them. They thought she was a crazy. She was the hysterical mother. She couldn't know anything.

Mandy, the cat, crept up and snuggled under the afghan, stretching along the length of Ruth's legs.

Ruth considered what she knew was the reason they were not taking her claims as fact. The problem was that she wasn't hysterical. If anything she was angry they would not listen to her. She stretched her perma-clenched jaws. How could she get them to listen? Hot, as Ruth turned, she unsettled the cat.

This wasn't real. This couldn't possibly be happening to her. These things happened to other people, people who could handle it. She wasn't one of them.

It wasn't so long ago that she could see Annie here on the floor beside her, playing with the cat, giggling. Ruth's arms ached with longing to hold her girl.

Her life was two rooms. She stood in one and watched her daughter walk into the other. Annie turned and waved. French doors and billowing gauze curtains separated the two rooms. The doors closed, the curtain came across, and the other room went dark. Her daughter's last wave faded away into memory. From the moment of her daughter's birth all she had ever wanted was for her to be safe. But she hadn't been—not in Texas, and not here.

She stared at the ceiling. It was too much to bear. She wanted one more chance to spend time—to untie her life, wrap up all her moments, and invest everything in her daughter.

Today dredged up the very worst parts of her life, especially those days spent with her ex-husband. Before he had come along there had been good times: her mother's laughter at her jolly father, childhood trips to Galveston, the hot brown sand, the warm brown water. They would stop to eat at Gaido's where she always ordered the crab au gratin.

In the dim light, swirls in the ceiling plaster formed into shapes in her imagination. She saw through the mists that the purls and eddies had become a face. As an artist, she could always see extra things in ordinary places. As she watched, the ridged, wild forms became a Dali mustache across a broad face. Tiny flecks of plaster shadowed crazed eyes. The face morphed from a human face into that of a monster. Anger? She wanted to show him what anger looked like. What gave him the right to take her daughter? Where was Annie?

A car rumbled slowly up the hill. The car's lights flashed across the curtains and slowed. She sat up and looked out the window. Was it the postmistress's old beat up Mercedes? The car drove away.

The night called her. She pulled on a warm coat and went outside. The bracing air was damp, but warmer than it had been the past few days. She set out to listen to the surf. She walked past Perstow's cottage, Frog's Turn.

Perstow's house was nestled firmly into a hill. The stone drive leading to the rear garden wound around between the house and a single car garage. A garden shed attached to the garage had been transformed into part greenhouse. It occurred to her that the upper windows must command a decent view of the shore, and she wondered how much of it she could see from up there.

She went to the rear of the house. What was this? Who lived in the camper trailer? She could just hear Annie admonish, "They are called caravans here." It sat next to the greenhouse/shed. There was a low light coming from inside. She should leave. Some might find her presence here really strange. She hesitated, thinking that now would be a good time to turn back, and then she heard it. A shrill lament turned to sobs like a child crying. It came from the trailer. She would just peek in the window.

She lifted the latch to a short picket fence. The gate creaked. The whimpers from the trailer ceased. She stopped to listen. There was a tiny whimpering. It sounded like a dog.

She crept forward and had only just reached the trailer's door when it swung open barely missing her. She took a step back as a chemical smell hit her with a blast of foul air. A hulking dark shape rushed at her. She flung her hands out and up to shield herself. Sharp words—"You stupid policeman!"—were followed by a terrible screech. Something heavy shoved against her. She twisted to avoid falling. Pain stabbed her skull above her ear. Bright light and heat washed across her.

As Jon neared his caravan, he caught a whiff of ammonia and saw some movement near the door. With a flash of light the far side of the caravan whooshed into flames. In front of the open door a man stooped and drew back a fist to hit a prone figure.

"Hey!" Jon shouted.

With an inhuman growl, the person swung around to face him. The man clutched at several scarves that encased his face, before taking off across the garden and disappearing into the dark.

By then the fire had engulfed most of the caravan. Jon ran to the person on the ground, grabbed him under the arms, and dragged him away from the heat and flames.

As he set the person down it registered that the "him" was Mrs. Butler. The realization set him back in shock. At the same time a flush of terror seized him. He fell to his knees beside her and touched her face. "Mrs. Butler, Mrs. Butler, can you hear me?"

24

Jon flipped open his mobile, punched in 999, and explained what had happened and where he was and what was needed. Then he punched in another number. At the first ring Peter Trewe answered and Jon said, "Jon Graham at Sergeant Perstow's house. At the rear in the garden. The caravan. Mrs. Butler—"

"What is it?"

"I've called emergency services. Someone's set fire to my caravan and Mrs. Butler's hurt."

"I'm on my way. Is Perstow there?"

"I'll check." Jon banged on the Perstow's rear door. The door jerked open as if Perstow had been standing all this time on the other side.

"Mr. Graham?"

Jon yelled into the phone, "Yes, he's here."

Trewe's voice sputtered from the mobile. "Detective Inspector, have you any idea why Mrs. Butler is there?" A car's wheels ground to a halt on the gravel drive. A disheveled Trewe raced around the corner and knelt beside Mrs. Butler.

Jon wondered how Trewe had arrived so quickly. The backyard became a surreal scene recorded in slow motion and lit by the flames. He called out, "Here!"

Trewe attempted to bring Mrs. Butler around. He muttered loud enough that Jon could hear, "Perstow didn't tell me he was going into the tourist business, keeping caravans in the garden. A true holiday spot in the making."

"Sar!" Perstow careened from his house to where Mrs. Butler lay near his patio.

Trewe yelled to Perstow, "Ambulance, man! Where's the ambulance?!"

With an exclamation, Trewe knelt to pick up Mrs. Butler.

"Don't touch her." Jon grabbed Trewe's arm.

"Don't tell me what to do." Trewe yanked his arm away. "We need to move her farther from the flame. If there's compressed gas canisters, there's danger of explosion."

"But we've got to do it right." Jon looked down at Ruth's face bright in the light from the fire. Her breathing was shallow. Blood leaked from an ear. "And no, I have no idea why she is here. She was being attacked."

Perstow huffed toward them. "Sar! The ambulance will take her to a clearing so she can be airlifted."

Trewe checked the pulse at her neck. "I hope they hurry. Look, you brace her neck the best you can and I'll pick up the rest of her. We'll move her around to the front of Perstow's house, away from the flames."

Jon noted the contusions on Ruth Butler's hand. The flesh turned dark where blood seeped close to the surface of the skin. He ever so gently laid her hand across her stomach to keep it from further damage. Working together, the two men picked her up. As they came around the cottage, a fire crew passed them dragging water hoses. An ambulance drew near, the crew already scrambling out. The emergency team crowded around, bent over her, blocking his view until she was whisked away.

Jon overheard Perstow's wife yelling, "If this is what one must put up with having a caravan in the rear garden, then someone best remove the caravan!"

A disheveled Trewe lurched toward him. "Mr. Graham, there must be a reason Mrs. Butler was at your caravan."

"I can't think of one."

"The fire's out now. Take a look, make sure nothing is amiss aside from the obvious fire damage, if you would."

It took him a moment to observe his heavily scorched personal effects, his ruined books, and what was left of his tattered clothing. The monitors were melted or smashed. *Damn, and Trewe had seen them.* The copies of the VHS tapes he hadn't reviewed, the flash drives, and the DVDs were gone.

When he descended the two steps to the ground, Trewe said, "Come with me, Mr. Graham. We'll make sure nothing else befalls Mrs. Butler."

The hospital was an uncomfortably silent one hour and six minutes' drive.

Inside the hospital Jon leaned against a wall, staring at the swinging metal doors which led to A and E. "Accident and Emergency is busy for this time of night."

Next to him, Trewe crossed his arms. "Not necessarily."

Somewhere close by, a phone rang. Metal trolleys loaded with boxes rolled down the hallway. Despite a cheerful demeanor of pastel-colored wallpapers and framed watercolors, the cavernous corridor gave Jon a dread feeling of being swallowed up. He hummed a tune to himself.

"My caravan is wrecked."

"I was there."

"The other person, who was in fact going to beat Mrs. Butler more before I interrupted him, must have set the fire. You'll be coordinating an action team to investigate?"

"In process of being assembled as we speak."

"Area's cordoned off?"

"Have done."

The phone did not stop ringing. Why did no one answer? Jon jingled coins in his pocket. The noise didn't help jangled nerves. The cracks in the granite floor spelled "do" in crooked capital letters. He wondered if it were irrational to think the imperative was meant for him. The phone went quiet. He glanced at Trewe. "Coffee? I'll get it."

"Machine's over here." Trewe led Jon to an automatic dispenser.

Coffee, tea or hot chocolate? Too bad the answers to all of life's questions weren't in multiple-choice format. Jon put his coins in the machine and pressed the selection button. "Seems you have everything lined up."

"Seems some things are out of my hands." Trewe mashed the button for his choice while Jon fed in more coins.

Jon saw his investigation slowly sink into the oblivion of the lost causes file, which would in this case be located beneath the rubbish bin. Trewe would suspect that all was not kosher with Jon Graham and his holiday in Cornwall story.

With disposable cups of black coffee in hand, Jon pointed out that he would like to wait where they could watch when Ruth would be wheeled out. He resumed his former spot against the wall. "I'm assume Perstow told you I followed Mrs. Butler the other night. She has a habit of wandering at night."

"He failed to mention it."

"Apparently, someone else was following her, too."

"Do say."

Jon couldn't tell if the man was being sarcastic or actually wanted him to report his movements. Surely Trewe wished to know. He repeated his story of taking Tavy for a drink and learning of the woman's nocturnal rambling. The more he thought about the shadow figure, the more convinced he became that the shadow figure did not have Mrs. Butler's best interest in mind.

When he finished, Trewe glared and pouted without a word for some minutes before finally saying, "Sounds as if Annie Butler wasn't the only intended victim, or because of her daughter, someone has targeted Mrs. Butler. I don't know, but I'll take no chances from here out. She will be guarded now."

A rolling cart burst through the door to A and E. Mrs. Butler was trussed from head to toe in bindings and sheets. Her golden brown hair was splayed across the pillow. Her cheeks were as pale as the bedding.

Coming along behind, a short, red-headed man brushed past, intent on his chart.

Jon stepped forward. "Excuse me, you were attending Mrs. Butler?"

"Yes." The man's eyes finally left his chart as if noticing Jon for the first time. "Family should be notified."

"Her mother is on the way. It's bad then? Dr.—"

"Mr. Matzelle."

A Mister? A rank above god in heaven. What was he doing making hospital rounds?

The doctor closed the chart with a metallic click and eyed Jon. "And you are—"

"Detective Inspector Jon Graham. This is Detective Chief Inspector Peter Trewe, Devon-Cornwall CID."

The doctor sighed. "There's been a serious injury to the woman's hand. But the main concern is her head. With an injury of this nature …" His expression was grim.

Trewe asked, "Her injury is consistent with being hit with a heavy object?"

"The injury to the head, yes. The hand was crushed possibly with a boot." The doctor paused, staring at them over his glasses. "Now, if you will excuse me." He started down the hall away from them.

Jon did a quick sidestep to block the doctor's path. "There was a lot of blood."

"The cut was superficial, but head wounds bleed copiously. Why CID? Is there a criminal investigation?"

"Yes."

"Then is this official? This questioning?"

Trewe stepped forward. "You said other injuries?"

The doctor held up one hand. "Nothing of a sexual nature. She was likely unconscious when the contusions occurred."

Jon was shaken by that. "You mean she was unconscious before the beating?"

"That's what we believe. As I said, the head injury is what we need to watch. She's not responding as well as we had hoped. When the brain gets knocked about in the skull, there's risk of closed head injury—bruises to the brain. But there's also the hand; one bone may require surgery as soon as she comes around." He craned his neck to look around Jon. "Now if you'll excuse me."

This time Trewe stopped him, "Is she able to answer questions yet?"

"We can't be sure she'll ever be able to speak again," the doctor snapped. "People die from this type of head injury. You might want to save your questions." With that, he nodded curtly and sidestepped past them and into the next room.

Jon shook his head. "What could she have ever done to have this happen to her?"

Huffing, Perstow joined them. "Mrs. Butler's mother is here. She'll spend the night with her."

Trewe sighed and turned to Jon. "It's late. We'll discuss this tomorrow. There is one thing I think you should be aware of."

"Yes?"

Trewe glanced at Perstow with something like hatred, and then the icy glare fell back upon Jon. "I was given video footage and still photos of the scene of the crime and told they came through natural channels which were presumed at the time to be CCTV footage. Now I discover a caravan loaded with monitors I assume were not smashed before this evening. Yesterday I asked about a photo Mrs. Butler found taped to her door, which I suspect came from you."

"It did."

"I want to see you in my office at noon tomorrow, Mr. Graham. You can rest assured a call will be put in to Superintendent Bakewell this evening."

WEEK TWO

Time Was

"Yes! in the sea of life enisled,
With echoing straits between us thrown,
Dotting the shoreless watery wild,
We mortal millions live *alone*."
– Matthew Arnold –

25

Sunday morning, 9:13 a.m.
Day eight

Charles made his way down the hospital's corridor with geraniums from his hothouse. He moved to within a few doors of the room where the American woman was. He'd had his chance and didn't know it until it was too late.

The hissing sound in his ear pulled him aside into the shadow of another room's doorway. *"Can you not see the room is guarded?"*

"Yes!"

"Well? What are you going to do about it?"

"All I *can* do: keep walking as if I am visiting someone else."

"Fool!"

The man shoved off from the doorway, just as it opened, and an old woman stuck her head out. With his head lowered, Charles marched down the hall without turning. Through clenched teeth, he said, "I've been successful in some things, mother."

"Not in the important things!"

"There's not enough time in a day."

"What is time?"

"I know." He sighed. "I love you."

He paused, listening. He said again, more insistently, "I love you."

Silence.

His eyes burned. Would she never say it? He found an exit door and left the hospital more upset than when he entered. As he stepped into the cool morning air, he slammed the flowers down into a privet hedge. As he drove up the road, he counted slowly to calm himself. His mind filled with conflicting thoughts and feelings: one, he should have stayed there, two, he could have waited for his opportunity, three, he did the right thing.

"No, you never did anything right."

In the privet hedge outside the hospital, a young wasp, wings still untried, fell dead—then another, and another. The liquid cyanide slowly evaporated from the broken vial. An empty syringe lay on the ground amongst broken flower stems. Fourteen wasps, beginning their insect life on this earth, jerked spasmodically in the last throes of insect death.

In the hospital room, Jon timed Mrs. Butler's breathing—in, out, in, out. Beneath the blanket, her chest rose and fell as the wall clock ticked. The machine clicked in rhythm to the red light blinking—off, on, off, on. It was maddening.

He stood and stretched, checking her mother who was sleeping sitting up in another chair. She stirred and mumbled something. He bent over her and whispered, "Mrs. Thompson, do you want tea? Coffee?"

"What? Oh no! I'm fine. Thanks, such a dear." She went back to sleep.

He left the room to find something approaching caffeine that might be drinkable, and wondered for the millionth time why Mrs. Butler had been near his caravan the night before. What connection did she have to whoever had torn through his things? Video equipment, video footage, and all the archived copies of everything were gone. And just as importantly, the files of the other missing girls had disappeared.

Another thought made his blood run cold. What was his own connection? Why had he been the one to find objects connected with the child's disappearance? Was it merely coincidence or was it someone else's plan? Had he in some way been led to the body and the shoe? If so, why had the victim's mother ended up battered nearly to death at his caravan?

Was some psycho toying with them all, as a cat does a mouse before the fatal blow?

Had Mrs. Butler been in danger all along? Had the killer followed her until he could corner her in Perstow's rear garden? Or what if the killer knew the caravan was his? Perhaps in the dark the attacker thought Mrs. Butler was Jon. She'd been dressed in jeans and a heavy coat. Had he seen the killer on the cliff Thursday night, and had the killer seen him clearly enough to want to make sure Jon wouldn't recognize him again? And if so, was there some identifying mark or mannerism to give him away?

Or had Mrs. Butler, out of curiosity, stumbled upon someone ransacking the caravan? So many unanswered questions. What a muddle.

If only she would wake up.

What would he do about Trewe? Confront him about the money and then let the cards fall where they may? After all, it isn't likely the man would deny having the money. The bank records were clear. On the other hand, the detective chief inspector had done absolutely nothing suspicious in all the weeks of observing him. But since Trewe found himself with an officer from Complaints on his doorstep, he more than likely has shut down any wrongdoing. What a conundrum—a double muddle.

Jon made his way back through the claustrophobic corridors to Mrs. Butler's guarded room. He nodded at the tall, thin constable standing outside. There were no other beds save Mrs. Butler's. It was surprising

Trewe had arranged to have her in a private room. Her poor mother could do with a bed instead of the chair she had slept in.

A doctor was bent over Mrs. Butler. He straightened when Jon neared. The quiet form on the bed murmured something he couldn't hear. She was still asleep. One cheek was swollen, the skin around both eyes was bruised dark brown, and yellow-green streaks connected the swollen cheek with her nose. Her head was wrapped. It hurt to look at her. This fragile woman had taken a beating.

She was still beautiful.

Stop, he thought, *don't think like that.* He couldn't stop his heart doing a triple flip-flop.

The doctor left and from beside the hospital bed Jon watched Mrs. Butler, so silent and still buried in the white sheets. Machines beeped. The room smelled of antiseptic and laundry soap. Jon sighed, shook his head and went to sit on a chair in a darkened corner, his head in his hands. She had not regained consciousness. Who could have hurt her? Was it his fault? Why was she at his caravan? Over twelve hours had come and gone. If she did not come to by this evening, the neurologist would do further tests to determine if there was a bleed in her skull forcing this lack of response.

Jon scooted his chair closer to the bed. He couldn't sit. He stood and leaned over her. Any response would be preferable to this human shell bound and hooked up to beeping machines, with tubes splayed like wheel spokes from her form. At least she was breathing on her own.

Everything was undone. Nothing was safe any longer. Nothing. Ruth floated sideways, turned over, reaching with both hands to grasp … what? … some small thing she had forgotten … She had to remember. Oh yes, the past. She wanted it back, wanted it back more than anything in the world. She longed for it so much she could taste it. It was bitter. Her past was not her imagination, and she was not hysterical.

Don't lie. No, she was intolerably honest. Her thoughts twisted obsessively as she tried to figure things out. Somebody was a killer. Hysteria hadn't produced a murderer, and she hadn't imagined the dead girl's body. There was another mother out there, missing her daughter. So what did this real, flesh-and-blood killer look like? What kind of work did he do when he wasn't killing? Had she spoken to him today?

She was flying. A face closed in. This was what the killer looked like. Jesus wanted her to forgive. *I know,* she thought, *but I can't.*

She fell a long way and landed on a cloud. Her head throbbed. It took a long time to think of anything besides the smoke and the heat. The smell hurt her nose. Smoke and lava flowed as frightened villagers ran for their lives, their homes engulfed in flames. She watched. Her skin hurt. She needed water. Her mother's face loomed over the mountain and spoke, "Buy the Pink Lux Shampoo. Run, the volcano is dangerous." She ran into the smoke. A man blocked her path. He smelled like breath mints. A curtain moved between them. She pulled it aside and saw a lion in a corner, baring claws. What? A child! She jumped between them. She swung her arm to hit the lion, and a tearing pain shot through her and made her sick to her stomach.

She woke up, and couldn't understand what she saw. Why was the clock upside down? And who put her in shackles? "Where am I?"

Jon bent over Ruth. Her eyes had opened and she mouthed something he couldn't make out. His face was no more than ten inches from hers.

Ruth's eyes opened wide. "Scary face."

Jon backed away. "Oh! Thanks! Now it's back to the ego shop for repair. I'm happy to see you awake. You gave us a scare."

"He had a scary face," she whispered through dry, cracked lips. "He called me …"

"What? Mrs. Butler, what did you hear?"

"Why can't I be still?" Her voice was barely audible. She winced with a spasm of pain. "Everything floats. Make it stop." She opened her eyes. Closed them. "Make it stop," she whispered.

"Make what stop?" he whispered back.

"The world." Her eyes opened and sought his. She stared at him for a moment. Her mouth formed a lopsided smile. "You're no angel." She closed her eyes again, and before Jon could react, her eyes closed and she breathed deeply—asleep.

Shaken, Jon stared at her for a moment.

A rough voice whispered, "Mr. Graham! What happened?"

Jon hadn't heard Trewe enter the room. "She was awake briefly."

"What did she say?"

"That I wasn't an angel."

"I could have told her that." Trewe tugged Jon's sleeve and motioned him away from Mrs. Butler's side. "Why are *you* here? I have a uniform guarding the room."

"What happened to Mrs. Butler concerns us all. Besides, I couldn't sleep. My bedroom's in a bit of a mess."

Standing in the doorway behind Trewe, the uniformed officer's face flushed and his brow furrowed.

Trewe swung around to the young constable. "Has anyone else tried to enter this room?"

"Just Mr. Ketterman, sir. I turned him away. I didn't think you'd mind the Detective Inspector—"

"You're not paid to think," Trewe almost hissed. The patient stirred. Trewe glanced in Ruth's direction, then back at the officer. He whispered, "No others without contacting me. And *that* is final!" Trewe closed the door in the constable's face. He turned back to Jon. Mrs. Butler's mother stirred. Trewe watched her for a moment. His voice a whisper again. "Is this her mother?"

"Yes."

Trewe glanced at Mrs. Butler, and shook his head. "Perstow tells me you chased the bugger off."

"Seems so."

"He could have killed her."

"Probably his intention."

"Mr. Graham, tell me why there were six monitors in the caravan you say you lived in momentarily."

"I can't pretend I don't know what you are talking about. I was sent here with the Regional Crime Squad on another matter."

"I know. From Complaints. Truth out, is it?"

"You don't seem at all surprised, Chief Inspector."

"It's about my department isn't it? Oh, you don't have to tell me." Trewe rubbed his chin. "I've already talked to your super. It was time we had a few things out. Though he had no answer for me."

Jon wondered what Bakewell had said and why Trewe sounded so bitter. He glanced at the sleeping beauty again. Trewe looked at Mrs. Butler's mother and then at Jon. "I'll just have a brief word with her mother before I leave. I won't be back by noon for our meeting. I'm not sure I'll be in my office until later. I'll give you a ring."

Jon went to the door. "I'll be waiting."

A lone young man, dressed in black from head to toe, strolled along the cliffs. A breeze carried a faint, dried-shellfish scent. Tugging on a multi-pierced earlobe, he watched the sun transform dark clouds to pink sheets that spread above a glistening, purple sea. He tried to unlock his creative spirit by listening to Mozart on his headphones. When his foot came down on something hard, he didn't give it a second thought until he happened to glance down and see it was a videocassette.

"What's this?" Brushing aside the dyed black hair that hung over his face, he picked it up. No markings. He thought it might contain something interesting. Why else would it be lying here with no one about? After meeting up with his mates, he would slip home to view it. He could maybe add it to the other interesting tapes he had hidden in his room away from his mum's prying eyes.

He did not peek over the edge of the cliff, so he failed to see the other videocassette trapped in a crevice, gutted and exposed, film blowing like streamers in the wind, or the DVDs smashed to smithereens reflecting the light like so much glitter.

By virtue of not looking, he was spared the sight of the human body, split and broken among the tapes and DVDs. That picture would have destroyed from his mind all the benefits of the Mozart.

The hollow echo of dripping water never stopped. With a worry at the pit of her stomach, Annie was finally able to slip the scarf from her eyes. He wasn't there. She'd already figured out that she was in a cave. She hated the nose-numbing cold and the smell of wet stone. The dark was darker than anything she'd ever experienced before. Daylight was dim. Light came from an opening about fifteen feet from her, the one with the grass and leaf mat over it. The door was a flimsy nothing. The freezing wind blew in with force and, finding nowhere to go, sat down with her to stay and tickle her shins with ice-fingers.

The walls were rough and pitted. In the pits were jars. There were tons of jars. A metal band around her wrist was melted to a chain that was bolted to the wall, or she would have left long ago.

She shivered, teeth clattering. Despite the archaic oil heater that ticked on and off, heat only teased her. Unlabeled cans were stacked against the wall. She wondered if they were food cans. She didn't have an opener. She could bash one on the rock to open it, but what if it wasn't food? He hadn't brought her anything to eat today. A gnawing gripped her tummy. She could eat anything, but there was nothing.

The skin under the plaster strips on her arm itched, but if she scratched, it hurt. There were holes in her skin that she imagined were needle marks. What had he done to her?

The dripping came from the ceiling when droplets formed and fell into a puddle at the center of the cave. All around her were rags and pieces of material. The mattress with the loose button lay beside her. It had been on top of her when she first arrived. It stank. She was sure the brown stains must be blood. Whose blood was it? Thinking about it made her head hurt worse.

She tried to see everything she could before pulling the scarf back over her eyes. The creeper told her to keep it there. Her head hurt when she shifted around, so she lay still and thought about how to remove the metal cuff off and where to find real clothes that weren't rags—or something to eat or some shoes that fit.

Time passed in centuries. She hated the nights, alone in the cave, thinking about the creeper. It's what she called him because it is what he did. She couldn't figure out the days. The fuzziness in her mind must be from her fall. She'd had a fall—that's what he told her. The fall gave her a concussion. He said her mother wanted her to stay with him while she healed.

That was crazy talk.

She still had her thin windcheater. There was an old quilt. She worked hard to stay on the dry side of the quilt. It wasn't easy because the damp coated everything. He'd left an anorak there beside her, and woolen socks, and trainers that were too big, but it was better than having no shoes, because her feet were the coldest part of her—her feet and her hands.

She pulled the scarf over her eyes. Just in time. Soft rustling.

26

As Jon didn't need to be in Trewe's office until later, he went to secure anything salvageable from his wreck of a caravan that was now cordoned off as a crime scene. What the fire didn't get had been slashed or smashed beyond recognition. Graphite smears and glass shards coated everything. A few of his books he could dry out or repair, and he had more in his car. He knocked on Perstow's rear door again and had a brief natter. "Did Mrs. Perstow hear anything last night?"

"Not a thing, sar. The wife said all was quiet till the ball of fire from the caravan drew her attention; it didn't make a sound that she heard. She saw a flash o' light, and soon after, you raised the alarm at the back door, just as I arrived home."

After asking for recommendations and then directions, Jon took himself to the Hasten Inn B & B with only a change of clothes and the toiletries kit he carried in his car at all times. The bed and breakfast was a quaint affair, set in a sturdy white house at the top of the village. Those flats-to-let and B & B's closer to the police incident room were fully booked with the teams of police. They came from all over Devon and Cornwall to help with the search and the investigation.

After a brief wash, he took a nap, then decided to check to see if there was any change with Mrs. Butler. He had to find out what took her to his caravan after dark. He picked up WPC Craig in order to question the patient without complications arising if Trewe were to discover a second visit in one day.

He entered her hospital room and the first thing he noticed was the new wrap that encased the top half of her head and far fewer tubes sprouted from her arms. The entire side of her lovely face was starting to turn purple. He greeted her with, "You've got two, lovely black eyes."

"Oh, thank you. Not only is the man observant, but complimentary, too."

"Think nothing of it."

Ruth closed her eyes and then opened them again. The tendency to smile was curtailed because any muscle movement on her face hurt something awful. He sounded like a policeman, but didn't look like one, wearing a casual shirt and jeans. He wore jeans like he was born in them. Despite the pain, she wanted to keep looking. Allison Craig stood by the door. What were these two up to? She said to the man, "I assume you're police, too."

"Detective Inspector Jon Graham. I'll leave my card." He put a card next to the flowers on the stand by her bed. "I brought WPC Craig with me. I met your mother this morning."

"My mother said there was a policeman here earlier. Why did you come back?" She closed her eyes again. It took such effort to keep them open. "I don't have anything to add to what I've already told Detective Chief Inspector Trewe. The attacker said, 'you stupid policeman,' then … He must have realized I wasn't who he thought I was. He yelled or screamed, or someone did. He hit me. I punched him away, but he must have knocked me out."

"I'm the policeman who lived there. At the risk of sounding blunt, why were you there?"

"I didn't know about the camper. I was restless. I was curious about the view of the shore from Perstow's shed. There's a little wood deck. Oh! Sounds crazy in the daylight, doesn't it? But the nights are my worst time. I can't stop thinking. I keep asking myself how I could have prevented this."

"It wasn't your fault."

She looked at him then. He had a nice nose in a Romanesque way and sensuous lips on a generous mouth that curved up on both sides in a natural smile. Dark eyelashes, why did men always get the good lashes? Not handsome, interesting maybe, nothing more. "The sergeant showed Annie and me the view last summer. I hadn't seen it at night. But when I arrived ... When was it? ... last night ... I couldn't help but be curious about the camper—excuse me—caravan at the bottom of the garden, so I walked over to it. The door must have hit me. That's the only way he could have grabbed me. I know how to defend myself. Both Annie and I have taken self-defense. I used to teach kick boxing."

"That *is* impressive."

"I'm sure I look impressive. Great at self-defense, right? What is it you wanted to ask?"

"Do you have any idea why that man would have been there?"

"No idea. Except he was angry at you."

"Why? Did you recognize him?"

"No. He called me the stupid policeman. Then ..." She looked into his green eyes, and she knew instinctively that she could trust him. "It sounds mad ..."

"Tell me."

"As I walked up to the camper—er, caravan—I heard the person inside say that the American woman was the devil. The voice was a loud whisper. It was the voice on Annie's mobile. I knew I would know that voice again. Before I could get away, he was lashing out."

"I'm sorry, Mrs. Butler. I'm sorry he hurt you, and I'm deeply sorry for your loss."

"My daughter isn't dead," she said. She leaned deeper into her pillows and closed her eyes because it was hard to keep them open. *Thank you, Lord, for such a calming voice to listen to.*

"I must go, but I have one more question, Mrs. Butler."

"Of course."

"Why do you walk the cliffs at night?"

She blinked to clear her view. *Wow, where did the sudden tears come from?* "I walk the cliffs because I need to get out of the house to clear my head and think. I thought we were safe here." Wiping the tears made her face hurt. "When this happened I thought he had found us. But the thing is—he died. Two weeks ago."

His eyes widened in surprise. "Who died?"

"My ex-husband. I've been hiding from him. That's why we came here." She looked into his eyes. She saw the a sudden sadness. It's a special person who is empathetic. Her free hand, as if it held a will of its own, moved to his hand and grasped it. His hand tightened around hers. She could sink into those eyes. "I thought it was safe. I guess I got real complacent."

He must have suddenly become aware they that were holding hands. He let go and took a step back, his face flushed. "Pardon me … I'm sorry."

Ruth closed her eyes again. It hurt too much to keep them open. Something still nagged at her—someone not there. "Where's my mother?"

"I understand she's resting at your house."

"If this happened to my daughter, and then to me, my mother isn't safe."

"I'll see to it she's safe."

"Thank you. I can't help but think that if I'd only reached out to whoever was sending those emails …"

Jon Graham said, "He wouldn't have been stopped."

"But he might tell me where Annie is." Her voice caught. She willed herself to be stronger. "That's the real reason I go walking at night. I know I'm being watched, but he is the only one who can tell me where my daughter is. I tried to follow him. She is still alive. No one believes me, so no one will help me."

There was silence. She looked at him. His face had gone pale except for two splotches of color on his cheeks. "What is it?" Her breath caught and held. "What else has happened?"

He said, "You are not the only one who believes the way you do."

Ruth's breath whooshed out of her. "What are you saying?"

Allison Craig cleared her throat. "We better be on our way."

Jon Graham edged toward the door. "Look, I've said too much. I have an appointment to keep."

Ruth struggled to sit up. This man may be her only hope to start a new search for her daughter. "Tell me what you know."

He paused at the door. "I'll come back to talk with you after I've kept my appointment and made sure your mother is well."

She strained against the tangled IV tubes. "Wait!"

"Please don't move, Mrs. Butler."

"Mr. Graham, my feet aren't hurt. I'm getting out of here."

After seeing her settled, the doctors explained to Jon that agitation was a symptom of her head injury. They gave her a mild sedative to help her relax. He and WPC Craig stayed a short time longer to make sure she wouldn't try to follow him from the hospital.

According to the uniformed officer guarding the door, Detective Chief Inspector Trewe had taken Mrs. Thompson home earlier. That must have been an interesting ride; he wished he could have witnessed it.

Like every other cottage on her street, Mrs. Butler's cottage had been constructed with locally quarried granite, but she had painted red shutters and a red door. He could tell a true gardener lived here, not like his pretension to the title. Miniature azaleas bloomed in decorative pots beside the stoop. Forsythia branches draped in graceful yellow over the low stone wall that lined her front garden. Primula had been planted along the top of the wall.

Near the front path, in a rusting toy wagon full of potted flowers, toy bears and dolls had been placed amongst the cards and flower bouquets, a bright memorial to the child who had lived here.

Ruth's mother opened the door and ushered him inside. "I'd say 'Howdy' because that's a cheery hello we say in Texas, but it sounds strange to say it here—like a shoe that doesn't fit. And I'm not cheery." She jerked and put her hand to her mouth. "I shouldn't have said 'shoe.' When I think about those little black shoes of Annie's ..."

"It's hard not to think of them, Mrs. Thompson. You can feel free to speak with us," Allison Craig said as they entered.

The room was warm to the point of hot. A large window opened onto the front garden and gave a clear view of the street. The white ceiling was not so low that Jon had to duck around door frames and beams to get around, which was unusual for a cottage as old as this one must be. The walls were a muted peach color. It was furnished with comfortable-looking sofas and chairs, with bookcases full of books on the far wall. Soft guitar notes strummed from a speaker nearby. A laptop was open on a tiny table in a corner opposite the book wall and next to a door that led, presumably, to the back of the house. There were canvasses everywhere, some on the walls and some leaned against the walls. Jars of paint lined narrow shelves; the colorful effect was very artistic. Some of the canvasses on the walls were paintings of Annie in various locations at the beach, sitting in the churchyard among the flowers, or holding a white cat.

Jon took special note of the watercolors of herbs haphazardly placed across a work table near an easel. The area would be a dining room for most people, but this was obviously where Mrs. Butler worked. Her herb illustrations must be a work in progress.

Upon the sofa table was an opened bottle of Madeira, and there were several empty wine glasses around the room. On top of a drinks cabinet sat a nearly empty bottle of Glenlivet. Judging from the neatness of the rest of the room, Jon figured the incongruous bottles and glasses must be a new development, possibly from Mrs. Thompson, as she had a glass in her hand.

He said, "I hope you're able to stay in England for a time, Mrs. Thompson."

"I'll stay as long as Ruth wants me."

"I wanted to let you know that your daughter is awake and speaking."

She raised her hands to the ceiling and whispered, "Praise be!" She rubbed a hand against the sofa's back, straightened a pillow. "I just got off the phone with the doctor. He told me he thought she was out of the woods."

The stout woman's American accent was like something out of a Clint Eastwood movie. Jon was very glad indeed that Ruth had a loved one to care for her, albeit the loved one was a mother who seemed drunk. He said, "She is very awake and aware. I left there with assurances to her that we would keep you safe. Be sure to lock everything and keep a careful eye out."

"I'm fine. Say, with you being a policeman and all, I've got something worrisome to talk to you about."

"Anything I can do to help."

"The phone calls are frightening!"

"Phone calls?"

"The horrid, whispering ones."

He was taken aback. "I didn't realize."

"They say things like, "wish I had done you." Horrid. What does that mean? What in tarnation is happening, I ask you." She poured herself a generous drink from the bottle of Madeira. "Want one?"

"No, thank you." He didn't care for fortified wines. This business with the calls was worrisome.

She paused and stared hard at him. "A policeman? Where is your uniform?"

"I lost my things in the fire. And I don't wear a uniform."

"Oh my gracious! You're the one from London? Are you a Scotland Yard detective, Mr. Graham? Aren't they the ones who investigate murders?"

"Scotland Yard is a part of the Metropolitan Police, Mrs. Thompson. The Criminal Investigation Department investigates murder. Any officer with the designation 'detective' in his title is with CID. Of course, in my case, I happened to be here for other reasons when the crime took place, so I'm only an observer with the murder investigation, offering any help I can."

"Well, I've always been a fan of those BBB police shows on TV, but I didn't know all that. The distinctions—tricky. I have to tell you, love the accent." She raised her glass to him.

She must mean the BBC. He handed her a card. "We want to keep you safe whilst you visit. Ring my mobile anytime, for any reason. We want to know about the calls as soon as they happen." He pulled out another card. "This is DCI Trewe's number. Have you mentioned these calls to him?"

"Oh! I have his card. He gave it to me this morning. He's the good-looking man with the baby blues."

Baby blues? "So you've spoken to him about the calls?"

"Yes, but I wanted to know what you think."

If Trewe had charge here, Jon didn't need to interfere with tracking down malicious pranksters. "I think these types of calls are horrid. Probably the result of someone's torrid imagination. I must not interfere with what DCI Trewe is doing. Now, if you'll excuse us, we must be off. It was a pleasure—"

She practically jumped at him. "Ruth told me the top detective on the case wasn't married. That would be Mr. Trewe. I didn't realize he would turn out to be such a handsome devil, too." Mrs. Thompson studied the card Jon had handed her.

The devil part is correct, anyway. "I don't know anything about Mr. Trewe's private life." *Wish I did, is the ironic part.*

"We met yesterday, the first time. And then this morning he offered to bring me here from the hospital. Said he lives at the top of the lane—at a farm? Is he a farmer? I would not have imagined that!"

"I believe his son-in-law runs a dairy farm."

"A dairy farm! It's all just so quaint. And tell me, which is higher, Detective Chief Inspector or Detective Inspector?"

"Chief Inspector is a higher rank."

"So he is your boss?"

"If I worked under his jurisdiction, he would be."

"A tongue twister, getting that 'detective' in front of saying the rest of the title." Mrs. Thompson turned to WPC Craig who had been standing near the door looking distinctly uncomfortable. "Are you a detective, also?"

"No, I'm a Woman Police Constable. A WPC for short."

"Seems a bit sexist. But that's just me being American. They're a good-looking bunch over here, aren't they?"

"If you say so, Mrs. Thompson," Allison murmured. Jon could see her face turn red beneath the hair wisping from under her hat.

Clearly this conversation was uncomfortable. Jon stepped away from Mrs. Thompson. "We really must be going now."

But Mrs. Thompson didn't let up. "I had hoped to go to my daughter, but I have to find a way to get to the hospital. You see, I could drive her car, but I'm afraid I wouldn't be able to get the hang of driving on the wrong side of the road. It would scare the living daylights out of me. A car accident would be more trouble than I'm worth."

She needed help. He hadn't the heart to run away. He leaned over and patted her arm. "After my appointment, I could offer you a ride."

"That is kind of you, Mr. Graham. You're a good-looking one, too. Are you married?"

Jon drew back and looked away. "No."

"Now, don't go getting the wrong idea. I'm asking for Ruth's sake." Chuckling, Mrs. Thompson took her drink and trounced toward the door that led to the back of the house, talking the whole way. "My daughter thinks I'm as old as dirt, like I've got one foot in the grave. But there's still an ounce or two of piss and vinegar in *this* bucket!" Ruth's mother raised her voice to be heard. "I took the liberty of thawing fish."

The WPC did not leave her advantageous getaway spot near the door, but urged Jon to follow Mrs. Thompson. He stepped through the door and past a pantry area and found himself in a well-appointed kitchen. The stone counters were clear of anything and sparkling.

"Mrs. Thompson—"

"Call me Samantha Jane." She pulled out a chair for him at the kitchen table. "Look at this kitchen. Can you believe anyplace this old could look this good? Of course, since I've been here I've rearranged things. Ruth doesn't seem to mind. I'm adding decorative embroidery to the bottom of the curtains. And I've alphabetized the cupboards. Wouldn't you and Allison like to stay for lunch?"

Twenty feet away Jon could hear Constable Craig clear her throat and say, "Thank you for the invitation, Mrs. Thompson, but I'm very much afraid we must decline."

It was as if all the air went out of the woman. She plopped down at the table, and appeared lost and disconcerted. "I understand from my daughter, and Annie's friends, and everyone who knew her that my granddaughter had a mind of her own. I wish that I'd known her. I nursed Ruth's father through his last illness and found I had time on my hands. But I was afraid—afraid of my own shadow, if you must know. I never held my own granddaughter. Have you ever heard of anything worse than that?"

"I'm certain you did what you could," Jon soothed. The poor woman was lost with the future prospect of no one to care for. The drink, the banter, and her bonhomie were all covers for a terribly broken heart.

"My sister keeps up with the latest video communication devices, but I couldn't have it on my computer with the police looking for her, 'n' all. So I've been able over the years to see and talk to her on the computer at my sister's. But I should have come—snuck over here, despite the ex-son-in-law. What a human disaster he was. When he died, I thought, 'now I can go over there and give her a hug.' It's all I ever wanted to do. Now it's too late." Mrs. Thompson gulped the rest of her Madeira and then wagged a finger in his direction. "I don't want anyone else giving my daughter false hope. She is under the impression that the dead girl isn't Annie. Don't fan the flames, mister. Don't go leading her down some bunny trail with that notion. She has to face facts." Her voice broke. She looked away.

But what if? If Annie was still alive, they could not wait for this killer to kill her. It would be like having two funerals for the same person. He thought of what he'd read of the other girls, the fact they were found dead months after they were taken. He reached to pat the woman's shaking shoulder. "But what if she's right?"

27

Jon drove east away from Perrin's Point the eighteen miles to Treborwick and found Trewe in his office. Despite the clutter of computer, printer, wire bins with stacks of papers, stacks of paper on the floor and along the walls, and the jumble of file cabinets, his office was much more spacious than Sergeant Perstow's cramped police cell of an office.

"Have a seat, Mr. Graham."

"Thank you."

Trewe held up the envelope he'd been carrying. "This was found on the ground outside your caravan. Your name's on it." He dropped the envelope on the desk where Jon had to reach for it.

Jon examined the outside of the envelope. It was a large brown clasp-type envelope. Where the stamp would have been a picture of a stamp had been drawn with colored chalk. His name had been scrawled by someone trying to disguise their handwriting by using their non-dominant hand. It was addressed to "Jon Graham, nosey police." He looked up and met Trewe's eyes. "Do you have something I can open it with?"

Trewe handed him a letter opener.

Jon carefully slit the envelope wide and turned it upside down. A single piece of paper slid out, heavy with pasted newsprint. What he read chilled him to the core. He read it aloud:

Little Johnny Snooks was fond of his books
And loved by his super and master;
But naughty Mrs. Butler has broken her hand,
And now carries her arm in a plaster.
p.s. I would have done more but for your interference. You will regret it.

This was from the person who had set fire to his books. It was personal. The words had been cut from newsprint and pasted to cheap copy paper.

"He has a thing about Mother Goose." Jon glanced at Trewe. "I was the intended victim."

"What about Mrs. Butler?"

"I asked Mrs. Butler why she was near my caravan. She said she went to look at the sea from Perstow's shed. There is a clear view of the sea from there."

"Had you met Mrs. Butler before you came here?"

"No."

"But the man targets you? For what reason?"

"Several reasons come to mind." He told him how he had possibly thwarted the killer doing harm to Mrs. Butler on the cliffs.

Trewe exploded, shouting, "And why the devil did you think to follow her?"

"To see her safely home."

"Bakewell in no way gave you permission to have any contact with the victim's mother." Trewe was breathing hard.

"Granted, it was against regulations but …"

"I would rather you continued in your role as observer, Mr. Graham, but circumstances have involved you much deeper in this investigation. I understand you have had your own job to do, but now whatever it is that brought you here can wait."

"Sir—"

Trewe held up a hand. “Let me finish. Superintendent Bakewell has charged me with the task of instructing you in these things. If you have questions or concerns, call your office.” Trewe leaned against the wall as if he were overcome with exhaustion. “I want you to meet with the team for a daily briefing first thing tomorrow morning. I’ll try not to let the fact you came from Bakewell’s office interfere with how I feel about you.”

“I thought you were friends.”

“I said we went way back; I never told you as what.”

Jon swallowed. “I’ll keep that in mind.”

“You’ve met his wife, Neena?”

“I’ve met her.”

“Yes, well …” Trewe paused, his sharp eyes studied Jon’s face. “Neena used to be *my* wife.”

THE CAR PARK ACROSS FROM THE SPIDER’S WEB

Sunday, 10:32 p.m.

Dark was good, a perfect time. Charles watched the comings and goings of stupid people. The pub had a busy clientele. Quitting time was in less than half an hour. He had nothing else to do but sit here and wait for people to clear out and settle down.

Time stole everything. He was determined to retrieve what time, and his mother, had taken from him.

Everything began with Cecilia. He had been only twenty years old and had worked his way up to head gardener on a decent estate just north of London—never took any classes—but he knew his onions. He had lost weight with the work, slimmed down, and muscled up; he looked completely different from when he lived in the council flat with his mother in London. Cecilia, a children’s tutor, had loved him and told him so on more than one occasion. He had taken her to visit his mother.

That's when the trouble started. His mother hadn't approved. She detailed Cecil's shortcomings—nothing the girl said made sense, she was foreign, nobody foreign would make a good wife for her Charles, she was too tall, too broad, too talkative, too blond.

He had ignored his mother as best he could, but her accusations haunted him.

The nights, the dark nights when Cecil had brought him fresh linens from the big house, and everything had smelled so clean in the dark, felt so smooth and firm in the dark. He had declared his undying love forevermore, for her and her alone. It was in the daylight that she had informed him she was pregnant, and she was a good girl, and he must *do* something! He had been torn. He loved her, but he had a lot of living to do. He couldn't settle down yet. He had begged, he had pleaded, without result. She insisted that he marry her and take her away from the house where she worked as a glorified *au pair* under the guise of children's tutor. It was her long weekend, so they had time, she had said. She wanted to visit his mother in London again and get her blessing.

So, they had gone to London. He had told Cecil that he intended to marry her, and had told his mother, as well. His mother had been outraged. She railed against her, railed against him, railed against the natural order of the world. Her vehement accusations had left him shattered; he couldn't go on. His ardor dried to a hollow husk. Cecil had had a fit and said if Charles didn't marry her she would tell everyone that he had made her pregnant by force.

His mother had told him to make her quiet or *she* would make her quiet. He tried to calm everyone, but Cecil wouldn't listen—wouldn't be quiet. His mother would not stop yelling, and Cecil would not stop talking. He had pulled Cecil away to the car where she had continued to not be silent, his mother's words rang in his ears. It wasn't his fault. He couldn't take all the noise. He *made* Cecil quiet then.

His life, his world, his being, was torn asunder. He carried her off to Cornwall in the trunk of his car. The countryside was less crowded back then, more empty space and beach. That was when the idea of flowers and herbs had first come to him. The gesture was a requiem of his love.

From that point onward emptiness plagued him. Regret grew to remorse. He had to bring her back, had to find her again.

When Cecil hadn't come home from her day off and couldn't be located, the police arrived. When his turn came around, the police had grilled him for what seemed like hours, but he remembered distinctly how surprised he was to learn, when all was said and done, that he'd been with the police for about a quarter of an hour. He had answered as naturally as if Cecil had only been one of his prized lupines, nothing more than something pretty to look at. He told the police that she had had many admirers, how she had often complained about the lack of money working there, how she had had greater plans for her future, that lately she had become quite secretive about her comings and goings, and that he believed she had had a lover in Devon. The police never suspected that he'd made it all up. They put her down as a runaway.

It was while he experimented with crossbreeding lilies that the idea had first come to him. If he could turn back the clock, make a wrinkle in the fabric of space and time, he might be able to undo what he had done. Perhaps he could bring back his one true love. One idea that he'd read about was blood replacement. So he took it a step beyond. If he changed his blood to the blood of someone younger, then he would become younger—he would reflect that change. It only stood to reason that, if he could turn back the clock of his own body, he could turn back the clock altogether.

If he could go back in time, he could retrieve Cecil.

He noticed the traffic had increased. He should move. Getting the video footage and other evidence had been easy. If the slightest thread of real information had been on the policeman's tapes, he would have received a visit. Now, he need not worry about such mundane things. He needed to worry about the transport of food to his hidey-hole. He didn't want to have to bury another so quickly. She was doubly important. Her blood was tasty, but without her alive, how could he lure the American woman near?

He witnessed a dark-haired, young man so bone-thin as to look near starved enter the Wicked Flowers storefront on the other side of the pub. His curiosity made him wonder what the boy was doing, but then he remembered that there was an apartment above the shop.

What he could not observe was the young man from the cliff-top walk, after entering his home, tossing his rucksack on a rickety chair inside the door. The rucksack slid across the chair and opened, partially revealing its contents: a few tattered paperbacks, a broken pencil, some candy wrappers, and a black videocassette.

The young man's mother came out of her kitchen, wooden spoon in hand, and told him to get ready—his supper was on the table.

28

Monday morning
Day nine

After last night's uncomfortable confrontation with Trewe, Jon took himself to the daily briefing and then back to the Inn to put a call through to Bakewell at home. He explained in short order the bomb that Trewe had dropped on him last night about Bakewell's wife Neena.

"A mare's nest," was Bakewell's reaction. "I'm certain you will sort everything."

"Wait a tic, it's you has the trouble with this man."

"Our troubles happened many years ago."

"That's a laugh. You know, I get the impression he isn't over it."

"It's none of your—"

"I would have appreciated a heads-up on this one, boss."

"Look, if he makes an issue of something that took place so long ago, then that *is* a problem and I apologize to you. But it is not very professional of the man, and if I remember correctly, he was the definition of professional when I knew him. So this must go to the issue of what the present issue and very likely has something to do with his sudden windfall. Sounds as if you've touched a nerve, something that makes him emotional enough to get personal, so get to the bottom of it and find out about the money. I shouldn't have to remind you why you're there. Try to avoid discussion of your assignment, and Jon …"

"Sir?"

"Stick to every directive Trewe passes down. Do not think you know best, even if you do. Your main assignment depends on Trewe trusting you enough to let you get to know him. This murder inquiry gives you the perfect opportunity."

Jon thought, *Yes, it is very convenient, isn't it?* But he said, "I'm not sure I like this."

"Don't put a foot the wrong way now."

"Why did you hand-pick me for this assignment?"

"You were the best man for the job. I don't believe you should take my decision lightly. And one more thing …"

"Yes?"

"Don't get too close to the victim's family. Their lives are miles away from yours, and I know you. You tend to take things to heart. You get involved. I don't want you to. Don't forget, you won't be there much longer."

Jon rang off. His super had taken the piss and thrown it back at him. Maybe he was feeling the lack of sleep. He had just spent a night walking hospital hallways. He'd had a short nap, but he needed true sleep to think straight.

He was the only police officer at Hasten Inn Bed and Breakfast. Mrs. McFarland, the proprietor, had fussed over him as if he were a helpless fledgling. He made the mistake of telling her that he needed a few hours of quiet.

She waved her oven mitts. "And that you will have, dear. And you'll let me know if you need *anything*, will you?"

"I will."

She followed him to his room. "You'll just call down to me. I'll be listening."

"I understand. Thank you."

"Just you call."

It didn't take long to figure out what she needed was constant assurance she was doing a top-notch job. "I'm fine. Wonderful place you have here."

"Thank you, dear."

"Yes, well, I'll just get settled then."

"Oh! I'll see that you have quiet. You need your rest, because of this terrible business. Soon you'll be right as rain." She flapped her ever-present oven mitts at him and floundered away toward the kitchen at the back of the old house.

But the promised quiet had done him little good. He couldn't stop his brain thinking, especially now that he knew he had been the intended target, not Ruth Butler.

So the mystery remained. Why?

What Trewe had told Jon about Bakewell's wife was a real shocker. His mistake had been not getting more information from Bakewell in the beginning. If he'd asked, he wouldn't have wasted time trying to picture why Trewe left London for Cornwall. Or why after all these years Bakewell and Trewe were still at odds with one another. It wasn't just because of the marriage breaking up. By keeping silent with the others at the station, Bakewell had let everyone believe Trewe had something to hide and therefore had run away home or worse had a mental problem. But he didn't have anything to hide. He left because his marriage ended. Bakewell had not only taken his wife but his reputation as well. Everything made sense now. He would tread carefully around Bakewell.

He didn't know how much time had passed, but the sun shone right into his room to wake him. He ran a toothbrush over his teeth and shaved. He was very impressed with the comfort of this B & B with its modern appointments and spacious, brightly lit rooms. He could sit back, relax, and really think. A shower with hot water, what a delightful concept. What would they come up with next?

He dressed and went to search for food.

Mrs. McFarland scampered around wiping crumbs from the sideboard with her oven mitts. "Oh Mr. Graham! What can I get you?"

"Some eggs would be nice, Mrs. McFarland."

"Veggies?"

"No, thanks."

She brought out a steaming dish of eggs and added it to a side table where several other dishes were being kept warm. He helped himself and was soon quite satisfied. He was on his third cup of strong coffee when a group of six student-types, gesturing and speaking in staccato bursts of Italian, crowded into the room. They spotted him and gestured "hello" wishing to speak "the English." He nodded, smiled, and excused himself before he had to commit to a word of it.

He drove back toward the beach. The incident room had its own car park, which was great because parking in the village was a problem. The village had begun as a port. There were no cars—only horses, carts, and, if you were wealthy, carriages. The narrow streets allowed for no turning around of cars. The car parks across from the Spider's Web and next to the incident room were the only places for cars to get turned around in the area. He parked and locked his car. On his way into the building he almost ran into Perstow.

"Sergeant, tell me what happened after the fire."

Perstow seemed surprised to see him. "Oh! Not much—a few villagers hung about after."

"Anyone stand out in your opinion?"

"No."

"SOCO turn up anything unusual?"

"Your fingerprints. Some footprints. They'll need shoes of those who entered the yard for reference."

"Were any videocassettes or DVDs found?" Jon said.

"None."

"Thank you, Sergeant, that'll be all." Jon walked down toward the beach. None. The flash drives he'd sent to Bakewell turned up nothing new. The VHS cassettes had yet to arrive. He was still kicking himself for not hiding the copies of the tapes in the boot of his car.

The incident room was empty save for two officers busy at computers. He skimmed through the reports. So many villagers had been interviewed. These officers were likely adding to the nominal index of Home Office Large Major Enquiry System, or HOLMES, a record of each person of notice during an enquiry. Apparently some interviews were flagged for further investigation having to do with other cases. They could wait.

He turned to leave.

"Have you been helped?" came a voice from the back of the room.

He turned. It was a young officer he didn't recognize. "No, I was looking for DCI Trewe."

"He'll have gone back to Treborwick, something about another message found. Are you Jon Graham?"

"Yes."

"He was looking for you."

"Right. Thanks very much." Another message. What fresh hell has been uncovered?

Wind whistled around stone. The muffled sound of waves came from out beyond the grass and leaf door. The heater gave off its occasional warmth. The rest of the time Annie shivered under her rag piles, clutching her button tightly in one hand. Even with the mattress it wasn't easy to get comfortable on the knobby, damp cave floor. Her school used to have a guinea pig. She had had to clean the cage when it came to her turn. This cave smelled like the urine damp shavings.

There was water in a pool at the center of the cave. At first she wouldn't drink it, no matter how clear and cold it was. But her resolve passed when thirst and dry heaving drove her to gulp it down. Within no time she had the runs. The illness left her feeling like a deflated balloon. Her toilet needs ran through the tissue. She had to use what was nearest at hand: her windcheater. Afterward she had to toss it down the hole. She hoped creeper wouldn't notice the missing jacket.

The worst thing about sitting chained to a wall was the nothingness. She yelled a lot at first. She cried. She kicked the wall and strained to get the chain loose. Then came the nothingness, because nothing she did did any good, so she had nothing to do.

She thought about things she would do to the creeper if she were ever free. Because when she got her chance, she would do something. He crept around the cave, and whispered low so she could not understand but it sounded poisonous. She hated him. She would hurt him if she got the chance to escape.

She had uncovered some marks on the cave's wall when she rearranged the rags around where she was supposed to lay. Marks had been etched into the stone, tiny straight lines about as big as her thumbnail, all in a row. There were eighty-nine of them. Marks to count the days, perhaps.

Her skin tingled when she realized what it meant. There had been someone here before her. She hurt all over when she thought of it.

Flashes of memory surfaced from the time when her eyes were still covered and she had sneaked a peek. A groan escaped as she remembered. It had not been a nightmare—the grotesque, hollowed cheeks and sunken eyes, the white face with a gaping hole where a mouth should have been, the limp, rag-doll quality of body and limbs, the feet with *her* socks, and one of her new shoes being crammed onto a foot. In that half-out-of-mind moment, she had witnessed her fate.

She curled up and closed her eyes, grinding her teeth. She willed herself to stay calm. If she had seen what was to happen to her, there was nothing left for her to do but to make it unhappen.

TREBORWICK POLICE STATION

Trewe was in rare form. "So I went looking for you at the B & B and Mrs. McFarland said you were asleep. Tired from all your time spent at the hospital?"

Too late, Jon realized he'd dumped four teaspoons of sugar into his cup. "Yes, sir."

"Bakewell assures me you're the best. I don't know if I share his opinion. I can't police my police apparently. You've been asked to keep your distance from the victim's family?"

"Yes, sir."

Trewe glowered for a few moments, then let a file drop from his hand to his desktop. "There are a few things we haven't made public about this investigation."

Jon stared at his coffee. He hated sweet coffee, but he'd have to drink it. "I'd be interested in hearing about these things."

"There's the bunch of twigs found tangled in the string around her neck."

"Twigs?" He swallowed against the lump in his throat. "What kind?"

"Forensics called in some local plant specialist." He paused. "As it turns out, we needn't have called a specialist. Perstow fancies himself a gardener and smelt of the twigs. Common thyme."

"Common thyme," Jon pondered aloud. He felt his chest tighten as the implications hit him. The world around them ground to a halt as the center of the universe rested in that moment. Plants and herbs with the body, the shoes—this confirmed his suspicions beyond a shadow of a doubt. He took a sip of the coffee and had to hold his breath to keep from gagging.

"Yes," Trewe said, "and stranger yet, the twigs had had blooms, possibly when they were stuck in the string."

"Isn't it too early to bloom? And how'd they know there were blooms? Hadn't the waves and water taken care of that?"

"Experts could tell there'd been blooms. The wild thyme that is common to this area is *not* blooming yet, but Perstow saw thyme in bloom in Mrs. Butler's back yard. I suppose with the sun and the walls reflecting the heat …"

"The killer had to have had access to her yard." His mouth went dry. "She isn't safe."

"What's that?"

"Tell me, was the body identified by the mother?"

Trewe nodded. "They shouldn't have allowed it. I gave those officers some thoughts to take home when I heard about it."

"But what did she say about the body?"

"That it wasn't her daughter, naturally. There wasn't much to recognize. But she did identify the clothes and the shoe as her daughter's."

"The famous shoe. What about DNA?"

"Mitochondrial results aren't conclusive enough, so we've ordered a nuclear DNA result. Takes weeks. Meanwhile, the blood type matched Mrs. Butler's."

That didn't answer Jon's questions about what he suspected was a series of murders, but it would be a long, hard road to convince Trewe. "I have a question for you. How could a person change their name? I mean, how could they—say, if they were wanted by Interpol for terrible crimes—how could they change their name and hide their identity so well they could assimilate into local society or village life without notice? People are naturally suspicious of strangers."

"They'd have to have money, lots of money. They'd have to be someone coming into a new area, with all the trappings of wealth, and a history—even an invented one which made sense or that no one questioned. Ever."

"Yes." *Exactly like you,* Jon thought. He rubbed his chin, and said aloud, "Police work has come down over the years to cleaning up, clearing away, and playing games with evil, hasn't it?"

"Aren't you the philosopher this morning?" Trewe took a sip of his own coffee and smiled as he looked pointedly at Jon's cup.

29

Jon set his awful coffee aside. "How can I help? What would you like me to do, sir?"

Trewe gathered a small stack of what looked like handwritten notes and handed them to Jon. "Mrs. Butler was receiving these, each with a handful of wildflowers, on a regular basis. We need a translation, if you're not doing anything."

Jon gathered the notes. "If this is Gaelic, there are likely books in the library … local historians … the Internet."

He glanced up. Trewe was gone.

Most villages and smaller towns had only a mobile library, but the village of Perrin's Point had a library. Unlike the Tudor Revival architecture of most of the rest of the village, the library was a square of yellow brick and few windows, and ugly as a bald goose.

As he made his way down a narrow alleyway to the building's entrance, a large black dog appeared out of nowhere, and shouldered him aside. A second's panic later he realized the creature was Chelsea, the dog that discovered the child's body. He gave the hairy head a pat. "Good girl."

The dog stared at him and sat down, barring his entrance.

"Right! Now, go home!" He snapped his fingers and pointed away from the door, a move he'd seen on a doggy training show. "Move, Chelsea!"

No response. The dog must not have seen the show.

"Come now, let a man past." With the toe of his shoe, Jon nudged the dog carefully. In response, it turned its woeful eyes up at Jon's face. Jon backed away. "Sorry."

The creature rested its head on its paws and heaved a sigh. When Jon attempted to pull the animal away from the door, she planted her feet so her already massive weight exceeded that of a small house. Jon decided to try something else: "Are you hungry girl?"

Her tail dusted the walk. Jon turned and walked back to his car. A half bag of leftover crisps was all he found. He grabbed it and walked back. She was still there.

"Here, girl. Here, Chelsea." He stood away from the door and knelt, emptying the greasy paper to the walk. The brute cocked its head sideways as if to say, "Humans do odd things." Then she lumbered over and made the twelve or so crisps disappear like the end of yesterday. She acted starved. Where was Tavy? He couldn't imagine the old man would normally let his dog wander the streets and bar entrance to county buildings.

He stepped past the dog and entered the library. Chelsea slowly ambled away. Jon shook his head and turned to his task. When he showed the librarian the inscriptions, the soft-spoken woman told him she couldn't read Welsh properly, but there were plenty of language references available. She pointed him in the right direction.

With stacks of books to keep him company at a quiet desk in a corner, he worked for an hour, referencing and cross-referencing. He sat back and rubbed his eyes. The notes were not meant to harm but to warn. Did the person who wrote them know something? Why did this person not come out and say it plainly? What were they afraid of?

Despite the tide of opinion in some circles and efforts to explain evil away with platitudes and reason, no one could explain it away. Evil manifests itself in innumerable forms in any environment, no matter how bucolic. Evil had affected the village and all the surrounding area. The very nature of a peaceful environment made shattered peace all the more traumatic.

He stacked the books into a wall surrounding his notes.

Years in the force had him desensitized, to a point. He could usually witness the effects of evil without emotion, but today raw emotion swept him into an anger he hardly recognized. In those moments of fury, he wondered if he should give up the job and call it a day—call it a lifetime.

He'd often thought of advancement in the police ranks, but it was crimes like this one, that involved a child made him wonder if his temperament wasn't best suited to do just what he was doing. Some people wanted a desk job, but even an hour at this desk in the library had him tapping his foot to get away. A regular desk job would probably kill him. Take the super in his role as a liaison between policing agencies: he worked hand in hand with Policy Authority Inspectors, HM Crown Prosecution Service Inspectorate, HM Inspectorate of Court Administration, HM Inspectorate of Probation, and HM Inspectorate of Prisons in their process of drawing up a joint inspection scheme and associated framework. The job kept Bakewell busy with written reports and contributions to the content of the AMIC website. Bakewell had become the hand watching the hand watching the hand of various agencies of police where they intersected with the public. It was a desk job.

However, where *was* the public in all this framework and scheme drawing? The core purpose of police officers was the prevention and detection of crime, not drawing up frameworks for schemes. The higher the rank the more obvious the politics. Policy had become more and more about finance, soothing grievances, and reaching targets.

He didn't want that. He wanted to be in touch with the people he had to work with and with the public. The death of the girl had affected him deeply, eaten him up with cold anger, the kind that grew colder, harder, and more determined with each day.

As he closed the last book, a voice coming from above his head startled him out of his thoughts.

"Halloo, sir! Halloo!"

Jon looked up to see an older man with thin hair slicked to his head peering at him over the top of the wall of books on Jon's desk. Jon backed away slightly at the overwhelming scent of aftershave.

"I've seen you about and would love to make your acquaintance. My name is Quentin Malone. Local magistrate. Local." The man extended a hand over the books. His long jowls quivered and bloodshot eyes squinted when he flashed a toothy smile.

Jon grasped the hand before him. "Mr. Malone. Jon Graham. This is a fine library you have here."

"Oh! Not mine. Not mine. Only do the odd job, volunteer you know. Love the old books, the feel of the place. Wonderful place."

"I meant, for a village this size, to have a library."

"Ah yes, of course, of course, I see what you mean. Yes well, just thought I'd introduce myself. I heard you were a policeman. A policeman from London."

"I am."

"Yes. Well, so the local Bobbies can't do it on their own when murder hits the village, eh? They call in reinforcements? Even more than there already are?" Malone cocked his head to the left when he asked a question.

"I'm here on holiday. I've only recently made Detective Chief Inspector Trewe's acquaintance."

"I see. Well. If you need anything, anything, or would like to know the best tourist spots, you can count on my help. Like to help out the tourists. Like to do all I can. Time on my hands. Pensioner, you see. Only volunteer here one day a week. If you wish to visit with me in my office, you'll find it at the combined county courthouse. Or come by my home. You'll find the local history quite fascinating. I've always fancied I know a little something about the history of this part of the world. Ask away! Ask away!"

Malone pressed into his personal space but Jon would not give an inch. "I'll keep that in mind, Mr. Malone."

The pear-shaped man moved away a pace. "Do come round. Don't feel you've interrupted me. I'm available. Pleasure to meet you. A pleasure, to be sure." With one last shake of the jowls and a quick wave of his hand, the effusive Malone walked with jaunty quick steps to a stack of books which he set about replacing on a shelves.

Looks the part of dapper country magistrate, dressed and pressed in tweeds as he is, Jon thought. *Funny, the vanity of some men—the way he wears his hair. Yes, I would like to know something more, Mr. Malone, but not about history. The present is what I'm most interested in.*

It was then he realized his notes were turned so anyone leaning over the stack of books could read them.

Monday, late afternoon

Ruth left the hospital with a reminder to "mind your health" and with many a "thank you" from the staff. Though she tried to say her own thank yous, she was still outmatched in that department. So with final "cheers" and "taras" from the staff, she was released to her mother's care.

A police constable had taken them home.

The door of her cottage home opened as they stepped across the stoop. Ruth's heart skipped a beat, but no, it wasn't Annie at the front door.

Sally greeted her with a hug. "How are you now, my duck?" Sally asked, her red hair floated around her face like a flare.

Ruth held up her plaster-bound right hand. "Hurts like the dickens."

"Ah! You've picked up some Texan since your mum arrived. Look, table's set. I've warmed some stew. That's it then. I'll be leaving. Ring if you need anything—I'm on the phone."

Ruth was grateful, but when her friend left, she collapsed on the sofa. Every square inch of her house brought another remembrance of

Annie, only now they seemed to be hitting her painfully by twos and threes. Her home couldn't have felt more desolate.

Despite her mother's protests, she couldn't rest, so instead wandered around the house checking things, touching things. If she stopped, the sadness would catch hold and she wanted to avoid feeling anything.

She checked her email and found several poems that had come in before the last three days. Whoever sent them must have known she was in the hospital. All of the emails were disjointed and confusing. She forwarded them to the police, but only after she printed them out and saved them on her computer. She reread the most recent:

As time would birth events
in their separate spheres, two people
meld in death when their worlds collide.
Hopeless love
becomes sorrow's guide
in the monstrous eternal
of such return.
There is no place to hide
For such as this
would our hearts burn.

No place to hide? She shivered. The poems she received were nothing compared to the one entitled " An Ode to the Stupid Police." Either someone or a group of someones in the village got their jollies from sick persecution, or there really *was* a madman loose. She tried to one-handedly wrap her shawl tighter and sit beside her mother on the couch.

"I can't believe you don't have a TV in the house, honey." Her mom's voice held a thin whine, "I don't know how I would have raised you without one. Funny, I never thought about that—but you thrived, didn't you?"

Ruth rested her aching head on the back of the couch and listened to the click of her mother's knitting needles for a moment before she answered. "We had television when we first came, but it took a lot of my time that I could use for work. I kept it for Annie. But honestly, now we both find television boring. I didn't want to pay another license fee for it."

"A license fee? What in the heck is that? You know I'll pay."

"No, we're fine." She saw her mother's hurt look at her sharp tone. "Sorry."

"I feel so blasted cut-off from the rest of the world without it."

"You said 'blasted.' It sounds so foreign coming from you."

Her mother chuckled, "Well, it's not really cussing coming from me, either."

She patted her mother's leg. "Don't worry. I'll get a paper. We do get news here."

She hoped to set her mother at better ease than she could muster for herself. Should she tell her about the constant stream of news on the Internet she kept online at all times? If she did, her mother would want to get on the computer, and then she would accidently see the emails. It would be just another thing for her mother to worry with.

But who was she to dictate what her mother could worry about? When she could gather her wits, patience, and physical strength she would set her up in front of the "blasted" machine and let her make her own choices.

The sound of the surf came from outside. It seemed to come from below also, and this was worrisome. Annie's stomach couldn't settle. Were the waves real, and how close were they to the sea? What if water came in and drowned her, chained to the wall as she was? Everyone knew the caves around Perrin's Point were too dangerous to explore because they were underwater at high tide.

Water had formed most of Cornwall's caves. Over time the sea's tide had washed out the softer layers of sediment between the heavy granite, which caused the layers to collapse, and sometimes spaces were left behind. Some of the caves weren't caves at all but adits, those engineered tunnels that lead from earth's surface deep into the mines. Breathing tubes for the miners, her mother called them.

Mummy help me.

She counted the links in her chain: twenty-five. She'd managed to work the bolt in the wall loose, but it would not come out. If she twisted it around and did a body flip she might be able to unscrew it. How long it would take she couldn't tell. There were no clocks and no sun. Her sleep and awake times seemed to be running together. She stopped working on the chain when the blood ran down her hand from where the cuff bit into her skin.

Her clothes were filthy. Everything smelled putrid. Her mummy kept everything clean at home. Oh, how she wanted to go home. She squeezed into a ball on the filthy mattress. Both arms hurt now. She wiped her snot onto the greasy material and wailed, "Mummy!"

No. No mummy.

There was no one to help her.

She stretched the chain as far as it would go and could only reach the little pond of water. The effort had her tuckered out. Why did no one come? Why couldn't she get to her mother? Someone whispered, "Let me go. Let me go. Let me go." The words came from her own mouth. *Ugh,* she thought, *Shut up!*

She would kick him where it counted. Except if she did, what good would it do if she couldn't get the chain from the wall?

All this movement was exhausting. Her mom would say it made her "bone tired."

She lay down and stared at nothing. Her heart thundered inside. She pinched herself and it hardly hurt. She gulped back tears. Why couldn't she feel anything? She turned to her side and curled up, holding her tummy. Tears dripped to the mattress and the rhythm of the crashing waves out beyond the doorway cradled her into dreams until she jerked back to the present.

It seemed that she slept all the time. No matter how much sleep … she always wanted to sleep more. Why could she not shake the urge to close her eyes? What was wrong? She could hardly lift her arms above her head. When she struggled to stand, she couldn't stop trembling. Her legs went rubbery until she crumbled into a heap again. She tried. Every time she woke up, the first thing she would do was stand on legs that didn't feel like legs.

Were her legs real like the real of the walls, of trickling water, of hissing waves? She cradled her head and sobbed, "Get me out of here!"

This real—the little tufts of long hair hung on the wall, the bits of rag, the jars of blood, the blasted *drip, drip, drip*—repulsed her until she wanted to scream. What was real was no good.

11:30 p.m.

Charles didn't like to talk to them, didn't like to think of their needs or their names. He liked to think of what they were—tiny flames, so delicate, so easily extinguished. But while they were alive, they had to eat, and so he had to feed them.

He tied a string around each trouser leg to keep the material from snagging on the rock along the cliff's side as he made his way down the slanted and very narrow path. The turquoise water below foamed around the rocks at the base of the cliff. Above, turf overhung the edge to within six or seven feet from the path. The wind whipped his hair aside, and he paused to smooth it back before pulling the grass mat aside to squeeze into his little hidey-hole. He laid the platter down and lit a torch he kept near the door.

He checked to make sure the heater had oil, and he made sure the temperature gauge was correct before picking up the platter to set it near the girl. She lay on a mat about ten feet from the cave's entrance. Her portion of the cave was perfect. She had her toilet, her watering hole, and her bed. He brought her food. She had it made. He hoped that in time she would learn to be grateful for his thoughtful care.

She didn't stir, and he decided she was asleep. He didn't want to check on her yet. He had other things he could do with his precious time.

He played his torchlight across the keepsakes on his special wall, in the niches he'd carefully crafted in the rock—the small jar of teeth, the tube of lipstick, the snatches of hair, blond, brown, and red. There were slots for more, like that lovely golden brown of the American woman. Next to the hair were the lovely knickers, white with lace, blue, the pink ones with Sunday written on the front, the funny little stringy thing—what good was it, but it did make the juices flow didn't it? Knickers—that was what they called them in the old days before this spoilage of language made them "pants." Such a wearisome word. Knickers brought titillation to the thing, which was the way it should be, the way it should remain.

Then he let the light dance across his little collection of shoes. They had come in so handy.

He always saved the next keepsake for last. He liked to take his viewing of it slowly. It was the best prize of all. First, he slid the light down the object, and his breath caught from the delight of seeing how the light reflected on the blade—so pretty. The handle came down just so. He liked its heft. When he was ready—when the power was coursing through his veins and he could hear it sing to him—he would go forward with his plan to take back his true life.

He heard her shifting, the scrape of her foot against the stone. She uttered a small groan. He'd have to bring her more medicine. Her head injury made his gleanings puny, as he was ultimately afraid of losing her too soon if he took too much.

The place reeked. The water and soap that he'd scrubbed the floor with didn't do much good. He needed to grab a couple of bunches of the thyme that grew at the mouth of the cave and spread the floor with it. He would crush it underfoot; its fragrance would mute the stench of death he couldn't wash out.

30

Tuesday morning
Day ten

A cool breeze blew in from the sea to where Jon and Trewe sat at breakfast in the Hasten Inn B&B's terraced garden. Jon smoothed his hair down and faced Trewe, whose grizzled head-mat never moved, and not for the first time Jon wondered if it might be a wig or a bad hairpiece.

Beside them the garden glowed in lazy terra cotta colors reminiscent of a far-off Italian garden of distant happy memory. Across the courtyard they had a view of the village and the beach cove partly hidden by a curve of cliff. The village looked brilliant and peaceful, the roads empty of traffic.

The sun warmed the skin, but the air was brilliantly cold and carried the faint scent of briny fish. Jon leaned forward to stir his tea with a wary eye on Trewe's narrow face. Something was amiss. He was angry.

Tiny sparrows flew back and forth, tittering and chattering as they fought over crumbs under the table.

Mrs. McFarland brought tea and chatted pleasantly about the weather. She asked if they needed anything and said she would be more than happy to set out a fresh pot. She slapped her oven mitts together before her ample bosom like the poor mitts needed an airing.

"This is more than lovely, Mrs. McFarland," Trewe told her with a smile.

In Mrs. McFarland's presence Trewe seemed amiable enough, but as soon as she had gone back inside, he became glaringly quiet. Jon could provoke nothing but monosyllabic responses from him. *This does not bode well,* Jon thought. *A quiet dog is a dog that attacks.*

Jon split his scone and spread upon it the contents of the little condiment pots on the table. The strawberry jam and clotted cream slid in clumps off the scone, dripping onto the blue-and-white china plate, a hodge-podge of red, white, and blue. He bit into his scone, and then noticed Trewe hadn't touched his tea.

Trewe, his voice low, spit out the words, "You seem such a pleasant liar."

Jon dropped his butter knife. "What?"

"I cannot get around what was discovered in your caravan. And the cameras."

"The home office directed me in an investigation here, and I was told to stand down and follow whatever orders I'm given by you, and you did ask me to work on translation."

"Trust," Trewe said flatly. "Trust is the key to work with here."

"When I'm able to divulge the nature of my investigation, you'll be made aware of everything. Meanwhile, the subject is off-limits." He paused to stir.

Trewe looked as if he'd swallowed a pigeon and it still fluttered. "Tell me one thing. How many cameras are there?"

"Sixteen."

"I see. Have any of them contributed to the murder investigation?"

"Only so far as the footage that you received. None of it shows anything, at least not that I could see. There were some old cameras at the beach that record to VHS tapes. I didn't have a VCR, so I sent them to London. Bakewell never received them. I had copies, but they were stolen by the person who set the fire."

Trewe took another swallow of his tea and cleared his throat. He spoke carefully, as if he held back strong emotion. "The camera my team found, so well hidden above the road, was an extremely sophisticated piece of equipment—an extremely sophisticated machine, indeed. I've never personally seen anything like it."

"Most use micro- or macro-cards these days."

Trewe clawed at his scone with a finger. "So everything else is off topic?"

Jon kept his silence. The man was dying of curiosity—why was that? Was it because he did have something to hide?

Trewe eyed him. "So there was footage beyond the videos which were handed me?" He stuffed the last bit of scone into his mouth and talked around it. "I'm assuming your investigation had been in full swing that morning."

"Yes."

Trewe leaned forward jabbed a finger alternately between Jon's face and the sky. "If you had gotten the footage to me, I would have taken the bloody time to have every pixel dissected."

"They were the ones stolen."

Trewe stood. His voice rose a notch. "If I could, I'd have your guts for garters! You seem at the center of every mistake in the investigation, sir."

Mrs. McFarland came out of the house with her broom. "Mr. Graham?"

Trewe waved her away. "Mr. Graham, you're either with me or you're not."

Mrs. McFarland went back inside, but Jon noticed the curtain move. He wouldn't put it past her to jump out with the broom.

"I apologize. It was truly careless on my part," Jon said.

"When would you have filled me in?"

"We would have reviewed the footage together and straightened things out."

"What with?" Trewe growled. "More lies?"

"I beg your pardon?" Jon straightened his spine, ready.

Trewe remained standing, and gripped the table. Then his face went white and he swayed.

Jon reached before he could topple over.

Trewe shook him off. "I'm fine."

This extreme emotionalism was not a virtue for a chief inspector. But it could be there was something else. Trewe looked like a sick man. Jon indicated the chair Trewe had vacated. "Please. We really should discuss the other abductions and murders."

Trewe would not sit. "I don't understand your obsession with that. The perpetrators were found and convicted."

"There's DNA."

"Pixie dust!" Trewe shouted.

"Get with the times, man. You said a DNA profile is being run on the girl's body."

"Standard procedure doesn't make it foolproof."

The bees found the strawberry jam. Jon brushed his hand across the table. "At the very least get a forensic profile and a psychological profile of what type of person this could be. Mary Shelly wrote 'Our creature will be waiting in the shadows, waiting to view our slow and painful departure.' You see, Peter, I think he watches us. I think he is laughing at us."

Trewe took out a small vial from his pocket and emptied a white tablet into his hand. He used his tea to swallow the pill down as if there were nothing more natural. He pulled out some sheets of paper from a folder he had brought with him, muttering, "I bloody well would have wanted to see the other videos."

"Might we move on to the notes left on Mrs. Butler's doorstep?"

Trewe shook his head and finally sat down. He put the paper on the table, disturbing the bees. "I read the emails to Mrs. Butler as threats towards her. At best, cyber stalking."

"How did he get her email address?"

"The various neighborhood associations have address books. If she volunteers for anything, her email would be posted for the other volunteers."

"And you've followed up?"

"Yes." Trewe looked tired. The bees found his hair interesting. He waved them away. "She volunteers at the church with keeping up the grounds. The author of these emails is writing from various public access computers, not only in Perrin's Point, but in other villages and towns, as well. We're working to trace them to a central user, but there are different addresses for each email. Not an impossible problem, but it'll take time."

"Why didn't he send the emails to the police at the station?"

Trewe stared hard at Jon. "How many times a year do they let you out?"

"Sorry?"

"Have you seen our computers? Hand-me-downs. We only just graduated to color monitors. Our email is sporadic at the smaller stations; there's no budget for the online-all-the-time services. It's not been so many years since we received bulletproof vests. All around us they have things like the new Adams metal-detecting gloves. They handed them out like candy just south of us but do we have any? No." He paused to wave his hand at an errant bee. "Our crime may not be as terrible in quantity as it may be in the big city, granted. But the summers bring in the bad with the good, you know. It is crowded here then. We get our share."

"I just assumed your police stations were online." The pace here was definitely slower than London. Were the head-office technology people not aware that the southwest of England needed attention? He was certain they were aware, but budgets lately had taken even the London Met's expectations down a notch or two.

"Not in Perrin's Point," Trewe said. "Between four police stations in our area, there are two computers online at any given time. The server's down more than it is up."

"If I have anything to say about it when I return …"

"Don't trouble yourself."

"This isn't pretty." Jon shifted papers and scanned through a few of the emails. One bee still clung to the side of the jam pot. "Here's the email to the police. I suppose this one is for me. It's called 'An Ode to the Stupid Police':

> Come thou fount of blathering wisdom,
> Fount of misguided direction.
> So you slip and slide with Pete Trewe,
> A toast! Follies of combined detection!
> We spin our wheels on grounds
> of understandings, the wheels slip.
> Such a waste, I find you take up space,
> an inner place our history dictates.
> Death won't come too soon."

"Well?" Trewe asked.

"Scary devil. Spinning our wheels?"

"None of it makes sense and he isn't a poet. If we spend too much time on this, we are spinning our wheels."

"True, but I'm going to think about this. There may be clues in what he says."

"Let's move on to the scraps of paper tied to the flowers." Trewe waved the bees away again, as he slid the emails back into his case. "Damned bees."

"It's early. They aren't finding enough flowers." Jon pulled his notes from his pocket. "The notes—written in Welsh—are condolences to Mrs. Butler. And something more."

"Condolences! He should have written in bloody plain English." He waved his hand again. "Is it my imagination, or are there more bees than crumbs?"

As if on cue, the bustling Mrs. McFarland appeared. "My busy bees have found the sweets. Here, Mr. Graham, let me take that away."

"Bless you, Mrs. McFarland." Jon noticed at least one bee follow her into the house. He lay the strips of paper one after the other across the white wrought iron table, securing them with the salt and pepper shakers, the cream pitcher, and the covered butter dish so they wouldn't blow away. "If they're placed in order of the days they were sent, as per the notation on the outside of the evidence bag, they look like ... this. What was Mrs. Butler supposed to do with the notes, not being able to read them?"

"Save them for us—as she has done?" Butter dripped down Trewe's chin. He wiped it with his napkin, then bent forward to stare at the scraps of paper.

"Used the dictionary's translation as best I could," Jon said, "The first one—'*Gyda phob cydymdeimlad dwys,*' with every sympathy deep—doesn't look suspicious."

"Everything's suspicious," Trewe muttered.

"This one, in English, warns her to be careful—be vigilant— which indicates he was dead serious about getting the message across," Jon said. "Then in Welsh, *'Fel neidr yn y ddaear'.* Like a snake in the earth. There's a quote from Virgil that is similar, '*Latet anguis in herba,*' a snake lurks in the grass."

"Warning her of someone who is sneaking around."

The way Trewe said it brought something else to mind. He'd have to give it more thought. He leaned back to catch the full warmth of the sun across his chest. "The next one, *'gofalwch gofala,'* means watch out."

Trewe nodded. "That's plainly a warning."

"Who would know to warn her–" he caught himself and stopped.

"What is it?"

"I know who wrote these."

"Who is it?" Trewe swept crumbs into a neat pile and absent-mindedly waved away a bee or two circling his head. "Why'd he do it?"

Jon shook his head, baffled. "The deep depression of the pencil shows he meant it. He was writing these things as he walked to her house. He didn't plan it."

"Who is it then?

"Gareth Wren Tavish."

31

When Jon and Trewe entered the Perrin's Point police station, Jon recognized Harold Sonders, the barman from the Spider's Web, by his flame-red hair and familiar apron. In the light, the yellowed cloth looked as if its better days were long past. He reeked of cigarette smoke and fried fish as he intercepted Trewe, almost jumping in his path.

"Sir! Have you seen Tavy?" he asked.

"No. But we were on our way to see him."

Jon could see the man was near panic. "Why are you concerned, Mr. Sonders?"

"Chelsea, Tavy's Newfoundland. Sech a loyal, smart dog. Watches out fer him, if you were t' ask me." He leaned toward Jon and whispered, "Sump'n's happened to Tavy!" The man wrung his hands and rocked back and forth on his feet.

"Explain yourself, man!" Trewe demanded.

"Chelsea comes to the pub. When I comes close, her takes off," Harold swung his arm in an arch, "higgledy-piggledy."

"Look! Not biting anyone, is she?"

"Nae." The man shook his head, clearly put off by Trewe's impatience. "But he's not answerin' my texts."

"Dogs don't use mobiles," Trewe said, then waved a dismissive hand at Harold. "Yes, yes, you meant Tavy. What has that to do with a dog showing up at the pub?"

Harold's agitation increased. "It's the time he does, sir." He directed his words to Jon, "The time."

Trewe growled, "Time?"

"'Tis at the regular time Tavy comes to the pub, the dog shows up. Tavy shows up rain or shine, like clockwork, but not Saturday past, nor Sunday, nor Monday. Those days, the dog showed up without the man."

"Now, Harold, he's probably just under the weather. It's only been three days," Trewe told the man. Then he sent Harold off with assurances they were just on their way to check on the old gent.

"Harold is overly emotional," Trewe growled. "The girl's death has everyone on edge. We'll drop in at the Spider's Web and see if anyone else has seen him then."

Clouds tinted the late afternoon sky gray. In search of a dog's man, they entered the pub. Conversation stopped dead, and the patrons stared at Jon and Trewe in a smoky still life.

Jon asked the blond, busty girl at the bar, "Seen Mr. Tavish?"

She waved her hand at the patrons. "No. We were all wondering about him, really."

The man at Jon's right looked up from his drink. His glasses sat crooked on his face. "Might be ill. Not like 'im." He went back to contemplating the bottom of his tankard.

Jon started to speak but the bald, fat man on his left nudged his arm with an elbow. "Go over 'is 'ome, be the quickest way."

"Am I to understand you are all concerned about Mr. Tavish," Jon said, "but none of you has gone to check on him?"

Three other people started to speak at once in protest, but Jon heard the girl above the men.

"Tavy likes his privacy." There was a round of general agreement. "We would not be worried a bit but for the dog comin' here an' all. He keeps himself to himself, does Tavy. Besides that, sometimes he goes away for days on end. Course, he would take his dog with him, wouldn' 'e?" She dried the tankards and arranged them on a tray. The men nodded in agreement with her. She said, "Harold is the one worried half to death."

"Where is Mr. Sonders?" Trewe asked. "We just saw him."

"Off, isn't 'e? Likely gorne lookin' for him again."

The two men at the bar nodded.

"So, if we want Mr. Tavish …" Jon started.

"… go see him," the bald man muttered.

Jon shook his head. "Right. We'll be back."

Trewe said, "I've summoned Perstow to join us. He knows Tavy better than we do."

A crowd stood outside the pub's door. Chelsea appeared and received a grand welcome which included a plate full of sausage and chips. She lapped up the food scraps.

Jon watched and wondered. When the dog kept him from entering the library, had she been trying to tell him something? "Regular as clockwork?" he said to Trewe.

"And no sign of Tavy." Trewe's face paled. Jon wondered again if Trewe was ill.

A few minutes later, Perstow joined them with a plastic carrier bag. He held up the bag saying, "Best be prepared; never know what we'll be needing."

"Regular Boy Scout is our Mr. Perstow," Trewe announced.

Perstow snickered, his round belly jiggling with his mirth. *What a household his must be,* Jon reflected. The jester and the shrew.

"Should we invite the dog to go with us?" Jon asked.

"I'm not sitting in a car with a dog," Trewe gruffed. They took Jon's car. Perstow squeezed into the back seat. They drove past shops and even Ruth Butler's cottage.

Jon said, "Things look quiet at Mrs. Butler's house."

"Don't blame her really," Trewe said.

At the end of the road, the street took an abrupt turn left. They took a lane shooting to the right and then bumped along until they were forced to park and walk.

Tavy's home had been named "The Combe." Its front door hung partly open.

The three men moved toward it.

"This isn't like Tavy a-tall," Perstow said as they neared.

A huffing sound and a sudden movement sprang at Jon from behind. He pivoted into a defensive posture as Perstow shouted, "Chelsea, heel!"

Jon breathed in relief that his frightener was the dog. "She beat us here from the pub."

"Chelsea's path over the hills would be quicker," Perstow remarked. "In fact, anyone walking along the cliff could 'ave beaten us here. The coastal path is a rough walk, but short."

The stout police sergeant pulled a ham bone from his carrier bag. The canine grabbed it out of his hand, tail sailing back and forth. She lay down. While she chewed and gnawed hungrily on the bone, holding it down with one massive paw, Jon ran a hand along her back. "She's bone thin."

Trewe pushed the door with the toe of his shoe. "Mr. Tavish?"

An odor of moth crystals and *eau de dog* assailed Jon's nostrils. Above it all a high keen of sickly-sweet wafted. Jon's heart sank. It was the smell of death.

From somewhere came a ticking sound too irregular to be a clock.

Trewe switched a light on. The light revealed pale, olive-green walls lined with dark wooden shelves. Books were crammed in, stacked on their sides, or slumped against pieces of maritime jetsam. Ship instruments with polished brass and crystal-faced dials shown like jewels from beneath sheaves of papers. Various model ships sat on top of the bookshelves. Some were made with coconut husks and fragile dried palm leaf sails, some with bull horns and hooves, some with capuche shells and mother-of-pearl sails, and others with balsa wood and parachute silk sails.

Two large, over-stuffed chairs sat at odd angles. Around the chairs were stacks of books, used it appeared, as repositories for notes and pencils or as foot rests. Dust lay thick. On top of one of the stacks was a pair of wire-rimmed glasses, fingerprint-smudged, next to a mug with an inch of murky liquid complete with a scab of mold. A pair of worn slippers lay beside one of the chairs, waiting for the return of familiar feet.

Perstow gave a low whistle. "I've never been in this part of the house before."

"What is that ticking sound?" Jon paused to read a framed paper set against the wall. "A Certificate of Merit from the Coast Guard? For lifesaving efforts during the sinking of the Greek ship *Stavinous Steady*."

"Villagers frequently get involved in rescue efforts along the coast," Trewe said. "Maybe the ticking is coming from that?"

Jon and Trewe converged at a computer, which looked vastly out of place in the quaint, old-fashioned room.

Jon touched the mouse. The screen flashed awake.

Trewe exclaimed, "Bloody hell."

The words "The only good policeman is a dead one" were repeated over and over and shaped in the form of a skull.

Trewe bent closer and murmured, "Mr. Tavish has some explaining to do."

"Someone else did it." Perstow was behind them. "Not him."

Jon frowned. "What makes you so sure?"

"Tavy's a good man, through 'n' through."

"Any relatives? He may be visiting elsewhere," Jon said.

Perstow said, "His only relative, a great-nephew, looks like 'im, only younger." His round face was very grave. "Tavy wouldn't 'ave gone off without his dog."

Jon pulled a piece of paper out of his pocket. His copy of the quotes was folded into the paper. He unfolded it and handed it to Perstow. "What would you make of these?"

Perstow read them. "Oh! That's Tavy's handwriting, sure as sure. Likes a bit of mystery, does our Tavy. Leaves notes in Welsh for everyone. It's 'is way." He glanced at them. "Condolences." He frowned. "This one's a warning. Must 'ave been in a hurry."

"Too bad you weren't around much this past week," Trewe growled. "Would've saved us trouble."

Perstow's face turned red. "Her Indoors—"

Trewe cut him off. "We know."

Jon made his way to the closed door opposite the open front door. The odd ticking noise grew louder. "The sound is coming from here. Where's this go?"

"Kitchen," Perstow said. "It's the main door for visitors, really."

As Jon opened the door, a plume of black smoke enveloped him. He ducked and rushed in, shouting, "Something's on fire."

An ancient oscillating-type fan lay on its side with a piece of wood jammed into its tines, preventing much movement. It ticked as it jerked. Black smoke plumed from it. Jon lunged at the fan and jerked the plug from the wall. At the last squeak and groan of the fan, it was so quiet he could hear the dog just beyond the open front door gnawing the bone.

Choking, Perstow waved through the smoke and opened another door that led to the back garden, letting fresh air and bright light into the room. The kitchen was in disarray with chairs on their sides and crockery shattered on the floor.

Jon documented the room with his mobile's camera.

"Perstow," Trewe yelled, "call SOCO. I want official photos of this setup."

Jon stooped to look at the dog prints on the slate floor. He dapped a finger—it was dry. "Blood, not mud."

At the deep stone sink, flies arose with the incoming of fresh air from out of doors. Two plates, mucky with food scraps and alive with maggots, lay in the sink. They were the source of the horrible smell.

Trewe said, "Surely, a dog wouldn't sit quietly as her owner was attacked. This mess could have been made by the dog."

Jon coughed and sputtered. "It's the dog's fault there is blood on the floor?"

Trewe pointed to a spool of string. "Looks like the string used to tie the sack around the girl's neck."

"And the shoes in the tree," Perstow said, setting the dog's water dish on the sink's ledge. "The dog needs clean water."

Jon saw two little white tablets where the dog's dish had been. "What's this?" He scooped them into a baggie. "Perstow, don't change that water. Find another bowl to use. Get these and that water to a lab. The killer's playing a game with us. That's why he set this up the way he did. It's some bloody game and we have to figure out the bloody rules, because he's not bloody telling."

"Is that anger, Jon?" Trewe muttered.

"And what if it is?" Jon snatched up the iron fry pan from the floor. He took a deep breath. He knew being angry wasn't helping anything. He studied the edge of the pan. "White hair. And more blood."

Perstow backed into the table, jarring it against a wall.

Trewe whipped around to face Perstow. "Hell's bells, man! Do I have to tell you twice? Get SOCO!"

32

Tuesday, late afternoon

Ruth's mother suggested that she go sit in the garden. So here she was, sitting like a bump on a log. The afternoon sun was warm, though the occasional breeze had a cold nip to it. It was already late afternoon. Clouds on the horizon meant they would have rain again by evening. It rained a lot this time of year. Or maybe it rained all the time, she couldn't recall. She actually loved the weather here, especially when the sun shone. The garden was still and quiet and still muddy from yesterday's rain. She leaned back in the garden chair and let the sun warm her face.

She had so many questions. Should she approach Jon Graham? He seemed the only one willing to believe the impossible. Had she only dreamed what happened between them when she was in the hospital? Had it been a drug-induced fantasy? Her mother told her that Mr. Graham had watched over her early on after her attack.

She stood and pulled her cellphone from her jeans pocket to call Detective Inspector Graham. He answered but told her he'd ring her back, and he did within a few minutes. He told her, "I'll be by soon. I can't promise when."

She gripped her cellphone until she had to set it down or she would break it. Why could she think of nothing to do to help?

Jon set the phone down. He had only just washed the soot from Tavy's kitchen from his hands and face when he answered Mrs. Butler's call. He sat alone in the former jail cell now called an office. He caught his breath, then pushed it out. Whether he went against orders was not a question any longer. She wished to speak to him. He wanted no one in this small village to gossip or question his presence near her. The best possible course was to ask Constable Craig to assist him.

Before he could do that, he had been asked to wait. Trewe wanted to consult with him. He stared at the piles of papers accumulated across Perstow's desk. His mind filled with dark thoughts. Where was Tavy? The scene suggested foul play. Why would someone suddenly find Tavy a threat?

Annie Butler's disappearance was no isolated incident. But how could he prove it?

If he could place his hands on the man who killed the child, he would show him justice. If only a suspect would surface, someone to investigate. If only something concrete would come to light that would tie everything together so he could show Trewe what he meant about Annie's murder. And what about all the other girls from the past thirty years? No, it seemed even to him to be too fantastic. If only he could find a strong enough thread to hang his convictions on besides the twigs of thyme. All the other girls had had herbs on or near their bodies. Of course, there was always the matter of the shoes. But who would believe such flimsy evidence?

The current topic of conversation in the office was the disappearance of Tavy. Mr. Tavish had been known to take long treks along the coast, he and his dog and a backpack. But after viewing Tavy's cottage, Jon was sure the old man hadn't walked away willingly. Unless he had something to hide and staged the things at the cottage to look as if he'd met foul play. No, he wouldn't have left the dog. Even in the short time Jon had been acquainted, he knew the man loved his dog. How did this tie in to Annie's murder? Tavy was an old man. His death does not fit in with girls found dead in Cornwall.

Budgets were tight, and police officers don't lie around like spare change. He needed Allison Craig, but she and another constable actively made inquiries after Mr. Tavish. Everyone else had loads of work.

He listened to the constable tap at his computer in the front room of the Perrin's Point police station. The man had been pushed out of the incident room because it was too crowded. All the officers were on edge. They were tired. They were all tired from knocking on doors and interviewing villagers. The village wasn't huge, but because of the narrow streets and lack of parking they did a lot of walking. They worked twelve- and fifteen-hour shifts in the mud and wet weather, until they were a bedraggled lot.

The entire village seemed to be in lockdown mode out of fear from what was taking place. People didn't walk on the streets in the daylight, much less at night. The elderly hid behind locked doors afraid to even purchase groceries. Jon mused that fear gave crime fewer witnesses and greater opportunity.

At his desk, Jon watched dust mites dance in the sunlight, which streamed through the tiny window above the prison-plank bed. What else could he do to move this case forward? Time was a funny thing. When one wanted to have something over and done with, life crawled into an unbearable forever.

No fingerprints, no footprints, no suspects. *Spinning wheels.* The supposed poem from the killer—Why had he said that?

Jon pulled out his copy. *We spin our wheels on grounds of understanding. The wheels slip. Such a waste, I find you take up space, an inner place our history dictates.* Grounds of understanding? What does that mean? An acquaintance? A friend? Another police officer? And why start rhyming now? Waste, space, place, dictates, there's a clue here. *Why can't I see it?*

Without a suspect what could he do—test everyone in the surrounding villages and towns? It'd been done before: first the blood grouping, then the DNA profiles. He could stand to endure all the bloodsucking jokes if he could lay his finger on a murderer. But the initial narrowing down could take weeks of testing non-intimate samples. The scene played in his imagination. "Excuse me, gentlemen, if you would all queue up whilst we swab your mouth. Step right up!"

He steeled himself when he heard Trewe's voice in the outer office.

Trewe poked his head around the doorframe and said, "What trouble are you going to give me this afternoon? Have you found out anything more about Tavy? Have there been any answers to the television appeals about the girl's kidnapping?"

"Have you gotten any DNA back on Annie Butler?"

"No. Why?"

The antagonism wasn't getting easier. "I do fine when allowed a little respect for my opinions."

Trewe turned his face away. "I won't raise objections to anything you do."

"I hear an 'unless'?"

"I don't care a bit for vigilantes."

Jon didn't move. "I mean to look at the other girls' murders. I don't believe it has anything to do with vigilantism. I like to think I have initiative."

"I say you are wasting the department's time."

"Short of a miracle, this investigation might take time, which I don't have much of. I've got to return to London." He forced himself to remain calm. "But I don't want to leave you hanging."

Trewe eyes flashed slivered ice. "And to think I've been able to manage all this time without you."

Wake up, Annie.

No. I can't. Leave me alone. I want to sleep.

Wake up, Annie. It was her own voice in her head. Why couldn't she just shut up?

I want to sleep. I don't want dreams. I want Mummy. No more real. *Leave me alone.*

The dripping water made music like a distant piano playing. It was sad music. The music was more distinct just before she drifted into sleep, and she slept a lot; sleep was the best thing. The dripping water, the whisper of the waves outside, her hollow heartbeat, those didn't matter. Nothing mattered.

Wake up, Annie.

I don't know how.

Jon could not locate Allison Craig, and no one else was available to come with him. But he had a commitment to keep, so he found himself alone at Ruth's door. He would be in and out quickly, he told himself.

Her mother let him in. He wasn't sure how this was going to go, but at least he wouldn't be alone with the victim's mother and give Trewe more ammunition to fire at him.

Mrs. Thompson was speaking. "Everyone is so helpful. I can't imagine who would hurt Ruth-Ann or Annie, because every person I've met has been so kind. I just don't know."

"Thank you."

"Hot tea? That's what you people like isn't it?"

"Sorry. I don't want anything, thank you." He wondered when she said "you people" if she meant the police or the British. "Mrs. Butler called me."

"She's resting. I'll tell her—"

"No! Please don't disturb her." He turned to leave. "I'll be off."

As he turned, he saw her. She stood at the door opposite the front door. Despite the bound hand, taped head, and battered face, he could think of nothing else he'd rather see. *No, don't think.* Why couldn't he think? He was falling in love with this woman, and he was absolutely stupid.

She said, "I can tell by your expression, I must look scary."

"No. No, I wasn't thinking that, just … umm … you called?"

"I did." She moved slowly to a small desk in the corner where a computer sat. A long table was covered in paper and some jars with color-tinged liquid. Paint brushes sprouted from a coffee can. The drape of Ruth's gold-tinged hair obscured her face, so he couldn't guess at her expression as she checked the computer screen. On the wall above her head was an oil painting of a girl on the beach. He could see it was Port Isaac south, about fourteen miles from Perrin's Point. The painting had the boats canted on the sand, and visible cables stretched out to the sea wall. There were several paintings around the room of the same girl.

He said, "Annie's a beautiful girl. Nice colors you used, the way the light comes from all around. Is this what you do? I mean, as a business."

"I do research and some illustration. It keeps us in cereal."

"I like them. Not that … I know what I'm talking about. I mean, art … I'm no critic." He needed to stop talking. A small voice inside his head told him if he let her look into his eyes she would know more about him than he wanted known. He shouldn't have come. He must be crazy. He had a crime to solve; how was he helping? She rearranged papers. Jon had the impression of a bird in a cage, not able to stay still. "Mrs. Butler?"

"Yes, someone has been following me for some time, before this happened to Annie."

"Can you describe the person following you?"

"He's covered. Scarves or something on his face. He doesn't stand straight, or maybe he's deformed, like a hunchback … Whatever." Ruth's voice caught. Jon's heart did some kind of back-flip.

Jon knew that she had described the man who beat her outside his caravan. He said, "Don't you have any suspicion of who it was? Could it have been Tavy?"

Ruth looked up in alarm. "Tavy had nothing but kind words for me. How could you say such a thing? The reason I called is I want to know more about your suspicions that Annie was not or is not the only girl kidnapped in Cornwall. Why can't I find anything about it on the Internet?"

"Because they weren't kidnapped in Cornwall."

"But—"

"They were left in Cornwall."

"Dead?"

"Yes."

"And Annie ... it wasn't Annie I saw dead."

Ruth's mother must have been listening, because she hastened into the room with a mug of steaming tea in each hand. "Are you upsetting my Ruth?"

"I don't want to." He turned to Ruth, "Mrs. Butler, we have no real proof."

"Look!" Ruth pointed to the painting of Annie on the beach. "There's your proof. Look at her feet, then look at the dead girl's feet. You can see the proof. It isn't Annie!"

Tuesday night, 10:33 p.m.

The flickering firelight caressed Charles's features with seductive, warm fingers. He sat in the long, narrow sitting room of his home listening to the crack and pop of sizzling embers. The rain fell in sheets. He would have to go check the heater in the cave. Rain was good because it covered his footprints so well.

He had been so good, to accomplish all that was required so his mother would tell him how much she had loved him always. He intended her to say it.

He had his chance to capture the American woman and he had been scared off by the nosy policeman. He would not fail a second time.

It takes too long to grind the seeds to make cyanide, he thought. The Wife must have something in her medicine cabinet. The one medication had been perfect for the dog. Stupid to be so friendly, what good is that?

He sang softly, "pick-pack paddy-whack, give the dog a pill. That old man goes rolling still."

He slapped his knee and stifled a laugh. Sometimes he really exceeded himself.

Poison. Really effective stuff. Of course there were always lupine seeds. He could dig around in the greenhouse and come up with some. A few could kill a man.

He stood up, stretched and walked to the bar opposite the fireplace. He moved one of the decanters and saw the ring it left in the thick dust. He hadn't wanted The Wife to touch his liquor cabinet. He liked his dust just the way it was. A hissing beyond the fireplace brought him upright.

"Life is only a casing, Chubby, an exoskeleton, as it were, for death. Physical death is the final and glorious conclusion. The top rung of the ladder, Bubby. We only pass from one death to another. All of us are dead."

"I hear you, mother." He wanted to add that some were definitely more dead than others were, but why bring that up?

He fixed himself a small nightcap and a larger one for The Wife. If something happened before he could prepare more carefully, he could claim she killed herself with alcohol.

He started to take a long swallow.

"The German hussy has led my Charlie to an unhealthy way of living. I knew she would from the moment I laid my eyes on her. I always said ..."

He choked on his cognac. The fumes burned into his nostril, thrilling up into his forehead. "The German witch wants me for my secure position and good looks," he intoned. He had heard it more times than he could count.

"Health is paramount to keeping your body for the everlasting life, Charlie."

Old-fashioned gibberish, he thought, but there was no reasoning with her. "You are an everlasting memorial, Mum. The proof of the pudding!"

He positioned a Frank Sinatra album on the record player. He wondered why others found records so passé. "Come Mother! Let us dance as we used to." He held his arms out and up, put his head back and made a slow rotation, turning in wide arcs around the den.

The flickering shadows on the walls moved back and forth. Anyone observing would have imagined trickery as the one shadow dancing became two.

33

Wednesday afternoon
Day eleven

Standing above the beach, Jon watched the waves break against the rocks. He'd been over everything twice and had no breakthroughs in the case. He'd been briefed in the morning meeting with Trewe at the police station, and after filing reports and fielding phone calls, he wanted a walk on the beach. Nature always revived his good humor. A seagull perched on a nearby rock, pecking at what was left of a fish. Like Trewe, pecking at the subject of money while they were driving from Tavy's house yesterday. Jon couldn't remember why the subject got around to money of a personal nature, but he had said to Trewe, "Mrs. Butler may not have money problems, but if the killer has money problems, it may have set—"

Trewe had interrupted, "Or maybe the killer has lots of money and tucked it away so no one knows where it came from, and then the child stumbled upon some truth the killer didn't want her to know. Perhaps the child threatened to tell—there's a scenario I can believe."

Jon had wondered where Trewe would go with that. What about the money Trewe had tucked away? But the conversation drew to a close once they arrived at the police station.

The gull rose into the air and floated away.

Should he tell Mrs. Butler more about the investigation and his own suspicions? He dare not, not alone. He was too good an officer to be unmindful of the serious nature of the warning for speaking to a witness or anyone so closely involved in a case without another officer present. Trewe did not want anyone privy to the information about the other victims. Jon was convinced it was crucial to step up the investigation and begin again to search for a living victim, but he had no allies.

Of course, he was one for following leads—always within the law, signed citations, proper warrants, etc. He often got results, and results were not frowned upon. But in this he had to be cautious. He had developed feelings without encouragement or reason for Mrs. Butler. She had just withstood the worst thing to happen to any parent. She was in no way interested in him and never would be, but that didn't stop his heart doing what it did in her presence.

He went over in his mind all the particulars of the case. No eye witnesses, no witnesses to anything, but there were several strangers seen in or around the village that day, including himself. They were all accounted for and found to be there for legitimate reasons.

Why in this case was the killer taunting the police? He hadn't done it with any of the other girls. Those had been done without any notes or calls or anything. And Annie was ten years old, while the others had been older. Were these the reasons Trewe would not consider his theory?

In the process of acquiring every detail of Annie Butler's life from the past twenty-eight days, more questions were put to Annie's friend, Dot—the hope being that Annie had confided something, as girls do.

Seems that Annie had been worried about something a few days prior to her disappearance. Other friends, their parents, and Annie's teachers were questioned. Anyone who could possibly have had any contact with the girl at any time had been questioned. Other than the vague, unnamed worry, they had learned nothing new. Annie was a good girl who trusted others easily. She had strong opinions but sometimes changed her mind. She liked to do things her way if she could get away with it, she liked being outdoors, she was very creative and often made things or did things for others. She had a passable singing voice and enjoyed sport, particularly football. She and her mother both took part in a self-defense training class. She was a physically strong, though petite, child. She adored her mother, loved lemon ices and did well with her school work. What was it about her that made her more vulnerable to being a victim of murder?

He couldn't answer that. And if the child was the victim of kidnap and was being held, then the question remained, why? The only possible answer was because something of Annie Butler's was what the kidnapper wanted. What would that something be? Money? No, Ruth Butler did not appear to be so well off that her child would be held for ransom. Added to that, there had been no ransom demand. No, the perpetrator wanted something other than money. But what? Power? Sex? Were they dealing with a pedophile? The other girls had not been sexually molested. Though time and sea had wiped away most evidence, the body they had did not appear to have been sexually molested. And *that* was what was entirely strange about this business.

So, what kind of power was the murderer getting from these girls?

The blooming thyme had obviously come from Mrs. Butler's garden. Or had it? There were many possible places. If protected from cold wind and with the right amount of sun, it could bloom early.

Suspects? He had seen the postmistress near the hanging shoe outside Mrs. Butler's cottage. She was not perturbed in the least by any questioning, and there was nothing suspicious about her statement.

The flowers and strange Welsh notes had come from Mr. Tavish.

The emails. Had they come from Mr. Tavish's computer? After a forensic examination of the computer, it was determined that anything threatening had been written after the day of the inquest. And no one had seen or heard from Tavy since the inquest. The evidence suggested to Jon that Tavy had had a violent altercation in his kitchen that day, but they could do little until he was found except keep that line of inquiry open.

Money and lots of it was somehow involved here. He didn't believe in coincidences. Trewe had lots of money and it was time to approach the problem head on instead of dancing around it. Trewe's secret needed airing. The man would implode otherwise. He had even considered him as a suspect, but he didn't seem like a killer—which didn't mean much, Jon knew. Many sociopaths could function every day in their jobs and do terrible things without thought or emotion. They had a bent dial on their moral compasses. But that did not fit our Mr. Trewe, Jon thought. The man spouted emotion at every turn, which also didn't mean much if something had upset the balance of his mentality. He may not have displayed his volatile nature until recently. He'd have to check on that.

The string. The spool sitting so prominently on the stove in Mr. Tavish's kitchen was the same sort of string used at the post office to bind packages before taping. Could it be pointing at the postmistress? Of course, it is common enough. It could be purchased anywhere and used for anything.

The thing to do would be to locate Mr. Tavish.

He went back to the Perrin's Point police station and sat at Perstow's desk because there were no other desks available that weren't buried in paper. Where was Perstow? He should be here or at least have left a note or something. Why hadn't Perstow rung him to let him know what he was doing? Jon stared at the reams of paper strewn everywhere.

Just then, the station's phone buzzed. Jon answered and explained that Mr. Perstow wasn't available and asked if he could take a message.

It was the coast guard. Some fishermen had spotted something suspicious on a ledge of rock, just below the village, and noticed a lot of bird activity. They were there now. The light wasn't perfect, but it looked like a human body.

Wednesday night

The piercing, cold salt air stung the eyes and nostrils. Jon peered carefully over the edge of the rock precipice. It had taken time to get all the equipment together. Except for preparing for the incoming tide, there had not been any scurry to get set up. This was not a rescue.

Lights had been set up to aid the divers, forensics personnel, photographers and various other police technicians assisting SOCO with the scene of the crime. Some lamps had been lowered over the edge, about fifty feet down. There was indeed another body.

The sea should have been successful, Jon reflected, in washing away the physical scraps. But it had already been reported that the body's flesh had snagged and caught on the jagged rock. They were working against the tide. They needed to get in and get out before the waves washed away a few policemen.

With his constant pacing, shouting and arm waving, Trewe made Jon nervous. Definitely not a good thing to be nervous while standing on a precipice above the sea after dark.

"Mr. Graham! What do you make of this?" Trewe held a plastic bag up to Jon's face.

"Video tape."

"It's strewn everywhere down there along with cd shards."

With a creaking squeal, the winch attached to the back of a Range Rover hummed to life.

"The body is coming up now." Jon cupped his hands to shield his eyes from the glare of the lights. "It looks heavy. It isn't a child."

The winch pulled the black plastic-enshrouded body strapped to an aluminum stretcher from below. The men at the top of the cliff used a hook to grab the metal cage the body bag was in. They directed it to land and let it down. Once unhooked from the winch, they freed the parcel from its cage. With explosions of white light, the photographer shot pictures of every detail. Jon took a few pictures on his mobile. Technicians on all fours were going over the turf on the cliff's edge. The forensic staff would supervise the moving of the body to the Royal Cornwall Hospital's Mortuary.

The pathologist, Roger Penberthy, reached the top of the cliff in a harness and handed his medical kit to Trewe. With help from one of the uniformed police, he fought free of the clamps and buckles.

"Never so happy to be on solid earth," he sputtered, white mustache bristling. His breath vapor puffed as if coming from a steam engine. He squinted at them. "Peter, count your blessings you weren't hung above this frightful sea as I've been for the past hour."

Trewe glared. "Well?"

"Man's chief end is to glorify God and enjoy Him forever. This poor soul did not enjoy his final moments. I was not able to ascertain the exact cause of death"—he indicated the body-shaped parcel lying near where they stood—"except for the obvious."

The glare from the strobes turned the water-specked, black bag silver. The doctor unzipped the bag, to reveal a flattened, misshapen, greenish-red face, swollen in a death grimace that obliterated what should have been there—the laugh-lines around the eyes and mouth.

An unseen fist plowed into Jon's stomach. The body was Gareth Wren Tavish.

The doctor spoke over the waves, "Remarkably untouched. Lay with his arm covering this part of his head. Rest of him didn't fare so well. On the rock for the better part of three days."

"How can you tell?" Jon asked, sick at heart.

"Bodily fluids and gas build up after death, swell a body like a balloon, then they leak out—slowly. This balloon is deflated. Usually takes about three days. I'll have to do tests before anything is official, of course. I can be more specific once I've done the postmortem." The doctor pointed to the side of the head. "Either from the skull scraping against the rocks or as a direct result of the fall from the cliff, there's this ..." He pulled long strands of the man's beard away from the side of his head. Part of the skull was gone, exposing gray-white, bloodless matter.

The bulging material was brain. Jon looked away. "In your opinion, is there a way to that particular spot on the rocks other than straight down?"

The doctor shook his head. "Waves are too rough for boats to move close to the rocks. Even at low tide, the beach isn't visible, just the rocks. The spot the body was lodged in is compatible with a free-fall from the top. Pushed over? Slipped over? Don't know. That's your department." The doctor picked up his case.

Trewe swayed slightly. "How'd this happen?"

Jon couldn't separate his feelings into any kind of reasonable muddle. How ironic Tavy had teased him about falling over the edge when they first met. But some unanswered question niggled just now—something was missing. Seeing Tavy in such a state left him numb and depressed. He had really liked the old man. Tavy's body, the lost video, and whatever else the killer felt was important enough to destroy must have gone over the side. Then the niggling thought became clear in a flash. He said to Trewe, "The killer would have taken what he thought important."

"Taken? From Tavy?"

The doctor had started towards a waiting car.

"Wait!" Jon said. "Was he wearing shoes?"

"Shoes?" the doctor paused, looked puzzled before answering. "Now that you mention it, he hadn't any."

34

Thursday morning
Day twelve

It was six o'clock by Jon's mobile. He lay in the bed trying to think, but a mist had settled in his brain. Could be because he'd stayed late at the Spider's Web, with drinks all around, pretending to be interested in snooker, whilst listening to the locals discuss Tavy. But he'd left the pub with more questions than answers.

There was a rap sound at the door.

He struggled away from the thick duvet, threw on some trousers and opened the door.

In stepped Trewe. "Hallo, it's six o'clock. Are you sleeping in?"

"No, sir. I had a late—"

"Good, I need a word." He took the only chair available. "This place looks like a tip."

Because everything he'd had in his caravan had either gone up in smoke or been ruined by water and soot, Jon had had the files on the other girls found dead in the region resent from London. Papers were strewn across every surface. Jon worried that Trewe must see his room as completely disorganized. Here and there, colored paper tags dotted across the jumble didn't help. "It's my room, sir. I didn't think to entertain—"

"It's a perfect spot to speak without other ears overhearing. What is this mess? Looks like you've been working on something."

"It's about the other girls—"

Trewe held a hand up, interrupting Jon. "God, you don't give in easily do you? Suspects tried, convicted, period."

Jon was in no mood to coddle this jackass. He sat on the edge of the bed to face Trewe. "Two of the cases are still open. And those convictions were before 1989 and DNA profiling."

"What! You're going to try to dig up DNA on every case?"

"I've already done it."

"On whose authority?"

"I … I took the initiative."

Trewe glowered. "Blasted vigilante."

"Just hear me out." Without waiting for a response from Trewe, Jon picked up a sheet of paper from the desk and read aloud. "Cecilia Jaggi, twenty. Strangled. Hands tied together with ivy. A package of periwinkle seeds stuffed into her mouth. Ten weeks pregnant. Found by a walker along the A30 near Bolventor. DNA from saved fetal tissue being done, as we speak."

Jon glanced up and caught Trewe's glare, which he had expected. He didn't wait for more response but kept reading. "Next, Alice Dorset, twenty-four, rosemary twisted into a bit of her hair. Mother's name—Rosemary Townsend. Found alongside a church, near Boscastle. A small Elder tree branch under one arm, her shoes were missing. DNA, inconclusive."

"Hold it. What was the date on the first case?"

"1984."

Trewe shook his head. "I can't believe a case from so long ago would have anything to do with this murder. Why would he wait for so long to strike again?"

"He's getting more desperate or something set him off. I can't speculate as to what it was." Jon waited half a tic for Trewe to reply, but the

CI was listening. He finally had his absolute attention. "In the Jane Simmons case, the girl's bra was stuffed with rue. It was June 1995 when some hunting dogs unearthed her shoeless remains. The young lady at seventeen had already proven studies of the scholastic kind were not her thing. She was more interested in the opposite sex. She had been officially declared a runaway in 1992, though she rang up her mother sporadically to let her know she was all right. The calls stopped in February of '94. Her body was found near Rough Tor. The workup on all saved samples showed no foreign DNA."

Trewe leaned back. "And then there was one."

"That we know of anyway. Victoria Benton, age fourteen. Disappeared six months ago from Devon. Her parents received her shoes by parcel post." Jon set the list on the desk. "That must have been horrible."

Trewe growled, "So why do you include Annie in this fantasy of yours?"

"Because of the herbs and shoes."

"Herbs and shoes?"

"Each body was found with herbs or something significant about shoes. What I would like you to do, if I may be so bold—"

"Nothing has stopped you before."

"What I'd like to see happen would be that Victoria Benton's DNA from a hairbrush or something be compared to the body from the surf."

Jon noted the angry stance Trewe took, as if he were fighting a losing battle and would never admit it. He would have to allow the man to save face. "Look, the mere fact that he used the other shoe to hang in the tree speaks more than words, in my opinion. For her sake, man! There were herbs tied into the string around her neck!"

"What do the herbs mean, is the question."

"Herbs do have meaning. People study and write books about it."

"And of course, you would know your herbs."

"As it happens, I do."

"Why am I not surprised?"

The course Jon had taken had been boring. The real reason he had attended had been the girl he was seeing at the time. He realized Trewe was staring at him. "Cecelia Jaggi, the first girl, had ivy twined in her hands and a package of periwinkle seeds stuffed in her mouth. Ivy represents wedded love and fidelity, but the periwinkle is *Fione de Morte,* the flower of death, from an Italian tradition of laying wreaths of periwinkle on the graves of dead babies."

"And she was pregnant." Trewe tapped a finger against the wall. "I get it. Go on."

"The first murder seems disorganized. She was strangled, but the herbs suggest that he loved her and wanted to marry her. Did he not want the baby? Did she push him over the edge? By the next girl, Alice Dorset, he'd perfected his methods, or at least he was calm about murdering her. Rosemary and Elder branches were found on her body. According to an ancient custom, burying Elder tree branches with the dead protected the soul from evil. Rosemary is for remembrance, and her mother's name was Rosemary. So we can conclude by inference, the killer perhaps didn't relish the killing but was interested in her mother—or hated her mother."

"Amazing what you can learn in those courses." Trewe's tone was sarcastic.

They were interrupted by Mrs. McFarland when she poked her head through the door to say that breakfast was on the sideboard and ask if Mr. Trewe cared to join them.

Jon wondered if she'd been listening. She'd never before come to tell him breakfast was there; she'd always left him to find it. She flushed pink as Trewe stood.

"I don't want anything, Mrs. McFarland," Trewe said. "I've got to be going."

"I'll be down in a moment, thank you," Jon told her. He watched her walk downstairs before he shut the door. He continued, "Most of this I've been researching on the Internet since we last talked. The rue stuffed in the bra? Rue is for repentance or regret."

"And the girl had a reputation."

"Exactly. Only in this instance, the death was violent, so there was no regret there. He must have thought the girl needed to repent for something and she hadn't."

"Okay, I'm listening. Annie Butler had thyme in her neck cord," Trewe said.

"Thyme grows around here. In days gone by, specifically in Wales and probably here in Cornwall, thyme's flowers were thought to hold the souls of the dead. Hence, thyme for death. The fact is, he found a bit of thyme that had a blossom. He used it specifically, when a sprig from a wild bush, which would not be blooming, would be more convenient. I think this was not so much a murder as a burial."

"Deadly thyme. Sounds as if you have him figured out."

Jon took a deep breath. "I believe this is a man who believes he is above the law. He has been doing this for some time and has not been caught. Now he is flaunting it. But he is either quite superstitious, or he believes in ceremony. Why? Is it regret? Perhaps he believes he is humane so killing isn't part of his nature. Is he attempting some kind of atonement for himself by including ceremony in the burial? He forces himself to carry out some sort of elaborate burial practice where each time the plant material is tied in some way to the dead, but not to him. I believe he still feels some security because nothing's been in the press about any connection in the other deaths. Probably thinks he got away with it again. And there's one other thing."

"I'm listening."

"I've been wondering why he didn't molest the girl. Why not? He'd violated her by taking her blood. So why not sexually? Then, it came to me. He's impotent."

"That's hitting a little close to the bone, son."

Jon jerked upright. "That could be one reason he didn't."

"Or perhaps sex is just something you are fixated on, Mr. Graham. This is not a pedophile. And the herb theory is interesting but thin, very thin. Meanwhile, I'm pursuing the idea that Mr. Tavish knew more than he was letting on. There must be a reason he had his head bashed in."

"I imagine he did know something. How long has he lived in Perrin's Point?"

"About twelve years."

"So he hasn't been here much longer than Ruth Butler. Where did he move from?"

"Wales."

"I wonder how long the killer has been here and where he moved from. He can't be a native, because others would know and wonder about him. Being an incomer creates its own peculiar lack of anonymity."

Trewe stood, put his hands in his pocket. "With your *theories* there must be a reason Tavy had parsley tucked into his pockets."

"Parsley?"

"Don't miss your breakfast." Trewe huffed and exited Jon's room.

Annie studied the water in the pool. By some odd quirk of nature, a deep gouge at the center of the floor had filled with water from a thin rivulet of water streaming down one side of the cave. There must be a reason that the water never overflowed the pool and it stayed a constant level, but she couldn't see how.

The water was crystal clear. There were shiny things at the bottom.

A sound behind her startled her. It couldn't be the man, it was daylight. She turned too quickly. Her head pounded. The light made her dizzy and her sight blurred. A shadow moved. She knew it was the man and she needed to be in her bed pretending to sleep. *Move!* She moved—but not quickly enough. The great hulking shadow became *him*. She stared at her hands, and swallowed back tears. He had caught her awake.

"What are you doing?" he asked.

"Looking at the water."

"If you fall in, there won't be anyone to save you. No one will hear your cries."

"I'm careful. The chain will keep me here."

"True, true." He gave an awful chuckle. "I want you to do something for me."

"Will you unchain me?"

"I'll take you for a car ride. Fresh air."

"There's plenty of fresh air here."

"Don't be cheeky."

Think Annie, think! There may be a chance of escape. She said, "Yes."

"You'll write a letter to your mother?" He was drooling.

He leaned too close to her and she wanted to spit in his face, kick him where it counted, and gouge his eyes out, but she forced stillness into her limbs. She could endure his reeking breath. She had to be free of the chain. But if he laid a hand … "What do you want the letter to say?"

"That you will be allowed to rejoin her if she will meet me."

He was mad—stark-raving. The way his eyes looked when he spoke about her mother—there was something wrong there, bent, like a bolt hadn't been screwed in right and now everything inside this man had fallen sideways.

Her insides hummed. He was lying. The stark knowledge of something terrible became clear in her mind: her mother was in danger, more danger than even she was in chained to a cave wall inside a mountain of rock. Her mother would not escape this danger because she would not have time to think, time to whittle away the rock from around the bolted pipe. "Sure," she said, "Where is the paper to write on?"

"I'll bring it next time I come. Perhaps tomorrow. You'll do it, then?"

"Yes." What choice did she have? It wasn't until he had gone away again that she wondered why he would let her go if she did what he asked. She knew his face. She knew he must live in or near the village. He looked familiar, like she'd seen him around the village, but not acting weird like he was when he was in here.

No, she didn't believe he would let her live. She grabbed the chain, furious at it. She pulled it and jerked it around trying to get it loose. She screamed until she was hoarse and fell to the mattress. Sobs wracked her. No, he wouldn't let her go. He would not care what happened to her after he had her mother. He would not bring her food, he would not take her filthy rags away to wash them, and he would let her die. One thing she knew—and it was real—he must not be allowed near her mother. She must think of something convincing to write, something that would give her mother a clue.

The tiny cuts along her arms and legs itched. One in particular on her left leg looked infected. She splashed the cold water on it. She washed the cuts with soap he had left her, but this one wouldn't get better.

35

Thursday afternoon

Ruth finished with her workout. The activity not only helped keep her strong physically, but it also helped her to think clearly. She still needed a walk or a jog in the lanes around the village and along the coast. The sky and the land worked together to open everything up with fresh air, birdsong, and the distant bleat of sheep. As she rounded a curve in the land, she startled a group of four wild ponies. They tossed their winter-thick manes and flicked their tails and moved up the hill away from her. She jogged past.

Her mother had gone through everything in her liquor cabinet. She must have some secret helper buying her more, because Ruth hadn't been to the grocery or the liquor store since Annie disappeared. Then there was Sam. He had shown up with his new tactic of moaning, moping and sighing. She wasn't sure it hadn't been Sam who stuck to her like a coat of paint that needed to be peeled off. Sam was likely her mother's liquor supplier.

She ventured along the cliff path to one of her favorite spots among a grouping of huge boulders. There was a place she could sit and look out at the sea, the color of jewels sparkling in the sun. The boulders sat around her like quiet companions. The air was pungent with the scent of new spring grasses. With her back against the sun-warmed rock, the chill of the breeze didn't bother her. She watched the sea where white horses danced across distant waves.

She reflected on the conversation she'd had that morning with Sergeant Perstow. He'd caught her sobbing in the churchyard and he'd asked her to walk with him as he was just going to pop in to see his lovely wife for his lunch break. He was so kind to patter on so cheerily. Then he had said the thing that set her to sobbing again, "God is still listening, lass."

And she had said, "Have you ever left someone in anger, determined to never speak again? And then you find you have to, because without speaking to Him again the world didn't need to go on and may as well end?"

He hadn't replied, only nodded. And she said, "I hadn't prayed in years; now I can't stand not to. But I left God for so long, I don't think He wants to hear from me. Why doesn't He answer?"

"Sometimes it feels like He has fallen asleep, p'r'aps?"

"I'm scrabbling around down here, useless, while my daughter needs me. I pray and pray, but nothing happens. She's alive. God must know where she is."

"I understand."

"No one believes me."

"He sends His angels to watch o'er us, lass."

"Where were the angels that Sunday morning, Mr. Perstow?"

"Watching. And where e'er she is, they're watchin' still."

"You believe me?"

"A mother knows her own. If you say 'tis true, lass, I've no call disbelievin' you."

She had hugged the sergeant and walked away from him, then took the cliff path where she could be alone. She leaned back against a boulder. She wished she could *believe* as thoroughly as Sergeant Perstow. An unfamiliar dark car turned into the lane below the boulder patch. The driver was too far away to identify. The car slowed, pulled into the layby, and stopped in the shade of some trees. The motor was switched off.

Peering down from her high perch she could see there was someone in the back seat. She stood taller to get a better look.

It was then that she heard the noise, like a muffled scream. Could someone be in trouble? She stepped down the path. The car's motor roared to life. Gears ground and belts shrieked. The car kicked up gravel as it spun into reverse and whipped back onto the road.

Was that a little girl's hand clutching at the back seat?

Her breath left her. By now the car was too far to read its plate numbers. An old dark car—the police were looking for the driver to help them with their inquiries. She ran. The car crested the hill and disappeared over the far horizon, traveling away from the village.

The creeper chained her again and left the cave and Annie alone. She screamed, "Come back here, you filthy bastard!"—the worst words she could think of.

He didn't come back.

She could hardly believe that she had been that close to her mother. The creeper had been driving. She was strapped to the seat in the back and couldn't see where they were. When he turned the motor off, she had scrabbled around and was able to free a hand and use it to pull herself up and peek over the back of the seat.

Her stomach hurt so much. She crumpled into a sobbing pile on the nasty mattress. She had only wanted to warn her mother, but her cries brought her mother closer to the car. If the creeper had gotten out of the car then, with her tied up in the back, her mother might have been hurt. She couldn't let him hurt her mother. She would have to be smarter.

She strained at the chain again. Her wrist was raw and painful where the metal cuff bit into her flesh. Rock dust flaked to the knobby floor beneath the pipe in the wall. She would clean it up, drop it down the hole. The bolt was wobbly. Her heart beat double quick. She would get loose.

She had enough length of chain to move to the rough toilet built over a hole in the cave floor, to the pool of water at the center of the area, and to lay on the pile of rags he called her bed. Every few days, she would wake up with clean sheets. The wake times and sleep times blurred together. She couldn't understand why. He left her soup sometimes. After the soup, she always slept. He must be doping it.

The reeking, padded mat that kept the cold to a minimum at night, the thing with the dangling button in one spot—he never cleaned it. She ripped the button off. It was a large, cloth-bound button, soiled around the edges. She pressed the side with the metal grommet into her palm, rubbing the smooth cloth side with the thumb of her other hand. So far, it was the only thing she had been able to reach that was not tied down or soft. But what could she do with a button?

Ruth rang the police from her mobile, but hung up before anyone answered. What would she say? She'd seen a dark car? The driver had been wearing gardening gloves? Light faded beyond the cloud-blurred horizon as Ruth made her way along the cliff path back toward the village. On the way she saw the sign for the short path to the Hasten Inn Bed and Breakfast, where Jon Graham was staying.

She could tell him that she saw her daughter. Yes, and everyone would think she'd lost her mind. She had to have something definite, right?

She wiped her sweaty palms along her jeans. The sore hand was healing well. She had seen Annie. Her daughter was alive. She knew it beyond a doubt before, but now, now she had absolute proof. Even if no one else believed it, she did. Thank you, Jesus, it was an answer.

She kept to the wider path and walked toward her cottage, but just as she stepped down to High Street, she paused and looked back. Fifty feet back along that path, the B & B sign stood. Okay, she was desperate. So what? She could at least press Officer Graham for answers.

Ruth hesitated after entering the B&B's entrance. Mrs. MacFarland greeted her and, when she learned why she was there, directed her to the guest's lounge. Ruth didn't want to barge in and interrupt, so she opened the door quietly. Jon was bent over a large dictionary-like book that lay open under a lamp.

He shut the anatomy book. He turned as she came in, and when their eyes met, his opened wide in shock. He said, "Mrs. Butler?"

"Excuse me, Mr. Graham," Ruth said, "something's happened."

"Tell me."

"I saw a little girl in a car. It was an old Renault. I couldn't read the plates."

"Was there something that led you to believe the little girl was in trouble?"

"Yes." She rubbed her eyes with her good hand.

Jon pulled out his mobile. "Where was this?"

"Up the cliff path, just south where there is a bend. It's private land and there is a lane with a place to park beneath the hill. The car pulled in there."

"And what happened?"

"I think the girl was screaming." She held a hand over her mouth, breathed deeply with her eyes closed, then put her hand against her chest. "I hope she wasn't hurt. But I think she saw me because she screamed when I stood up."

"I'm calling DCI Trewe, Mrs. Butler, if you will take a seat." Jon punched in some numbers. Trewe must have answered immediately. "Yes. Mrs. Butler is here at the B & B. No, she came by herself."

Ruth heard him sigh.

He quickly repeated what she had told him, then said, "She is here. I … yes, sir."

"What happens next?"

"They will get the description of the car and where it was seen last."

Ruth heard herself scream inside her skull. *That isn't enough!* Her hand throbbed. She searched to come up with a reasonable way to get him to talk to her about her daughter. "My daughter wasn't a drug addict."

He jerked back as if she'd slapped him. "Mrs. Butler, we don't believe your daughter was a drug addict. The drugs were probably injected by the killer."

"I overheard DCI Trewe say that the still photo was from a video. Mr. Graham … You gave it to me didn't you?"

"Yes."

"You saw a video of her? What was she doing?"

"It looked like she was talking to herself. She sees something—or someone—and she walks toward the shadows. That was all there was."

She noticed his face went very pale as he spoke of her daughter. She asked, "What do you think she saw?"

"I don't know." He stood and fidgeted, rearranging books, checking his mobile. "I wish I had something more to give you than flimsy platitudes. You're worth more than that."

"And the handwritten notes I couldn't read?"

"Tavy. Apparently it was his way of communicating when he was emotional."

"And no one told me that."

"That was a mistake. I'm sorry. When we discovered him missing, the notes were momentarily forgotten. There is no excuse for not communicating with you."

"What did you mean 'you're worth more than that'?"

He cleared his throat. "You've been through a lot. You deserve better."

"Why?"

"I … you just do."

She waited for more but he would not look up from his mobile. So she turned and left.

11:52 p.m.

He couldn't take as much blood as he needed. The child couldn't handle the loss without dying, and even on days when he did have enough, his stomach wouldn't bear more than a cup at a time. He knew that once the blood passed the stomach it did him nothing but good, but he hadn't figured out a way to get it in without drinking it—and blood goes bad too quickly.

Charles bent over the garden bench in his shed. His roses were doing wonderfully with the leftover blood. He used some for his nightly disguise, and the rest he poured into the drying trays with screening to keep the flies from feasting. Then he would mix the dried blood into top soil to lay out on the beds.

Even The Wife had commented on how youthful he was looking. His efforts were working. He was readjusting his physical being for the turning back of time.

He fixed his goggles to his face, careful not to let any of the plant material touch his bare skin. This particular poison could be deadly if absorbed through any mucus membrane. He hummed a tune under his breath. The concoction he made was odorless. The white powder was not tasteless, though. He knew he would have to invent a way around that.

36

Friday
Day thirteen

It was early evening by the time Jon was ready to meet with Trewe with what he thought were good arguments for reactivating a search for Annie Butler. Jon went to the Perrin's Point Police Station, but Trewe was not there. Strange, because he said he would be. He overheard Perstow remark that Trewe was out for blood today.

He entered Perstow's cramped office through the break room where there was another package of chocolate digestives. "Who are you talking to?" he asked Perstow. There was a square-shaped uniformed woman in Perstow's office. Jon read her name tag. "Ah, Mrs. Trethaway, we meet at last."

Perstow stood. "I don't wish to be here when DCI Trewe comes along. I was asked to wait until you arrived and now you're here." The jolly man waved and rushed away.

Police Community Support Officer Sue Trethaway had mouse-brown hair and three pairs of glasses draped or perched on her person. Introductions over, she began with a well-told story about her son and his car. Seems the old rattle-trap was in long need of mechanical help and in short need of petrol all of the time. Her son had a good job in medical sales but spent a fair portion of his salary on the needs of his car, so he still lived at home. That story ended when the phone alerted her to other business.

An hour passed with no word from Trewe. Jon reviewed notes on his smartphone, set up some to-do lists, and reread a few reports. He had eaten some of the chocolate digestives, washed down with some tea. He would not sit here waiting all day. He stood and brushed crumbs from his trousers. Trewe burst through the door carrying a sheaf of papers. "I'm having the DNA of the spittle analyzed."

Jon sat back down, a little taken aback with Trewe's abrupt entrance.

Mrs. Trethaway nodded and smiled at him from the doorway. She said, "I'll just make sure you're not disturbed." She shut the door behind Trewe.

Jon realized what Trewe had said. "Brilliant. There will be something with the other murders."

"New developments. Fingerprints found in Tavy's kitchen were sent to the Police National Computer." He let the papers fall on Perstow's desk.

"The PNC matched them?"

"Beggars belief, it did! Name of Charles Darrin."

"He signed some of his notes and emails as Charles. But I didn't see there were fingerprints with the other cases. How was there a match?"

Trewe shifted files. "Found at another murder scene."

"Really? Which one?"

"One that you don't have in your nice, neat little stack, Mr. Graham. His mother, when he was twenty. He had a job in Wales. Supposedly came home that weekend and found her dead." Trewe frowned. "Here's a grainy photo of the mother."

Jon took the photo. His breath caught.

"What is it?" Trewe asked.

"This looks like Ruth Butler."

Trewe studied the photo again. "There is a likeness."

"This could be a motive."

"Seems a stretch to say that. Why hasn't something happened to her before? No one has recently moved to the village." Trewe pulled his readers from a pocket and fit them across the bridge of his nose. He studied the photo. "What do we do about this?"

"We need to assign someone to guard her."

Trewe huffed, "We have all available manpower on this as it is."

Jon leaned back, and rubbed his temples. "I'll make it a point to watch out for her then. What else do we have?"

Trewe gave him a look. "And I'll make it a point to watch you."

"I'm only saying that if the killer, this Charles, killed his mother, and Ruth Butler looks like his mother … Well, she isn't safe."

Trewe pursed his lips as if he was about to argue, but then said, "We'll add some officers to keep an eye on her house. The profiler believes the killer is presently employed in a job where he can control his own hours. The situation may be complicated by multiple personalities. The killer may believe he is invincible and so will take risks. He may act perfectly natural most of the time."

"Anything in there about a stunted social background?"

Trewe looked at Jon over the glasses. "How did you know that?"

Jon shrugged.

Trewe continued reading. "He might have had a speech impediment, some physical deformity, or something less obvious. May have been obese as a child—one underlying cause of social inadequacy. Childhood obesity was not such an epidemic thirty or forty years ago. The problem led to self-image issues. He would have had either an authoritarian father or an overbearing mother—but not both—one who would use the other against the world or their child."

"In other words," Jon said, "if he had a bad father, the father would use the mother against the child, or the mother would use the father against the child, in order to weaken their resistance, to frighten them to death. 'Just wait until your father gets home!' that sort of thing. And we can link the Mother Goose nursery rhymes to childhood. What else do we know about him?"

Trewe glanced down at his notes. "Age at present: late fifties. He'd have to be in pretty good shape, too. He was fingerprinted at twenty, after his mother turned up dead. Not enough evidence to pin it on him. The bloody fingerprint was explained away apparently—tried to revive her or some such nonsense—but too many others died around him. Always an alibi at hand, had our Charles. His father only recently turned up—as an old skeleton. The age of the skeleton put Charles at about eight or nine years old, meaning that he probably wouldn't have been the one to put a bullet in his skull and drive him into the pond. Just an odd coincidence, is all. The headmaster of his school was ruled a suicide, but guess who was the first on the scene."

"Charles Darrin."

"Got it in one. Imagine a fourteen-year-old kid pushing his old headmaster from the school's roof."

"You could say he is quite experienced," Jon murmured.

"I don't know what sort of job he has, but he has a good knowledge of chemicals. Managed to drug the dog with a drug prescribed for stomach problems."

"Ulcer?"

"Irritable Bowel Syndrome. The drug contains Secobarbital. He had to drug the dog and wait until the dog showed signs of drowsiness to have a go at the old man." Jon busied himself stacking the files that were scattered across the floor beneath Perstow's desk so they wouldn't tumble to the floor if shifted. "Have you had the local chemist checked out?"

"Yes, he's been cleared."

"Has anything come up about the car that Mrs. Butler saw?"

"No. I expect he has a hiding place for it. Something well concealed."

"I like the theory of hiding in plain sight. How many people around here have a dark, old-model car?"

"I for one. Perstow does. A lot of people, I imagine. It isn't exactly an uncommon color for old-model cars."

Jon shook his head. All this Sturm und Drang and nothing was resolved. "At least we have a name."

"Yes." Trewe stood. "But, that's all I've got. I'll not hold you back from your busy schedule, Mr. Graham."

"I'm not so busy that I'd turn down a pint." He wanted to discuss things a bit more. A pint was always good for easy talk.

"Not even in your mission to keep an eye on Mrs. Butler?"

"She's got plenty of eyes in the daytime, Chief Inspector." Jon followed Trewe outside, where they turned to walk toward the beach and the Spider's Web. Jon paused to look out over the tiered houses. A sliver of sea gleamed under the cold, gray sky. The sun seemed to be taking a vacation this week, only making an occasional appearance for appearance's sake. "It won't be easy to find him, will it?"

"Not unless he keeps shutting up witnesses. He'll make a mistake. They all do."

In search of an honest man, he could try walking through the streets in daylight carrying a lighted lamp like Diogenes. He doubted he would discover many truly honest people. No life was completely open. Everyone had secrets and ulterior motives. No one was without guile. Motive wasn't evil.

In practical terms, each human undertaking could be boiled down to a few fundamental objectives: power, money or sex. So why was Charles Darrin killing? From what he could surmise from reading and rereading the files, it seemed the answer was power. It was likely that his true reasoning was unreasonable. The man was mad.

The pub was crowded and loud, but warm. There was a party in the public bar—a wake, of sorts, for Tavy. Through the pervading smell of food and beer, cigarette smoke moved in waves of intensity about the main room. The no-smoking rule must have been taken lightly here. But he wasn't one to disrupt the proceedings. He and Trewe found an empty table in the quieter snug where a few oldsters had settled in with their pints and their thoughts.

"What can I get you, Peter?"

"Milk."

"Really?"

"Don't drink much. Stomach." Trewe patted the flat area above his belt.

Jon had been impressed since first meeting Trewe at the shape in which he kept himself. He must be close to retirement age. For an old guy, he looked good. He made his way to the bar to place his order. Their glasses clinked as he set them on the table.

"Cheers," Trewe said.

They finished their drinks in a silence broken by Trewe when he said, "I'm starved."

"I'm for one of those Cornish pasties. I'll buy this time around. Milk again?"

"Water. I'll have a ploughman's. Next round of drinks is on me."

"I won't let you forget. Back in a tic."

Jon returned with their drinks. "The manipulation of the bodies shows order and intelligence. With the other bodies being buried in the manner they were, over the last thirty years, we could say he was rational and orderly. No one could have predicted Annie Butler would meet him that day. What made him act impulsively?"

Trewe shook his head.

Jon pursed his lips and said, "I think it has to do with the mother and Ruth Butler."

"Perhaps you're right. I will assign someone to patrol."

The bell rang to announce their meal was ready, and Jon brought the two plates to their table from the bar. They set about making short work of their meals. The Cornish pasty was everything it was supposed to be, a thick, steaming meat-and-vegetable concoction enclosed in flaky pastry.

Trewe said around a mouthful, "This morning a motorist came forward. He saw two men walking along the road on that Friday evening. One had a white beard and brown felt hat. Sounded like Tavy. The other, a younger man, wore a hat much like Tavy's."

"Sounds like the nephew." He picked a matchbook with the pub's name on it from a bowl at the center of the table. Even though the non-smoking rule had been implemented, there were still scofflaws and the pub's owner apparently looked the other way. He had a lot of matchbooks. It was an unofficial record of where he'd been.

"It was."

"You checked him out?"

"Very thoroughly. Only living relative. Inherits the house. Not much else. The day Tavy died, the nephew had already returned to his girlfriend's flat in London. Plenty of witnesses. Everything he says checks out, down to the hats. They purchased them together."

"The hats?"

Trewe nodded. "The nephew and he found them in a little shop in Port Isaac."

"My money's on the postmistress," Jon whispered. A group entered the snug and were noisily engaged nearby. He leaned closer and lowered his voice. He didn't want anyone listening in. "Knows a lot about the locals. Has a reputation. Nosey. Good ingredients for a killer."

"Good ingredients for a victim, too. Charles Darrin is a male."

"There's that."

"We examined Tavy's computer."

Jon had to raise his voice a bit to be heard over the swelling crowd. "What'd you find?"

"All the emails and poetry on it were written after Tavy's death. So the killer was spending a lot of time in Tavy's cottage."

"Likely why you were able to find a print."

Neither of the police officers noticed the older man sitting on the other side of the crowded table next to them pull a hat on, excuse himself and leave the pub.

37

Jon and Trewe had been so engrossed in conversation, the Friday night crowd and the noise of the pub could just as well have been down south in Port Isaac.

Trewe's mobile beeped. Trewe looked at it before answering. "Yes, Perstow?"

He stood abruptly, nodded a dismissal to Jon and left.

Puzzled, Jon followed on his heels, but by the time he'd exited there was no sign of Trewe. His mobile sounded. It was Ruth Butler.

"Mr. Graham, there's someone in my garden."

He swung around full circle, searching for Trewe. He started off at a run to Ruth Butler's cottage. "Do you recognize him?"

"No."

"On my way. Call 999." He took off through the car park and over the footbridge spanning the River Perrin. The pathway ended at the alley behind Ruth Butler's back garden. He craned his neck to see what he could over her garden wall, but could make out nothing in the dark.

The shadow of a cat slunk between dark patches. A dog barked. Jon raced through the alley to the narrow walk between cottages and to Ruth's front door. The cottage was dark. Jon approached the front door and knocked. "Are you all right in there?" No answer. Had something happened to her?

Two uniformed policemen arrived, breathing hard as if they'd run uphill, which they probably had. "Check the doors and windows," Jon ordered.

Flashing lights raked across windows along the length of the street. Tires squealed as car after car arrived in front of Ruth's home. Just then, Jon heard several locks click undone. The door opened. The smell of fried fish wafted out. Mrs. Butler clutched her dressing gown around her thin form. From the darkened doorway her scared face looked pale green in the flashing lights. "You came so quickly," she whispered. "He got away."

Shorter than Mrs. Butler, her mother peeked out from behind her.

"He didn't go by way of the alley. I would have seen him. Might I have a peek from your vantage point?"

Mrs. Butler stepped aside and pulled the switch on a floor lamp just inside her front door. She was standing so close to Jon he could have reached out and touched her. He wanted more than anything to be able to take her in his arms, tell her he would protect her from any harm, and promise he would always be there. All these thoughts went through his head, but at the same time he thought, *What am I thinking?* He said, "Show me where you saw him. Tell me what happened."

"Mom and I were leaving the kitchen. I turned off the lights and saw his shadow through the blinds. He ducked down."

"Can you tell me anything about him?"

"No."

"How tall was he?"

"Not tall."

"How long do you think he stood there?"

Her good hand moved up and out. "I have no idea. I dialed emergency first, then you. I was very quiet. He couldn't have seen me. When I put the phone down, he was gone. Look, I can take care of myself, but this sneaking business has made my mother and me jumpy."

An officer entered through the open front door. He spoke to Jon, "In the garden, sir."

"Stay here," Jon told Mrs. Butler.

In the garden, two uniformed officers held torches over a dark pair of men's shoes, neatly set beside the bins.

"Those were Tavy's," Jon said, shocked. "He keeps bringing her shoes, like a cat dragging a bloody mouse to its master." He bent and with the blunt end of a pen, tugged at the paper showing just inside one shoe. He had one of the gloved officers place the paper in an evidence bag and seal it. "Bag the shoes, too. Let's take this inside where we can read it properly."

As they reentered the sitting room, Trewe was standing with Mrs. Butler and her mother speaking into his mobile, "Perstow, we need tracking dogs."

Jon wondered briefly where Trewe had gone between leaving him at the pub and now.

The beautiful woman's frightened eyes were huge dark orbs in her pale face, when she asked Jon, "What is it? What's out there?"

"There were some men's shoes in your garden, Mrs. Butler," Jon said. He kept the bagged note behind him. No use worrying her further. He made eye contact with Trewe.

Trewe stepped between them. "I wonder if I might bother you for a glass of water?"

"Of course," Mrs. Butler said.

Mrs. Thompson struggled up from her chair. "I could use something a lot stronger than water. Wouldn't you gentlemen care for something more substantial, too?"

"No, thank you," Trewe answered.

The two women left the room.

Jon smoothed the note in the baggie flat and read aloud, "And we look ahead, into the bottomless lake where nothing awaits us but death. Enjoy our future, love. For your daughter's sake."

"Definitely not another Mother Goose rhyme," Trewe murmured.

Mrs. Butler reentered the room with her mother close behind her. Mrs. Thompson made an odd, choking sound. Jon glanced towards her. Her mouth opened and closed several times. Her eyes rolled upward. Her arms dropped. Her glass crashed to the floor.

"Get him!" Trewe shouted.

Jon turned. Behind Mrs. Butler, a man dressed completely in black stood in the doorway reaching for her. Something was off about his face—it was hidden beneath material wrapped and bunched around his face. Jon had a glimpse of the whites of eyes as he leapt to grab Mrs. Butler away from this monster. He tripped. The lamp went out. A high-pitched scream rent the air, followed by a thud, an "oof!" like someone had the air knocked out of him, then silence.

Jon waved his arms in the dark. He felt nothing but empty space where Ruth had been, but he caught and held on to the person slipping past him. "I've got him!" he yelled.

"No, you don't." Trewe's voice boomed in Jon's ear. Jon released his hold. And the lights came on. Trewe had flipped the wall switch.

Jon backed away. "Sorry." He plugged the lamp back into the wall socket. The lamp flashed on. "Who was that? Where is Mrs. Butler?"

The room was a mess of bodies and pillows and furniture. The puffy chair had been shoved against the settee. Mrs. Butler sat near an overturned chair cradling her hand.

Perstow appeared at the door rubbing at his face. Other officers entered through the kitchen. Trewe yelled at them, "Go! Go! A killer's running amok and you're playing in the garden."

"Did you see anything?" Jon asked Perstow, wondering at his convenient appearance.

"A man covered from head to toe in dark clothing ran from here."

Mrs. Thompson lowered a pillow away from her face. She squeaked, "Where's Ruth-Ann? Ruth-Ann!"

Mrs. Butler said, "I'm okay."

"My lands and stars!" Mrs. Thompson grabbed her daughter's good hand. They helped each other to stand. Mrs. Thompson swayed.

"Mom, sit here." Ruth led her mother to a chair.

Trewe turned to Perstow. "The dogs. Where are they?"

"Just arrived."

"Is anyone hurt?" Jon asked.

"That man grabbed me, but I gave him an elbow to the face before I fell." Mrs. Butler bent down behind the settee. She came up with a large white cat, tail fluffed to maximum size. "I must have stepped on Mandy at the same time. Did you hear her scream?"

Jon crossed the short distance between them and patted the fluffy, white cat. "Such an unnerving sound."

Ruth crumpled to a chair. She was trembling. "I was able to kick him but I don't think it had much effect. I think the cat startled him into running."

An officer entered and reported a rubbish bin on one side of the garden wall and a shed on the other side. It was an easy access to the garden. The wall's gate was locked from the inside. "Likely using that shed to climb in and out."

"Have you secured it?" Jon asked.

"No, sir."

"Do I have to give you instructions for everything?" Trewe shouted. "Do something 'bout it and call Constable Craig. Secure this house. Station someone at the front door. These women need to be kept safe!"

11:04 p.m.

Charles limped through the thick mists toward his cave, cursing the night. The chilly damp penetrated his clothing, but could not quench the hot fury that burned deep within. He rubbed his sticky palms against his jacket. The night's cloud-shrouded moon cast a pale shadow across his path through the swirling of the thick fog. The mists didn't hide anything.

Dogs could track him despite the wet mists. The scent of grass freshly crushed by his shoes would give him away. The mist made the scarves he'd wrapped around his face heavy with damp. He walked through the stream down to the cliff's edge. Surely the heavy air would bury his human flakes and spores beneath its clammy fingers.

Something was wrong with his leg. He had received a severe blow to one hip and now his foot was numb. He rubbed his chin where the woman had elbowed him. He couldn't figure out how or what had hit him in the leg. That noise. Bloody cat! He hated cats—smelly, germ-ridden beasts.

"Only a fool would enter the American woman's house like that."

He ducked down, limping faster, tears oozing out of his eyes. He didn't have to listen to her. He was a grown man.

The cold salt air filled his lungs, giving him strength. The whisper of waves crept into the dead stillness of the air. A cool finger of breeze touched his cheek. All would be well soon.

He reached the summit of his climb, turned, and stumbled along the cliff top. The mists wrapped around his legs, then dispersed in his wake. He had to make several sharp turns to find the reed-thin route. He limped down the narrow path carrying the bowl of fruit and cling-wrapped sandwich he'd hidden earlier. He pushed, then pulled the moss-covered twig door into place.

Inside the tiny cavern, he groped along the familiar walls, set the bowl down near the mattress, then found and lit a candle. He could hear his blood pounding in his ears, keeping time with the surf. On his knees before the small pool in the center of the cave, he cupped his hands into the cold, crystal clear water and splashed a bit of the coolness against his burning face and neck.

"Pain. And for what?" he muttered.

He removed his shirts. He was out of the wind but not the cold. He fired up the heater. He only used it at night during his experiments taking blood, and then he kept the heater away from the entrance. He didn't need infrared cameras finding him. From a supply of dry clothes he took two heavy shirts and pulled them, one at a time, over his head. He threw his old, smelly shirts across to the pile of rags. Glancing around, he nodded. This place had been a smuggler's lair, now it was his. It was far enough away from The Wife, which was a glorious thing.

His attempt to get the American woman had been thwarted again. For so many years, he had never seen her face as she puttered about the graveyard at the church, her head down. He'd never paid her the least bit of attention until the fete. She had been there, and she danced! He had seen her face. Her face! Since then his mother's voice grew louder and more insistent every day. He couldn't escape. Everything was spiraling out of his control and he had to wrest it back. How could he lure the American woman to his lair without giving the police a way to find him? These are the things he needed to work out.

Lifting the bowl of food, he checked the freshness of the sandwich's bread and placed it near the heap of rags. The plums were good ones. She better appreciate his efforts. The place carried a stench. He would replenish and wash the stash of clothes tomorrow; the place needed an airing. He'd already tried to take her on one outing, and it proved too much. Though she was bound and gagged, her screams had attracted attention. It was by chance the American woman was at the boulders at the same place and time he had planned to let the girl sit in the sun. Such an odd, out-of-place feeling *that* had been.

It was quite late, and he knew the girl would be asleep. He would be very quiet. Undressing from the waist down, he examined the bruise forming over his hip and shook his head. *What to do?* He splashed cold water on the bruise. It would be better tomorrow, perhaps. It would have to be—a limp would give him away.

Then, he positioned himself over the tiny pool in order to place the object of his true loathing directly into the water. He writhed and groaned with the pain from the frigid water until he could stand it no more. He pulled away gasping. He glared down at his shrunken member and nodded. "Serves you right."

The candlelight revealed several flashes of gold beneath the water. Amongst the gold pieces, four tiny white objects lay as if randomly cast. Four tiny white teeth. Their owner did not miss them.

38

Saturday
Day fourteen

Jon showered, dressed, and tromped down the stairs, looking forward to Mrs. McFarland's fresh vegetables and farm eggs. Steaming chafing dishes lined the dining room's sideboard. He carefully tipped their coverings back to check the contents: rashers of bacon, warm scrambled eggs, fried tomato, smoked herring; toast done to perfection slotted into a silver toast rack; homemade jams, butter, and clotted cream; boxes of cereal and bowls of muesli; and pitchers of milk and orange juice.

He shook out a linen napkin and laid it next to his place at the empty table. No other guests had made it downstairs as yet. This was lovely. He soon topped a full plate with a piece of toast and set it at his place. He poured a cup of hot coffee and took a seat.

The door opened on silent hinges. "Oh Inspector!" Mrs. McFarland stuck her head in. "I'm so sorry. Excuse me. I had hoped you wouldn't be disturbed after yesterday—I'm so sorry about that—but he said it was urgent!"

Mrs. McFarland had "flustered" down to an art.

"It's alright. Who is it?" He laid his fork down.

"Mr. Trewe. He is here, in the guest's lounge."

"Right." Jon stood up.

"If you'd like, I'll make you something fresh when you return." She picked his plate up. "A policeman's work is never done, isn't that what they say?"

In the guest's lounge, Trewe was perched on the room's one extravagance, a circular settee, complete with gaudy fringe, taking up the center of the room like a velvet mushroom.

Dark circles under Trewe's ice-blue eyes gave his pallid face a haunted look. He held up a sheet of paper.

"What is it?" Jon asked.

"A copy of a note stuck to my door this morning."

Jon took the sheet and read, " 'Birds of a feather, flock together, and so will pigs and swine. Rats and mice have their choice, and so will I have mine.' Mother Goose again."

"Yes." Trewe did not look well. He winced and sat straighter, then collapsed forward with a groan, his face livid.

"What's wrong?" Jon attempted to lay the man back but his knees came with him as if he was in a full body cramp. His eyes were closed. "Mrs. McFarland," Jon shouted. "Call for an ambulance."

Mrs. McFarland rushed into the room. "Oh dear me! Not the old trouble." She ran out of the room, shouting, "I'll call for an ambulance."

Trewe stirred. His eyes opened. "What's happened?"

Jon kept his hand on his shoulder. "Take it easy, man."

"I'm fine. It comes and goes."

"It?" Jon stared at Trewe. The man didn't answer; his eyes were closed again. "Mrs. McFarland!" Jon called, "The ambulance!"

"Ambulance?" Trewe's eyes opened. He struggled under Jon's arm.

"Relax, man."

"Don't you dare! No ambulance!" Trewe sputtered. "If I need to go to hospital, I can bloody well drive there on my own. Leave off!" He pushed Jon away.

"You're not well."

"I'm fit as a bloody fiddle." Halfway to an upright position, he bent over double with a groan. "Bugger all!" he said, in a choked whisper. "Damn it to hell! I'll die in hospital!"

It didn't take long before an ambulance screeched to a halt outside the inn. Though bent double, Trewe insisted he walk to the stretcher. He complained the entire time. "I've things to do! This investigation needs me. Who'll feed the chickens?"

Though he *did* wonder about the chickens, Jon assured him he would see to everything. As the ambulance doors closed, he heard Trewe yell, "Call Perstow!"

Jon shook his head and ran both hands through his hair. Trewe had the entire department on edge. All the noise in the world couldn't disguise it; the man was scared to death. Why was that?

Trewe's well-being had now become a priority among many priorities. Which would be the urgent and which would be the immediate? And which of the immediate urgent would become the most important? He would follow the ambulance south to the hospital to make certain Trewe was well and settled. On the way to the hospital he passed the morgue. It wouldn't take a minute to stop and check on Tavy's post-mortem.

Pathologist Roger Penberthy held a jar of orange opaque liquid up to the light as Jon entered. The man's white mustache bristled. "Sorry to hear about Peter."

"How'd word get out so quickly?"

The man pointed to the radio nearby and Jon saw the long insect-like antennae. "I listen to the calls. Like to know what to expect."

Jon swallowed. *That's morbid.*

The man spoke in a thoughtful manner, his blue-veined hand touched his chin. "Can't imagine what could be the matter with Trewe. He's tough as nails. I'll drop by on my way home. You asked about Mr. Tavish's age? Nineties, and he's been dead since last Saturday afternoon, I'd say."

"How'd you come to your timeline so exactly, Dr. Penberthy?"

"Insects, flies, you know, cycle of life—we measure the stage of the insects in the body, and there you have it, to the day. Contents undigested of the stomach—egg—so his last meal was breakfast, I imagine."

Jon's stomach rumbled in disgust. "I'll take your word."

"One more thing."

"What's that?" Jon asked.

"He didn't have long for this world anyway—a month, maybe two. Our time is in God's hands. Who knows the hour?"

"You're saying?"

"He had lung cancer—inoperable, metastasized to the lymph nodes, liver, and brain."

Jon thanked the coroner and left. He wondered if Tavy had known.

When Jon entered the hospital ward, he found Trewe sitting up in a bed at the end of a long row of beds, most occupied. Jon stopped at the end of Trewe's bed. With eyes closed, the man's face looked almost peaceful. Trewe's eyes opened.

Jon asked, "What's wrong with you?"

"What?" Trewe muttered through cracked lips. "No preliminary small talk? No, 'How are you? Glad to see you're alive.'? You'd best be watching that. Someone may suspect you'd been hanging about with the likes of me." Trewe grimaced, though it may have been a smile. "The doctors know damned little, and what they do know would fit in that shit bottle. Here and I thought it was my heart. They say no. They've got me on bloody awful clear liquids. Don't happen to be carrying a spare pizza under that coat of yours? No? They'll run tests tomorrow—early morning. Going on some horrid fast starting at midnight."

"They'll get to the bottom of this, surely."

"Don't say bottom. That's one of the tests." Trewe moved uneasily under the covers. Glancing around, he waved Jon closer. "The curtains have ears and I want information. They'll figure something out about me by tomorrow. Can't keep me in here too long taking up a bed. Have you learned anything new about Tavy's death?"

Jon leaned in and explained what the coroner had told him about Tavy. Then he said, "You've got my number. I'll post a constable outside the ward's door. No, don't argue. The note taped to the door at your house this morning was addressed to you, not me. I'll be around again this evening."

"No, don't come. I insist." Trewe fluffed his pillows. "I've arranged for you to take charge till I'm out of here. You'll have plenty to do."

Jon stared for a moment and then said, "Why?"

"Why do I leave an investigation such as this in your hands? Because I was too stubborn to listen to a capable and inventive young man."

Jon was shocked speechless.

Trewe raised his voice, "But don't expect an apology!"

"Yes, sir."

"Just shake it up and see what falls out."

"Yes, sir."

Jon drove north to Perrin's Point. From the hospital it was about an hour's drive. His mind filled with lists of things to prepare for the general assembly's direction tomorrow morning. He made verbal notes on his mobile. The blue posters requesting any information concerning Annie Butler were still tacked up on notice boards or on shop windows. Some were already in tatters.

He slipped in the back door of the police station and startled Perstow who was going through papers on the desk Jon had been using which he had moved into the former holding cell.

"Oh! Sorry. Only straightening this for you." Perstow continued to pick up papers and place them in piles. His ears flamed red.

Jon filed away his suspicions. "I understand there is a psychologist's profile report. Is it here?"

"Yes. I was just seeing that." Perstow went around the desk, reached over to one pile, and glanced through quickly. "Not here." Scratching his head, he went into the other room and came back with the report.

"Something wrong with your leg Perstow? You're limping."

"Slammed the gate on a toe." Perstow's blue eyes creased to a squint. Funny how his eyes receded into his face when he smiled, like a shark when feeding. "Thank you for your concern, sar."

"I just met with DCI Trewe in hospital."

"I was not surprised he put you in charge, sar."

"Well, I was. He mentioned the investigation's been stepped up?"

"Combinin' Mr. Tavish's murder investigation with Annie Butler's. Trewe had already arranged several interviews with the murders team. Ye'll be wanting to attend the last few?" Perstow took on the persona of an eager puppy.

"Yes. Any leads, anything new?"

Perstow's face took on a tragic cast. "No, sar."

"Thank you, then." Jon dropped the papers to his desk. He didn't like a curt dismissal but he had so much to do before tomorrow. He reread the psychologist's criminal profile, and likewise an analysis of Charles Darrin. Mother issues, yes. He was suspected of murdering his mother—slit her throat. What were the mother issues that would suddenly come into play here after being benign for so long? Was this why he was after Ruth Butler? What would he do if he got her? Kill her as he had his mother? Stands to reason.

He was surprised when he glanced at the wall clock. It was still morning. So much can happen in a moment. He picked up the phone and called the incident room. He spoke to an officer and told him he wanted a twenty-four hour watch over Mrs. Butler.

He gave a quick perusal to the other reports that had accumulated. He gathered up the things he wanted to study further and added those to his briefcase to take with him. He put other reports in a stack. At the china board, he drew a diagram against an area map, correlating the time and location of each incident into a rough timeline—the time he entered the area, the moment that Annie was taken, the car bashing he received, the finding of the girl's body in the surf, and the finding of Tavy's body on the side of the cliff.

It was logistically possible for one person to have managed the harassment of Mrs. Butler and all of the other incidents. That is, if someone spent his entire time completely devoted to stalking her and tacking mad lines of drivel on doors.

Just as Jon was leaving, he ran up against Perstow again. The man skulked soundlessly. If he were not such a jovial man he might be creepy.

"I just had the thought, sar," Perstow said and handed two sheets of paper to Jon. "The DCI may have commented on what else we found on Tavy's computer."

Jon read aloud, "In marble walls as white as milk, and lined with skin as soft as silk, within a fountain crystal clear, a pail of wealth doth appear. No doors there are to this stronghold. No one can enter and steal my gold."

A pail of wealth, gold! Perhaps he should see the police commissioner about another officer brought in to reactivate the fraud investigation of Trewe. But Trewe was as helpless as a baby in hospital. How could he be the killer? No, it wasn't Trewe. Someone else had wealth, but not enough to look suspicious.

Perstow rubbed his elbow and shook his head sadly. "If you don't need me, sar, Her Indoors has it in mind to create a garden patio of sorts. It is Saturday, an' all."

"Sounds like work to me."

"It'll get done drekly, or it'll be the end of us. There's the phone. I'll just get that first." Perstow scooted back into his office to answer the persistent ringing.

Jon was familiar with the local word "drekly." In the slow pace of life here, there were a lot of things done "drekly." *Let us only hope murder is solved a lot quicker.* Jon tacked his timeline to the note-crowded china board. He would take this to the morning parade tomorrow.

Perstow cleared his throat and held the phone away from his ear. "Beggin' yer pardon, sar."

"Just on my way out," Jon said.

"Walkers have found a pink windcheater buried in the sand at the beach."

"Probably from a beach outing last weekend. Get Stark and the other constable on that. I've got a scheduled appointment and then I will stop by and check on Mrs. Butler. After that incident last night, I want to make sure she is doing well. Do you know where Constable Craig is?"

"She was interviewing one of the lads who works at the Nap."

"Tell her to meet me at Mrs. Butler's in an hour, please. I'm off to meet with Mr. Malone. After that, I'm conducting a telephone interview with the nephew. Just for my own peace of mind."

"You're visiting Mr. Malone?"

"He said he had some historical notes on Cornwall to show me. May help, he said. Looks as if we're grasping at straws just now. It's good to have such citizens willing to help out." Besides that, he was one of the wealthier citizens of Perrin's Point. His house was on the national registry, not that that meant much. It might be an ancient tip pit.

There was a visitor information kiosk in the car park across from the Spider's Web. Jon needed directions to the estate called Medlingham. It wasn't but a mile away by car, but the cliff paths would take him there faster. Apparently, Medlingham was the property just south of the B & B where he was staying. The skies were clear, so he decided to walk.

On the way, he watched the water, the waves, and his footing as the path had a tendency to dip or twist unexpectedly. An unsettled feeling of something left undone invaded every other thought.

He arrived at his destination, Medlingham spelled out in an iron arch near the entrance. He walked down an impressive drive, catching glimpses of a tower before him. Just as he came to the front of the large brick house, he observed a garden gate surrounded by huge fuchsia rhododendron. Curious, he walked closer to peer through the gate. He saw a lone stone wall, glassless window set high, and what remained of a Palladian tower attached—ancient ruins. What had befallen the original house? Wind? Rain? Damnation?

He walked up the pathway to the door of the newer house, a neatly symmetrical Queen Anne style country estate house that looked like it may have been built around 1700. Indeed, there was a small marker near the front step.

Green tufts of lichen grew in the crevices of the flagstone, softening his footsteps. Pressing his finger against the bell push, he could hear the chime faintly resound from a great distance. Footsteps approached the door. He anticipated a butler. The door swung open and Mr. Malone stood one step above, smiling down at him.

"Hello, Chief Inspector!" Mr. Malone stepped back. "I'm sorry, I meant Inspector. I was just thinking of Peter Trewe, poor man. I understand he is in hospital?"

Jon stepped inside. "Word travels fast."

The entry led into a longer hall. A staircase twisted around and up. Rugs on the floor brightened the polished stone.

"Yes, yes! In a small community such as ours the grapevine works extremely well. Extremely well. Much to our chagrin or benefit. Can be a benefit." Mr. Malone stepped aside and opened a door to the right.

The brightness of the room left Jon dazzled. He had noticed the open curtains in the wide, tall windows across the front of the house. Overstuffed white furniture pressed into the white fitted rug that looked as if it had never seen a shoe. The only color in the room came from oil paintings set like jewels against the white walls—nothing large or flashy, just expensive. There were no photos or small objects of any kind.

The one thing missing to create a picture perfect for a home magazine was a great slathering beast of a hound ensconced next to the fireplace. But this room couldn't afford a living, drooling canine. It was too perfect. The place smelled of disinfectant, like a hospital. The walls teamed up at him. He needed an open window.

"You look pale, officer. Pale."

"Just a bit claustrophobic."

"I'll open a window." Mr. Malone opened the window, which swung out. "Take a seat."

Jon took Mr. Malone's suggestion and sat on the puffy settee, hoping he didn't have anything on his trousers that would rub off. He noticed with regret his shoes had left marks on the carpet. He pointed at the mess. "Oh no! I am sorry."

"Not to worry. Liz will know what to do."

"Liz is your wife, then?"

"Yes. Good woman. Yes."

"She's home then?"

"No. Visiting friends for a few days." He fluttered his hands. "She'll be sorry to have missed you. We don't receive many visitors. Not many visitors at all."

"I'm not imposing on your time?"

Mr. Malone's thick eyebrows drew closer. "My time?"

"You said you were something of an expert on history."

Mr. Malone went to a table near the window. He rubbed the table with a hand, as if searching for unseen dust. "Used to teach it. Used to. What are you needing? History of Cornwall in general?"

"Tell me about the pirates of Cornwall."

Mr. Malone gave a curt nod and put his hands behind his back. "Before I begin, can I offer you something to drink? I was just going to have an afternoon sherry."

"I regret I'm on duty."

Malone opened an impressive wardrobe-type cabinet. "You don't mind if I do?"

"Of course not. Go ahead."

Malone poured and took a swallow. "Good. Good."

"Mr. Malone, you volunteer at the library but I don't see very many books. You must have a library."

"I don't care to display them. Ostentatious. Spoils the color scheme. I keep my books upstairs. Private library. Private."

"I beg your pardon. I didn't mean to offend."

"None taken. None taken." He took another swallow. It didn't take a moment for the man's demeanor to relax into a litany of stories so well told that Jon found himself listening with interest and enjoyment. The pirates had used the rough coast and the jutting harbors to their advantage again and again. Smugglers, too, had been a huge source of income for the residents of Cornwall for centuries. Mr. Malone finished with "I hope that answers some of your questions."

"It does. You have a way with stories, Mr. Malone." He stood up, prepared to leave. After some awkward remonstrations, Mr. Malone trailed him to the door. At the top of the steps Jon turned back. "You seem knowledgeable about many things. Is there something you can tell me about the history of herbs in England?"

"Oh my, my! I'm not an expert. Liz is the gardener." He leaned against the closed door and studied Jon. "One can learn a lot about herbs on the Internet."

"I expect I could find most of my questions answered on the Internet." Jon paused. "But my computer … er … crashed recently, I'm afraid. I have my mobile with internet, but the screen is small."

"Amazing how dependent we can become. Amazing." Malone appeared flustered. "My computer isn't acting right. Can't figure the bloody contraption—"

"I'm somewhat knowledgeable," Jon interrupted him.

"Liz would be extremely irate if I let anyone touch her computer. She has said it responds best with her. I expect when she returns she'll know what to do or take it in to get fixed. You see, there's a chance she'll know how to fix the thing. A chance."

"Mrs. Malone is a computer expert as well, is she?"

"An inalienable right of the young, being computer savvy. Born with it." Mr. Malone grinned. "I'm preaching to the choir."

Jon nodded.

"I expect she'll be back shortly," Malone added.

Jon took another step down. "Thank you. No. I'll take myself off. Thank you for your time."

"I certainly wish I could have been more helpful. I offer help and then turn out to be useless."

"No, no! You have helped. I found your stories full of information."

"I'll make us tea," Ruth Butler's mother, Mrs. Thompson, announced as Jon entered Mrs. Butler's cottage. Allison Craig followed.

"They may want coffee," Mrs. Butler said. "Would you, Mr. Graham?"

"Coffee would be nice."

Mrs. Thompson shook her head, "My land and stars! Coffee! What was the revolution for then? Do you like it strong?"

"Yes, thank you very much indeed."

"That's my kinda guy, Ruth-Ann."

Jon remained standing as Allison Craig took a seat next to Mrs. Butler on the couch. He had briefed the constable about what he would tell Mrs. Butler. Mrs. Butler was as beautiful as ever, though some bruises remained. She wore a flowing dress that accentuated her shape and form. He cleared his throat to give himself time to get over it. "Have you recovered from the fright with the stranger in the garden?"

Her eyes narrowed. He wasn't winning any "favorite's awards" here. She said, "We are survivors, not victims. He wants us to be victims. We refuse. You look tired. Why don't you sit?"

"The line of inquiry we're working on has everyone on edge. Everyone is busy. But I have a twenty-four hour watch over you."

Her mother brought in a silver coffee service set, and left again. The coffee set looked old and ornate, not really what he would have expected, but then it seemed nothing about Mrs. Butler was typical.

"A twenty-four hour watch? Why?"

"I believe he is after you."

"What about my daughter? This line of inquiry has to do with my daughter?"

"Possibly."

"You're either being obnoxiously cryptic on purpose or I'm just dense." Mrs. Butler poured and handed him a cup. "Please say what you've come to say and get it over with."

"This person left shoes at the front of your house and at the back. Shoes are symbolic."

"Of?"

"Travel, either a desire to go, to be somewhere else, or to escape."

"Would the fact that we traveled here from somewhere else be significant?"

"The first time something weird is found with a body, it's simply an odd thing. Second time? Coincidence. The third time some object is found with a body, it becomes the killer's signature."

"Keep going."

"Now, with Tavy's body being found, we have a fourth body found with herbs. We have shoes."

Her eyes grew large.

"The DNA isn't back from the lab yet. Getting your hopes up would be the worst thing you could do."

"Then why are you concerned?"

"There is still a girl missing without a body being found."

She seemed dazed. "You do believe me."

"Do not get your hopes up, Mrs. Butler."

"Can't you call me Ruth?"

Annie shivered. Weird noises came from the hole that she used as a toilet. At times, the wind howled across the hole. Other times it moaned. It was as if the wind copied her agony.

There was nothing warm. The heater hardly helped. She wore layers. She covered herself in the spare bits of clothing and the mattress and the quilt. It didn't matter. She could not stop shivering. Sometimes the sun shone across that outside mat-covered opening. The dapples on the wall opposite her taunted her with their possible heat and nearness. She strained to get close and only tore the skin under the metal wrist clasp.

Her arm hurt, her head hurt. The cut on her leg was drippy, the skin around it hot to the touch. When she was awake she would work at loosening the pipe in the wall. Then she'd make sure to pile the rags to hide her progress.

She would escape. If she could only stand without shaking. Her knees gave out. She had to get out and warn her mother. *Don't trust him, mummy. Don't listen to him. He is a liar. He wants to hurt you.*

Tears only made her head hurt worse. She didn't feel like moving much anymore.

Hunger gnawed inside like maggots at rotten meat. The creeper brought food on an irregular basis, enough dry bread to last a day or two before turning damp and disgusting. She threw it down the waste hole, wondering how far down the hole went and what was down there besides the rotted food and her waste—and whether she should try to jump.

The night before he'd left a sandwich. The day before he'd left some cheese. She still had an apple and a plum. Two days before he'd brought some cereal packed in a plastic container. She hadn't eaten it fast enough. He took it away the next time he came.

One time he brought her a bowl of spaghetti with red sauce and a meatball. It made her throw up.

He didn't bring her paper and pen to write the letter he wanted from her after the incident when he had taken her outside.

She had scratched her own marks on the wall by her bed with the metal grommet of her button. That is what the other girl had done. She'd scratched marks on the wall to count the days she had been here. So many marks, she couldn't stay awake long enough to count again. Some crossed each other out or overlapped. Had the other girl gone crazy after a while? The deep gouges represented desperate, she was sure of it. Would she get to that point, too? Could she do something hurtful to that man before she went bonkers? How long does it take to go bonkers?

Saturday afternoon

Jon waited for the connection. When he had it he asked, "Mr. John Burns?"

"Speaking."

"Jon Graham here. You are Mr. Tavish's nephew?"

"Tavy's nephew. Yes."

"I just wanted to confirm details you've already provided, and to check that there wasn't anything else."

"Only too happy to help. I can hardly take it in that he's dead."

"Did you know he was dying of cancer?"

There was a long pause. Jon waited. Finally Burns said, "He told me. He also said that he believed in living life to its fullest, you know." There was a catch in the man's voice. Either he was a good actor or he really was mourning his uncle.

To give him some time to pull himself together, Jon cleared his throat. "I understand you both bought hats together?"

"My mother used to tell me how I was the image of Uncle Tavy. She started it. Buying us the same shirt in two sizes when I was a lad. We bought the hats in Port Isaac late last month."

"Is there anything you can think of about that last time you visited that had you wondering about his state of mind?"

"Yes, as a matter of fact. I remembered after my interview with your sergeant. My uncle was boxing some things up in his house. I asked him what that was about, and he said that he was preparing to leave. I asked him where he was going and he seemed vague. Didn't actually answer me. Later, when I heard the details of his death and how bad his cancer was, I was shocked. But then I got the boxes in the mail. He'd sent me some of his best ship models." It was here the man's voice cracked and Jon could hear a sob. "Look, Mr. Graham. Could we talk some other—"

"Don't worry yourself further," Jon said, quietly. "I won't be calling you. If you have anything more to add, you've got my personal mobile number."

The interview only proved that Tavy did know that he would die soon. He was parceling out his best belongings. It made Jon wonder if knowing of his imminent death made Tavy a little more careless of his safety, but the catch was that the old man loved that dog most of all. He would have held onto her until he couldn't any longer and then seen to it that she was cared for. So, someone put an abrupt stop to Tavy's life when the old man wasn't looking.

He couldn't believe it was still Saturday. Jon put files in order, checked over reports from the police team and compiled his own reports. He never put off until tomorrow what could be accomplished today. Finished at last, he hurried back to the Hasten Inn. With the sun setting over his shoulder, he climbed the steps from street level to the entrance. He passed a sign reading "Garden" with an arrow pointing left, and he paused for a moment thinking it would be pleasant to enjoy the sunshine while he could. He entered the courtyard to sit on a bench. The cold of the stone leached through his woolen trousers.

Tomorrow would be a big day, and yet, he still could find no plausible evidence to renew the search for Annie Butler in an official capacity. It had been two long weeks. Reports had her health as excellent, so he could only hope she could hold up. He was certain the body they now had was the other girl. She had lived in captivity almost six months, being bled out slowly, losing her health, her teeth, her hair. He hadn't bled out his victims from long ago, so why was this man doing it now? What could he possibly gain?

Time. The passage of time meant he was getting older. He didn't want to get older. He couldn't molest the child, so he took her blood instead? A vampire in the making. He could rule out organic reasons. If there were someone with a blood disorder or need, with all the information they had fed to the press, they would have known of that person through witness reports. Nothing unusual had surfaced. How was he using the blood he took? What had it to do with the passage of time? Because he craved their youth? That could be a reason.

Children go missing all over the world. How many other victims had there been? Where were their bodies? This murderer had been practicing for a long time. That's the reason Victoria Benton had remained alive as long as she had. He drained their blood a little at a time, to keep them alive as long as possible. He was an expert at it.

Where could the killer keep his victims alive and how was it no one had noticed? A basement? A hidden room? But people don't normally hide others away without someone else becoming suspicious at odd noises. Walls aren't so thick that screams wouldn't go undetected with everyone on high alert, unless the perpetrator kept his prisoners some distance from civilization. If so he would still have to feed them and bring water if he wanted to keep them alive yet remain undiscovered.

The stacked rock wall, covered in vine cast a deep shadow over the B & B's garden entrance. Protected from strong wind, potted palms anchored the scheme of things like sentries battling with rattling fronds against the breeze. A chill passed through him as he stepped into the deep shadows of the evening garden.

Out of the corner of his eye, he saw that something didn't fit in with the rest of the garden. A figure waited patiently. He turned sharply. From the shadows Mrs. Butler stood watching at him.

WEEK THREE

Time's Past

“Light breaks where no sun shines;
Where no sea runs, the waters of the heart
Push in their tides.”
– Dylan Thomas –

39

Sunday morning
Day fifteen

Jon fought sleep then slept anyway. Images of Tavy alive and of Tavy dead floated in and out of his dreams. He tried to apologize to the old man, only to watch him turn away and disappear into mists. Then the nightmare really began—a table, a black cross grid on a large, white piece of paper with him racing to stick letters squarely into the puzzle. He knew the answers and inserted the letters as quickly as he could, rushing against a ticking clock. He couldn't move fast enough. The letters screeched. He overturned the table. The table came back around to attack. He fell through a thick, gray mist smelling of mint mouthwash. He woke with a thud. The screeches hadn't stopped—gulls.

He lifted his head off the pillow. A headache pounded around inside his skull, louder than the birds. What had he had last night for drink? Wine—he remembered the wine—had he had too much? The few locals he had spoken to hadn't been helpful. He pushed himself up.

Pots and pans clashed from a long way off—or was it church bells? Probably both, with it being Sunday and with Mrs. McFarland bustling about downstairs in her kingdom.

Clawing his way to the door, he opened it. A rush of cooked breakfast odor hit him. With a groan and much effort, he stumbled down the hall, gripping his pajama bottoms so they wouldn't slip to his ankles.

Before leaving his room, he had checked his smart phone. Half ten. How had he slept so late? The ringing church bells seemed far away. He took church in small doses when he had to, like medicine. Although he didn't think about God often, he had come to a place, not so long ago, where he realized he had squeezed an incorporeal God into a corporeal place the size of his smart phone—silly, really. Improvements should be made, adjustments to his beliefs, because he did believe in a higher power, one that was bigger than his mobile.

All this thinking likely stemmed from his discussion with Ruth last night. *When did I start thinking of her as Ruth?* Even if she had asked him to call her that, protocol dictated he remain formal in his dealings with the victim's mother. He intended to follow protocol, even though she was devastatingly beautiful.

Their conversation had rattled him. What if he were in her position? Would he have the kind of faith she had? Struggling with it as she was, she still held a deeply rooted faith. Would he feel as confident that his loved one would come back to him if their roles were reversed? He doubted it. And he hated to see that she felt that way. It would just lead to a soul destroying blow if her daughter was dead.

He winced from the cold water he splashed on his face, and thought about how we live in a sinful world and the best people have to endure it as hell. He was leading a group of investigators today in a murder inquiry. How was he supposed to present facts and set about leading a team of investigators in a clear and concise way with his own thinking so muddled?

The sun shone as he climbed into his car. Distant dark clouds foretold a storm. He stopped at the hospital. Trewe was snoring. On the bedside tray were the remains of his breakfast: one empty juice container. Must mean more tests.

He took off for the incident room in Perrin's Point. He would keep the car nearby because he might need it later. But driving meant he had to go the long route through the streets lined with cottages and shops. He passed a field of daffodils. On the sea side of the road to his left, a lopsided tree punctuated the bare rolling hills, and between hills were glimpses of water, the palest blue against a pale and endless beyond.

How would they catch the killer with no leads? The only thing left to do was to restart a full-scale search for Annie Butler again. They couldn't afford to wait for DNA.

He put a call in to Superintendent Tom Bakewell. He proposed another search.

Bakewell exploded. "What? Have you lost your mind?"

"We've had two murders now. It will be three unless she is found."

"The murder investigations team found nothing to suggest that the girl is still alive and nothing to suggest that the body is not the girl's. You're dreaming, wishful thinking, and all that."

"My 'dreaming' and 'wishful thinking,' as you call it, have nothing to do with … Never mind. I believe the search for the girl should begin immediately and should be much more thorough and broader in scope."

"You've got something on your mind besides the girl, and it may not have anything to do with anything, but I can hear it in your voice. I know you too well."

Jon took a deep breath. "I would rather not talk about it."

"You must."

"It's a stupid crush on the victim's mother."

"Use yer loaf, man," Bakewell huffed—Jon could tell he was considering what he would say next—"How will you feel about the poor woman next week, next month, next year? I've never thought you anything but the sanest young man I've ever known, but now this. The problem is your vision is clouded. I don't think you've been a bit rational in anything. This is where this request is coming from."

Life is a fragile thing. It was true that seeing the victims of murder had a sobering effect. Dealing with the families was an extremely sensitive sort of thing. Special officers were trained to do just that. He was not one of them. He said, "I believe I'm being reasonable. Another search for the girl—"

Bakewell interrupted, "Your timing—"

"And you're one to educate me on the finer points of love?"

"Are you referring to something that happened over twenty years ago? I could have you recalled, inspector!"

Jon registered this. His job really was on the line here. He swallowed. "You could have at least warned me."

"Never mind about that. Trewe and I have more than the past that keeps us at odds. Have you ever spoken to the man?"

"Of course! He does his job well. I haven't a notion about the other thing."

"And that is precisely why you are there."

"Murder has gotten in the way."

"Well, just keep your bleedin' snout away from Mrs. Butler. What a time to think of such things."

"I've fallen for her without a hint of anything on her part."

"DI Bennet is more than willing to take your place. You've got three days before you either have some concrete evidence and a report on my desk or I send him down. Any questions?"

"No, sir."

"Good," Bakewell said, then he murmured, "Hope you come to your senses before you make a fool of yourself."

Annie flew away, out of the cave, straight across the sea to a warm place—Texas. Her American relatives waited for her. Hugs. Warmth. The smell of food cooking. Chattering speeches.

Loud screeches.

She cringed, covered her ears. No, not warm. She had never been to Texas that she could remember. She lay on her pallet covered in the heavy quilt. The gulls beyond the door made a terrible racket.

Would she ever get to go visit her mother's family? She hardly knew them, though they were connected on the Internet. She'd never felt her grandmother's hug. She imagined it would be much like Sally's smothering hugs. She wouldn't mind it if she could only get loose.

Her mum never spoke of her father. She'd peppered her with loads of questions. Where was he? What did he do for a living? What did he do that was so wrong that she couldn't see him?

Was the creeper her father? No, he couldn't be. A father would never be so cruel to his daughter.

She wanted to go away again—go away in her mind. Hours and hours would go by while she thought and imagined and dreamed of not being where she was—in the real. She hated the real.

The thumping again. She hated the thumping, the tick of gears. It came from behind, inside the wall.

The first time she heard that thumping sound she had been dreaming of lying on the beach with her toes in warm sand. The sound of waves became a thumping hum. Then the sound was sucked away. That split moment or two of silence forced her to snap out of her dream and sit up in a horrid crash landing.

The bowl from the previous night's food was gone. She hadn't heard the twig door. A bit of rag hung midway up, in a crack on the wall behind her. The creeper had another way in, a secret door.

She didn't need to hear him any more to know he was there or that he had been there while she was out of it. He left a sickly sweet smell behind.

She curled up, trembling. She pulled the mattress pad over her head and clutched tight fists against her chest.

There were more jars of blood. Hers was there now.

She woke up again. In front of her was a little crate. On the crate was paper and a pen.

Now to put her plan into action. She had to make a way for her mother to escape.

40

PERRIN'S POINT INCIDENT ROOM

The incident room had been scrubbed of its former fishy smell. Come to find out, the development had stalled. Apparently, the economic disaster affecting the entire world had reached even the deepest of pockets in Cornwall. Funny how the bigger picture can take years to trickle down so far. There was talk of things looking up in America, and the political-television talking heads were taking this to mean this "hope"—whether real or imagined—would affect the rest of Europe eventually. At present, unemployment roiled on this side of the great pond.

The building had been renovated to look much as it must have for a couple of centuries, with brick, crumbling stucco, and purposely aged gray board. According to the notice board, the new "old" façade was to attract the buyer looking for a bit of history to live under, but with all the latest in electronics and appliances. Even the open sheds along the side facing the waterfront contained barrels artistically placed, as they must have been in past centuries to hold salted herring. Now the sheds were parking spots and the barrels collected rainwater to syphon to well-placed garden allotments for future residents.

Inside, plaster looked as if it were still drying. Electrical outlets were operational in some areas, and in others wires sprouted from holes in the walls. Small portable heaters sat here and there took the nip out of the air. One side of the room was lined with partitioned cubicles used for interviews. When Jon entered, there were only four officers present, their pasty faces and dull eyes glued to their computers. What happened to the dozens of officers considered the brightest and best combined to form the murder investigations team that Trewe was heading?

"Haven't I called a morning meeting?" Jon asked, amazed. For the moment, at least, he was in charge of the Murder Investigations Team.

"Yes, sir. But when you weren't here by nine, the others went for something to eat," one of the officers ventured, quickly looking away.

Noting the name and rank of the young man, Jon said, "Sergeant Bickers, right?"

"Yes, sir."

"Sergeant, call, text, tweet—I want them back here immediately."

Within ten minutes the room had filled with officers. Jon used that in-between time to get the names of the three officers who were present when he arrived. He called the meeting to order. "While I don't expect I can fill your DCI's shoes exactly, I cannot believe you would have done the same were he available to address you this morning."

Heads nodded sheepishly, murmurs of apology could be heard from all around the room.

Jon held a hand up to an ear, "Sorry, didn't quite catch that. Did you say you would be here next time I call a meeting?"

"They will be, sir." Stark stood up from his desk. "The men are exhausted, sir. They've been working almost round the clock since Tavy's death."

"Right, and I don't want to hear about that again. First, I expect you to make time for breaks. Take it in shifts if you need to. No one can function properly without sleep. I won't have it. Anyone here who has not slept in more than twenty hours is dismissed to find a place to sleep. I won't have zombies working for me. That's ridiculous. DCI Trewe is in hospital. I don't want any others to join him. I need every man I can find. We have more on our plate than ever with Tavy's death. And I'll tell you right now, I think there is worse to come. So, those who need sleep are dismissed; please report back in eight hours."

Seven of the twenty-two officers left. They really did look dreadful. Constable Bickers was one of them—the man could barely move. As the door closed behind them, Jon turned to the remaining men. "Right. There is something I will share with you that I believe you need to know. Tavy was dying of cancer. He may not have had the strength to fight off an attack, which might be the reason there were no signs of defensive wounds. His computer was used after his death. Several threatening emails and notes to police officers were left in Tavy's documents file. As most of you know from reports and interviews, Tavy would have been the last to write such garbage. DCI Trewe received a note taped to his door yesterday morning, and it certainly wasn't Tavy's ghost who put it there. I want anyone who receives anything, even the slightest hint of a threat, to report the action to me. I want all such documents to be kept and compiled.

"Second, it may be—though it is not supposed to be—common knowledge or even a matter for discussion, and though there is no official word, I believe that the body found in the surf was not that of Annie Butler."

The room buzzed with exclamations of shock. The officers stood or sat up straighter, their eyes suddenly sharp.

Jon continued. "There is no official word on this line of thinking as yet, so it's hush-hush. I want each of you to be more diligent than ever in discovering places where a child could be kept alive, hidden, fed, etcetera. Think—along the cliffs, whatever. We won't call out the troops until the DNA is conclusive. Most importantly, this is not to be discussed with residents or even other police teams. I do not want the killer to be aware that we suspect such a thing. It would put him on his guard and possibly cause more harm to the girl, if she is still alive. Any questions?"

After fielding several questions he made certain each man had his assignment, Jon reviewed what notes there were and studied the china board's scribbling and diagrams. He noted the photos that were there—one photo in particular. Half an hour later, he was still at it when Perstow interrupted, "Sar, we've got the interview room ready."

"What have you found out so far from the interviews?"

"Some villagers are working themselves up to hysteria because of Tavy's death. He seemed to have lived a peaceful life. No conflict."

"Not a bit?" Jon asked. In a village where everyone knew each other and everything, conflict was inevitably the main course on the everyday menu.

"A true gentleman was the general opinion—considered Tavy polite but not talkative, kept himself to himself but always ready with kindnesses. He was a regular evening fixture at the Spider's Web. The regulars at the Nap saw him for the occasional lunch."

"Yes, they knew him, treated him like one of the regular lads."

Perstow nodded. "He apparently always ordered the same thing. And he attended their weekly music fest. He really went in for the music, did Tavy."

Perstow continued with a recap of interviews with the regulars at the Spider's Web. Two ancient fishermen came in every afternoon as Tavy did, rain or shine. Tavy would share a table with them and listen to them tell their stories of life on the sea.

"That fits in with what we saw of his interests when we were in his house," Jon said.

Perstow went on, "As for the irregulars—that is, people who fancied an hour or two at the pub four days out of seven—there were several. Those who knew Tavy included one woman, of dubious past and present reputation, and four old pensioners who claimed he never said much to them. But then, according to the dubious woman, 'Them four never said much to nobody, so what would they know?'

"According to Mr. Sonders, the pub's regulars were DCI Trewe, his son the dairy farmer, and myself. There was the magistrate, along with his wife; two local gentlemen farmers escaping the late afternoon tedium (or the wife); the postmistress and her erstwhile live-in, both carrying the local gossip; and the librarian, a single lady who kept herself to herself. The librarian would read a book while having a pint or two. She seemed to take special care to say a word to Tavy every day."

Jon noted the first person to be interviewed today was the person who would have had the most contact with Tavy—Harold Sonders from the Spider's Web.

Obviously ill at ease, the Spider's Web's sonorous, flame-topped publican stepped into the portioned cubicle farthest away from the computers and phone lines. He looked different without his apron. His polyester yellow-and-brown-checked suit looked as new as the eighties, the material having acquired an oily sheen of age.

Sonders shook hands all around before Jon asked him to have a seat. "This is not an interview, Mr. Sonders, so I won't take up your time with the list of dos and don'ts. If you'll be sure and sign the paper acknowledging you understand you were taped, that will be all of the formality we'll go through. Remind me if I forget, won't you?"

"I'll do it, Mr. Graham. Find the killer an' ye'll be needin' ta remind *me* to keep from doin' the same to 'im as he done to my friend." Mr. Sonders wiped his eyes, his voice slowed to a low growl. "I'm that spun out."

"We understand. Tell me about Mr. Tavish."

Mr. Sonders suddenly rallied. "Tavy—'is name has auways been Tavy to his friends an' acquaintances." He snuffled, and wiped his sleeve across his nose.

"I'll remember. Did you ever witness trouble between Tavy and anyone else?"

"Nae. Quiet, but took guff off no one."

"Did anyone give him trouble then?" Jon asked.

"He was a humble man, kept himself to himself." The poor man's florid face appeared as though it would disengage like a space shuttle from his thick stump of a neck. His white shirt collar was obviously buttoned too tight as he kept tugging at it.

Jon believed there was something he held back. He would reword the same question and ask it again later. He wondered how to put the man at his ease. Perhaps he should tell him to take his tie off, but to do so would call attention to the fact he'd noticed, thus putting the man in a more awkward position of admitting he might have been wrong to dress up. This might be the most exciting and out-of-the-ordinary thing ever to happen to him. One could always hope.

"Any gossip around about him?" Jon asked.

"Never."

"You knew him well?"

The man almost burst a seam. "What do you think?"

Jon wasn't having it. "Just answer the question."

Mr. Sonders took a deep breath. "I knowed 'im. I loiked 'im."

"Had you noticed anything out of the ordinary before you saw the dog coming to the pub Saturday last?"

The man shifted in his chair, and pulled at his crotch. "Could not say. Tavy auways come round about four o'clock. I can juse imagine 'im now, in the corner." He rubbed his eyes. He might have been crying, Jon couldn't tell.

Perstow leaned forward, "Had you noticed him talking privately with anyone the week before he stopped coming?"

"Ace … Thursday last, over by the window." Mr. Sonders tried to wave his thick arms, but the coat wouldn't allow it. "Fellow's back 'us turned. Don't remember anythin' sketchy, nor who it may 'uv been."

"You didn't overhear anything?" Jon asked.

"Nae."

"Do you think he was aware he had terminal cancer?"

"Cancer?" Mr. Sonders jerked back as if he'd been slapped. "Cancer? What cancer? I didn't know."

"Would he have told you?"

"If he didn't tell me, he wouldn't 'uv tol' anyone." Mr. Sonders's eyes grew shiny. "Poor, poor Tavy."

"What *did* he talk about … lately, I mean?" Jon asked.

"He auways had a tale about 'is dog—trained to save drownin' volk was Chelsea. Once, I saw 'er leap in to grab a chile an' pull 'er to shore. 'Cept the chile wasn't drownin', was she? She an' her mum were not well pleased. Tavy had the dog trained professional. So 'er would know not to go after a chile havin' a dip in the surf." Mr. Sonders leaned forward rubbing his round chin. "Don't know who'll be taking Chelsea?"

Jon shook his head. He could see the man wanted the dog. And now he knew why Chelsea'd gone to check the body in the surf. The dog could sense the body's presence. And she had been trying to get his attention to save her master when he'd gone to the library that day. More fool he. "Perhaps the great-nephew will be looking for a home for the dog."

The publican brightened up and nodded. Any brighter and he would glow. "Would 'e let 'im know I do want the dog?"

"He'll be told." Jon leaned forward. "Before you go, one more question. Did anyone bring up any disagreement with Tavy that you were privy to? Or was he worried about something having to do with anyone else?"

"'E were auncy since the girl … er … since the girl went and …"

"You mean anxious—since the body was discovered?"

"Since she disappeared."

"In what way anxious?"

"Not like 'im to wander round, like 'e were lookin' fer 'er himself."

"I see. And do you know if he found something out?"

The man shrugged. "Why else did 'e get chopped?"

Mr. Sonders had been watching too many gangster movies, Jon thought. "If you think of anything you'd like to add, would you get back to us right away?"

"Yes, sar." Mr. Sonders signed his statement and went on his way.

41

Sunday afternoon

Jon put both hands to his face and tried to rub his weariness away. He stretched his legs under the table. A sour fug clung within the cubicle. He stared at the clock. "Only one interview in and I can hardly keep my thoughts in order."

Perstow placed a hand against his forehead, closing his eyes.

"Not you, too?" Jon asked, suddenly worried.

"I'm fine. Not much in the way o' sleep."

"Time for lunch," Jon announced.

A bright expression flushed across Perstow's face, as if Jon had offered him a raise in pay. "Sure!"

Out of doors, the gray sky glowered. The wind's chill bit through layers of clothing. Puddles of rainwater dotted the pavement. Before they had made it past the pottery on their way to the Spider's Web, rain burst from the leaded sky. Inside the pub it was a little less dreary than the weather outside, but not by much. Jon ran his fingers across cigarette-burned pits along his chair's arm. "They all say 'Tavy kept himself to himself,' do you think they decided together what to say?"

"I'd say the same of Tavy," Perstow offered. "I heard you went to visit Mr. Trewe? How did you find him?"

"He can't stand lying abed while the world is 'up to something.' Says it is like an electric current under the skin."

"Holdin' still won't lie easy with him, I reckon." Perstow smiled.

Jon wondered if, with Trewe in hospital, Perstow would feel more talkative. "He does like to be in the thick of things doesn't he?"

"Yes, sar. He was always one for such as that." Perstow rubbed his stubby-fingered hands around his glass. "He is a good man, the DCI."

"He seems well respected."

"I mean *sar*. Beggin' yer pardon."

"What?"

"He's a *decent* man." Perstow would not meet Jon's eyes.

Jon watched the man's expression. "You're referring to our surveillance. Because we haven't seen anything But his attitude - Surely he wasn't always so explosive. Don't you agree, he seems on edge?"

"P'r'aps here lately. Worried like, about his health. But that isn't him really," Perstow continued. "I'd like to say, he's the type who wouldn't let anyone down."

"You like him, I see. Let's order lunch." Jon studied the Pub's blackboard. The chalk markings were the same as yesterday and the day before. Jon supposed the special of the day was in reality the special of the month: plaice or cod, jacket potatoes, ploughman's, homemade biscuits, coffee or tea.

After a brief discussion on the offerings, Perstow insisted it was his shout and went to the bar to order.

Settled again, Jon asked Perstow, "What have you gleaned from the interviews so far?"

"One of the farmers is suspicious of the death of his prized racehorse. Colic, the vet told him. The farmer thinks it was poison. Another farmer reported an arson fire destroyed one of his barns the same week."

"When was this?"

"Just a few weeks ago."

"Who haven't you interviewed?"

"The magistrate, his wife, the librarian."

"So, they are next. And so I'll be there."

Back at the incident room, Jon called Mr. Malone in for his interview. He was anxious to see how he reacted to Jon's presence and the absence of Trewe. Mr. Malone seemed unperturbed. The man had a jaunty, energetic walk.

Just inside the door, Malone turned to Jon. "Is this a formal interview? Formal?"

"It is a customary visit to talk to anyone who might have known Mr. Tavish."

"Then I'm not necessarily helping the police with their inquiries?" Malone made the motion with his hands indicating quotation marks as if to underscore the meaning of "helping" in a sarcastic way.

"Just a friendly interview." Jon saw this interview start on the wrong foot.

Malone started forward when he saw Perstow in the interview room. He turned back to Jon. "Then you are taking over for Peter Trewe? Poor man. I hope he is well."

"He's better," Jon said.

"DI Graham is not taking over, Mr. Malone," Perstow growled. "He is only filling in."

A raw undercurrent of wariness flashed between these two men. Perstow didn't like Malone—or was it the other way round? Even with no door, the cubical had an airless feel.

Mr. Malone sat, elegant in his lightly pinstriped wool suit, cut to fit perfectly, a colorful, woolen scarf wrapped loosely around his neck. He didn't skimp on fine clothing. Jon had seen his Bentley. Where did a public servant and local tour guide find the money for such amenities?

"Ye know me. And you've met Detective Inspector Jon Graham." Perstow nodded toward Jon.

"Yes," Malone gruffed.

Perstow pressed forward with a surprising air of authority. "Mr. Malone, you're a regular at the Spider's Web?"

"Yes, my wife and I do try to go every day. Every day. Keeps us in touch with the people, you understand."

"Where is your wife?"

"She is coming just after me." The man looked down his sloping beak of a nose as if such a question was far below standard in his book.

Jon didn't appreciate the man's condescending attitude. "Tavy did not seem very sociable."

"Oh my! No, no! He was quite friendly. Quite."

"Did you talk to him very much?"

"Not really. No, no. Mr. Tavish and I were not really what you might call friends. He kept himself to himself. I am sure we spoke occasionally. Only occasionally. There have been many times when I go to the pub alone. Those are times I might have spoken to him. If alone, I usually watch the TV or the darts—or the characters at the pub—*the characters!* You understand what I mean? The regulars at that pub are characters, some quite sinister, actually, and some colorful, but all very interestin'. Listening to the talk, you can pick up all kinds of information."

He's trying to tell me my business. "Did you have something in particular you would like to tell us about these characters? Who would you say is sinister?"

"Well, there are the farmers who put on airs, but are no better than they should be."

Jon didn't want to pursue a self-righteous diatribe. "Do you believe any of these characters had anything to do with Annie Butler's or Tavy's murder?"

"I don't know anything about that."

Perstow pushed a clipboard toward him. "Then if you'll sign here, you may go."

Malone's mouth opened and closed a few times, his bow tie bobbed up and down, with no sound forthcoming. He finally managed to sputter, "That's it? Didn't you want to know if I had seen anything suspicious?"

"Have you seen anything suspicious?" Jon asked.

Mr. Malone settled deeper into his chair. "Well, now that you mention it, and I'm glad you have, I did see something. I saw a man talking to Mr. Tavish on Friday afternoon." He leaned forward. He whispered and nodded like he was telling dirty secrets. "Friday. I was there on Saturday when the dog showed up and everyone remarked about the fact the dog was alone. So the day before?" He pointed to his head. "It sticks!"

"What did this man you saw talking to Mr. Tavish look like?"

"I only remember the beat-up, old hat the other man wore, pulled down. Suspicious."

Perstow leaned forward. "Where did you see them?"

Mr. Malone seemed to swell with the importance of what he was saying, "On the cliff side. I was walking to my car; it was parked up the lane from the pub. I like to walk sometimes. Walking—good for the back."

"Can you describe him?" Jon asked.

"A young man. Young. The man waved his arms around. I noticed. I noticed." Mr. Malone watched Jon for a few moments, eyes sparkling.

Jon did not normally feel any animosity toward anyone, but this man irritated him. And he wasn't forthcoming. Rather, he seemed to take pleasure in forcing them to ask him more questions. "Could you hear them talking?"

"I could hear them shouting."

"What were they shouting?" Jon asked.

"I could not hear specifics." Malone pointed to his ears.

Jon glanced at Perstow. Could he tell if Malone was lying? Or had the great-nephew been lying?

Perstow said, "Mr. Malone, if you think of anything else will you get in touch with us?"

"Of course. More than pleased, of course!"

"One more thing." Jon leaned forward. "Before you leave, do you mind telling me how a public servant, lecturing tourists and volunteering as village magistrate, can afford a Bentley?"

Mr. Malone gasped. "As if *that* is any of your business. I acquired my car in probably much the same manner Mr. Perstow afforded his, Mr. Graham. My wife bought it for me."

42

Jon Graham watched the obviously offended man stomp out of the cubicle and across the room to where his wife was sitting.

"Ne'er liked that one so much." Perstow glowered.

Jon glanced at Perstow. "I didn't know you had a car."

"I do keep a car in the old lean-to, but there's not much need for driving it about except on holidays. I'd rather make use of my trusty push bike. But what he says is bothersome. I had always believed Liz Malone came from humble circumstances and came up in the world marrying that one."

Jon decided to thwart Mr. Malone's plans and bypass his wife on the interview list for the moment. The next person to be interviewed entered the cubicle with shoulders slumped and face averted. The tall woman's mouse-colored hair was pulled back severely into a knot, though some strands had escaped, and feathered along the sides of her head to frame thick-rimmed glasses. The silky, smooth skin on her face covered a delicate bone structure most women could only hope for. If she took the time, she could be a classic beauty. Jon wondered why she chose to hide behind herself. He pulled out a chair.

"Miss Karen Gower?"

She nodded.

"You're the Perrin's Point librarian? We've met. You helped me with some research."

She nodded again.

Jon noted her clothing was a good quality but not the latest style, by any means. Her hands lay calmly on the table in front of her. Well preserved for a woman of forty.

"Could you tell us what you knew of Mr. Tavish?" Jon wondered if she would nod her way through the interview. She leaned forward. He was surprised at the tears running down her face. She made no attempt to brush them away.

"I would not be alive right now," she said, her voice deep and softly melodic, "if not for Mr. Tavish."

Jon took this in. As far as he knew, this was the first person to reveal Tavy might not have been entirely consistent in keeping himself to himself. "What do you mean, Miss Gower?"

She stared straight ahead. What he could see of her eyes revealed irises of deep Wedgwood blue. Her expression was hard to read. Strength? Hardness? Unbearable sorrow?

"When I moved here it was to … bury myself away. Tavy came to the library often. It started out … We talked about books mainly. Gradually, we became friends. He told me about his daughter, how much he missed her. Told me I reminded him of what she might have been like if she had lived." The tears started again. "I loved him for that. He didn't have to say it. He talked about forgiveness … at my lowest point … He sensed my despair. He talked me out of it."

"It?"

"Killing myself."

Jon waited for more. Her posture suggested she expected a challenge.

Very softly Perstow said, "The past is behind you, Karen."

She turned to Perstow as if seeing him for the first time. She had a dazzling smile. "That's what Tavy would have said." She pushed back a thick strand of hair that draped across her forehead.

Jon held in an audible gasp. A thin red scar cut across her forehead from side to side, as if someone had tried to scalp her.

She caught his eye. "I see my past every day."

Jon found his voice. "Can you think of anyone who would want to do Tavy harm?"

"That's just it. He was the kindest man." Miss Gower stared down at her hands. "I can only think he must have frightened someone. His way of talking, saving his words for important things, I imagine he knew something, or he knew … the child's murderer."

"Did he mention living family members, how he felt about them?"

More hair fell forward into her face when she dropped her eyes. She pushed it back. "Yes! A great-nephew. He was very fond of him, I recall."

"Did Tavy ever indicate to you there was trouble with the great-nephew?" Jon asked. "Think hard, Miss Gower. This is important."

"He spoke warmly of him, said he enjoyed his company whenever he came to visit."

Perstow leaned back. "Thank you, Karen. You've been a great help. You will miss him. I'm sorry for your loss."

She signed papers and left.

Jon looked over at Perstow. "I wonder why Mr. Malone would've lied about the shouting great-nephew. Or did someone else wear a floppy, beat-up hat like Tavy's?"

Next was Mrs. Malone. Jon walked out into the large room and motioned for her to come. Mr. Malone glowered in a corner.

Mrs. Malone stood. She was a woman of understated elegance from the style of her hair to the tips of her shoes.

After they were settled in the interview room, Mrs. Malone leaned forward and touched Jon's arm. "I am so sorry for Mrs. Butler. This latest tragedy has me losing sleep."

"Why's that?" Jon asked.

"The village has always been so … so quiet."

He watched her slender hands move gracefully up to finger a gold chain around her neck. She said, "In the few months of tourist season we get noise. As for me, I love the quiet. Now ... I don't feel comfortable here, or free, the way I have in the past."

"Did you know Tavy well?"

"Not really. At the pub, we would talk sometimes—about gardening. He knew the names of the plants and trees. I tried his herbal remedy for colds. It worked."

"What was it?" Jon asked.

"Tea made from the wild thyme. Stopped a cough." She smiled and played with the end of a strand of hair.

Warmth flushed from deep within. Here was something important. "Did Tavy ever discuss other uses for thyme or its meaning?"

"Yes. He said it meant courage. It's good for the digestion. If, every day, you take a teaspoon of honey the bees have made from the thyme flowers, you won't have allergies. He was brilliant."

"Seems he had a good student in you," Perstow offered.

"Did he never mention its local connection with death or rituals?" Jon studied the way she fidgeted with her hair and pulled on her fingers, practically wringing her hands. She seemed to have lost weight from a week ago.

She looked horrified. "No!"

"Does your husband share your enthusiasm for gardening?"

"He says he hates gardening. Black thumbs. But he knows a lot about it. He says he studies it to aide in his guided garden tours."

"Did your husband use any of the remedies you made with the local herbs?" Jon asked.

"My dear husband insisted he would never take anything made with local herbs."

"Why's that, Mrs. Malone?"

"Said I was trying to poison him." Mrs. Malone perched at the edge of her chair.

"Why would he say that?"

"I used thyme one evening in the pork. Something upset his stomach that night and he said it was the supper. Forbade my using anything freshly green to cook with again. It's all very frustrating."

"Does your husband have stomach problems?" Jon asked.

"Not usually."

"You had a nice friendship with Tavy?"

"Oh yes."

Jon went on to ask more questions. She hadn't talked to Tavy in weeks and hadn't seen him in all that time. Interview terminated.

By the time Jon made his way back from the men's toilet, Mr. and Mrs. Malone were gone. He glanced over the notes from some telephone interviews and looked over the china board, adding a detail here and there.

Perstow and Constable Stark stood in a corner of the incident room talking quietly. Whenever Jon saw Stark he thought instantly of a stork, so remembered his name. Stark dabbed at his red nose with a handkerchief.

Jon called out, "Constable, weren't you in charge of tea and crumpets?"

Stark held up both hands as if he was giving up.

Perstow bantered back, "Something wrong with the electric kettle."

The officers grumbled about no tea as they signed out of computers, gathered papers and joined Jon in the main common area. Several mobiles trilled sporadically with officers answering or turning off the volume. Some were mashing at their mobiles, sending hurried texts.

Jon sent one of the men out for some sort of machine that would provide reliable hot water. In the break area there were plenty of biscuits and tea bags—useless without hot water.

Perstow piped up, "Just heard from the DCI. He's coming in tomorrow."

"Good," Jon said. "Well, Stark, anything on your end?"

The tall constable cleared his throat. "The only thin' stands out is the one statement by the postmistress."

"How so?" Jon asked.

"I've talked to her many a time about the murder. She'd give me bits and bobs." He swiped at his long nose. "Tavy came into her shop Thursday week and wanted to know if any farm animals had been poisoned or lamed, and that's not all." Stark peered at his notes. "He wished to know who received the most mail-order catalogues—in particular, from plant centers—and if those same people received pharmaceutical supplies from mail-order chemists."

"And the postmistress would remember that?" Perstow sounded amazed.

"She said she never paid any attention to that sort of thing."

"I bet. Well, it *is* interesting," Jon said, wondering.

"The postmistress seemed so adamant about not remembering," Stark said and sneezed.

"You think she was lying?" Jon asked. Of course she was lying, he thought, but wanted Stark's impression.

"I'm certain of it."

"I would like to interview her again." Jon nodded at Perstow. "It might be good to get the answers to those questions."

Stark looked hopeful. "Getting on for dinner time, innit?"

Jon glanced at the time on his mobile. Just because he and Perstow had had a late lunch didn't mean others weren't going hungry. "It is. You may go."

Stark grabbed up his jacket.

As Perstow prepared to follow, Jon stopped him. "Do you mind waiting back a bit?"

"No, sar."

"What's the story on Miss Gower?"

"Ah!" Perstow said. "Noticed the scar, did you? Happened in the village where she's from. A girl jealous of Miss Gower's looks had her boyfriend attack her. He took it to levels not planned. Raped her and cut her. Almost didn't survive. Poor, poor lady."

"So she hides out in the Perrin's Point library. Sad story."

"Aye! Sad indeed, but she's better for being here. Good place to live—before now." Perstow shook his head and made a sucking sound through his teeth. "Before this."

43

Early Monday morning
Day sixteen

Jon looked up from his reports when the Perrin's Point police station's door opened. Trewe walked in. He held his back straight, but an unhealthy pallor still marked the area of skin around his eyes and lips. Jon was surprised. "Well, you're back then?"

"Aye, part of the day, if the doctors get their say, which they won't. Bollocks. I'm too close to retirement, I told them, I'm not putting in for sick leave now."

"But you really should listen—"

"I said bollocks!"

Jon wondered how Trewe would react to his initiative to rekindle the search for Annie Butler. How much time did they have before he called off the search? Would there be any progress made at all? The clock was ticking. He wondered how Annie Butler was doing. He didn't want to think about what might be happening to her. He checked his mobile for messages. There was nothing he had to respond to immediately.

He stared at the typed sheet in his hands. This would not make Trewe's day much better, but it certainly had his. He ventured to ask, "What did the doctors say?"

"IBS. Irritable Bowel Syndrome or some such, unlikely business. Could have knocked me over —thought it was the heart—twas that painful."

"So I've heard, poor—"

"Do not say it. I'm well enough to walk, I'm well enough to be here. Tell me the latest." Trewe's relief that there was nothing deadly eating away at his insides was obvious.

"Well, it may not be on the top of your list of happy news ..."

"What is it?," Trewe growled, sounding his old self again.

"Right." He handed over the urgent fax that had just arrived from the crime lab.

Ruth had not slept well. Her hand still hurt. She huddled on the step outside her front door, drinking a mug of hot sweet tea. She stared without seeing the trees across the road, her bandaged hand cradled in her lap. She waited like a fly caught in a web. The spider hadn't shown itself yet. To complicate matters, Sam confessed to being too in love with her to think clearly, asked would she please forgive him, and said he would leave her alone. She felt like a complete lout for throwing him out on his ear. Maybe she should consider asking him to represent her with her imminent deportation problem.

The American IRS had already phoned her about back taxes. The American Bureau of Vital Statistics had sent her a letter about her name and Annie's name. The American FBI had emailed her informing her that they needed to schedule a meeting. She wasn't in much trouble—she was in loads of trouble. She had heard that she could possibly face prison time for using an alias to exit the United States and enter Britain.

It was too much, all of this bureaucratic mess combined with losing her daughter. It was too much. She had even snapped at her mother like she was a teenager all over again. This crazy anger wasn't rational, but she couldn't help but be a little bitter towards her mother. Why couldn't her mother have come when Annie was alive? Annie needed her grandmother, too. Things might have been different if she'd had another pair of eyes—an older, wiser person who loved Annie, too. Things might have been different, and Annie wouldn't have been abducted.

When Annie first went missing she couldn't function, couldn't feel anything. Every reminder of Annie brought tears, from Mandy staring at Ruth with her wise cat-eyes, to walking anywhere around the village. Bits of her heart and soul fell off every day. Losing Annie had been her fault. It was her fault. Overwhelming sadness had become resentment towards her mother for not being there, even if that was an unreasonable thought, added to fury at Sam for being a dolt, added to rage at herself for being stupid-angry at everybody.

She forced her thoughts to anything else—like travel, someplace she'd already been. An overnight in Nice? Paris? London? London was charismatic and claustrophobic all in one thought. She enjoyed London for short bursts, but it was too car-exhaust smelling and the traffic noise at night kept her awake. But she couldn't go anywhere without Annie. Annie was out there somewhere under the same sun, the same sky. If only she knew where. She often thought of this when she thought of her mother and her loved ones in Texas. They were over there, west, under the same sky.

It is funny how a place can settle a restless soul. Most people sought out their roots. She, however, had been glad to see Texas behind her. She had taken her child and searched for she knew not what until she came to Cornwall. She realized now that she had been searching for what she found in Cornwall all along. Attracted as one can be with an old friend, Cornwall, with its wild open-places and ever-changing weather, touched in her soul a familiarity with the Texas coast. Here, she developed a new sense of the delicate balance in nature that she could not remember from her past. The only color that she could really remember from Texas were the many variables of brown. Here, she had the many hues of the sea and the greens of the fields to keep her bursting with creative joy.

Absorbed in thought, she didn't hear the white Mini until its tires scraped against the pavement edge in front of her walkway. A white Mini ... seemed like she knew whose car it was. Oh yes. She heard the handbrake being set. Detective Inspector Jon Graham exited first, then Constable Craig and Sergeant Perstow. Mr. Graham rounded the car's hood. He looked eager. She wondered what he wanted as he walked toward her. He had a neat, compact way about him. "Mrs. Butler, we have some news."

Ruth swallowed, her heart did a backflip. She jumped up. "What is it?"

"Wouldn't you rather we talked inside?"

"Tell me now."

Jon looked at the windows of neighboring cottages, clearly uncomfortable. "You don't want us standing on your front step."

"Of course." She opened the door. "Take a seat."

Jon looked as if he needed more sleep. Ruth wanted to touch his face, let him know he didn't need to be uncomfortable around her.

"Didn't you sleep well last night?" she asked and then thought, *What a ridiculous question, don't embarrass him.*

"I haven't slept. The news came through early enough to catch me at the station, and I knew I could not sleep then. So I finished a lot of paperwork."

"Can I get you tea?" Ruth offered. She tried to figure out what Jon's expression meant. "I'm not so sure I want to hear what you have to say. Just tell me."

"Mrs. Butler," Perstow stood to one side of her. His voice struck a note of calm despite what his words said. "Ye might want to have your mom here with you, actually."

Constable Craig laid a hand on Ruth's arm and positioned herself near Ruth's other shoulder.

"What?" Breathing hard, Ruth pivoted toward Jon. They must have horrible news. "You better tell me now, Mr. Graham."

"We did get the DNA back. The body of the girl in the surf was not Annie."

44

The quiet swallowed up Ruth Butler's cottage. For half a second the world came to a standstill. Jon wanted to rejoice with her, but there would be no joy until they found Annie alive. Sunlight streamed through the cottage doorway, caught each painting of Annie, and pooled on the floor where the white cat took up a curled position. The light brought to Jon's attention the awards and school honors that were taped to the wall between each of the paintings.

Jon stood near Ruth. Her face was too white. He stepped closer to her and took her arm. "Perhaps you'd like to take a seat?"

A whistle rose from the kitchen.

"The kettle …" Ruth mumbled.

"How about that tea now?" Jon offered. *Stop being so stupidly cheerful, no one has given her anything she didn't know.*

Constable Craig said, "I'll get the tea."

Jon turned toward Ruth. Her eyes glistened with unshed tears. It broke his heart.

"I knew it," she whispered. "I knew it."

"We tried not to get your hopes up."

"Any thought of Annie not coming home and I shut down, as if one tiny thought might get through the crack. What am I to think now? Am I supposed to be happy?"

She gripped the back of the chair so tightly her knuckles turned white. "Who was it? In the surf, I mean." Her voice was barely audible.

"The girl, Victoria Benton, missing now six months."

"How did this happen? This mix up."

"The blood type matched yours," Jon said. "Annie's clothes were on the body, the hair, the same type and color. She was the same height as Annie. The shoes fit. We made a mistake."

Constable Craig returned with tea steeping in mugs.

Perstow offered, "We didn't question. We should have."

"I mean how would a dead body last that long so well-preserved?" Ruth rubbed her eyes.

"She had only just died."

"Oh God, no! He kept her alive? That poor child. Oh, that poor mother. Where is her mother?"

Jon said, "She and her husband are on their way. They are in a state of shock. It's been especially hard for them. They accepted she'd died long ago."

Ruth stared at the floor and whispered, "Now they'll have the guilt of being wrong, and wonder why they didn't persist in searching."

"They've also identified an anorak found buried in the sand at the beach as hers. Forensics doesn't think it had been in the water long and it was found long after the body."

"What does that mean? Why was the jacket buried recently? Where has it been?"

"All questions we have no answers for, Mrs. Butler. We don't think it was purposefully buried. It must have fallen into the water at some point. The action of the tide and waves left it partially covered in sand."

"So … so this means that he has Annie hostage now. But to what end? I haven't had a ransom demand." Ruth's hand shook as she put it to her lips.

She rocked in her seat. "He's keeping her alive. Oh Annie!"

"Keeping who alive?" Ruth's mother walked into the sitting room in a fluffy pink robe. "Ruth, what's wrong?"

Jon caught Ruth as she slipped sideways.

"Ruth!" Her mother dashed to Ruth.

"Where is my daughter?" Ruth's eyes streamed tears.

"We don't know," Jon said. "We've got teams trying to be discreet, but the search has been stepped up. We are intensely searching everywhere. We don't want to alert him that we know. It might make things worse."

Ruth's mother zeroed in on Jon. "Young man! You'd better explain! I'm not deaf, and I'm certainly not invisible."

"Mrs. Thompson," Jon said, "we'll get this sorted."

"Why does he go to all the trouble to keep someone alive just to kill her?" Ruth asked, "To what end?"

"Annie is alive?" Ruth's mother screeched.

"Mother, please! I've told you all along. You wouldn't listen."

"This is an ongoing investigation," Perstow told Ruth.

"Look!" Ruth said. "We're talking about my daughter. What else do you know?"

"We must keep this new information to ourselves," Jon said. "If the killer knows we know, he'll run to ground. We can't begin a full-blown search and alert media and so on."

"That's ridiculous!" Ruth snapped. She jumped up and left the room. Annie's paper awards fluttered as Ruth dashed past them. She came back moments later with her keys and shoes.

"What are you doing?" Ruth's mother asked.

"I'm going out to search for her."

Jon shook his head. He didn't know how to reason with her. He didn't want to tell her about the stains on the jacket that were being analyzed.

"Didn't you hear them, Ruth-Ann?" her mother said. "They just got through telling us we must not let the killer know we know. We've got to act as if they'd never told us, or we could put Annie in more danger."

"This is stupid! I've said it all along and no one would listen, and now that you all know, too, you're telling me to stay home and pretend? My daughter is out there. Are you all crazy?"

Jon stood ready to keep her from running out the door. "Please, Mrs. Butler . . ."

Ruth's mother muttered, "Sounds as if we could all use a little whiskey in our tea this morning."

Jon stepped aside as she brushed past him on her way to the kitchen.

Monday morning, 11:10 a.m.

He went to the small garage where the old car sat. Oh, he could afford better now, sure, but why draw attention? He only took her out on special occasions.

He ran his fingers along the smooth, cold metal on the car's roof. The oxidizing paint left a gray residue on his fingertips. He wiped his hands thoroughly on his handkerchief.

Sunshine filtered a dusty yellow haze through the old shed's window. Cobwebs were draped from the exposed beams above him. The scent of hay and rodents mixed with petrol assailed his nostrils. Wattle and daub walls were spattered with different colors, a result of his renderings on canvas from earlier years. He remembered the liberating feeling of throwing paint. Stupid galleries didn't know what excellence was.

His windfall money had afforded him the more important things. Who knew all this would be the result of the discovery in the cave so many years ago? Now, he had a new spot on the map, a different world to travel within freely—and a faked university degree. With enough money one could buy just about anything.

He and The Wife had had a row the morning the other girl died. He had stayed with her late that last night. Sad really, the choking last gasps, the pleading eyes. He couldn't help it. He needed the blood. He could see improvement—his skin was smoother, he had more energy—it was working. The Wife thought he was out too late, too many times.

Her opinion didn't matter. The morning after, he had taken the American woman's daughter. Ha! Lady Luck was good to him.

He just needed a little more time and some more blood. The American woman was bent on distracting him, but he would overcome the distraction. He didn't need her blood. Just her life. A life for a life. Isn't that how it worked?

Then he could complete his mission to turn back time and reclaim what his mother had taken from him. He would be young again. If he couldn't have Cecil back the way it had been, he would find another Cecil. He didn't care about the baby. He wanted to tell her that. He didn't care about the baby. He just wanted her back. He would do whatever she wanted if only he could have a second chance, if only he could tell her that.

Hardly three words passed between Allison Craig, Perstow, and Jon as they drove from Ruth's house to the car park. Finally Perstow broke the uneasy silence, "Beggin' yer pardon, sir, but you do seem different around the lass."

"I make myself ridiculous in her presence." Jon caught the secret smile Constable Craig sent Perstow. "Don't go reading into the situation, you two."

He negotiated a turn, slowing to take a right. He offered a honk to make sure no one was barreling down the lane towards him on the blind curve. "Surely there is something more we can do than sit on our hands at this point. We've got men combing the lanes and fields looking for some clue. We can't be too obvious."

Allison Craig said, "Someone would have noticed if he is keeping her in a house."

Perstow added, "Not in a box, not with a mouse, not with a fox—Mind the rabbit!"

Jon swerved to avoid a hare that chose that moment to dash across the road in front of them. "You've been reading too many children's books."

"It's Her Indoors, wishin' for a child. I'm afraid I'm a bit over my past due date."

"Aha! Allison did you hear that? You are witness."

Perstow turned red. "Now, sar!"

"You're as young as you feel," Allison offered.

"I feel old," Perstow moaned.

Jon slowed the car to turn again. He swept an arm out to indicate the area. "See this spot? I chased him and lost him on the cliffs, about here. The dogs lost the scent at the stream up on the rise just over there. I'm thinking, wild animals will decoy themselves to protect the young in their lairs or nest from predators. The killer would guard his lair. If we get too close, he pops out and leads us away, in a different direction to distract us. Could there be a place on the cliffs to hide?"

"Smugglers have hidden their goods along the coast of Cornwall for centuries," Allison said.

"I bet the local youths know some good places to hide along the cliffs." Jon pulled up to the village car park. "Perstow, get on to that. Someone here knows about places to hide things."

"Should we get the dogs to try again, tracking something of Annie's?" Allison asked.

"There's an idea to float by Trewe. Caves. Caves and abandoned mines. Are there maps?"

Perstow nodded. "Aye. We'll have some at the library, p'r'aps."

Jon dropped Allison and Perstow at the incident room and drove back along the High Street to the Hasten Inn. Mrs. McFarland burst from the direction of the kitchen to greet him at the entrance. Her cheeks glowed. "Is Peter Trewe out of hospital? Poor man, all those grandchildren. The *noise* in that house. It's proper baked goods he needs. I'll bake him a cake. He'll like that."

Exhausted from almost twenty-four hours without sleep, Jon made excuses and stumbled upstairs to his room. He'd laid down the law to the Murder Investigations Team, but he was the one who should have been listening. His brain was as muddled as his sock drawer. He lifted mismatched socks up. It wasn't as if he wasn't used to mismatched socks, but Mrs. McFarland was quite diligent with his laundry usually.

Would he fail in finding Annie? Would he give DI Bennet back in London something more to hold against him? "Can't finish the job can you? A failure is what you are." Would that prediction come true now he couldn't think straight?

He stared back at himself in the dresser's mirror. *Who do you think you are? You can't do any good here. Go home!* He slammed the sock drawer shut. *No!* After all this time, he would stay and he would straighten out this business with Trewe, and he would find the lost girl.

45

Tuesday morning
Day seventeen

It was about eighteen miles northeast of Perrin's Point to the Treborwick Police Station where DCI Trewe worked. The drive took Jon Graham thirty minutes. The night's rained left puddles on the roadway, but the sun was bright that morning. The regional station was a square gray building that posed against a rise of land. The time had come to resolve issues. He pursed his lips and stepped through the glass front door into the dimmer interior. His eyes hadn't adjusted, but he kept walking and almost ran over Perstow, who was leaving in somewhat of a hurry. He must not have noticed Jon entering. Why was he here and not at Perrin's Point police station in his office?

"Since you are here, do you have a moment?" Jon asked.

"Of course." Perstow stood back and smoothed his shirt over his protruding front.

"Follow me then."

Perstow didn't say a word as Jon walked past several desks and rapped on the door to Trewe's office. He heard Trewe yell, "Enter." Jon nodded encouragement to Perstow and walked in. A clutter of coffee mugs, pencils, papers and take-out pizza boxes were scattered across every surface. Jon wondered why Trewe ate pizza with his digestion problems.

Standing at the window, Trewe turned when they entered. "Yes?"

Without prompting, Jon sat. "The hospital rest put you in a good mood, I see. Pizza and coffee?"

"I'm in a perfect mood, and someone else was here eating pizza last night."

Perstow scooted into a chair before being invited.

Trewe huffed, "What is it?"

"After yesterday's revelation," Jon said, "the entire direction of this investigation has changed. Now we believe Annie may be alive. I've asked Mrs. Butler and her mother to keep quiet until after the second inquest. And I believe that Mrs. Butler may still be in danger."

"We know this. So why burst in here? I'm up to my eyes. Get on with it."

It sounded as if Trewe was angrier at him than he usually was. Jon said, "If you would prefer, I'll ask Mr. Perstow to leave the room."

"I was completely prepared to speak to the dead girl's real mother." Trewe's pale eyes narrowed, cold as ice. "I wasn't so sick I couldn't drive to the Benton's home in Devon."

So that was it, Jon thought. Trewe still thinks of him as a vigilante who over-stepped his responsibilities.

"I'm sorry that I did not consult you. The police authorities in the girl's district needed to be the ones to tell the poor parents."

"That isn't all, though, is it?" Trewe swung towards him. "Why have you come so formal-like and with a witness?"

"My mother always said if she were going to cook something, she had to clean the kitchen first."

Trewe rolled his eyes. "And?"

Jon said, "In order to arrive at the truth, I need something cleared up."

"Bloody hell!" Trewe yelled, "What's this about?"

"About the investigation that brought me here in the first place."

Trewe shoved empty take-out boxes aside. "Talk!"

"I'd like to get Bakewell on conference call with your permission."

"Right." Trewe punched some numbers into his desk phone.

Bakewell's voice boomed a loud but normal, "Bakewell here!"

Trewe told him who was calling, and Jon chimed in as well. "Sergeant Perstow is present, also."

"So the whole circus?" Bakewell exclaimed. "Well, Trewe, it's come down to this. I wanted this assignment badly, especially when I found out who the subject of the home office's investigation was."

"Who?" Trewe's face looked pinched. Jon thought he saw wariness and stark suspicion in his eyes.

"You."

Trewe's face changed from storm to tempest, developing a dangerous, wild-eyed, veins-standing-out-at-the-neck look. "What?"

"Look, it's the money, man," Bakewell boomed.

A change came over Trewe. The standing-out veins disappeared. The rigidity and the wild-eyed dangerous look, gone. In its place was something close to a smile. "Money? What money? What are you on about?"

Bakewell's voice filled the room, "The nine hundred, eighty-two thousand pounds or thereabouts transferred from National Westminster to Lloyds."

Jon watched Trewe carefully. Shock registered. Then, a trace of a grin played at the edges of his lips, where it gradually spread into a smile. A chuckle started and grew to a laugh. It took him a few moments to gain a modicum of control. He reached for a tissue to wipe his eyes. "Brilliant. I had no idea … What a waste of our tax payers' money."

Jon stared at Trewe. *What was this?*

Trewe took a tissue and blew his nose. "I won the money on the pools."

"The pools!" Bakewell yelled. "There's no way in hell you won that money and didn't spread the word."

"People change, Tom," Trewe said.

Jon glanced at Perstow who looked like the canary that had been nabbed by the cat.

With a gigantic grin spread across his face, Trewe wiped his eyes again. "My son-in-law talked me and my son into joining the pool. Split three-way it was a grand thing!"

Suspicion remained at the back of Jon's mind. How could this man, who wore his emotions like Christmas-fairy lights, have hidden his tremendous fortune for this long? "How is it no one knew?" Jon asked.

"Only the three of us knew. I swore them to secrecy until I was pensioned." Trewe waved his hand in the air. "I don't want a lot of long-lost relatives popping in, acting like pigs in clover. And I don't need my past sneaking up thinking I might owe more alimony. Pardon me, Tom. So I kept quiet."

With a parting growl, Bakewell cut the connection from his end.

"Nothing's changed except … my deposit account." With that bright non-customary smile plastered to his face, Trewe leaned forward. "How is it my account is of interest to anyone?"

"Someone at the bank reported a policeman had deposited a large amount of money," Jon said, "and demanded an investigation."

"I did wonder at the manager's reaction at the time I transferred the funds. Wouldn't stay with that bank after what they did to my son in law, charging him interest on savings!"

"But what are you going to do?"

"What would you do?"

Jon laughed. "Early retirement and a holiday in the Greek islands or the States comes to mind."

Trewe snorted. "Everything else keeps interfering."

"We can wind up the fraud investigation, if you can prove all this, of course," Jon said.

"I've filed a cover letter from Littlewoods … here," Trewe pulled a drawer towards him and withdrew a sheet of paper, "here it is." He handed it to Jon. "And all along I thought you just wanted to keep me company."

Jon glanced at the paper and handed it back to Trewe. He could hardly take it in.

Trewe smiled, calmer now. He shook his head. "The way people react …"

Perstow beamed. "I'm in the room with a rich man."

Trewe leaned back in his chair, crashing into the wall behind, gouging yet another mark. "You see?"

46

Midday

The postmistress jerked back and almost slipped off the stool behind the counter. "What! Charles? Don't find the door open enough as it is, yer sneakin' through the back door where no one is allowed?"

Charles stood before the postmistress and smiled, more to himself than at her.

"I hoped to bring a package in early," Charles said, "as I haven't much time later in the day. Won't you humor me this one time?"

"I may be deaf, but blind I'm not, sar. Ye 'aven't any package. I know what's what," she raised her voice as she pointed at the computer, "and I stick to schedule even if no one else does! That's the way things are, like it 'r not. What are ye up to? Yer not comin' back here!"

"You know my name. No one gets that privilege any longer." He pushed the rag he had prepared into her mouth, forcing it open. She choked, then gasped and took a step back, grabbing at the rag. He shoved her. She ricocheted off a cabinet to the floor, slamming the back of her head against the flagstone. Between the chemical on the rag and the force of her landing, she was senseless to the world. Her dress had flown up.

He looked down, shocked.

"She is such a liar!"

Sin upon sin, as you would say, Mother!

Ruth looked out the kitchen window to the back of her home where the thyme cascaded over its pot. It was a partly cloudy day, and much too humid. *Annie is alive and I must keep my mouth shut.*

Dear God in heaven! she wanted to shriek.

Crepuscular sunlight strained through the haze in the west. She stared out across the next cottage's roof below her window. A wide stone wall divided the properties. Movement caught her attention—a single gray feather, weightlessness on stone. She looked again. It was gone.

It had been two weeks and three days.

Her stomach churned. She paced across the kitchen and back to the window. Was Annie cold? Hungry? What would she do if they couldn't find her? What if they couldn't find her for six months, like the girl in the surf? She rubbed her hands up to her shoulders. She bent and stretched her lower back. She readied her stance and kicked out with her heel. She swung around, jumped away, and kicked with the other leg, back kick, push kick, evasive side kick. She then paced back to the window, turned, and repeated her kicks, imagining the hurt she could do if she only knew who to hurt.

Somewhere there was another mother going through what she had gone through already. Perhaps for six months this mother went through this not knowing and wondering. That would make the death so much more horrible. Not knowing is worse than knowing, really.

She paced the length of the kitchen again and glanced at the clock on the wall—past twelve—an excruciatingly long day. It was amazing how long a minute took. At exactly this time tomorrow the second inquest would take place.

And Annie may still be alive and will stay that way as long as I sit in my house and keep quiet about it.

❧

She had been experimenting with paper, wadding it up and tossing it into the little pool at the center of the cave. How long did the wadded up paper take to sink? The paper floated better if it was less tightly wadded. She had written notes then crushed them into balls and sent them down the hole.

The first time Annie wrote anything it sounded crazy:

Mom, I'm in a cave. I need you. Please help me.

He wouldn't let her mother see that. No, it would be worse than writing nothing. That one went down the hole.

This is Annie Butler. I'm in a cave.

Which cave? No one will know which cave. Tears turned her cheeks to ice. She rubbed them to revive some warmth. The heater's tick, the dripping water, and the waves outside worked together in a sort of weird orchestra of a thrumming music that never ended.

She had thought so hard about what to write, but when she put it to paper her words sounded so stupid.

Mom, don't worry. Follow the man's instruction and you'll find me.

Less frantic, but no, that was bad because she didn't want her mother to follow the man's instructions. The creeper was crazy. The creeper would hurt her. She crushed the note up and tried again:

Mom, I'm well. I will let you know soon what to do. Do not worry.

That wasn't bad but she did wish she knew the man's name or something so she could slip clues into the words. How could she slip clues into words?

The first letter of each sentence—she could code it like the kind of messages they texted. What would it say? How could she hide it well enough?

She had nothing else to do but think. The cut on her leg was oozing. The skin around it was red and painful to touch. It was hard to think when her leg felt like it was going to burst open.

❦

Jon had a good, strong cup of coffee in front of him. He and Trewe were on a sort of truce, sitting across from each other at Trewe's desk. He and Perstow were at the Treborwick station to see Trewe, who had not resumed a full schedule.

Trewe nodded. "It's wonderful the body was not Annie Butler. But that still leaves Annie out there somewhere, and we're back on square one. How is Mrs. Butler taking this?"

"As well as," Jon said. "I told her we have to be discreet. Don't want the fox to know the hounds are after him. The second inquest is still on, public notices up. We'll stage it as if it were Annie's. Mr. and Mrs. Benton, the *real* dead girl's parents, will be coming later to make arrangements for the remains so they can bury their daughter. We've asked them to remain incognito so the alarm is not raised. They've been more than cooperative because they want this as much as anyone. We want to flush this person. There has to be a reason for taking a child and keeping her alive."

"He drains their blood. Maybe he needs it fresh."

Jon leaned back. "Surely this one is different. He grabbed her so near her own home."

There was a soft knock at the door.

Trewe murmured, "What fresh hell…Perstow?"

Perstow got up and when the door opened, he nodded at whoever had interrupted.

The door cracked wider. Trewe thundered, "What? Speak up!"

Perstow turned to him. "Another body, at the Perrin's Point post office."

47

On the way to his car Jon listened intently as Perstow told what he knew.

"Old Mrs. Davies went to the post office at a quarter past the hour. When she entered she saw the one counter overturned and came over scary. Found the postmistress on the floor behind the counter, 'n' she turned and stumbled out. Someone noticed her about the time she screamed. It had just happened, I reckon. The blood still flowed when the first unit arrived. There was no helpin', though."

They were thirty minutes away, but they hardly spoke as Jon took curves at full speed with a honk before each turn. As their car drew closer to the old post office, they pulled to the side of the roadway and walked through the thick crowd of villagers gathered around the door of the combined county courthouse where the post office was. A white-haired lady was at the center of the most attention. Several people bent over her as Jon and his colleagues drew closer. A constable barred the door to keep the curious out of the building. SOCO had arrived at the scene.

"Is that Mrs. Davies?" Jon asked.

"That's her, poor dear," Perstow said. "Bad heart. Wonder we didn't have another body."

Trewe told Perstow, "Call for reinforcements from Devon. You need to work as liaison between the teams. I'll contact you later."

Perstow left with Constable Stark. Trewe motioned for Jon to join him. "Let me talk to Mrs. Davies before we see the body."

Trewe walked over to where Mr. Malone sat next to the tiny Mrs. Davies. Malone moved aside to make a space for Trewe to sit. Jon stared at Malone, but the man ignored him.

"I'm sorry, Olivia," Trewe patted her hand. "Not a pleasant thing."

"The blood. The blood!" Olivia Davies wailed. Jon saw the lady was trembling. "Oh! I can't get it out of my mind. I never imagined anything so horrible could happen. What with that little girl, and our Tavy, and now this! In broad daylight! What are we coming to, Peter?" She sobbed.

"There, there, dear." Trewe put an arm around her. "Nothing you could do. You'll be right as roses soon enough. Mrs. Jeffers is going to take you to your house and sit you down and give you a nice cuppa. Aren't you, Mrs. Jeffers?"

Jon noticed another lady nod emphatically. She was not quite as elderly as Mrs. Davies.

"I'll see she gets home and comfortable, Peter," Mrs. Jeffers said.

These people really like Trewe, Jon thought. They looked up to him, yet called him by his given name.

Trewe stood as Mrs. Davis was helped away. The crowd parted to make way for Jon and Trewe to get to the door. The pathologist, Roger Penberthy, beckoned from just inside the post office's doorway.

Trewe exclaimed, "You've arrived soon enough for once!"

"We were nearby."

They filed after him into the building. The metallic odor of blood overpowered the smell of postal supply-laden shelves that lined the walls. Lying face-up behind the counter, the postmistress was very dead. Blood had pooled beneath her. She was outlined in the dark liquid like a large custard in raspberry sauce.

"What have you got for us, Roger?" Trewe asked.

The doctor moved behind the counter, careful to avoid the blood. "At first glance, I surmised massive brain hemorrhaging had killed her."

Jon pointed at the bloody shoeprint near the body. "Do you know who did that?"

"No."

"Hold up," Trewe said. "Is the wound consistent with being hit on the head with a blunt instrument?"

"You can see for yourself."

The three police officers leaned over the body. There was an obvious dent in the side of her skull and a large bruise on her forehead.

The pathologist continued, "At first, I would have said it is a very straightforward case of blunt trauma."

"Would have?" Jon asked.

"Yes."

"How long would you say she's been dead?"

"After a preliminary examination, about an hour. I would put a guesstimate at around one o'clock. The post office would have been empty for only a small frame of time." The doctor coughed and smoothed his generous mustache with one hand. "The postmistress was very strict about her break. She took a regular tea at midday sharp every day, rain or shine. Wouldn't let anyone else touch her mails during that time. Wouldn't allow Postie Pauline in. Not even her companion, Thomas, came round then—she was that particular." The doctor shook his head. "She said that was the way of it and anyone can wait half an hour to buy their stamps." He looked from Jon to Trewe. "But, what with the method of killing used, a thorough autopsy will better determine the time."

Jon noticed the sweat beaded on the doctor's forehead and wondered what had so perturbed the unflappable man. He couldn't help musing aloud, "Well, this lets her off the short list."

"Cause of death," Trewe demanded.

Jon moved closer. A heavy, partitioned shelf had been ripped away from the wall and now lay next to the postmistress's skull. As if she had just stepped out of them, her large shoes lay to one side.

"There is the shelf edge here," the doctor pointed.

"Killed her?" Trewe snapped.

"I'm getting to that. First thought: she fell into that shelf, knocked it from the wall, fell forward, hit her head a second time on the counter, and fell backward. I would have said that was it."

Tiredness eked out of Trewe's voice. "I know you're dying to tell us how she really died."

"Well, I wouldn't say dying." The pathologist took out a handkerchief and blotted his forehead. "At first I thought the shelf *was* the instrument of death. There's the dent at the front of the cranium and blood on the counter here." He pointed to the edge of the counter. It seemed obvious.

"But wait, there's more," Trewe said with a touch of sarcasm.

"He'll get to it given time," Jon muttered.

"Well," the pathologist explained, "I examined the body a little closer, and Peter—" the doctor gave a long sigh, and whistled through his great white mustache. "I've been the doctor here for many years. She never registered with my surgery. I understood she went to a doctor in Port Isaac. I never questioned … wasn't my place. I actually had never thought much about it."

Trewe slammed a palm against the counter. "Roger, we'd like to get on with our jobs."

"Well, Peter, if you'd only be patient. I've just received the shock of my life. You're not being very sensitive."

Jon wondered why death would shock a pathologist.

"I've never been accused of being sensitive, so tell!" Trewe bellowed.

"The cause of death wasn't blunt trauma at all, though I've no doubt the injury to the brain was serious enough to cause eventual death."

"Make short work of it!"

"You see, gentlemen, with the amount of blood around the body, we can surmise that the body has lost a lot of blood. There are only a few places where a cut can be made to cause this kind of serious blood loss in a relatively short period of time: the neck, of course, then the main arteries under the arms and legs—a deep puncture wound in the chest area could pierce an artery around the heart, which would cause blood to pool in the chest cavity. Then there is this, if you'll just have a careful look here." The doctor pulled the postmistress's skirt. The cloth came away with a soft, suctioning noise.

So much blood.

The doctor yanked her blooded knickers away from a red gaping hole in her flesh.

The other men gasped.

The doctor said matter-of-factly, "The postmistress was a mister. With a deliberate stroke of a very sharp knife … sexual organ deleted. That is where the loss of blood took place. Then it was conveniently covered with the clothing."

"Oh God!" Jon saw black specs in the blood and leaned forward for a better look. Plant leaves of some sort were intermixed into the deep, red liquid. "He's becoming more violent."

Perhaps because Trewe hadn't moved, Jon glanced at him. Trewe's face had turned as white from loss of blood as the floor was red with it.

Jon motioned for the pathologist to help. Together they gently tugged Trewe toward the door.

Trewe jerked away from them and turned back to the doctor.

"Where is it?"

The doctor looked at him with question in his eyes.

"His Tom, Dick, and Harry! What do you think I mean?" Trewe spit the words out, as distasteful as they sounded.

The doctor glanced down at the body. "Sorry. Haven't found it."

Trewe swayed.

"I'm taking you home, Peter." Roger Penberthy grabbed his arm.

As Jon helped get Trewe out the door, he said to the pathologist, "Have the lab discover what kind of leaves those are mixed with the blood, and see the shoes are handled with care."

48

HASTEN INN
Wednesday afternoon
Day eighteen

Mrs. McFarland had provided an impromptu lunch. She didn't normally provide lunch to her guests, much less guests of guests, so Jon was grateful for the cold meats and toast that she had set out with her usual, unflappable energy. Trewe and Perstow were eating as Jon pushed his untouched lunch away. They had spent the evening and night garnering forces, comparing notes, and assigning tasks. After four hours of sleep they were ready to start again.

It had been three weeks since Jon had stumbled after Tavy on the coastal path, when Chelsea led them to Victoria Benton's body dressed in Annie's clothes. Today was another inquest. The condiment jars rattled when Jon's fist hit the table.

Perstow stopped munching to stare at him. "Sar?"

"Do policemen go mad with inactivity?"

"No," Trewe growled.

"How is it," Jon demanded, "someone like the postmistress could get away with keeping such a thing quiet for so long?"

"Wouldn't have been easy, keeping that secret," Trewe cleared his throat. "Lived with about twenty cats and a couple of canaries and Thomas. Such a secret—don't you know the villagers are going to look a bit askance at that fellow? The postmistress didn't garden, didn't attend church, didn't socialize at the pub. Didn't, didn't, didn't." Trewe blew air through pursed lips and kept his voice low, "Question is: why was she killed?"

Jon took a sip of tea—good, strong stuff. "Seemed to me she was a professional busybody. She must have found out something she wasn't supposed to know."

Perstow nodded. "Snooped into everything. She could tell when Uncle Elmer last wrote from Australia, or when Joe's sister in Sidmouth would have her eightieth birthday."

"As to the 'why now?' ..." Jon pulled his chair closer to the table. "That isn't so hard. It was because of the computer!"

"Her computer?" Perstow said, sounding surprised. "Why is that?"

"There's a public-access, for-pay computer in the post office. She would notice who uses it. The killer likely intended to knock her on the head hard enough to kill. When she fell, the dress went up. The murderer, perhaps as surprised as we were, went mad and whacked it for the lie. That would put a self-righteous spin on this character if it were true."

Trewe nodded. "But do we know yet what the leaves in with her blood were?"

"Dried parsley flakes," Perstow said.

"I thought so," Jon said. "Makes sense the killer had them with him."

Trewe looked pointedly at Jon. "But what does the parsley mean, dear expert-of-all-things-herbal?"

"Well, parsley used to be called the Devil's herb, because it takes so long for the seed to germinate that it was said it would go down to hell seven times before reaching for heaven. Honored as a plant of death, the customary thing to do was put the leaves on the corpse or to make them into wreaths for decorating tombs."

Perstow whistled through his teeth. "You're sayin' he was honoring the dead?"

"Not in the postmistress's case, but likely in Tavy's. Remember the parsley in Tavy's pockets was fresh, but these were crumbled flakes. Probably leftovers he still carried in his pockets."

Trewe finished his tea and set the mug down with a thud. "There should be a law against people knowing too bloody much. We've another inquest to attend. We've put paid to one mystery only to have more open up."

Perstow's face paled. "Whatever is next?"

The weather had turned unseasonably warm and oppressive, but they were able to walk from the Hasten Inn to the courthouse because it was only a little ways along the cliffs. To the north across the sea-filled horizon, the clouds were a deep blue-black while, where Jon stood, the light was bright as blazes. *Storm front,* he thought, *Just wish it would get on with it.* He removed his jacket as he entered the long, narrow courtroom of the combined county courthouse and walked down the aisle between the rows of pew-like benches that faced the podium.

The police tape blocked off the area around the post office and though it attracted the gawkers, there really wasn't anything to see even if they could get past all the curtained windows and closed doors. The post office was only a small portion of the building in the front and was completely separate from any of the official offices or the courtroom.

Extra chairs had been added around the court room in anticipation of a crowd. It was almost empty save for a few people along one wall. They had laptops open, or notepads, so were likely reporters. There was a news crew outside. Cameras were not allowed in the courtroom. As to the laptops, they were probably going to have to put them aside at some point because most of them had video.

Trewe sat alone near the front. Taking a seat behind Trewe, he leaned forward and said, "Someone mentioned a package left near the incident room with your name on it?"

Trewe turned slightly and muttered, "Not a pleasant subject."

"Someone trying to tell you your business?"

"He isn't alone then." Trewe turned completely around and gave Jon the eye. "The postmistress's pocketbook with the severed organ tucked inside did me a turn. It was left in one of the rain barrels. Someone saw blood on the outside of the barrel."

"So I heard. Nasty."

"There was a note to Mrs. Butler. She confirms it is her daughter's handwriting, says there was a message from each first word."

"How did she figure it out?"

"Something about text message abbreviations. At any rate, the message was 'don't follow the man.' "

"Good Lord!"

"The fact that he let her write anything at all … I don't know whether the killer wants us to know the girl is alive … whether we are fooling ourselves into thinking we'll catch him out …"

"… or whether he is laying a trap." Jon noticed others take their seats. "Were the cameras functioning on the street near that rain barrel?"

"They were."

"And?"

"There was a figure—bundled, face wrapped in a dark scarf— the sort everyone has. The person was short, or huddled over to look short. Must have known there were cameras—so many cameras." Trewe gave Jon another look.

People drifted in by twos and threes until the room filled. Murmurs, coughs and scuffs of chairs diminished into expectant silence.

The new coroner from Exeter moved purposefully to the front of the large room. He used one hand to whisk his wave of sandy-colored hair off his forehead. With the motion, the hint of a smile disappeared as he took a seat in the front row.

A barrister by the name of Mr. Ackerman moved to the podium. He turned with a flourish before sitting.

A showman, Jon decided.

There was more coughing and scraping of chairs against wooden floors. Perstow lumbered toward them. He nodded to Jon and sat next to Trewe.

"This is the second inquest into the death of Annie Grace Butler," Mr. Ackerman called out. "The law requires a second inquest in the event of a murder being done and no killer apprehended. When the killer is apprehended, there can be no question of injustice in the examination of the body with the opinion written by an independent coroner, thereby expediting the release of the body for burial."

Jon listened to the precise litany of words. The loved ones needed to bury the body. His mind wandered. Who in this room knew the body to be released to Ruth Butler was not her daughter?

Mr. Ackerman called Perstow to testify. "Are you able to proceed?"

Perstow faced the coroner. "Your Honor, I would like to defer to Detective Chief Inspector Peter Trewe. I reserve the right to add anything I might wish to include, in due time."

Mr. Ackerman nodded, "Of course. Let the record so reflect. Thank you, Sergeant. Detective Chief Inspector Trewe, take the oath."

Trewe cleared his throat. "I swear by Almighty God that the evidence I give shall be the truth, the whole truth, and nothing but the truth."

"Thank you. Proceed."

Jon glanced across the other attendees toward Ruth Butler on the other side of the room. She turned in his direction. He gave a quick nod. He'd kept quiet despite his frustration at not being able to add anything constructive. He had no hope of impressing her. But he would solve this case no matter how long and frustrating it became.

Trewe gave his name, rank, and number, then said, "We received a call ..." and he went on to report what had happened after the call came about the body in the surf.

Jon thought about what he had been doing on that day: checking up on Trewe, walking the cliffs wondering how the man had come into so much money, seemingly all at once—and now that he knew, he still didn't understand why Trewe didn't retire. His mind was pulled back into the flow of Trewe's voice.

"... and immediately alerted police officers in the area to respond."

Trewe went on to recount the investigation's progress before and after the discovery of the body. Jon listened to the facts but remembered how his discovery of the body had left him heartsick and furious. What a jolt that had been. And now the real girl's parents are hearing this for the first time.

Another witness was speaking.

The criminal profiler from London was a woman, Dr. Sarah Manning, whose bottled-blond hair contrasted sharply against her florid face. She spoke distinctly. "This type of killer's thoughts fester in his mind, and create pressures that need an outlet. If at any time he or she were afforded opportunity to kill with impunity, he or she would consider them opportunities to perfect the killing technique. Each incident feeds the murderous urges and the effect is a release of pressure …" She used the words "steps to moral decline," which made her sound as if she were reading from a textbook.

An intelligent-sounding combination of words later, she concluded that this killer had likely reached a tight place of no return, which meant, to Jon's way of thinking, that the killer could not stop killing.

Ruth's mother fidgeted in the seat next to her. The room was already stuffy. Ruth leaned forward, determined to hear everything. She repeated to herself that this was not about her daughter.

During the first inquest she had been sick, numbed, and unable to understand most of what went on. This time she felt her time was being wasted when she would rather be out looking for Annie. Tears burned her dry eyes. She glanced around at the blurred colors in the courtroom. No one stood out. No one called attention to themselves. Of course, the person responsible had been a chameleon all this time; he wouldn't be any different today. Not unless she did something to force him.

On the other side of her was Sally in her flannel jumper, her face a bit red from the heat in the room. Sally gave her hand a squeeze. Sally didn't know that Annie was not the subject of this inquest. How would she react when she told her that Annie was still alive? She wasn't supposed to, but she had decided to tell her after the inquest. She wanted her perspective.

Sam sat behind her, so she could see him if she turned sideways a little. He looked like a whitewashed beach pebble, all clean and neat, but not at all outstanding. He had offered to represent her in this inquest but she told him that everything about it was routine because they still had not discovered who the killer was. She couldn't in good conscience ask someone to cross-examine any witnesses. But he promised to help her with her immigration problems later.

Ruth didn't want to jump up and yell, "Who did this?" but not doing anything was becoming more difficult by the minute. Her mother squeezed her hand. It was good to have her here.

Jon Graham was across the aisle. She thought about how he had told her the body was not Annie. Her heart gave a painful lurch again. That's right, not Annie. It was someone else's precious child, but not Annie.

She wondered what to make of this man. He seemed as outraged as she did.

Sally wiped a hand across her forehead. She moved her face into Ruth's line of vision and raised an eyebrow. "What is it? What are you looking at?"

"Nothing. I'm fine." She looked towards the back of the room.

Mr. Malone stood near the door. He caught her eye and gave a jaunty half-wave. She noticed Sergeant Perstow leave. He seemed to be in a hurry. She shivered. The room suddenly felt cold. It crept all the way into her bones.

A sudden movement caught Jon's eye. Perstow moved quickly to leave, brushing past Mr. Malone who stood at the open door. Malone's dark eyes swept the room. Jon was reminded of a ferret with his quick movements and his beaked nose sloping to a point. He wondered why Perstow exited the room so abruptly. He wasn't supposed to leave.

The video expert, Mr. Clark Grimly, had his projection screen set to face the courtroom. One of those PowerPoint slide shows, very up-to-date. It must be his own equipment; it was doubtful the Perrin's Point police had anything like it. Grey-haired, be-spectacled, and altogether the picture of respectability, Mr. Grimly spent the next few moments composing himself by straightening his bow tie and flattening his hair down to his skull. Now that all eyes and ears were giving him absolute attention, the esteemed Mr. Grimly stammered and sputtered until he noticed a smudge on one of the photo displays. As he set about wiping the spot, his manner smoothed.

Jon wanted to raise his voice and say, "Get on with it!"

When asked if the photo could show anything about the child's death, Mr. Grimly replied, "The present formatted images don't point toward any solid pictorial evidence.

For Christ's sake would someone put a stopper in this man's mouth and tell him there were more important things to do than listen to words like "formatted images." Jon couldn't sit through much more of this. Where had Perstow gone? Had he gotten sick? Perhaps he should check on him. He stood and moved down the aisle to step out into the hall. A spike-haired youth stood by the door speaking in low tones to Perstow. Was it a male? Who could tell? Very skinny, no boobs, must be male. He wouldn't be out of place in London, but here, he looked lost. As Perstow became more animated, the youth appeared increasingly disturbed.

Jon stepped toward them. "Can I help you?"

A mass of dyed blue-black hair stood out all over his head except for bangs flattened and plastered down straight over the front of his face all the way to his chin. Jon imagined he must have to crane his neck to see in front of him. Of course, he could not bend his neck too far back because his skull would become pierced on the vicious spikes protruding from the thick leather collar buckled around his neck.

The boy whispered, "Are you the one in charge?"

"I'm one of them."

"I've got this for you."

When he reached into a pocket of his black trench coat, Jon froze. Did he have a knife? A bomb?

The youth pulled a videocassette from his coat. With the peculiar singsong lilt of Cornwall, he said, “I picked this up on the cliffs. I thought it might have something interestin’ on. It did, but not for me.”

“What’s on it?” Jon asked, taking the cassette.

“Her from the posters.”

Jon turned the plastic casing over in his hands. There, written in his own handwriting was the word “Beach.”

49

Jon reentered the courtroom, resolutely made his way to Trewe and handed the videotape to him.

"What's this?"

Jon leaned forward and whispered, "The beach tape. Fellow found it on the cliffs. I haven't seen it as I didn't have a VCR, but the boy says Annie is on it."

Trewe growled, "Do say."

"Excuse me, gentlemen," the coroner said. He and the video expert glared from the front of the room.

Trewe nodded in Mr. Ackerman's direction, and turned to whisper. "We'll need to record the tape's receipt."

Jon nodded. "I will get it in writing how the young man found it and all."

Trewe stood up.

Mr. Ackerman stared pointedly at him. "Detective Chief Inspector Trewe?"

"Sir. We have just been presented with a videocassette, which may contain possible evidence. We haven't been able to review it as no one has a VCR."

Mr. Malone tromped to the front of the room and waved a hand as if there were a taxi to stop. "As County Magistrate, my office is here. I have a VCR. If you would like to use it to view the tape," Mr. Malone announced, "it's just through that door."

Trewe interjected, "I'd like Mr. Grimly to review it, to see what it contains."

Mr. Ackerman shrugged. "An hour adjournment. No more. We have a duty to perform and it is important we do so in a timely manner."

Murmurs and low conversation swelled to full-voiced clamor as chairs scraped and the doors opened to outside sounds and fresh air. Distant thunder rumbled. A storm was brewing. It was probably the reason for the dead air and stuffiness of the courtroom.

Jon's attention focused on Ruth. She had stepped up from her seat and made her way to where they stood at the front of the courtroom. She grabbed Trewe by the arm. "I want to see it."

Trewe carefully extracted his arm from her grip. "Mrs. Butler, we don't know what's on this."

"Let me see it."

That's the way! Jon silently encouraged her.

"Let me make myself better understood," Trewe said. "We've been told Annie is on this tape. We don't know if this is the tape of her on the beach, or …"

"Or?"

"Or if the killer has recorded something different on this tape."

Jon watched Ruth's face as the implications of what the killer may have filmed of her daughter sank in. "I've been through hell these past few weeks. I don't expect anything worse can happen, do you?"

Jon interrupted, "I imagine there can be worse piled upon worse."

"But—"

Jon noticed Malone by the door of what he presumed was his office, waiting on them. They would not let him view the video until they had run through it once.

"No," Trewe told her, and he and Mr. Grimly went into Mr. Malone's office.

She turned to Jon. Her eyes flashed heat enough to take the skin off his face.

"They have to make sure of what is on the tape," he said quietly.

"Someone's got to *do* something!"

"I understand."

"How could you?" Ruth turned away.

"What's going on?" Jon hadn't heard Sam walk up from behind them.

Ruth growled, "A video. There may be something on it about Annie. They won't let me see it. Everyone seems to forget that this is my daughter."

Trewe came out of Mr. Malone's office. "Mrs. Butler."

Ruth jumped to her feet. "Then you'll let me see it now?"

Trewe sighed. "It's almost identical to the other videos, Mrs. Butler, but yes, you may view it. And we need the computer expert to manipulate things, enhance things. There might be something."

Mr. Malone waited with the coroner at the podium. "I would like to view the evidence myself."

Mr. Ackerman pointed to the two television monitors in the room. "And why not use these?"

Trewe's face had grown progressively redder. He sputtered, "It's a bloody circus. No, we'll use the computer and VCR in Malone's office only!"

Jon leaned toward Trewe and murmured, "I'd like another constable or two in the room with us. Aren't there some firearms officers on the team? Someone with a gun?"

Trewe frowned.

Sam interjected, "May I join?"

"You can wait," Trewe said.

Jon was surprised with Trewe's calm but firm response and whispered, "Besides the mother, the person most interested in seeing this would be the killer."

Sam waited some feet away. His face had gone scarlet. He looked as if he would say something, but instead clenched his fists and muttered to himself.

Trewe paused, considering. "Yes, Mr. Ketterman. Do join us." Then Trewe excused himself and came back a few minutes later with two uniformed officers that Jon didn't recognize. Perstow, Mr. Malone, Mr. Ackerman, Jon, the lab's video expert, and Ruth crowded forward. Trewe more or less pushed the group through the door.

As Jon entered, Malone switched on another light. The room had been dim in order, Jon presumed, to see the video better. The eminently respectable magistrate had turned this room into a comfortable office for village business. Jon swallowed. Comfortable wasn't the correct word to describe it. Decadent would be a better word.

"Oh, wee!" was Perstow's exclamation.

Jon crossed the room to glance out the window and get his bearings. They were about four meters from the cliffs. He turned back to face the room, the air permeated with scents of lemon oil, old leather, and quiet. Except for the desk and a few side chairs, there was no other furniture in the room. The colorful vase near the door was a bit startling. Then again, the walls behind Malone's desk held their own surprises. Inlaid light and dark woods held a central disk of carved semi-precious stones and mother-of-pearl. Jon leaned in to examine the relief carvings. On closer inspection, he realized the sculpted figurines were set in risqué situations.

Trewe coughed. "I've never been in here before, Quentin."

"In the eighteenth century, this room was a meeting room for gentlemen's pleasures. Pleasures, if you catch my meaning." Mr. Malone stood behind his gigantic desk, waiting. His grin seemed a bit over the top. "This wall had been paneled over, if you can believe that. I've brought it back to its original grandeur. True grandeur."

Trewe cleared his throat, "Down to business."

Chairs had been dragged from the outer room to the desk. The uniformed officers stood by the door. Malone turned to loosen the gold brocade rope from the curtains covering the windows. "To darken the room a bit to view the video better. Just darken it a bit." He moved around to the back of his desk to stand behind them.

Trewe and the video expert, Mr. Grimly, seated themselves in front of the computer, with Jon standing on the other side of Mr. Grimly. They had moved the VCR and the television monitor to the desktop. Ruth stood behind Trewe. Sam stood to her left, closer to the door. Perstow stood next to him. They could all see the monitor. They waited while the expert plugged VCR adaptor into the computer and then added a device of his own to the computer. It looked like a flash drive. "Will only be a moment, while this loads. I've got a special video enhancing software program, should do the trick. We want to record what we see. I will remove it entirely when we are done, Mr. Malone. You won't even know it's been on here."

"Fine, fine, anything for the experts. Anything," Malone grumphed.

Mr. Grimly pressed "rewind" on the VCR and then pressed "play."

The light from the monitor brightened the room.

Jon glanced at Ruth. How would she react to seeing this? He heard her gasp as the picture flashed of the girls as they picked up shells and laughed together in the blue-gray morning. The familiar shoes—God, this must be horrible to see her daughter's last free moments.

Dot mouthed something and ran off. Annie turned. Her mouth moved as if she was singing. There was an undecipherable muttering. The video expert stopped the action and moved the cursor to bring up a separate window of colorful panels that he minimized to fit alongside the video. He brought the tones up and down and adjusted a video resolution file. Jon watched the bars change; it was like looking at the front of a stereo as the bass, treble, balance, and tone bands were manipulated. But this had to do with tones of the shadows in the video. It didn't help. They couldn't decipher words.

Mr. Grimly paused the action and looked at Trewe and Perstow. They shook their heads. Jon heard Ruth give an audible sigh next to him, and beside her Malone shifted his feet.

The expert pressed "play." On the tape, Annie stopped as if listening. As she turned, her face registered shock, and then she walked toward the camera and looked up. Surprise? Annie started to say something, then there was a flash of black to one side, behind the girl, then the screen went darker—shades of dark, and shadows—then the screen was filled with blackness. The expert used another window block to manipulate the tones. It made matters only worse.

Trewe muttered, "Back it up. Play it again."

The expert quickly did as he was told and pressed "play" again.

Jon leaned forward in his seat. He pointed, "There—pause it there."

The flash of black in the corner was the dog running across the screen in the background, then quickly disappearing. But forget the dog. Chelsea distracted the eye from the really important part. "Wait!" Jon grabbed the mouse from the expert and stopped action.

"What?" the video expert sputtered, "We've been over this."

"Quiet." Jon backed the footage to the part he might have seen in that instant. "Here," he let go the mouse, "advance frame by frame, and stop it when I say."

Trewe gave him a look. Mr. Grimly growled, "If you say so, sir."

He did, and Mr. Grimly stopped action when Jon said, "There."

The picture framed not Annie's face, but the side of the sheer cliff. The sun had made a brilliant appearance in that brief second and the reflection cast shadows dimly, barely discernible. Frozen on the screen a ghost of a shadow fell across the tall shelf of stone behind Annie. The shadow of a man drooped across the stone. Though distorted, the shadow of the distinct facial profile was easily recognizable.

50

Jon swiveled at the muffled scream from where Ruth had been behind the desk. Quentin Malone, county magistrate, had Ruth in his grip. They leaned against the back wall. He stood not five feet away from them. He stepped closer.

"You'd best stay where you are!" A strange woman's voice rang out. Then a man's voice, "Mother, stop! Don't make me do it this way."

"Fool!" the woman's voice screeched. "Can't do anything without losing it."

Jon saw the gun and froze. "Mr. Malone, you can't get away."

"No?" Malone, of the distinct penguinesque nose, held the gun under Ruth's ear with one hand and gripped her tightly in a strangle hold with the other. "Looks like we have you all where we want you."

For all his training, Jon could do nothing against bullets. "You don't have to do this. We can help you."

Malone jerked Ruth around like a rag doll. The metal gun barrel clicked against an earring. "Bullets enough for all. Who first?"

A woman's cracked falsetto voice rang out from Malone's mouth, "Kill the woman."

"Don't tell me what to do!" Malone screamed. Saliva flew. He switched from voice to voice with eerie precision.

"Chubby Charlie!"

"Stop calling me that!" Malone whipped the gun up and waved it across the room. His hand shook.

Jon reached for Ruth.

A gunshot. The vase by the door exploded. Jon ducked.

Dust billowed around the vase. It must have been a burial urn. Jon pivoted around to see Malone standing with his back against the decorated wall, holding Ruth in front of him. Malone fired two more shots into the ceiling. The gun clicked. Malone threw the gun at Trewe. It glanced across his head. Trewe slumped down. Malone leaned against the wall. Jon thought, *He's boxed in.* Air whooshed. A dark place gaped in the wall. Malone pulled Ruth backward. The opening in the wall narrowed. The gap was closing.

"Jon! No!" Trewe yelled.

But Jon had already dived through.

Ruth struggled against the crazy man. A scream rose from deep within and poured long and loud from her mouth. Her pulse raced and her thoughts with it. She had to get away. He had squeezed her into a skinny hallway with gobs of dry plaster sticking out of rough stone walls with half-hidden timbers. Cobwebs scraped off the walls and clung to her. Pain from her injured hand shot up her arm. As soon as he pulled her completely within the enclosed place Malone let her fall to her feet.

"Walk!" he commanded.

"I'm going," she muttered, furious at herself for getting caught and equally terrified of what this man was. She jumped to her feet and turned to give him a swift kick. The torch light in her eyes was like a blow. She stumbled backward, off-balance, but caught herself before she fell down a flight of stairs.

"Go!" Malone ordered and grabbed a big hank of her hair. He held so tight she couldn't move her head. She mostly slid down the steps with Malone on her heel.

She heard shouts behind them.

At the base of the stairs an old timber door blocked them, but Malone was through it and had it locked behind them as if he'd practiced the move many times. In that moment she was able to twist and step away from him and would have gotten farther if he hadn't grabbed her bad hand and spun her around. He loomed, his face a mask of hatred.

She clutched her hand to her chest and shouted, "Why did you take Annie?"

"She was to help me get you," he hissed. His fist smashed into her mouth and a tooth sliced through her lip. She fell backwards on the rough stone floor. Sparks of light exploded behind her eyes. The pain took a second to register. She choked back a sob and swallowed blood. Her stomach rebelled. He pressed a knee squarely onto her midsection and pressed so she couldn't breathe. Her lungs burned. She choked on her own blood. He made a cruel hacking sound through smiling lips as he snarled, "You've been a challenge."

With a violent convulsive movement, he dragged her.

The knobby stone floor scraped every inch of her backside. Sweat ran down her chest. Spitting blood, she yelled, "What do you want?"

Malone responded with a sharp bark of laughter. About ten feet later, he stopped. She ordered her mind to register what kind of hell Malone had created. It stank of dead and rotting things despite the cold. But all she could see was the wet rock walls and a black hole in the floor.

When Jon Graham stepped after them, his foot found nothing to land on for a heart-stopping second. He flung an arm out and caught himself short against stone. With the click of the closing wall behind him, there was a cutting off of sound, a deadness—a lack of echo. The space he found himself in was no more than two feet across. He was trapped.

He choked and bent double fighting nausea. He pulled himself up. He had to save Ruth Butler. He had to. His arms knocked against the walls. His breath came in short gasps. He clutched at his throat and heard a little boy screaming, "Let me out!" It wasn't him. He wasn't a kid stuck in a cupboard beneath the stairs any longer.

Then he remembered that Perstow had given him a penlight. Pulling it out of his pocket and switching it on, he started down a short hall. When he heard a muffled banging from the other side of the wall, he called out, "I'm here!" but realized his words went nowhere. Pulling his mobile out, he dialed.

Trewe answered. "What's there? Do you see another entry?"

"You've got to get through. It's dark. There's steps leading to God-knows-where with a door at the base. I'm going down. The signal will be cut as soon as I'm below ground."

"Do you see any lever on that side of the wall?" Trewe sounded desperate himself.

"Nothing."

"We'll keep trying. There must be another way in."

"What's below me?"

Trewe conferred with Perstow, "Abandoned mines, tunnels reaching miles in every direction."

"Great," Jon said. "That's just great."

Trewe shouted at Perstow, "Surround the building. We need reinforcements. Jon, I'll get someone to break a hole through from this side."

"I'm going after her, Peter. I can't let him hurt her." Feeling his way down the narrow passageway, Jon held the phone against his ear with one hand and the penlight in the other hand.

"Tell me what you see," Trewe yelled.

"I'm trying … I don't like small spaces. For Christ's sake, don't go away."

He placed his phone on the step, then lay the penlight on the step above so it shone down across the door. He braced his elbows against the brick walls to leverage his weight and concentrate the force of his kick against the door. Nothing. He tried again. The wood gave. He kicked again. His foot smashed through. He tried the lock from the inside. The door opened on well-oiled hinges. He picked up the mobile.

Trewe was yelling. "What happened?"

"I'm through. It's cold. Smells bad, like rancid meat."

Silence on Trewe's end, then static.

Jon muttered, "Oh God."

Trewe's voice suddenly burst into his ear. "Jon! We may know a way to get to you. There's a mine shaft west of you on the coast. We'll have someone try from that end. Infrared cameras are on the way."

The connection died as Jon said, "Gotta go. I heard Ruth."

As long as his mobile's battery lasted, he could use the compass—and the torchlight app didn't hurt—and he could message. In the event that signals reconnected, they would discover his last thoughts, if nothing else.

51

Ruth felt her loose tooth with the tip of her tongue. She held her arms across her belly, bent into them, gulping air. She fought the desire to throw up.

Malone waved the flame of his torch over a small box. He lifted out a necklace that looked like it was made of colored glass, but something told her that he wouldn't be this crazy if it were only glass. A snake-like quality oozed from his voice. "Fascinated? Take it."

"No."

"I've never offered you such riches before."

She turned her face from him.

He spat at her, "Am I so disgusting you cannot look at me, Mother?"

Ruth didn't answer.

"Then go." He stood and pushed her ahead of him.

She hit her head on the rock ceiling. She stooped, but another shove from behind sent her scrambling to stay on her feet. Malone's torch made the shadows dance around her. Her head swirled with the smell and the horror and the shadows. Sweating, she clutched her hand to her chest and tried to slip her shoes back on because they had come loose. He pushed her. Her shoes came off. He made a sudden movement and she leapt forward to avoid his touch. She had to abandon the shoes. Many steps later they came to another wide place. He hardly allowed her time to stand straight before he shoved her again. Twenty paces into the tunnel, she tripped and fell to the floor, landing on her good hand before whacking her bad hand again.

She ground her teeth against the pain, knowing that she wasn't going to survive unless she took control. She jumped up. Her socks made her feet slip on the wet floor, but she dashed back the way they had come. He was quicker. Maneuvering his body in front of hers, he smacked her across the face.

His hair, which had been wound around his head in a massive, flattened mess to hide the baldness, now stuck out in greasy strings. With a finger held to her nose, he cackled, "You can go with pain or you can go without pain. But go, you must." And he stooped and threw her over his shoulder like a sack of rice.

From her position as human gunnysack, Ruth struggled for breath each time Malone's bony shoulder jabbed into her abdomen. Once she'd gotten breath, she twisted around until he dropped her. She had a fistful of his tweed jacket. The material stunted the brunt of her fall, but a sharp rock dug into her back as she landed. She bit her lip to keep from screaming. She wouldn't give him the satisfaction of hearing her scream. She wanted room to maneuver and hurt him and get away.

But what if he took her to Annie? She heard a tapping noise. Footsteps? She yelled, "Help!"

Malone back-handed her. She fell.

"We are being followed," Malone muttered. The torchlight jerked crazily across the shining walls. "Get up!"

From somewhere nearby came the sound of running water. Her heart thundered in her chest. She'd read somewhere that the mines sometimes went under the sea, where the miners could hear the waves push and pull boulders across the ocean floor above them.

"Where's Annie?"

Malone leered. "Weren't you scheduled to bury her after the inquest?"

"That isn't my daughter."

"So they know, do they?"

"I don't know." She huddled over her bandaged hand. The pain so great that the light blurred into rainbow flashes. She yelled, "Where is she?"

"Wouldn't you like to know?" Malone towered over her. "Murdering slut!"

She leaned away and used the momentum for a sidekick—and missed. She had miscalculated and he leapt aside. By the yellow glow of the torch, his face shone oily and pockmarked. His nose ran rivulets into the drool from both corners of his mouth.

"Get away from me." She brought her knee up as he leaned over her. It glanced off his leg. He held her down with a foot. She wrenched sideways but was unable to budge the reeking hulk.

He reached and pulled her up by her hair, then wedged her neck into a headlock. Her wet socks slipped on the rock. He ranted in her ear, "Don't you think I am sick to hell with always explaining myself? You would never leave me alone."

"I never did anything to you."

He yanked her around so they were face to face again. "Of course not, you never knew me at all, did you?"

"I'm not your mother."

"I always wondered." He stared hard at her and growled, "If you were truly dead we would all have peace."

She moved her shoulder down for leverage and gave an upper cut to his belly, but he stepped away, so her fist caught him lower. He bent double with a retch. She raced back the way they had come, but there was no light. It was so dark she couldn't see her hand in front of her face. In a crouch, she tried to think. Where could she go? The cave held a strong smell of death. *Mustn't stop.* She stumbled forward and fell on something that squished beneath her with a horrible stench. She felt around and recognized the feel of another hand, cold and lifeless. She gagged and realized she was able to distinguish shapes—light meant

Malone was coming. She glanced down and saw a row of human limbs, rotting and shriveled.

She retched and pulled herself up. She had to get away. Too late. Hands grabbed her and shoved her head against the wall. There was a loud explosion in her mind and the dark folded in on her.

Spurred on by Ruth's cries, Jon rushed forward. He stopped at a wide place in the tunnel. Timbers held up the roof and walls, and the floor had been roughly hewn. His light revealed a juncture of three tunnels. Another cry came from the tunnel on the right. The low ceiling forced him to stoop double. He stepped over a small box with an open lid and played the light over gold coins and jewels. So this was Malone's secret.

A residual dankness of long-gone sweaty bodies permeated his sense of smell until it seemed he could actually taste body odor.

Malone. The man had been a wealth of information, filling Jon in on the history of Cornwall and of pirates, about the wreckers and the Spanish ships carrying gold to finance political schemes. The fitted wall panel that hid the secret passage for men and goods to come and go. Jon had half-listened like a foolish schoolboy. School's out now, Jon Graham.

He flashed the penlight across ancient, rotting timbers. One slip against a bulwark, one knock against a piling, and the whole works could come down on top of him. He wondered how many tons of rocks suspended by these few strips of dead tree waited above his head. Every creaking sound, every shower of dust raining from the ceiling reminded him that a few miniscule, soft, squashable humans crept under it all. He knew how being trapped felt. He tasted fear, a metallic, hollow taste that coated his tongue, and dried his mouth.

He held himself against a wall to decide which way to go. Two dark, rough-hewn holes gaped before him. *Ip dip, sky blue! Who's it? Not you!* What a stupid thing to have flash across his mind. In this horrifying chase to save Ruth, he found his mind wandering. There must be bad air. He heard a cry. He pitched forward as he tripped over a wide board. It had been covering a hole. The fresh breeze blowing from the hole cleared his head. He got up and kept going. From somewhere before him came the sickly smell of rotting flesh. There was a pair of women's shoes, laying as if tossed aside. The floor rose steadily. The walls gleamed with streaming water.

Passing a ridge of dark granite, he saw from the corner of his eye a reflected flash from his light. He played the beam into the deep shadows and saw three small legs, severed and neatly lined in a row. He came to a full stop.

A pretty bracelet on an out-flung arm led his eye to Liz Malone, who lay toes up, as if peacefully asleep. Her dress, blue like her eyes, was one Jon had noticed before. Her head was turned slightly. As he stared at her, her eyes opened.

He gasped, heart thudded to his throat. "My God!"

Liz moved a hand and then tried to sit up. Jon rushed to her. Her head was bleeding. She said, "He wants to kill me. My husband wants to kill me."

"Can you stand?"

"I need air. What smells so bad? Where am I? What has he done?"

Jon didn't want her so shocked she couldn't move. He needed her help. "Tell me what you know."

"It was after breakfast. He told me he wanted me to see something at his office. I followed him into the wall. I thought … it was amazing, but then I don't remember anything else. Except once we were here, he said …" She cried out, "He said he wants to kill me. Why?"

"You've got to get back down this tunnel. Here's my penlight. There's a hole in the floor you've got to miss. Do you think you can do it? Can you walk?"

"Where will you be?"

"I've got to keep going. He's got Ruth Butler."

"Oh my, no!"

“Can you get back? They are trying to break open the wall. There is no way to contact them this far underground. You can tell them where we are.”

“I know how to open it. He showed me because I wouldn’t follow him unless he showed me.”

“Please, go help them.”

Liz stumbled back the way they had come, leaving Jon in the dark.

52

Jon turned his mobile on and pressed the flashlight app. It was brighter than the penlight. He clambered farther into the tunnel until he found himself at a dead end. Somehow he had taken a wrong turn, except there had been no turns. An enormous wall of smooth rock blocked his path.

His light revealed an amphitheater of rock that could fit his entire London flat. Water dripped and gurgled with a hollow sound but he couldn't see any water. There were moaning sounds nearby, but he couldn't see anything. The ground was knobby rock like the rest of the tunnel, but there was mud and leaves and twigs. Large boulders were firmly ensconced around the area. There must be an opening to the outside that he couldn't see. He would look behind the boulders.

An old-fashioned oil-rag torch had been jammed into a crevice on the floor. It had been recently extinguished because one end still glowed in places. He was glad he still had the matchbook he'd picked up at the Spider's Web. Kneeling, he balanced the mobile, lit a match, and stuck it to the dark mass on the end of the stick. It didn't ignite. He hit the torch against a rock to knock off mud.

He struck another match. The torch flared. An inverted, funnel-shaped black hole in the ceiling intrigued him. He held the flame higher. It was a shaft filled with cobwebs. He stuck the torch in and air currents flirted with the flame. They were close to the surface. This was where the leaves came from.

He punched Trewe's number into his mobile. Bloody unlikely any signal could be picked up at this point, but nothing wrong with trying. He saw it did connect and was about to exclaim to Trewe that he was not far underground when he felt a sharp pain, heard something crack and saw the ground rushing at his face.

Ruth gasped as Jon's body crumpled to the floor. She had tried to scream as Malone snuck up to Jon as he was lighting the torch and hit him with a rock. Nothing came out but a high moaning sound from around the gag Malone had stuffed in her mouth. Her feet and hands were trussed roughly with a piece of rope behind her so she couldn't even squirm. When Jon arrived, she had tried to make some sound, but Malone's thin bony fingers pressed against her throat. *Oh Lord Jesus, help us!*

On the ground near Jon's out-flung hand, the mobile phone squawked.

"Wakie, wakie, Jonnie boy!" A maniacal giggle came from Malone. He picked up the mobile.

"All will be well in the end, you know," Malone said into the mobile. "You think you're so very important, policeman Trewe. How do you feel now?"

Malone hummed a senseless tune and danced around the rock room in the flickering torchlight. As he swung around near Ruth with his hand arched toward her face, she ducked instinctively.

As Malone hummed and danced in his own, sick little world, she worked her way to her knees for her own little dance. If he were to look her way, she thought, perhaps he would think she was on the same mental wave length or something crazy. Soon her arms were raw. Warm blood dripped between her fingers.

Her fevered maneuvers had her arms finally free. She crawled to Jon. *Dear God!* She threw herself across his chest.

His heart thumped in her ear. Alive? He was alive!

The flame from the lit torch danced across the walls joined by Malone's gyrating shadow. He danced closer and with a swift step lifted her away from Jon. He leered at her and pawed at her breasts. She rolled away from him. He was working himself into a frenzy. Shuffling in a wide circle again, he sang out, "Oh! Your lover's dead." The sweat rolled off his face. Saliva dripped from his mouth onto his dirty shirt.

"He isn't my lover."

"Mother, we both know what sort of company you keep. No use pretending."

"I'm not your mother."

"I recognized you. Aren't you glad I did? Time is. Time was. Time's past. That's us. Mother, I've always loved you!" He had to pull his hair out of his mouth. He stood very still, his eyes dark empty pits. "Mother, no one can compare to you. The circle is never broken is it? You always said you would come back to haunt me."

His voice cracked, and became high-pitched again. "I say what I mean and mean what I say."

He suddenly focused his attention on Ruth. The stare he gave her was lit with its own cold fury. In his own tone, Malone said, "But you see, I have figured this through. You want to die. You want it."

Her thoughts came slow but she scrambled for words. "Why did you kill those others? That girl?"

"I didn't kill anyone. They died."

"Why did you keep her?"

"I … I wanted her … youth. All of them. They tried to give it to me. I can't find Cecil. She's missing. I want her back. I can't have her back unless I'm young again like she is."

"Why Tavy?"

He appeared confused. "You told me to rid myself of hindrances." He whispered, "The old man knew my name. He tried to convert me.

What would I do with a god? That hypocrite the postmistress—she figured it out." He paused, and then said, "And that German whore wanted what I couldn't give her, didn't she? She wouldn't let up with her insistent demands—sex, sex, sex. That's all she ever wanted. I told her when I was young again … but then … then she laughed!"

"Liz? You killed your wife?" *Dear God!* That dear woman who made her good soup.

With a sneer, Malone bent toward Ruth. Then he jerked away, chanting, "Not yet. Not yet. Not yet." He took off his jacket and climbed atop a boulder, teetered, then balanced. He slumped down and stared at her. He looked like a vulture.

"Why did you take my daughter?" Ruth said.

He seemed puzzled.

"Take your daughter?" He crouched like a bird of prey on top of the boulder.

"She's a little girl."

"Young girl. Yes. Her blood is good."

"No!"

His voice rose to a higher pitch. "I followed you, Mother. That girl was going to tell her mum. I tried to stop her to explain. You saw it, Mother. She fell. Knocked herself out. Her fault." He held his arms out to Ruth and whined, "Tell me you love me."

His red-rimmed, bloodshot eyes protruded from his oily, swollen face. He was more than mad—he was desperate. In an anguished voice, he cried, "Just this once. Tell me you love me."

He leapt off the boulder and loomed over her. "Tell me!" Malone's shirt, drenched with sweat, clung to his shrunken chest and bulging stomach. The animal smell of him was overpowering. His wild eyes went unfocused and he turned away from her and spun in a circle around her. He moved his hands above his head as if they were flapping wings as he bobbed and swayed to unheard music.

She looked at Jon. *Lord, please.* If only he would wake up. If only she could find Annie. The thought seared into her head, what if I can't? No, it's best if she didn't think like that. She watched for an opportunity to do something because, if she had to die, she would take Malone with her.

Malone's scraggly head appeared from the shadows like a death skull. The whites of his eyes showing, he stared in her direction but didn't seem to be able to focus on anything, but seemed to be looking at something just above her head. He scooted forward and caught her up before she could brace herself. Her feet slammed against the floor as he dragged her towards the wall. He pressed a spot on the rock.

The wall's mechanics figured out by wily smugglers a century before worked as well as it must have always. It slid aside with hardly a whisper. He held her against his foul shirt, his face next to hers. She turned away. He shoved her through the doorway into a pocket of fresher air. It took a moment for her eyes to adjust to the light glaring from a diamond-shaped hole in front of her. She heard the wash of surf. Her heart leaped. The sea was near.

The stone door in the wall closed behind them. Jon Graham! He was still in there.

Jon swam up through layers of gray. Something near his ear hissed. Something tickled his cheek. His head throbbed. He cracked open one eye. For a moment he couldn't remember where he was. The torch was still stuck in the crevice in the floor. It hissed. He remembered Trewe on the mobile. Where was it? Funny, he didn't remember leaving it over there. He didn't recall that piece of cloth on the floor, either. Squeezing his eyes shut, he huddled into a tight fetal position, wondering what part of him hurt the most.

As he struggled into an upright position, his mobile yelled. He grabbed it.

He held it to his ear. "Hallo? Hallo?"

"Jon! Is Malone still there?"

Ruth looked frantically around the place they were in now. Green, brown, and yellow lichen spotted the walls. Striations of white streaked the black rock. Water shimmered in a small pool at the center of this grotto. Red and white rags lay everywhere. To one side was a wall studded with trinkets and swatches of what looked disgustingly like human hair. There were signs of human habitation—mucky dishes, rotting pieces of fruit, metal buckets, and a feral smell.

A pile of filthy rags moved and Ruth's mouth went dry. The rags heaved. Dirty streamers of hair appeared. Behind the straggles Ruth saw the eyes. Human? It couldn't be.

"Mummy?"

53

Jon used fingers to force his other eyelid open. It was caked with dust and blood. He scrutinized the cavern. "I don't see Malone. Or Ruth. He spoke to you?"

"Yes. What happened to them?"

"There are drag marks on the ground leading to the wall."

"Liz Malone showed us how to operate the wall. We've got men coming your way."

"Doesn't matter if he has another way out."

"We wanted to use infrared cameras to find them from the cliffs, but two storm fronts are colliding out there. It's bad. We can't use the helicopter."

"I'll keep trying on this end to get through." Inch by filthy inch, Jon continued his slow and methodical pushing against the wall. He worked at his third strategy. The first and second had resulted in nothing. He began at the top, as high as he could reach standing, slowly nudging inward each inch of the flat rock, working his way horizontally across, then back again.

"Annie!" Ruth cried. She glanced at Malone framed by light in the cave's doorway, muttering to himself. Wind howled across the entrance. There was a storm out there. She leapt over the cans and piles to get to Annie. She grabbed and held on to her.

"He's mad," Annie whispered. "You've got to get away. He means to kill you."

Her daughter's wonderful face was dirty and streaked, her lips cracked and swollen. She had purple bruises around one eye. Her hair was dark and matted, and she was chained.

Ruth's heart soared. *My daughter.* "What has he done to you?"

"He leaves me alone in the dark. I hate him. But I tried to warn you not to come."

"I couldn't help it."

"But you've got to get away. I'm almost loose. I'm going to get away. You need to push him into the waves. He'll kill you if you don't."

Ruth glanced around. Malone watched them, his brows knit in a scowl. She held her girl. She whispered in her ear, "We're going together."

"Now is your chance. He doesn't care about me."

Malone would more likely kill them both. Ruth shook her head. "I'll distract him. Get away as soon as you're free."

Malone's eyes took on a strange cast. He rushed over and grabbed Ruth. She knocked his hands away, but he pulled her roughly up, his grip like a vice around her middle. She swung her arms and kicked.

"No!" Ruth despaired. "Let me take her. I'll do whatever you want."

His lips brushed her ear. His voice like a hissing snake, he said, "She's nothing but bag and baggage."

He pulled her through the doorway. As they emerged from the cave there was a clap of explosive thunder. Stinging rain drenched her. They teetered on a precarious ledge. Thirty feet below, waves crashed on the rocks. She reeled, gasping, against the side of the cliff. Malone held her hair twisted in his fist at the nape of her neck. She yelled above the growling waves and storm. "You have me. Let my daughter free."

"I want you to tell me you love me, Mother." He leaned toward her, pulling her face towards his. The wind whipped his stench-breath across her face. "I've waited all these years. You'll tell me. Or we die together on the rocks."

Blinding rain hammered upon her face. Ruth shouted, "Whatever you say, son!"

"That's not good enough!" He tilted her face to his. "Say it."

Sea spray stung her nose. Sky and churning water were the same shade of gray. Rain poured.

Malone pulled her farther up the ledge. She placed her feet for an evasive side kick. Her dripping socks hindered her. He bundled her closer, foiling any movement. His grasp on her tightened.

Rivulets of water snaked across the ledge's pathway. She pulled one sock off with the other foot and stumbled. Malone's grip never let up for an instant. She slipped and ended up hanging midway between the edge of eternity and the end of his arm.

Jon watched, amazed, as the block of stone moved aside. Squeezing through the space, he found himself in a grotto. He stumbled to the opening to the outside and shouted into his mobile, "We're on the cliffs!"

He looked around the rock room—definitely a crime scene. Blood was spattered up one wall, there were blood-soaked rags everywhere, and one wall had chunks chiseled out where tiny vials and jars sat. Beyond that were a pile of rags and a mattress dotted with brown stains in the pattern of a body. There was a strong odor of urine. Water dripped from the ceiling into a tiny, clear pond in the middle of the floor. For one impossible moment, he imagined hiccups coming from the rags.

He pushed aside a rain-sogged mat that covered the cave's entrance and reeled back from the stinging rain. The narrow ledge dropped off abruptly to the surf.

Wind moaned across the entrance. The rain brought a respite from the reptilian, mud scent of the cave. Leaning out, he was just in time to observe two sets of feet slipping and stumbling up the path that curved around and up the side of the cliff.

Behind him, a low sound became an insistent wail.

"I said I want my mum!"

54

Jon turned at the sound of the girl's voice.

"Help me get the pipe loose, Mister," she said.

His eyes adjusted to the light. The pile of rags had eyes. The cloth shifted. Annie Butler's face looked older than ten.

"My God! Annie Butler!" Jon rushed to help her to her feet. She swayed. A thin chain went from her wrist to the wall. He took the metal clasp at her wrist and twisted it, worming fingers from both hands beneath. He'd seen this type of manacle before. It was cheaply made and could be pried apart. "Annie, this may hurt a little." He squeezed his fingers around the clasp and pulled. The metal clinked apart.

He held her steady. "Are you able to walk?"

She wiped her eyes and took an unsteady step, reeling sideways. "Hurry. My mum. He plans to kill her."

He caught her. "I'll carry you."

"No! I can do it." She managed to get to the doorway and pull aside the mat.

"I'll lead," Jon said. "Don't argue! The ledge is too narrow."

Storm and surf roared in concert. Waves rolled closer. Sea spray splattered across the path now. Jon took a firm grip of Annie's bone-thin wrist and helped her out. Cold rain soaked them.

Malone and Ruth were locked in a fierce struggle on the path just ahead. Ruth twisted in Malone's grip. She fell backward and hung toward the water for a second longer than eternity until Malone pulled her toward the cliff.

Jon crouched down. The cliff top was still a bit too high up to lift Annie to it so she could run to safety. The marginal ledge narrowed as they crept forward.

Lightning flashed.

Ruth screamed, "Annie!"

"Damned interfering police," Malone screamed. The rain glistened off his bald pate, strings of hair fell across one shoulder.

Ruth shoved from his grasp. Malone grappled for her.

"Malone!" Jon shouted.

With a roar Malone swung a fist. Jon ducked and grabbed Malone's belt. They grappled nose to nose for an instant. Jon muttered, "Stand still, old man."

Annie pushed past Malone and rushed into her mother's arms.

Malone crashed to the wet path. In a last-second lunge, he grabbed Jon's leg and slid over the ledge. Jon floundered until he flipped onto his stomach and dug his fingers into the dirt, mud, and stone path.

"No!" Annie cried. She reached toward him but Ruth pulled her back.

"Mother!" Malone screeched. "Your fault!"

A dog barked. A dark shape ambled toward them along the cliff ledge.

"Chelsea," Jon called. "Get help!"

"Bloody hell." Malone's curses became incoherent as he continued a steady descent, pulling Jon with him. Malone dangled over the ledge. Jon's fingers were slipping. He was losing ground.

"Hold on, Jon." Ruth knelt and reached for Jon, but Jon grabbed her bandaged hand. She cried out in pain, instinctively grabbing him with her good hand. Their hands were slippery wet.

On his stomach, Jon dug into the muddy path with his elbows, one knee and the toe of his shoe and held onto Ruth. Buffeted by the wind, his grasp loosened. He tried to kick free of the screeching weight clinging to his other leg.

The dark sky and churning sea would engulf them the moment they lost their tenuous hold. He was face to face with Ruth.

"Let go!" he yelled. The wind flung his words back.

Instead, from the corner of his eye he saw Annie crawling to the edge. "Annie! No! Get back!" he screamed.

Ruth, holding onto Jon and leaning back away from the ledge, cried, "Annie, no!"

Annie leaned over Malone. "Hey! I've got something for you!"

She tossed something into Malone's open mouth.

Malone made a strangling sound, grabbed for his throat with both hands. He fell away, silent.

Jon pulled his knees to the ledge and got entirely onto the ledge. He leaned into the cliff. He saw Annie scoot up the path behind the dark shape of Chelsea. Next to him, Ruth's foot slipped on the rock path. He lunged to grab her before she slid to the edge.

Like a restless monster jarred awake from a long nap, the sea rose up with an angry roar, spit and foam without end. Wind and water joined forces. Waves, as big as houses, surged up to the cliffs.

With a ruined mine house shielding them from the gale-force wind, Trewe had gathered half a dozen officers to map out how to proceed in finding the outside entrance to the tunnel that Jon—and presumably, Malone and Ruth—were in. Perstow was directing a group of men to search along the cliffs when a shout sent his group scrambling. Most had fanned out along the cliff top, but Trewe had a feeling about how the mine's shaft ran perpendicular to the cliff. There would be long, narrow shafts called adits in the rock, fashioned to let fresh air into the mine. But when he heard the shouting he didn't hesitate. He ran, his electric torch swinging from side to side.

Allison Craig caught up to him. “Sir, the men saw something this way.”

A wet child and the big black dog made their way toward their lights in the rain. “My God! It’s Annie Butler,” he managed to say.

Annie stumbled toward him. Her leg was bleeding. She cried, “My mum! Save my mum!”

Trewe nodded and yelled over the wind, “Which way?”

The girl pointed back the way she had come and almost fell over, but Allison Craig caught her. Trewe yelled, “We’ll figure it out. Allison, get her dry. Annie, you stay here.”

“No,” Annie yelled. “I’ll show you.”

Trewe hesitated. He couldn’t risk the girl, not after what she must have been through. Perstow ran up. “I hear shouting! Over the side of the cliff.”

Allison pushed a wave of rain-sopped hair out of her eyes and waved an arm, “We can’t waste time, sir.”

Trewe started forward. “Carry on.”

When Annie led them to the ridge, he noted the windswept land with a group of woody shrubs clustered and bent to hide the area where they would have to make their way down. It didn’t look any different than any other part of the cliffs along the coast. He wondered how long it would have taken them to find it without help. Didn’t bear thinking. Trewe stepped down the slope but had to use his hands, scratching at the rock and grit to remain upright in the wind. Rainwater streamed around his feet. He stared into the endless rain. It made it almost impossible to see three feet in any direction. “Line the men up to shine their torches across this way, and another group over that direction. Work across with the beams of light.”

“Do you see anything?” Perstow shouted.

“Not a bloody thing.” Trewe waved his torch all around.

Silver rain fell in blankets across the beam of light.

“Someone take the child to safety.”

Annie yelled, “I’m not leaving without my mother.”

❧

A wave reached up and drenched Jon with freezing water. Salt spray stung his eyes. Wind pushed rain into his mouth. But he no longer slid, and he was able to pull Ruth a bit more and a bit more up the path.

Ruth gasped, "I'm okay. It's okay. Where's Annie?"

"She went up ahead of us." He helped her the last few feet. It was slippery going, but they finally tumbled onto the turf away from the cliff's edge. Annie was at the top of the cliff with Chelsea.

Clutching her daughter, Ruth bawled, "Thank you, Lord. She's alive. Thank you."

With a subtlety antithetical to the storm's emergence on this stage, the wind and thunder subsided with hardly a murmur, leaving only a steady rain in its wake. There were shouts and police sirens.

Jon wrapped his arms around Ruth to help her up. "Let's get somewhere dry."

"Wait," Annie said. She launched herself against Jon with a hug. "Thank you."

Jon asked Annie, "You shouted at Malone—something about 'I've got something for you.' What was it?"

"A button. I dropped it in his mouth."

There was a crashing sound as Trewe barreled toward them, flushing two magpies from a clump of gorse. He yelled into his radio, "We've found 'em."

55

Two months later

"Ruth-Ann, someone's at the door. It's for you." Her mother patted her shoulder and took Ruth's place at the sink.

"Oh Momma, don't bother with dishes."

"No, really, there's someone at the door for you. Go!"

"All right, already." Ruth watched her mother bend over the washing up, her face turned away. *She's up to something,* she decided. Who would be at the door at this time in the morning? "There's a dishwasher, you know."

"Go!"

She jerked the door open. She was startled to see Jon Graham standing on her stoop.

"Hello," he said.

"You're here? I thought you were working on some project?"

"Project finished. By the way, I've been commended for exemplary service, so you're now in the company of Detective Chief Inspector Jon Graham."

"A promotion? That's nice."

"That's nice? Is that it? And without even inviting me in?"

"I haven't heard from you in three weeks."

"And I knew a phone call wouldn't do."

"Texts? Short and sweet, no bother?"

"Not good enough. I'm fully prepared to give you an explanation." Jon gave an exaggerated bow.

Ruth leaned against the door's frame. "Oh? And where shall you begin, hmm? Certainly not in my living room."

"Walk? It's summer and promises to be a gorgeous day."

"Ya never know."

"Fair enough."

Jon's smile appeased her. She hadn't forgotten how disappointed she had been when he left, promising to keep in touch, and then his messages by email and text had been sporadic at best. The last she'd heard from him he had an assignment in Scotland, then intensive training at Bramshill.

"Right." Ruth leaned away from him and pulled a jacket from the back of the big chair by her door. "Mom, don't miss me. Going for a walk with a mysterious stranger!"

They traipsed up the road towards the sea and the top of the cliffs.

"How's Annie?" Jon asked.

"The cuts are healing. She still cries out at night, still afraid of the dark. She has a tutor. Her teachers have been great." She tightened her jacket around her middle. "What did he expect to get from her?"

"Annie was the stepping stone to you. The writing we found in his study indicated that his scheme was to rid the world of you."

She shivered.

"He hated his mother, but his family was twisted. His mother apparently murdered his father for insurance money. Charles had only been about eight at the time."

The lane took a turn, the air held a brighter quality. She nodded. "Speaking of money and good old Captain Perrin, The Portable Antiquities Scheme at the British Museum was very intrigued. There was actually a formal inquest to determine how to treat the find. I've heard that the Perrin's Point Council has voted most of the money will go to the National Trust to use in conservation of the coastline, and the rest will be used to restore the village common areas."

"What about your immigration status?"

"That was a rough patch for a few weeks. I'm surprised you haven't heard." Her voice held sarcasm. "I'm still Ruth Butler. The name change wasn't as difficult as I imagined. Under the circumstances I was granted some leniency, being a model citizen and all. Both sets of grandparents emigrated from Scotland, so I was granted ancestry entry clearance and my application for residency is being considered favorably, Sam tells me. So I'm more or less a permanent fixture."

"Are you? That's brilliant. And you're well? I mean, you've talked about Annie, but what about you? How are you?"

"The whole ordeal ... like a nightmare still. I wake up with the shivers some nights. It helps having my mother and friends close by." She studied his reaction, wondering if he picked up her sarcasm.

"I see. I hope I can be a better friend."

She broke a twig from a bush as they passed. "Mom's only here for a few more weeks. She's having lunch with Peter Trewe. A regular event with them."

"So I've heard. Interesting, that."

"He's pensioned."

"I know."

They walked in silence for a while.

"They never found Malone's body," she said. "Don't you think that's strange? Bodies usually wash up don't they?"

"That was a serious storm that evening. Chances are the body was washed out to sea and eventually sank or was eaten."

She closed her eyes. "Change of subject."

Jon held up both hands. "As God is my witness. From now on."

They had reached the top of the cliffs. White crested waves crashed against the rocks below them. Far out across the dark blue of the water could be seen cresting white horses, the tumbling foam-topped waves.

Sunlight peeked through layers of clouds and bounced across the water. The sea breeze brought the sounds of laughter from the harbor beach. There was a couple with small children. Seagulls wheeled in the air above them.

Ruth laughed. "The gulls look like they want to land on them."

"Gulls are crazy for crisps." Jon stood next to her. "It's a normal, summer morning in Cornwall, full of tourists, isn't it?"

She shook her head. She had to say it. "After what we'd been through, why did you just stop communicating?"

"Last I checked the phone lines work both ways."

She sucked in a breath. "What?"

"You're right. I have no excuse. I admit it."

"And you've been busy." Ruth turned to go back home. "You just don't get it, do you? I don't know why you bothered to stop."

"I've thought of you all of the time."

"Poor you." She walked farther back down the trail. It was dry and slippery in places.

"I've wanted to call," Jon said, catching up, "but the things I want to say I couldn't say on the phone. I couldn't text or email; in print it looked stupid."

"Okay." She turned toward him feet planted, and pointed to her face. "Here it is. Say it and go. Because that's what you're going to do, isn't it? Say it and go. That's the way it will always be with us. Won't it? I can't take that, Jon Graham. I don't—"

"I've been transferred here."

That stopped her with her mouth open. "Transferred?"

"Someone had to fill Peter Trewe's place."

"I see." She pursed her lips, and with a tiny shrug, kept walking. "So, I guess I'll be seeing you around."

"I certainly hope so"—he kept up with her, his face turning a nice shade of pink under his tan—"and I hope more … than just seeing you around, I mean."

"Is that what you wanted to tell me to my face?"

"Could I tell you over dinner?"

She sighed and crossed her arms. "Look, here's the deal. The Dev'lish Pipes will be at the Nap this evening, and well, I wouldn't mind seeing them."

"Could you hear me over them?"

"You might have to shout." She leaned closer. "Perhaps you'd better tell me what you were going to say now, so that you don't have to—shout, I mean."

"You win. I was going to ask if you would let me see you, you know, on a regular basis." He stepped in front of her and took hold of her shoulders. "Blast it, woman! I've loved you since I first laid eyes on you."

She covered her mouth with a hand to stop the wave of joy that bubbled up.

He stuttered, "So … um … I know I haven't proven myself to you."

"What's to prove?" She wrapped her arms around his neck and kissed his gorgeous lips.

Jon noticed a half-dozen people gathered around a skiff waiting to board for a ride to the nearby fishing boat moored in deeper water. Taking tourists out to see the Auks nesting on the islands was more profitable than fishing this time of year. The road above the beach was crowded with people visiting the shops. Even at this distance he could hear cars honking. A procession of cars twisted from the beach up through the village like a shiny-scaled snake basking in sun.

Jon and Ruth joined the lines for the boat ride around Gull Island. She held his hand and it gave him no end of pleasure to watch her smile. He pulled his eyes away on occasion to watch what they had come to watch. The tiny Auks were amazing as they squabbled over nest sites. Looking inland across the sparkling azure water, it surprised Jon to see a number of caves pitting the dark cliffs.

Because they were so far out, he didn't see the blooms along the base of the caves—flowers fertilized with blood.

THE END

ACKNOWLEDGMENTS

A long time ago, a critique group led by Roger Paulding told me that my five-page short story needed to be a novel. That was the beginning.

There are so many people I have in my life who made *Deadly Thyme* a possibility. My family allowed me the solitude to write. My wonderful copy editor Rhonda Erb knew just what she was doing. She was so patient with me, which was needed with all those redundant hyphens. This book is so much better because of her! I want to also thank her brother, Darren Doyle, the linguistics magician! Meghan Pinson helped make the story hang together better. Heidi Dorey created an amazing book cover that fits perfectly.

I wrote the story, but then the location found me. It is a fictional location created from several small seaside villages along the northwest coast of Cornwall, one of which is featured in Doc Martin. On my research trip there I found the perfect bed and breakfast called The Old Rectory in St. Juliet outside Boscastle. It is run by a charming couple, Chris and Sally Searle. Everyone must be sure to set their vacation plans and make reservations. They serve the best food in the south of England. Also, I want to thank an unforgettable woman who helped me with so much of my research. Thank you, Sharon Bates!

I met a young man on the train who gave me some super pointers as I shared my cheese crackers with him. Thank you, Jaimie Atallah, friend for life.

Whatever does not ring true in this book is the fault of this author. I had the most amazing helpers sorting out fact from fiction for me. Thank you to Inspector Graham Clark of the London Metropolitan Police for police facts, a tour, and a delightful tea. Thank you, Constable Michael in Camelford, for your insights and humor and artwork. Sergeant Suggs of the Devon-Cornwall Constabulary helped me with my inquiries. Retired Detective Sergeant Jim Bakewell was most helpful with some pertinent facts that I would have gotten wrong were it not for him.

My critique groups fueled my passion for the completion of the story. I'm grateful for the advanced writing course I took with teacher and writer Chris Rogers.

Thank you also to so many people who read early drafts that were full of holes. They helped me plug them. These include Graham Clark, Chris and Sally Searle, Kimberly Morris, Maria Durham, Carnie Littlefield, and Amy Nolen.

If I've missed someone I should have mentioned, I'm sorry. It's late and I'm old.

ABOUT THE AUTHOR

Rebecca Nolen writes, draws, paints and cares for people she loves at home in Houston, TX. She has been a member of SCBWI, The Houston Writer's Guild, and Sisters in Crime for many years. She has won many writing awards, including the top prize for *Deadly Thyme* at the Houston Writer's Guild writing contest. She attended Emmaus Bible College and the University of Houston more years ago than she'd like to remember and she has participated in many writing conferences, workshops, and advanced writing courses. Her books will soon be available at bookstores. At the library ask for the book to be ordered, or if the author could send the library a copy. Contact Rebecca at: rlnolen@hotmail.com to request a copy and be sure and include the library name and location.

Read more at www.rebeccanolen.com

For a glance at Rebecca Nolen's middle-grade novel *The Dry* http://www.amazon.com/The-Dry-Rebecca-Nolen/dp/193988912X

CPSIA information can be obtained at www.ICGtesting.com
Printed in the USA
LVOW10s1727100516

487548LV00005B/623/P

9 781939 889140